# The Prophecy of Death

## Michael Jecks

D1007334

**headline**

First published in 2008
by HEADLINE PUBLISHING GROUP

First published in paperback in 2008
by HEADLINE PUBLISHING GROUP

1

Cataloguing in Publication Data is available from the British Library

ISBN 978 0 7553 4977 7 (B Format)
ISBN 978 0 7553 4415 4 (A Format)

Typeset in Times by Avon DataSet Ltd,
Bidford-on-Avon, Warwickshire

Printed and bound in Great Britain by Clays Ltd, St Ives plc

Headline's policy is to use papers that are natural, renewable and
recyclable products and made from wood grown in sustainable forests.
The logging and manufacturing processes are expected to conform to
the environmental regulations of the country of origin.

HEADLINE PUBLISHING GROUP
An Hachette Livre UK Company
338 Euston Road
London NW1 3BH

www.headline.co.uk
www.hachettelivre.co.uk

This book is for Barbara Peters of
the Poisoned Pen Press,
with huge admiration for the marvellous work she does
in support of crime writing and writers.

However, it is also for Ian Mortimer,
one of the very best experts on medieval
history and a wonderful drinking companion.
There are few men with whom I can go to the pub
and discuss Edward II into the early hours!
(There are even fewer with whom I would *want* to do so!)

# Glossary

**Assart**  A clearing in a forest, in which a farmer had created arable land by cutting down trees and grubbing up the roots.

**Bellatores**  Medieval society thought itself composed of three groups: religious, who prayed for men's souls, peasants, who gave their labour to provide food and clothing, and the warrior class, the *bellatores*, who maintained order.

**Buttery**  King's office which was responsible for ales, wines and other stores.

**Castellan**  The man in charge of a castle.

**Cokinus**  Literally, 'Cook', but was used as the term for messengers who went about on foot rather than on horseback – and older term, used before 'Cursor' came into vogue.

**Cursores**  Late in King Edward I's time, this term began to replace the older 'Cokinus'.

**Fewterer**  The officer who had responsibility for the packs of hunting dogs.

**Frater**  This was the room in which the monks would eat.

**Host**  The King's army. Army was a new term to the later fourteenth century.

**League**            An ancient measure of distance, roughly equivalent to three miles (although no medieval measures were standardised across the country!).

**Lords Marcher**     Also known as Marcher Lords, were the knights and barons who owned estates on, or near to, the 'marches'.

**March**             The lands along the Welsh and Scottish borders. They had their own customs and laws which gave great independence to the Lords who owned them, mainly because they were almost permanently in a state of war – especially on the Scottish March.

**Marshal**           The man in charge of the 'Marshalsea'.

**Marshalsea**        The stables, and those who worked in them.

**Murdrum Fine**      'Murder' was so termed because of this fine. In short, after the Norman invasion, the rebellions against the invaders were so regular, that unless a corpse could be proved to be that of an Englishman, by men coming forward to assert the dead man's 'Englishry', the body was assumed to be that of a Norman. The death of such a man meant heavy fines to be imposed on the vill where he was found – the 'murdrum' fines.

**Nuncius**           A messenger on horseback.

**Palfrey**           These were better quality horses for riding.

**Porters**           The men who were responsible for the gates to cities, or to castles or halls.

**Rache**             A specific form of hunting dog which was used to hunt by scent rather than others, like greyhounds, which depended upon sight.

**Reredorter**    A toilet that was at the back of the dormitory in a monastery.

**Rounsey**    A general, average quality horse used for riding, carrying goods etc, but not for pulling carts.

**Sewer**    The attendant on a lord who would serve his master, and who would see to the setting of the table, as well as tasting the King's food in a royal household.

**Sumpter**    Packhorse.

**Tranter**    A wandering salesman of various essentials.

# Cast of Characters

**Sir Baldwin de Furnshill**
Keeper of the King's Peace in Crediton, and recently made Member of Parliament, he is known to be an astute man and shrewd investigator. From his past as a Knight Templar, he has a deep hatred of injustice or persecution.

**Jeanne**
Baldwin's wife, Jeanne is mother to his two children.

**Simon Puttock**
Baldwin's friend for many years, Simon was a bailiff to the stannaries at Lydford, where he gained a reputation for honesty and fairness.

**Margaret**
Simon's wife.

**Edith**
Simon and Margaret's daughter.

**King Edward II**
the feckless king of England, Edward has gone down in history as one of our most brutal, sly, and devious kings. His reign is noted for the disasters, natural and otherwise, which dogged his rule.

**Isabella**
Edward II's queen, Isabella was the daughter of King Philip the Fair of France, and was thus the sister to the

| | |
|---|---|
| | current ruler, King Charles IV. |
| **Sir Hugh le Despenser** | probably one of the most unsavoury characters ever to gain influence at an English court, Hugh Despenser the younger was noted for his avarice, his cruelty, and his ruthlessness in the pursuit of his own personal ambitions. |
| **Edward of Windsor** | the son of King Edward and also called the Earl of Chester, the Earl was never officially made a Prince. He would later become King Edward III – one of England's most successful monarchs. |
| **André** | mercenary and guard to the Bishop of Orange. |
| **William Ayrminne** | a canon, Ayrminne is a close ally to the queen. |
| **Sir John of Bakewell** | one of many knights serving King Edward II at his coronation. |
| **Thomas of Bakewell** | the brother of John, and later a king's messenger. |
| **Matthew atte Brook** | the owner of an assart in Ashdown Forest, near Crowborough. |
| **Agnes atte Brook** | wife to Matthew. |
| **Richard of Bury** | a royal clerk who was based in Chester, in 1324 Bury became tutor to Earl Edward. |
| **Henry of Eastry** | the Prior of Christ Church Priory, Canterbury. |
| **Mark of Faversham** | steward and bailiff to Prior Henry. |
| **Brother Gilbert** | a monk at Canterbury. |

| | |
|---|---|
| **John** | son of Peter, John is a strong fighter too. |
| **Joseph of Faversham** | a King's messenger. |
| **Jack of Oxford** | one of the guards of the Bishop of Orange. |
| **Hal** | assistant to Mark of Faversham at Christ Church Priory. |
| **Bishop of Orange** | one of the Pope's trusted emissaries, Orange is attempting to bring peace between France and England. |
| **Peter** | one of the men-at-arms in Canterbury under the castellan, Peter is a ruthless fighter. |
| **Pons** | a friend of André's and guard to the Bishop of Orange. |
| **Walter Stapledon** | the Bishop of Exeter is a wily politician. Twice the Lord High Treasurer, he is known to be a loyal servant to the crown – and deeply suspicious of the queen. |
| **Sir Robert of Westerham** | the King's Coroner at Canterbury. |
| **Nicholas of Wisbech** | a Dominican sent by the King to negotiate with the Pope. |
| **Richard de Yatton** | Herald to the King, Richard is a trusted messenger. |

# Author's Note

This book was intended to be a very different tale originally. The main bulk of the story was to be set in the later part of the year 1325 in France, but things have conspired against me, as usual.

The problem I suffer from, and the attraction to me of my writing, is that the stories are set in 'real time' through history. This means that the stories have to stack up logically with the events of the period. When there was a famine, I have to mention it. Likewise, when there was a massive scandal over the princesses in King Philip's court in Paris, I have to incorporate that, too. It also means I have to be accurate about where people were.

I cannot, for example, cheat and suddenly have Edward II lifted from England and set down in Paris, just to facilitate the plot. He didn't go there. Worse, I know where he was in April, so I have to be true to the history and have the plot working around him in Beaulieu.

Equally, though, it's hard to jump from *The Templar, the Queen and Her Lover*, which was set in March and April, and suddenly move the action straight to September when the Earl of Chester was sent to France to pay homage for the English territories. That would be a large gap, and one which would take a lot of background flashbacks to explain.

So, to the despair of my editor, I threw the synopsis for

Book 25 (untitled) into the box marked 'Stories to return to', and started again from scratch.

And came up with this plot.

It is different from earlier stories, but the main aspects are quite correct. There was a prophecy regarding the 'Boar from Cornwall' and the story of the Oil of St Thomas was also well known. No, it's not made up by me.

Nor is the basic story of the coronation. I am afraid that John of Bakewell did die during a mad press at the time of the coronation in the manner described. It was only one of a number of aspects of the coronation day that struck chroniclers at the time as being proof that Edward II's reign would be enormously unlucky. And they were not wrong, as events were to prove.

The nature of the King's son, Earl Edward of Chester, is very much my own interpretation and guesswork, but set on solid foundations. I would refer any serious investigator of the period to look at Roy Martin Haines's work *King Edward II* (McGill Queen's University Press), and the truly excellent book published by Random House, *The Perfect King – The Life of Edward III, Father of the English Nation*, by my good friend Ian Mortimer of Exeter University.

To a large extent I can blame Ian for this book. It was his mention of certain aspects of the younger Edward's life that tempted me to look at this story from the viewpoint of the Earl. The idea that the next king would have grown to manhood in a febrile, dangerous environment, with a father who was so alienated from his mother that she lost her properties, her income, her servants, even her children; all taken away because her husband considered her too dangerous, was too appealing to my novelistic imagination. He feared she might pollute their children with treasonous thoughts. All this, because her brother was considering (how actively, I am not sure) invasion of England.

To look at the boy, and then consider his tutor, the strange Richard of Bury, who was an avid book collector (although detractors said he was illiterate!) and taught his charge all about the Greek and Roman heroes, and then to see the kind of man into which Edward grew, with the various influences which had shaped his life, this was fascinating.

Earl Edward (I am reliably informed by Ian Mortimer that he was never created a prince, and the title was not in those days automatically passed on to the King's sons, so he was at this time a mere earl) must have been an impressive character. It is true to say that he was one of our most revered Kings up until relatively recently. Attitudes have changed, largely as a result of politically correct rethinking, but, bearing in mind his dreadful upbringing – he would have witnessed his role models being executed, even his father's cousin, seen his family broken up, and the hatred that surely existed between his mother and his father's probably homosexual lover, Hugh le Despenser – it is astonishing that this lad developed into such a spectacularly effective king. Not only that, by all accounts he was also a loving, generous father and husband. A marvellous role model – if you can ignore the numbers of dead from his wars, the devastation of swathes of France, the consequential destruction of much of Europe when mercenaries swept over the continent, and the obscene cruelty aimed at the general population by arrogant and largely barbaric men-at-arms.

The trouble is, it is easy to admire men of his stature for what he achieved in his time – but his time was not the same as ours. It is hard to imagine living in a period when, to take the John Hawkwood example, two men arguing over which would rape a nun first were told that their leader would cut her body in two and they could both have 'half each' as some sort of Solomon-like judgement. The simple fact is, these were appallingly vicious people living in a harsh and uncharitable environment. Those who won were those, like Sir Hugh Despenser, who were the most appalling, the most cruel, the most ruthless. Pacifism was not a successful trait.

Those, like King Edward II, who wanted a more gentle, kindly existence, were forced to accept the facts of their era and become more cruel.

And after saying all this, the final comment has to be that this is my twenty-fifth book in the Templar series. It is rare for any author to be able to write these words, but for me to write them in the knowledge that the whole of the backlist is still available and selling, gives me a wonderful sense that the effort is worthwhile.

In my research, I have referred endlessly to so many books, from Mary C. Hill's *The King's Messengers 1199–1377*, to Ian Mortimer's book on Edward III mentioned above, and his superb *The Greatest Traitor*; Alison Weir's *Isabella – She-Wolf of France, Queen of England*, and many of the Selden Society records, that it is hard to know which books should be mentioned and which need not be. So I shall take the easiest line, and suggest that if you really want to learn more about the period, refer to my website at *www.michaeljecks.co.uk* where you will find a more detailed bibliography for the period, based on my own library.

As always, though, the mistakes are my own. And I

confidently expect Ian Mortimer to point them out to me!

I hope you enjoy this book, and that for a little while it gives you the distraction from modern life which so many of us crave.

Michael Jecks
North Dartmoor
November 2007

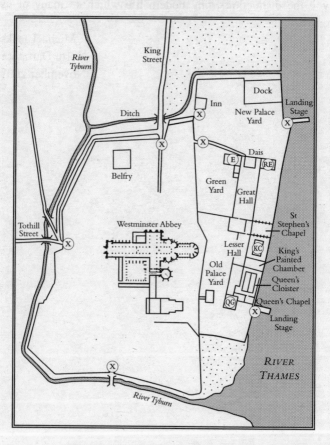

# Thorney Island 1325

**Gate** (X)

**Exchequer** (E)

**Receipt of Exchequer** (RE)

**King's Cloister** (KC)

**Queen's Garden** (QG)

River Tyburn

King Street

Ditch

Belfry

Tothill Street

Westminster Abbey

Inn

Dock

New Palace Yard

Landing Stage

Dais

Green Yard

Great Hall

St Stephen's Chapel

Lesser Hall

King's Painted Chamber

Old Palace Yard

Queen's Cloister

Queen's Chapel

Landing Stage

RIVER THAMES

River Tyburn

# Canterbury 1325

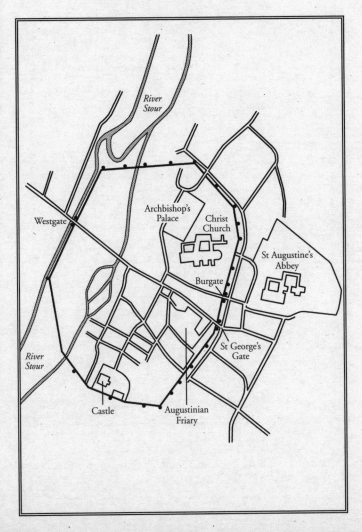

River Stour

Westgate

Archbishop's Palace

Christ Church

St Augustine's Abbey

Burgate

River Stour

St George's Gate

Castle

Augustinian Friary

# Prologue

*Saturday following Maria Visitatio, beginning of the reign of King Edward II*[1]

### Westminster Abbey

Within his burnished steel shell the knight looked utterly impregnable, standing close to the place where he was about to die.

To the boys all about he was a *giant*. Tom could see that. Massive, with all his limbs looking larger than natural, larger than life. It made his heart swell to see John, his brother, looking like that. He couldn't keep his feet still. His toes were tapping a staccato rhythm as he stood, waiting with all the rest.

This was the most exciting day of his *life*! All his life, he'd lived under the reign of the old King, Edward, but now for the first time in many years, five-and-thirty, some said, there was going to be a coronation again! Everyone was thrilled by the idea. All the apprentices were here, most of them drunk as usual; they hadn't the decorum of a bitch on heat, most of them. They were contemptible. But there were also all the rich ladies and their squires. He could see some merchants from the City over there, where the main gate to the abbey lay, and

---

[1] Saturday, 8 July 1307

nearer were some Aldermen. Everybody had come here to witness the great event.

Flags were flying, there were songs being sung outside near the taverns, and from here Tom could hear the chanting from inside the great abbey church. It made his whole body tingle with anticipation. He'd never seen a king before, and today he was going to see the King, his Queen, and all the glorious chivalry of the country. It was just *brilliant*!

There was a sudden tension, and people started shouting and cheering. People behind him started to push forwards, and he found it hard to see over those who were standing in front. He jostled along with all the others, staring. Looking over the other side of the way, he could see John. He may be a knight, but John himself was straining to see, peering round the doorway as keenly as any boy in the crowd, his back to the new wall.

Then there was a blaring of trumpets and shouted commands, and the regular tramping of many booted feet, and . . . and there they were!

First in view were the prelates, all with hands clasped before their faces, mouthing their prayers for the King, asking God's divine support for him; after them was a group of barons, one carrying the gilded spurs which would be placed on the King's boots, another with the sceptre, another with a rod that had a white dove carved on the top – a beautiful piece of work, Tom thought; after him came three great knights – earls, he heard later – with the great swords of state. Then there were more men carrying a massive wooden board on which all the King's royal clothing was set. Oh, there was so much! And all were knights, lords and earls. Tom could hardly breathe for the joy of the sight.

The King was behind all these, barefoot, walking on the

carpet that had been laid between the palace and the abbey church. And as he passed by, the crowds grew silent, from respect and from astonishment. Such good looks didn't seem possible on a human face. 'Such a physique, such deportment,' people were saying approvingly, and then he was past and the whole group of knights and others strode into the church.

He saw John again just then. John was at the wall, staring up at the altar. It was Tom's hope afterwards that John was even then praying, and speaking with God. He was always a good man, John, and it would have been good for him to have been in a state of grace.

Because suddenly there was a low rumble and a splintering sound, and even as Tom's head snapped up to look at it, the wall behind John suddenly crashed to the ground, smothering John with the rubble and dirt from the timbers and lathes and plaster.

Small fragments and a cloud of dust swept over everyone, getting into their eyes and noses, making everyone choke and cough. People panicked, running hither and thither, and some at the back were trampled as those who had seen the disaster tried to escape. Although Tom fought them, pushing and shoving, it took him a while to get to John. By the time he did, there was nothing he could do.

'Back, bratchet, or I'll have you beaten by the bailiffs,' a man snarled, and Tom tried to explain that the knight was his brother but, before he could, he had a cuff round his ear, and he fell to the ground in the midst of the plaster and dust, staring up in horror at the arrogant young knight before him. He saw the man's badge, and would have said something, but the knight spat on the ground near his head, and then strode off, bellowing for servants to clear up the mess.

'John! John!' Tom whispered, but although he tried to reach

his brother's hand, he could see that there was already no life in his eyes. John's head was crushed.

### *Fields near Crowborough, Sussex*

Agnes thought it was an auspicious day to be married, the day that the new King was crowned. It would set the seal on her happiness.

The field was still, with a fine haze rising in the brilliant midday sun, and they were all lying in the shade of a tree, eating their bread and cheese, drinking cider from their small barrels, tired after a long day already, gathering up the sheep from their little flocks and washing them in the stream that passed by the pasture, all the folk ending as wet as the sheep themselves. The filth that ran from the fleeces was extraordinary, and she thought to herself, 'Aye, they must be glad to lose all that weight, the poor beasts.' A short while after that, she fell in fully, her shift all sodden about her. She could feel his eyes on her immediately, running over her body as he would have liked his hands to. When she looked at him, he didn't stop, either. She liked that. He was bold, but so was she, when she wanted, and now, seeing him stare at her breasts, she arched her back a little, teasing.

For all the splashing and effort, she and the others soon dried off. More than half the flock had been washed, but there would be more to do that afternoon, and she would have to do her part.

She would do it at his side.

He was called Matthew atte Brook, and his father was a freeman, quite rare down here. While Agnes and her family lived here, near to Crowborough itself, Matthew's family had a little hovel inside the woods. The great forest of Ashdown surrounded all this area. Villages and towns might encroach on the trees, but the trees still remained. Assarts sprang up amongst them and flourished for a while, but all too often the buildings would decay and collapse, and the trees would return. But Matthew's father had maintained his house. It had survived much, with storms that had destroyed so many places in the last years, and a fire that had almost encircled his land last year, but for all that, he had managed to expand his holding little by little, and now he had two cows as well as his pigs. He made money by selling the cheese his wife made in their dairy.

Agnes gave him a cautious glance from under her long lashes. He was strongly made, her Matthew, with arms corded with muscle already, and his eyes were dark and broodingly intense. Oh, she wanted him! So much!

It happened at long last when she decided to wander into the woods to empty her bladder. Soon, as she rose from her crouch, she heard steps in amongst the trees, the crunch of twigs and the rustle of leaves.

'Matthew?'

'Agnes, I thought . . .'

She knew what he'd thought. It wasn't fear for her safety that had brought him here. No, it was the thought of her tight shirt over her breasts, wet and glorious. She didn't care. She wanted him as well.

He stood beside her, looking away, suddenly shy in her presence. He'd never been like that with her before. She had to take his hand and hold it to her cheek, and when that didn't work, she drew it down to her breast and rested his palm over her nipple, letting him feel it harden. She reached to his head and pulled it down to her, kissing him softly at first, gradually allowing her desire to transmit itself to him.

When she put her hand on his thigh, she felt him shudder,

and the proof of his lust made her tingle, and then chuckle throatily. 'You want me?'

'Yes!'

'You can't just 'ave me without the proper form, Matthew. Got to 'ave that.'

He didn't move away. He kept his arms around her and shoved his head into her shoulder. 'I'll do that.'

'You'll take me?'

'I will.'

'Now?'

'Yes.'

'Then come on,' she said quickly, and drew him after her, back to the stream.

'Listen! Listen!' She waited until all the others were quiet and watching her, and then she turned to him again, holding both hands, looking up into his beautiful face.

'Matthew, I take you to my husband, to have and to hold from this day forward, in love, to honour and obey you, in sickness and in health, from now until I die, and there I give you my oath.'

And as soon as he had said the words too, they left the others at the stream. And while the others laughed and screamed and played and then carried on with their work, Agnes, new wife to Matthew, lay on her back and let him take her virginity, her love and her soul.

She only grew to hate him ten years later. By then all her love had been squandered by him.

*Thursday following Easter in the thirteenth year of the reign of King Edward II*[1]

### Chester Castle

Bad news deserved lousy weather, the friar thought to himself bitterly.

At the very least, such news should be relayed at dusk. There ought to be a lowering sense of foulness in the air, the sort of malevolent fume that would make a man realise his life was about to be ruined. Not today, though. No, not even though his career was now effectively ended.

Nicholas of Wisbech crossed the court in front of Chester's castle in the south-west of the city with his mind numbed. The bastard had sat there smugly as he spelled out Nicholas's 'difficulty'. The *prickle*!

Master Richard of Bury was not the sort of person whom Nicholas would ever have warmed to. A slightly short man, chubby, and with glittering little eyes in his podgy face, he didn't inspire anything but contempt from a man like Nicholas. Nicholas was a friar, in God's name. A Dominican. He was a papal penitentiary. And what was this Richard? A royal clerk, a man whose life revolved around writing letters and collating information on accounts, and fattening himself at the King's expense. His flabby body was proof of his laziness and lax intellect.

He had tried to cultivate a different atmosphere, of course. Master Richard had begun to collect books, and now he sat among towers of them, although Nicholas reckoned he had not the wit to remember anything from any of them, even if he had read them. Which the Dominican found doubtful.

---

[1] Thursday, 3 April 1320

Master Richard's voice was as oily as his manner. 'Friar, I am *so* glad you could come to see me.'

'Your message said it was a matter of royal importance?' Nicholas pointed out.

'Aha! Well, yes, it is in a way. It is a matter which is embarrassing to the King. So, rather, it's a matter of some importance to you.'

Nicholas knew full well that the fat fool in front of him wanted him to enquire what was meant by that, but he refused to play his game. Instead, he stood silently, unmoving, his hands hooked over his corded belt.

He had once been told that he would make an excellent inquisitor, because with his sharp features, dark, intense eyes and ability to remain utterly still, he could drag information from the most reluctant witness. It was not the path he wished, and he had rejected the proposal, but now he made full use of his unsettling frown, fixing his cold, searching stare upon the clerk.

Richard moved a wax tablet from one side of his desk to the other. Then he fiddled with the binding of a scroll, as though gathering his thoughts. Richard thought he was trying to appear at ease. He failed.

'You see, Friar, it is like this: we have the rumour from you of this marvellous oil—'

'You dare to doubt the evidence of Saint Thomas?'

'Hardly.' Richard smiled, but uneasily, at the snarling tone. 'No, it would be fine so far as I am concerned, but there are others who're not so certain. The Pope himself . . .'

Nicholas could barely control himself. It was so unreasonable! He knew what had happened, of course. The others who'd spoken to the Pope had warned him of the unpopularity of the King, and warned against becoming embroiled in English politics, which was fine, but this could potentially have rescued the King, and with him, saved the realm from further damaging dispute.

'. . . The Pope himself refused to listen to our King's petition, didn't he?'

'I did all I could to persuade him!'

'Of course you did,' the clerk said suavely, but also absently, as though other, more pressing matters were already occurring to him, and he wished not to be detained. He glanced at a scroll on the table top at his left, moving it with a finger as he peered. 'Um. But you know the whims of a king. I fear he is about to write to the Pope.'

'To complain about the Pope's decision?'

'No, I rather feel he will complain about *you* and demand that you lose your post as penitentiary.'

'Why? What have I done?'

But there did not have to be a reason. As the fat clerk shrugged and concealed himself further behind his piles of books, Nicholas knew the truth. A man who put himself out to help the King must always succeed, for to fail was to bring down the full weight of the King's enmity. He was a weakly man, this king. Nicholas had noticed his flaws often enough before in their meetings, and weakly men in powerful positions always tended to punish those who were unable to stand against them.

'So I am ruined?'

'I rather fear you will not be employed by the King again. But never mind. As a friar, you will be happier to be released from the arduous responsibilities of working for King and Pope. It must have been a terrible effort, trying to persuade the Pope to send us a cardinal, after all.'

He could have no understanding. The weeks of formulating

the best approach to the Pope, the long journey to Rome, the difficulty of explaining how important this matter was . . . all had taxed his mind and body enormously. And now, simply because he had tried and not succeeded, he was to be punished.

'I did my best.'

'But the Pope didn't listen. Yes, I quite understand. But you do see, don't you, that it would be impossible for me to keep you on here? I am afraid that the King's largesse will no longer apply to you.'

'I have never sought it,' Nicholas hissed. 'Look to others who may seek only self-enhancement in the King's service. I toiled as a loyal subject must.'

'Without any thought of future appointments?' Richard said, and his pale grey eyes were turned upon Nicholas. With a strong tone of sarcasm, he added, 'How *very* noble of you.'

For that, if nothing else, Nicholas could have thrust his fist in the clerk's face. But no. He remained calm and restrained, and left the room a short while later.

And now, as he left the castle and walked down the lanes to meet his brother friar, he could not even pray. There was no prayer he could utter that might express his feelings adequately.

'Ach! God *damn* that fat fool!'

It was embarrassing, Richard reflected as the friar stormed out. The man hadn't really done anything wrong, after all. He was just unfortunate. But, as Richard sighed sadly to himself, all too often weaker men were let down. The strong never were.

He patted a book nearby. It was a fascinating book, this. A history of England written by that great man Geoffrey of

Monmouth. He had an appreciation of the importance of history, and of keeping an accurate chronicle of events. Monmouth had set down all the great events since the arrival of Brutus after the sack of Troy, through the great period of King Arthur, and beyond. It was clear from this that those who were bold and firm in their resolve, as well as dedicated to God, of course, were the men who would achieve great things. Other books in his stacks told the same story. Alexander did not conquer through laziness! No! He was a proud, chivalrous adventurer.

But that poor friar was not built from the same clay. He had failed, and because of his failure, the King was sent greater distress, because he had hoped for this late release.

It was all because of the prophecy, of course. The prophecy of St Thomas's Holy Oil. He had it here.

Richard moved his books about until he had a space before him, and then he blew dust from the aged parchment, smiling as he did so. Merely handling these ancient pages was enough to give his heart a sense of warmth and excitement.

He had not heard of the prophecy until some four years ago, when rumours of this came to him. The friar himself had told him.

There had been a dream given to St Thomas Becket while he was exiled in France. The Holy Virgin sent it to him, and in the dream she told him that there were to be six kings after his own. She showed him a marvellous Holy Oil, which he must keep safe, for the King who was anointed with it would be a lion among men: he would conquer large tracts of France once more, and throw the heathens from the Holy Land.

The oil had been secreted in a phial safe from danger, in St Cyprian's Monastery in France. It was to be kept there, secure, concealed, until the coronation of the fifth King after Becket's own king: Henry II. That meant it must be brought out now, for Edward II.

Even so, the King had not been anointed with the special oil. And King Edward II blamed all the misfortunes of his reign on that failure. The friar who had brought this matter to his attention was suddenly the King's best companion. Anything the friar wanted must be provided. And all he had to do was help the King. He had sent Nicholas to the Pope, to tell the story and explain the importance of the oil. And to ask that a cardinal might be sent to anoint King Edward with the Holy Oil – the use of such a high-ranking cleric must give the oil additional potency.

But the pontiff had demurred, saying that any of the King's bishops could perform the service. It was plain enough what his reasoning had been: the King was enormously unpopular already, and wasn't aiding the Pope in his attempts to bring peace between the English and French kings, so why should he help Edward? The King was thwarted in this one act which could, so he believed, save his reign and bring him the fortune he deserved.

And the messenger who had brought this news? That friar was no longer the King's favourite, of course. Failure was never rewarded in England.

But this matter of the oil. It was interesting, nonetheless. Richard gave a fleeting frown, patted his book again, and set it aside, but as he did so, his eyes narrowed and he wondered whether, just whether it was possible that the oil was genuine.

That would be a powerfully effective oil if it truly had been given to St Thomas by the Blessed Virgin.

*Tuesday before Easter,*[1] *eighteenth year of the reign of King Edward II*

### *Assart in Forest near Crowborough*

Agnes set down the milk and leaned back, hands at the pain in the small of her back where the muscles were so tense, and then took up the butter-churn's paddle and began the laborious work of converting the milk.

There was a time when she had been small and wisp-like, she remembered, but childbirth and the famine had stopped all that. When first she had been married, she had been a child, really. Only fourteen years old, and yet old enough to wed and conceive. She hadn't needed too many muscles in those days. All she had known was some easy cookery, a few chores about the house, and then the grim effort of suckling her boy. And then the girl, too, and another boy.

The priest had been a great support at first. She told him about her vow when her father kicked up a fuss, and the priest listened to her and Matthew, and checked with all the witnesses to make sure, before declaring the marriage perfectly valid. After all, a marriage wasn't something that was a Church matter. If people wanted the blessing of the priest at the church door, that was fine, but it didn't invalidate the wedding if they chose not to have it. No, and so Agnes was married.

It was the famine that did for her, though. All the children starved during the winter of the second famine year. One after another, as though they couldn't bear to stay alive amid so much sorrow. There was no food for anyone, but it was one thing to see men and women with their gaunt features and

---

[1] Tuesday, 2 April 1325

swollen bellies, their arms and legs withering, eyes sinking, teeth falling out, until only skeletons clothed with a thin layer of skin appeared to remain and another to see the children suffer.

All suffered, but families in the woods suffered more than most. Their scrappy land wouldn't support much by way of crops in good years, and they must depend on the grain they could buy from those with better land. But during the famine, they lost their animals, for there was nothing for them to eat. The animals that could eat, succumbed to a murrain before long. All were dead. And with them Agnes and Matthew's wealth.

Matthew had never been particularly demonstrative. He'd not taken to beating her before the famine. Only a couple of thrashings a week was his norm. But it had eroded her confidence even then. When Matthew's father had roared at her for making his pottage too thin, too garlicky or too cold, Matthew had taken his side, and would slap her face to show his discontent. But that was nothing to the pain she endured when she must pay the marriage debt. After her third babe, it was unbearable, but he wouldn't listen to her, and forced her to take him. That was why she grew to hate him. The routine manner of his beating her was one thing, but forcing her to open her legs each night when it felt as though there was a dagger in her belly already, made her despise him.

The sound of hooves came clearly, and she leaned on the paddle, listening, before continuing with her work again, the paddle thudding more heavily as the cream began to separate into buttermilk and butter.

'Maid, you look good enough to eat!'

She turned and felt her face break into a broad smile. 'Richard!'

The King's herald grinned and opened his arms, and it was then that she heard her husband's roar, and she saw him hurtling towards them with a billhook in his fist, and she screamed as it rose and sliced down at Richard's head.

# Chapter One

*Monday following Easter in the eighteenth year of the reign of King Edward II*[1]

### Eltham Palace

He was not yet thirteen years old, but he could still remember the horror of those days. Three years had passed, but he would never forget them. Not if he lived to be a hundred.

At first he had been confused. Only a boy, he had grown to appreciate the men of his household, great men, *good* men, who were entirely trusted. Knights, squires, even lords, had been his companions all his life, and he admired them, all of them. Everyone did. They were the pinnacle of nobility.

Many great men lived in his own private household: Damory, Audley, Macauley – they were the men he could look up to. Other than the King, they were the men he respected most in the world.

But his world was about to collapse about him.

It was no sudden shock. He knew that now, but to a lad of only nine and a half years it had come with the vast speed of a river in spate, washing away all before it. He had listened in horror to the tales of death and torture with utter incomprehension. In truth, the catastrophe was a long time building, had

---

[1] Monday, 8 April 1325

he but known it. But he was so young when the civil war began, he couldn't see that this was a ponderous disaster that had been constructed on the foundations of hatred over ten years – before his birth. It was the result of the King's capricious nature. King Edward II had long resented the attitude of the men who thwarted his whims. To the King's mind, he had the inalienable right of the Crown. God had made him King. None other. So no man had the right to overrule him. There was no one with the right to stand against him, and yet many tried.

The first rebellion, so the King said, was when his close friend Piers Gaveston was captured and murdered by the earls of Hereford, Lancaster and Warwick. Gaveston had been the recipient of too much of the King's largesse, and the earls resented royal generosity at the expense of others who had more noble birth. So they took the King's adviser and killed him.

When Gaveston was removed, the King seemed to settle and willingly spend his time with his other friends and his family. The birth of his first son gave him enormous pleasure and pride, so they said. But the King was not content. And soon he found a new favourite – a man of such rapacious greed that he set all the land against himself and the King: Sir Hugh le Despenser. It was his fault that there was a fresh civil war.

The Lords Marcher allied themselves with the lords of the far north and rampaged over the territories owned by the Despenser. They burned and looted all the vast Despenser estates, and then marched upon London, forcing humiliating terms on the King, demanding that he exile his friend and agree to rule within limitations set by them. It was degrading for a man of pride; shameful for a King. So, at the first opportunity, the King took action, and the war was finally concluded when he encircled the rebels at Boroughbridge.

If only he had shown tolerance and demonstrated that magnanimity which was the mark of a great man . . . but King Edward II was driven by baser motives. Instead of accepting apologies and forgiving those who had shown him such disregard, the King launched a ferocious attack on all those who had set their standards against him.

His own cousin, Earl Thomas of Lancaster, was led to a field on a donkey, and there beheaded. The Lords Clifford and Mowbray were executed at York, and up and down the country lords, knights and squires were hanged. The tarred bodies were left there on the gibbets, pecked over and desiccated, for two years and more, proof of the vindictiveness of the man who ruled the nation.

Except he didn't. Not alone. He had left his wife, and it was he and Despenser who controlled the management of the realm together, for all the world as close as lovers. Both of them feared by his subjects; both of them hated.

No king could be universally loved, of course. The boy may be just twelve years old, but he knew this; he had been well tutored, and he had read enough of the lives of Arthur, Alexander and others to know that a powerful leader would always have his enemies. But this was taking matters too far. It was one thing to alienate certain members of the nobility, but another entirely to turn even a wife against him. And her children.

Especially, Edward of Windsor, the Earl of Chester and first-born son of King Edward II, told himself, when it meant losing the trust and love of your own heir.

*Night of Monday and Tuesday following Easter*[1]

### Christ Church Priory, Canterbury

It was the howling of the blasted creatures that woke him –
again – and Mark of Faversham rolled over in his little cot
with a grunt and a muttered oath, rubbing at his eyes.

By the names of all things Holy, they were terrible. Here he
was, a man in his middle forties, worn, old, and in need of his
sleep, in God's name, and each night the damned creatures
would wake him. And if they could wake him, they could
wake anyone. It wasn't as though Mark was a light sleeper. If
they could get through to him, they could wake half the monks
in the cemetery.

The things were worse than bloody wolves descending on
an innocent flock. Locusts had nothing on them. He had
managed this estate with efficiency, with economy, and with
cautious good sense over some years now, and built it into a
modern, profitable little manor. And it still would be, if it
wasn't for *her damned hounds*!

The prior hadn't wanted them. Hounds were an expense
Henry of Eastry could well do without. Who on earth would
want them eating the priory's wealth week in and week out?
Not Prior Henry. He knew the way that they could eat through
food. It wasn't as if you could throw them all the crusts from
the table, either. Oh no. Dear God in Heaven, what would *she*
say if she heard that? And she would. There was always
someone looking for a small reward, and the hope of largesse
to follow, by speaking out of turn.

He pulled on boots and, without bothering to lace them,

---

[1] Night of Monday, 8 and Tuesday, 9 April 1325

stomped over the floor to the truckle bed in the eaves, kicking it. Twice.

The first served only to set the figure snuffling and grunting, which was at least better than the rumbling, discontented snoring, but at the second blow, there was a short rasping snort, and the fellow sat upright, bending over to the side of the bed so he didn't brain himself on the rafters angled over his head. 'Hey? Wa'?'

'The bloody hounds again,' Mark growled unsympathetically. 'The Queen's hounds.'

'Not again! Sweet Jesus' pains, can't the things sleep like everyone else?'

'Not everyone, Hal. Not you and me.' Mark took the candle from the wall's sconce, and set it on the floor beside him as he knelt, reaching for his tinderbox.

'Thanks, Brother. Thanks for reminding me,' Harry said.

He flopped back on his bed as Mark struck again and again with flint and steel to light some tinder. It was hard in the dark. The flash of sparks illuminated the tinder at the first attempt, but that brief explosion of light blinded him for the next three, and he kept missing the target, sending sparks flying uselessly to the rough timber floor.

Hal had been a Godsend to Mark. For too many years he had tried to manage this estate with the help that the lay brothers could provide during those odd moments when they had time to spare. But it was never enough, and when a man had a sudden emergency, like when he discovered that the shepherd had fallen and broken his head on a rock, and the sheep were all escaped, a man needed more than the promise of some aid towards the middle of next week, in God's name!

Prior Henry was good, though. When his steward went to

him and explained about the problems, he listened sympathetically, and told him to leave the matter with him. Mark had
thought he meant he'd to dispose of Mark's complaints in the
same way his predecessor always had, by ignoring his troubles
and hoping that the problem would go away. It was often the
way that priors would deal with their more difficult staff – tell
them not to bring problems but solutions, and threaten
punishment if they continued to bother their betters. And then
Hal arrived, young, strong, keen, and eminently capable.

At first Mark made the usual uncharitable assumption: that
the boy was the love-child of the prior, and the prior had found
him the best post he could while not admitting paternity. But
more recently Mark was forced to consider that the lad was
nothing of the sort. Apart from anything else, he came from a
place some distance from the priory, and Mark had never
heard that the prior had ever been up that way. Then again, the
prior seemed to show no interest in the lad's development. No,
Mark was forced to conclude that Hal was nothing more than
a boy whom the Prior had heard of, who happened to be bright
enough, and who Prior Henry considered might be a useful
additional body to have in the priory. He came from a good
area – other novices had come from his part of Kent, like John,
Simon and Gilbert. They were all from the same vill, almost.

'Ah. Good. At last!' he grunted as a tiny glow glittered in
the tufts of tinder. It remained, golden, even as the flashes
played with his eyes. Picking up the tinder in a bundle, he
blew gently until a flame caught, and with his other hand he
patted the floor looking for the candle he had placed there. At
last he found it – it had rolled under his leg – and set the
blackened wick to the flame. As soon as it caught, he carefully
extinguished the tinder and replaced it in his box. Tinder took
so long to find, to dry, and prepare, it was best not to waste it.

The candle he set back in the sconce, and retrieved two more from the box beneath, lighting them. 'Come on, boy!'

Hal was more a man than a boy now, but he'd remain 'boy' to Mark. Maybe eighteen years, slender as a willow-wand, tall, lanky and with the gangling clumsiness of so many youngsters, it was hard to think of him as ever growing up.

'What is the matter with them?' Hal demanded as he took the candle, shivering slightly in the middle-night chill.

Mark went down the ladder, muttering, 'Goddamned hounds. They're no good to man or beast. If they were warning us of invasion or the end of the world, that would be one thing, but these monsters only ever bark at the moon. They were disturbed by a cat or something, I daresay. Blasted creatures.'

It was a common enough occurrence. The cellarer had a cat, a promiscuous and undiscriminating little draggle-tail, who had just borne another litter. Several times in recent weeks the mewling things had irritated the hounds beyond restraint, and one kitten had fallen in among the pack. It didn't live long. Perhaps this was another of the little brutes, sitting up on a ledge and taunting the pack below again. However, it could be something else. They had to check.

The Queen's pack had arrived unexpected and un-announced about a month ago, as she passed by on her way to the coast. The Prior had remained urbanely calm about it while she was there, but all knew how problematic looking after them was going to be. She left them no fewterer to look after them, and as for money ... well, all knew that her own finances had been curtailed since the outset of war with her brother, the King of France, last year. Since then, it was said, the King and his main advisers did not trust her, and they wouldn't let her have the income from her lands. So, in effect, she had nothing.

That was probably why the French wench had deposited her beasts on the priory, Mark told himself grimly.

They had been housed in the old tithe barn. It was a great building over at the farther side of the priory grounds, unused for some months since the new barn was completed. In time, they had planned to pull down the old building and reuse the stones and timbers for some new storage rooms nearer the priory itself. Now they'd have to wait for the blasted hounds to go first.

'What is the matter with them?' Hal asked.

Mark made a snarling noise. There was nothing for them to make all this row about. It was the contrariness of hounds, that was all. If he had his way, the things would be loosed tomorrow and the devil take them. All Mark wanted just this minute was his bed again. The thought of the well-stuffed mattress, the roped frame, the soft pillow filled with hens' feathers, was all enough to make him scowl and want to kill a man.

There had been other little disturbances as well, of course. A couple of days ago there had been the arrival of the envoys from France on their way to find the King. Prior Henry had been able to direct them to Beaulieu, where he had heard the King had descended. God be praised, the envoys and their assorted train had departed yesterday, Monday.

At the door to the barn, he passed his candle to Hal before struggling with the great bolt. It should have been greased, and he reminded himself again to see to it. The old timbers of the doors had dropped, and the iron bolt was firmly fixed in its slot. He was forced to haul and jiggle it, gradually making it move side-to-side before he had loosened it enough to draw it free, and then he had to pull at the door while trying to lift it at the same time, the ancient timbers scraping across the paved entrance way.

Inside they had fenced off the left-hand side. This was where the hounds were supposed to live, while opposite was being used for hay storage. The two were cautious with their candles in here, for all knew the dangers of lighted candles and hay, and Hal's wick was already spitting dangerously. Mark made a mental note to trim it in the morning.

The noise was deafening here. Baying and howling, some of the beasts jumping up at the partition, while others prowled, heads low and suspicious.

Mark took up a switch from a peg by the door. He never liked dogs, and certainly wouldn't trust them. The first time he had been bitten by one was when he was nothing but a youngster, and the experience of seeing that enormous gaping jaw in front of him, smelling that foul breath, and feeling the teeth clench over his puny forearm, was one he would never forget. All he could recall was screaming in a high tone, like a hog feeling the knife open his throat. The memory was enough to make him shudder, and now, as he stood there in the gloom, candle high overhead, switch in his other fist, he was taken with an urge to destroy the lot of them. Just toss his candle into the hay, and all the hounds would soon be gone. Burned to ash, all of them.

Except he couldn't. The Queen would delight in repaying the priory for such dereliction. And Mark himself would be blamed. He was the man responsible, after all.

So no. He would have to see what the problem was.

Hal had taken hold of a small whip, and flicked it at a dog trying to leap the partition. It fell back, yelping. Another took a cut across its nose, and fled to the rear of the pack, howling

– although whether with rage or pain, Mark couldn't tell.

'What's the matter with them?' Hal demanded, trying to speak over the noise.

'They're beasts! Just hounds. They don't need a reason to make this row. They do it for fun,' Mark shouted back. God, but it was so tempting to throw his candle down and . . .

His eyes caught a glitter in the straw even as the enticing thought caught at his imagination. There was something there, he thought, and peered more closely.

'What is it?' Hal called, his attention split between the hounds leaping at the screen and his master, who had crossed the floor and stood staring down at the straw. 'Master?'

He cast a glance at the hounds once more, but then something made him walk over towards his master. 'Master?'

'No! Keep back, Hal!' Mark exclaimed urgently, and tried to stop the lad. But he was too late.

'Oh, Christ! Oh, God! Gilbert, no! What's happened to him? Gilbert . . .'

Mark tried to turn and shield Hal from the scene, but the boy turned and retched against a sack of grain, face white-green, clearly visible even in the warm light from the torches. He had already seen the obscene gaping wound, the pale, yellow cartilage, and the blood that lay all about Gilbert's body, smearing the hay in foul clots and puddles.

Run! He had to run! The noise of the hounds behind him was swelling all the time, and he had to escape the row. He didn't think they were after him, but the noise – *Christ Jesus*! He had to get away from the town as fast as he could. The castle was a short distance in front now, and he could see its battlements. There were only a few yards to the door, and then he was inside, panting with fear and exertion, feeling his heart pounding, the sweat cooling on his forehead. Or was it the blood? God's body, but there had been so much *blood*!

Three men waited just inside. They said nothing. There was nothing to be said, only a nod of mutual recognition, all aware of the great danger they ran. All knew that if their act tonight was discovered, they would certainly perish. Painfully. He gave them the small phial, and that was his part done.

Soon he was bustled out, still no time to rest. A man took him swiftly, all the way from the castle's outer gate, back into the town, quietly now, the pair of them scurrying like mice through the deserted streets, and out to the little postern. There was no guard here – it was the castle's men who were supposed to look after this doorway, so close to the castle itself – and then he was outside, in the open, the sky a purple velvet cloth overhead, sprinkled with clouds and shimmering sheets of silken mist. It was a strange sensation, standing there in the open, suddenly still, with no animals, no sense of urgency, no need to run . . .

Except there was. He would be running for the rest of his life now, unless the plan succeeded.

Of course, if that happened he might even win a great reward. Become a knight, even. Either that, or he'd be found dead one day in a ditch for his perfidious behaviour. The King would have his balls for what he'd done.

But for now, he must escape. He moved swiftly along the roadway, keeping the castle on his left, until he reached the cross on the Wincheap way, and there he turned south and west, heading towards the leper house of St Jacob. A short distance before that, he found the track off to the left into the trees, and met with the men who had the horse.

He took the reins, and with a sense of relief to be safe again, the man in the King's herald tabard sighed and clapped spurs to the beast. There were many miles to cover before he could rest properly again.

Since getting here from France he felt as though he had been in the saddle all the time. He only prayed he might find some peace soon.

# Chapter Two

### *Château du Bois, Paris*

Baldwin sipped his wine and tried to look appreciative.

The musicians were not all bad. Some were really quite talented. That fellow Janin was rather good with his vielle, and Ricard was a competent gittern player, although he did tend to make a little too much of a show with his playing for Baldwin's taste. He seemed to wave his instrument about overmuch when the women were watching him. Still, at least he was making a pleasing sound. Not soothing, but definitely pleasing.

But it was soothing which his soul needed just now. He had been here in France for a month or so, which meant that it was . . . what? Two months, no, three since he had left his wife and children back home at Furnshill. However long it was, it felt a great deal longer. That was certain. His son was only a matter of three months old when the King's summons had arrived to call him on this journey, travelling to France with the Queen, protecting her from dangers on the road, so that she might arrive safely at the French court.

Queen Isabella was a strong-willed woman. She had come

---

[1] Tuesday, 9 April 1325

through many disappointments with her husband and his choice of friends. In recent years she had seen all her properties confiscated, her income taken, her servants exiled and even her children taken into custody. All this while her husband ignored her and took to carousing with his favourite adviser, Sir Hugh le Despenser.

Many women would have been broken by such cruelty, but not Queen Isabella. Baldwin reckoned that at the heart of her there was a baulk of English oak, resilient, impervious, unbending. She grew more resolute with every setback, he thought. For all the hardship and the sadness which it must have brought to her, still she acted like a Queen. There was no apparent rancour in her spirit as she conducted her embassy with the French King. King Charles IV, her brother, was a man of great intellect and enormous cunning, Baldwin felt – but he tended to feel that about any king. Men with such enormous power were best avoided, in his opinion.

She was here today, sitting at her chair, listening to the music with enthusiasm as the players cavorted, her eyes sometimes straying to the little boy who sat at the back with the covers for the instruments, discarded along with the musicians' paraphernalia.

To Baldwin's relief the lad was playing quietly with a ball and causing no trouble. He was the adopted son of Ricard of Bromley, the musician with the gittern, and seemed content enough with his life just now. That itself was good to see.

Baldwin glanced across at his friend of so many years, Simon Puttock. A tall man, some ten years younger at nine-and-thirty or so, Simon was a strong man, used to long hours in the saddle. He had been a bailiff on Dartmoor, responsible for upholding the King's peace on the moors. His grey eyes were set in a calm, sunburned face and had seen their share of violence in over ten years of trying to seek out felons. His reliability had led to his promotion to the post of officer of the Keeper of the Port of Dartmouth, but the reward had been bitter, as it meant leaving his wife and family behind.

And now he did not even have that post, for his Patron, Abbot Robert of Tavistock, had died, and arguments had arisen over the abbey's choice of successor. Simon had no idea what his job would be.

Baldwin's face twisted wryly. Unlike him, he thought. His own position was fixed: he was the Keeper of the King's Peace, a Justice of Gaol Delivery, and most recently, a member of the king's parliament, a council which even the king distrusted. He only used it to raise revenue.

For Baldwin, such a post reeked. He had been a Knight Templar, a member of a holy and honourable order, which had been attacked by an avaricious French king and his partner, the Pope. The Templars had been destroyed by those two, to their dishonour. Baldwin had been fortunate enough not to be in the preceptories when all were arrested, and was never caught. Yet the experience of seeing the persecution and deceit had left him with an abiding hatred of politicians and the clergy. He could trust neither entirely. Only his friend Simon seemed absolutely trustworthy.

Simon was now standing at the other side of the room – naturally all those in the chamber here listening with the Queen, the knights, the men-at-arms, the ladies-in-waiting, were all standing; none might sit in the Queen's presence – and was stifling a yawn. Baldwin felt his own jaw respond, and vainly attempted to conceal it, sensing his mouth puckering like an old hag's who had bitten into a sloe, before he managed to cover it with a forearm.

The Queen displayed no such weakness. She remained

upright in her chair, listening with every indication of enthusiasm, as though all the tribulations of the last months were dispelled by the music, hard though Baldwin might find it to believe. And yet, he knew, for much of the time, she was bitter. She concealed her anger at, and detestation of, Despenser, the principal architect and cause of her misery, but for Simon and Baldwin, who had grown to know and understand her moods and behaviour in the last few weeks of travelling with her, the fact was that her mood was generally easy enough for them to read. It was clear that she was here to do the very best deal she could for her adopted country and her oldest son, so that he might inherit a good kingdom, but for all that, if there were any means by which she could embarrass or offend her husband, she would surely not hesitate to grasp it with both hands.

'That,' Simon said as they walked away from the Queen's chamber to their own, 'was boring in the extreme. I don't know about you, but I'm not sure how much more of this I can bear.'

'It's all right for some,' Baldwin admitted. 'Fine wine, good food—'

'Too damned rich.' His friend grunted. 'Give me some plain rabbit roasted over an open fire rather than all this coloured muck.'

'. . . and yet I want to be at home to see my son. I worry about Jeanne,' Baldwin finished. His wife had been so tired when he left her to set off for London, and all he could recall was that paleness about her features and the pinched look she had worn, as though his beautiful lady was overtired and cold.

'I'd like to see my Meg again, too,' Simon said sharply, adding, 'and my daughter should have been married by now. All this wandering about France and back has delayed her nuptials. I doubt whether she, or her mother, will be too happy about that.'

It was true. Simon's daughter, Edith, had been betrothed for an age – certainly more than a year – but she was almost seventeen now. He would have to allow her to marry as soon as he could, and that may well mean as soon as he returned home to Lydford. He had kept her waiting too long.

'Simon, I am sorry. I have been growing irritable without my own wife and children. I forget others may have the same regrets.'

'How much longer do we have to stay here?'

Baldwin shook his head. He had no answer to that. They had been sent here on the orders of the King, and their duty was to remain to ensure the Queen's safety.

It was a most peculiar situation, though, and one fraught with dangers for a rural knight and bailiff.

### Prior's Hall, Christ Church Priory

The Prior rubbed at the bridge of his nose and ran through the events again, from the moment the idiots had woken him.

It was not only him. Mark and Hal had woken the whole priory. All had been deeply asleep, waiting for the bell to toll for Matins, and instead they were jerked awake by the screams of those two. Old Brother Anselm had thought that the end of the world was coming and nearly expired on the spot, poor devil. In truth, it was a miracle the deaf old stoat had heard anything.

All had rushed to the barn as soon as the fools had announced their discovery, and the priory had been all of a twitter ever since. It would have been bad enough if the man was just one of the brethren. Yes, that would have been dreadful. But worse still was the fact of who he was: a friend of Sir Hugh le Despenser. No one disliked poor brother Gilbert. The man was a pleasant fellow, bright, studious, and keen to please.

What was he doing there in the hounds' barn? The man should have been asleep, like all the other brethren. Yet there he was, in the hay, with his throat cut. Something must have awoken him and made him rise and walk outside. A disturbance? No, surely not – if there had been something of that nature, someone else would have heard it. Another monk would have woken.

Prior Henry swallowed uncomfortably as this thought rattled about in his head. Because perhaps another monk *had* woken. Perhaps it was a brother monk who had slain the poor fellow?

But that would mean that someone had hated him enough to all but hack his head from his body. Surely that was no monk from Christ Church.

No. It couldn't be.

## *Château du Bois, Paris*

It was while Baldwin and Simon were settling down in their chamber that the messenger arrived to ask them to return to the Queen's rooms.

'What now?' Simon muttered as they trotted across the courtyard. 'She wants a brief demonstration of sword-play to help her sleep?'

'You grow impatient with our Queen?' Baldwin said with a flash of his teeth.

'Not impatient with her – just with our position here,' Simon protested.

'Yet you think she seeks our company for a diversion?'

'She appears to enjoy little diversions,' Simon grumbled.

It was true – and yet she was also possessed of an intellect which was quite the match of any man's, as Baldwin told himself. The mere fact that she was here, in Paris, at her husband's expense, was proof of her wiliness. She was no fool. When she wanted something, she tended to win it.

'Sir Baldwin, Bailiff Puttock, I am glad to see you return,' Isabella greeted them as they walked in. She was still in her seat, while, instead of the ladies-in-waiting, William de Bouden, her comptroller and personal adviser, now stood at her shoulder.

Bowing, his face to the ground, Baldwin could not see her face. 'My Lady, naturally we came as soon as you commanded us.'

'There is no need for formality just now. Please, stand, both of you,' she said, graciously motioning with her hands for them to rise. 'I called you here to hear what my good friend William has to say. William, tell them too.'

The comptroller was a slightly chubby man, but square set for a clerk. He had eyes that were grey, steely and determined. He had the appearance of a fighter who had somewhat gone to seed in recent years. Now he looked at Baldwin and Simon with some doubt in his face. He had not come to know either of them during their journey here, and since arriving in Paris there had been too many calls on all their time.

'As you know, we are all here to negotiate a lasting peace. We have the objective of having all the King's territories returned. We cannot lose lands such as Guyenne.'

'It's a matter of pride,' Simon said, trying to sound as though he understood perfectly.

William turned his eyes on Simon, and when he spoke, his voice oozed contempt. 'You could say that. On the other hand, when you appreciate the fact that Guyenne brings more to the

King's purse than England, Scotland and Wales combined, you may understand that it is more than mere pride which makes it an attractive territory.'

'What!' Simon blurted, and gaped.

De Bouden pursed his lips, then, seeing he had their full attention, continued in more detail, explaining the history of the disputed territories.

Last year there had been a flare of battle over a *bastide* at St Sardos. The Abbot of Sarlat tried to build it with the permission of the French King, but English locals had deprecated the construction, and thrown down the works. The French tried to stop them, and the mob rose in anger, killing a French official. It gave the French the pretext they had wanted, and all the English territories had been confiscated by them.

Now the French King, Charles IV, insisted that the English King, Edward II, should come to France to renew his pledges of allegiance over the French territories under his command. But King Edward had no wish to put himself under the authority of this latest French King. King Charles IV was a dangerous opponent, wily and astute, and, the way his mind worked, it was surely hazardous to the English interest, and perhaps to the English King's personal safety, for King Edward to cross the channel. Which was why the Queen was here. She was French by birth, so she understood them, she could speak the language fluently, and her brother would hopefully not wish to embarrass her. He may even give the lands back as a matter of chivalry.

That had been the hope.

The reality was that King Charles IV was a shrewd negotiator who knew the strength of his position and intended making full use of it. The idea that he would willingly give up the lands he had taken was farcical.

'What is he asking?' Baldwin said.

The Queen herself responded. 'He demands that we surrender Guyenne, Ponthieu and Montreuil, until the King my husband comes here to pay homage to his liege lord. The Agenais will remain in my brother's hands until the ownership and rights are decided by a French court.'

'You think our King will accept that?' Baldwin said, shocked.

The Queen looked at him. 'Hardly,' she said.

'So we will have to make an accommodation,' William de Bouden said.

'Of what nature?' Baldwin asked.

'It is easy,' William began. 'Our King cannot come here himself. He could be in danger. There are many men here in the French court who are no friends to our King, and—'

The Queen cut him off impatiently. 'The King will not come, and there is only one other who could. If the King were to elevate my son by giving him all the King's possessions in France, then my son Edward could come here and take the oath. My husband need not come here himself. I want you to go to the King and explain this.'

### Eltham Palace, Kent

Unaware of discussions taking place over the seas in France which would lead to the ruin of his family, the end of his father's reign, and which would have a terrible impact on his own life, Edward of Windsor, the Earl of Chester, was yet assailed by dark thoughts.

He sat silently while food was brought to his table, surveying the men before him as he dipped his hands in the bowl presented, and dried them on the towel. In front of him, ranged in two lines, were the great trestle tables, and two thirds of his household were there, seated at the benches, while the remaining servants scurried to and fro with the dishes of food, one to each mess of four men. At least it was only his own household, he thought. His father was off at Beaulieu in Hampshire now.

It was a relief that his father was gone. The peripatetic life of a King was the same as that of any important lord, and involved a lot of strenuous travelling from manor to manor, because the size of the King's household was so vast that it would drain any location of its stock of food within a few days. So the King was forced to land upon a site, despoil it, and then move on again.

But it was not the poor peasants of the area near Eltham which caused Earl Edward such relief at the King's departure: it was that it was so hard for the Earl to control his anger and frustration in his father's presence. How he wished, sometimes, that he had been born just a normal man. Not a peasant, but a knight who would never seek to be more than a knight. A man who had a set position in the world, maintaining the King's Peace, controlling the mob, and making sure that the third class, the working men and peasants, kept to their allotted tasks, producing food for the *bellatores* and the men of God.

The life of the King's son was different from that of ordinary men. Christ's pains, but he knew that well enough. An ordinary man would respect his father and seek no reward. He must only show the correct reverence. But not Earl Edward. The King's first-born son was different. From early in his life he was separated from his father. He was of the royal blood, so like his mother, he had his own establishment, his own household. And it was like his father's in every way. The three lived more or less unconnected lives. Each with their own comptroller, their own guards, their own cooks, their own squires and heralds. When all three together descended on an area, the locals groaned under the weight of the demands on their stored foodstuffs.

But when they were together, Earl Edward was constantly aware of conflicting emotions: the natural filial love mingling with gratitude for the magnificent gifts which his over-generous father lavished upon him, competing with the bitterness and rage caused by his father's treatment of the rest of his family. Not to mention the other issues.

Not one of them could be raised in his father's presence, though. The way in which he had lost the trust and goodwill of his nobles, the irrational way he dealt with the French, which risked all the foreign possessions, and, most of all, the shameful way in which he acceded to each and every demand from that snake, Sir Hugh le Despenser. All these were enough to make the Earl's soul revolt, and yet he dared not raise them. The capricious, unreasonable way in which the King responded to any comment that could be viewed as a criticism made the very idea unthinkable. It was too dangerous.

Just as it was to bring up the way that his father was treating his brother and sisters. All of them taken from their mother and put into the care of others. And his mother, who was a *queen*, in God's name, had even had her private seal taken and put in the safe-keeping of Despenser's wife. That was disgraceful treatment, and humiliating for Queen Isabella.

But the way that the King treated his mother was none of his business, as he had been told. It was hard. Very hard. He had adored his father all those years. When he was a boy, there was nothing his father wouldn't do for him. All through to the day when the despicable Despenser arrived. From that moment, practically, his mother had been set aside. It didn't matter that she had remained loyal and loving to him, King Edward just ignored her. Or, worse, tolerated her presence. For the daughter of a French king and sister of three others, this was worse than contemptible.

And no, Earl Edward was not allowed to raise the matter. Despenser might discuss the queen and her children in that sly, fawning manner he had, but not the King's own son. King Edward would brook no criticism of any sort. The subject was closed.

Even for his son.

Earl Edward of Chester was at the same time a minor, just, and one of the most senior peers of the realm. A confusing position for anyone to cope with, especially a man who had responsibilities like his. For he was not just any earl. He was an earl who would be a king to rival Arthur himself.

After all, he was to become the 'Boar from Windsor'.

# Chapter Three

***Château du Bois, Paris***

Baldwin and Simon left the Queen's rooms and strode over the court by mutual unspoken consent, straight to the chamber where the guards were given their ale and wine rations. There they demanded a jug of wine each, and sat at a table with them, raising them to each other in silent thankfulness, and drinking steadily.

'You be careful, old man,' Simon said to Baldwin, only half jokingly. 'You aren't used to too much wine.'

'Today it will have no effect, Simon. Today I am already flying high on the fumes of the wine. I feel as though my head could touch the ceiling of the chapel, I am so light-headed with pleasure. We're going *home*! At last I'll get to see Jeanne again!'

The beaming smile on his face told Simon all he needed to know about his delight.

Simon took a long pull at his drink and sighed with satisfaction. 'I feel the same. Perhaps at last I can plan for Edith's nuptials with an easy heart. Because I tell you this, Baldwin. Once I get home, I don't intend to leave it again for any reason. I don't care whether the King himself comes and orders me to travel – I won't do it unless there's good reason!'

'Nor I, Simon. Nor I. I will be content to stay at my home

and take up the life of a rural farming knight once more. To hell with the position of Member of the Parliament! To hell with keeping the King's Peace and acting as judge of Gaol Delivery! I will sit at home and raise my family. I need nothing more!'

'So all we need do is take this man back and protect him, and then we can get off home,' Simon said, grinning broadly.

'Yes.'

The Queen had asked that the two travel to the King with a personal message for the King from her – and another for her son, should they meet him. They would be journeying in the company of one of the papal legates who had first helped to persuade King Edward II that his wife should be sent on this peace mission: the Bishop of Orange. Bishop Stratford of Winchester and William Ayrminne, who had helped arrange the latest truce between the two countries, were already assumed to be with King Edward, and briefing him on the latest developments in their discussions.

'There appears to be a general marshalling of all who may be able to sway the King's thinking,' Baldwin said.

'Even us, you mean?' Simon grinned.

'Two English bishops, the Pope's envoy, us . . . there were others in the party with the Bishops, too. I saw Isabella speaking at length with a King's herald, who was surely being sent back with private messages,' Baldwin said. 'When a Queen feels the need to accumulate such a powerful party to her, you may be sure that the message is important.'

'How will he react?' Simon asked. He had no interest in the great and good who had been sent home. He was just keen to set off himself. 'It is not all good news for our king.'

'Hardly. Still, the Bishop of Winchester is a sound fellow, I think; a diligent, thoroughly responsible man. He'll weather the storm. After all, he is more or less used to the King's temper. He's suffered from the King's anger before.'

'In what way?' Simon asked.

'When he was given his bishopric, the King had expected another to be given it, and he punished the Bishop by confiscating all his lands and assets. It cost Bishop John twelve thousand pounds to recover them, so I'm told.'

Simon winced at the sound of such a fortune. 'At least he is reconciled to the King now, though? After all, he's been sent here on this embassy to negotiate for the King, so there must be renewed trust, I suppose?'

'Not necessarily,' Baldwin said. 'But Bishop John has more skill than almost any other in the King's service when it comes to careful, practical negotiation. The King needs him, whether or not he likes it, or Bishop John!'

'And William Ayrminne? Will he weather the stormy blast?'

'He is a skilled negotiator, who's spent plenty of time in the King's service. He's wily enough to see himself safe, I make no doubt. Personally, I wouldn't trust him further than I could hurl him.'

'Why?'

'He's a canon at Westminster Abbey, but he spends a great deal of time with the Queen. I think he's looking for a new position with her as his patron. Never trust a man who is seeking advancement! He will trample anyone in his ambition.'

'And in the meantime, we shall travel with the Bishop of Orange. Do you know him?'

'I saw him briefly in Westminster. I think he's a sound enough man.' Baldwin shrugged. He did not add that any man whom a pope might choose as his legate was not to be trusted. Simon already knew his trenchant views on the papacy and the corruption of the curia, so did not press the matter.

'In any case, all we need is to return to England with them, and we can forget all about France and get on home,' Simon said with a broad smile.

Baldwin grinned back, nodding. There was nothing that could spoil their pleasure this day.

### On the road near Crowborough, Kent

He was riding past at full tilt, when he reached the place. Someone had once told him that a man could always remember a place that was fearsome to him. Well, he didn't need to be told that. Not now. The horse itself could sense what had happened here, even though the beast was not with him when he had originally come past.

There was not a sound. Even the wind had died. As he sat in the saddle, the beast beneath him pawing at the soft soil here in the woods, he was struck with a revulsion so distinct, it was almost a physical barrier to his dismounting. But he could not ride past. It wasn't possible. He had to do this to ensure his safety. It was a little thing, nothing, in the scheme of things. And it wouldn't hurt the man. Not now.

No. No sound. Not of wind, nor of people. No rattle of chains, creak of harness or regular step of man or horse. Nothing. Just the occasional song of a bird of some sort.

He dropped to the ground and stood a moment, holding the reins. Still nothing.

In a hurry now, he went to the bundled clothing and untied the thong holding it to the saddle; his fingers revolted at the touch, but there was no time to delay. He was off into the bushes, his nose leading him to the spot.

Argh! The smell was foul! After only a few days there was no disguising the odour. The weather had been too hot, and it was disgusting; he felt a trickle of ice shudder down his back at the smell. Enough to make a man puke, this was. He had to block his nose and breathe through his mouth, like he would when cleaning a gutted pig. The smell was so bad, he could hardly brace himself to continue, especially when he saw those already-empty eye sockets, but he had to do it.

It was a relief to be back on his horse. He set off at a steady trot as soon as he could, but then he had to stop.

To throw up.

*Wednesday following Easter*[1]

## Christ Church Priory

Prior Henry Eastry left the refectory and walked the short distance to the cloisters, which he began to stride up and down, considering.

The King's Coroner had arrived already, and was studying the body. Not that there was overmuch to learn from it. A corpse with the head almost removed. That was all that there was. Poor Gilbert. Mark and Hal had been instructed to look to see if there was anything which might explain why Brother Gilbert had been out there, but they had found nothing. And although the prior had questioned all his brethren himself, none admitted to knowledge of the crime.

'Prior? May I speak with you?'

'Of course, Coroner. I would welcome your views.'

Coroner Robert of Westerham was a shortish knight with the look of a man who would prefer to be in the saddle than idling indoors. He rested his hand on his sword hilt, and tapped at it whenever he was thinking. There were many

---

[1] Wednesday, 10 April 1325

coroners whom Prior Henry had known who had been less than honourable in the way in which they conducted their business, but this one at least seemed to try to be fair. At least, he was in his dealings with the priory.

'Your man was killed by a sword, I reckon. When I looked at him, the blade had sunk into the bones of his neck, so that means a heavy bladed weapon struck him. Not just a knife drawn over his throat.'

'I see.' The prior was able to take some solace from that. 'That means it is less likely to be a brother from the convent, then. I am relieved.'

The coroner nodded. 'Whoever it was was experienced in the use of swords, if I'm a judge. I suppose many of the brothers will have learned swordplay, but how many would have practised recently? There's another thing: whoever did this would have been covered in gore. The blood splashes went all over the hay, and the man who killed him must also have been smothered. But none of your monks' habits seem to have been stained. I have checked.'

'Good. But it still leaves the question of who could have done it.'

'Clearly someone from without the priory. Is there anything stolen from the church?'

'It was the first thing I considered. I had a full account of all the silver and plate made as soon as I was informed of Gilbert's death, just in case it was a robbery.'

'Nothing gone?'

'No. All our church ornamentation is still there.'

The coroner mulled this over a little while, frowning at the ground while he kicked at pebbles. 'In that case . . . is there anything else here of value?'

The prior smiled. 'We have much of value. St Thomas's

bones, our books . . . but nothing that a common thief would consider.'

There was no answering grin on the coroner's face. 'This was no *common* thief, Prior. This man was prepared to hack a monk to death.'

'Sweet Mother of God!' The prior's face paled. 'I will tell my sub-prior to search all our relics immediately.'

### Eltham Palace

Richard of Bury sighed and leaned back in his chair, a deeply contented man.

This place was as comfortable as any palace in the land. For his money, it was one of the most beautiful, too. The great hall was quite new – only about twenty-five years old, and there was a magnificent park to the south which the last owner, Bishop Bek, had added. The park and the great buildings, with the massive stone walls strengthened with brick bastions, had been improved when the Earl's grandfather, Edward I, had been given the place by the Bishop. A magnificent gift. The kind of thing that showed that Bishop Bek was looking for something significant in return.

Richard grinned to himself but his face soon hardened. There was a time when he would have said he was getting cynical, but any man who said that now would have to have been deaf and blind. Cynicism was unnecessary now, in the reign of King Edward II. Not something a man might dare to say in front of anyone else, of course, but it was a fact nonetheless. The King was mad.

There were times when a man might have a degree of confidence in his king. The best kings were undoubtedly those who sought to reign fairly and rationally. Logic was essential in a king. Promising one thing, then doing another was not rational. It was unsettling. And a king needed a kingdom that was settled and calm, if he wished to rule in peace.

Bury patted the book nearest him. It was a history of the life of Alexander, a tome he often picked up and browsed through. This was the kind of man a king ought to be, he thought. Honourable, chivalrous, strong of purpose, determined in battle, and magnanimous in victory. That was the sort of king England needed. Not like the present king. He may never be able to mention such things to others, but the king was dangerous to himself and the realm. Even when he was triumphant, he was vindictive to his defeated enemies. Not only to them, but also to their families. That was hardly chivalrous.

If there was one thing Richard of Bury was determined to do, it was to show the Earl in his care that there was a better way to rule a people than this. And thanks to God, Earl Edward seemed a keen and willing pupil to his tutor.

And God had also put in his way the means by which the King's heir might exceed all expectations. The oil of St Thomas would make him *more* than a mere King.

With Bury's help, the boy would become a king to rival Arthur himself – as the prophecy predicted.

*Thursday following Easter*[1]

### Château du Bois

Simon was already on his horse and eager to be away before even the Bishop's guards were prepared. Although Baldwin tried to hold a world-weary disinterest on his face, he too was noticeably present from an early hour, his rounsey saddled, bridled and ready.

---

[1] Thursday, 11 April 1325

A bishop would normally require a large force to travel with him, and wagons full of provisions and plate and cash for payment along the way, but to Simon's surprise, this Bishop of Orange apparently required little in the way of comforts. There were five pack horses and a couple of small carts, and a total of only five men-at-arms to guard him on horseback, not counting Simon and Baldwin.

'He's keen to travel fast,' Simon said, nodding towards the party.

'There is need for speed if the embassy is to be successful,' Baldwin said. He swung himself up on his rounsey, a large beast with spirit to match. He was stamping his feet and raising sparks from the cobbles, irritated at the noise all about. Men were hurrying to and fro with baskets and sacks, while dogs milled about, some darting under the horses.

There was one dog in particular that caught his eye: a large, mastiff-like dog, but although it had a mastiff's size, it lacked the pendulous lips and excessive flesh of a brute like Baldwin's late and sadly missed Uther. This was an entirely different type, with a long, silky coat in several colours. Baldwin had seen dogs with these markings before, but rarely if ever quite so pronounced: black all over, but for brown eyebrows and cheeks, with a white muzzle. The paws were all white, as was the tip of the tail, while there was a large white cross on the dog's breast. He moved with a heaviness, as was to be expected with an animal that must weigh three stone, but there was a spring in his gait that spoke of his liveliness and strength, and he ambled around the place, casting looks about him at all the people with such a benevolent, amiable expression that Baldwin was smitten.

'Stop dribbling,' Simon said caustically.

'He's a beautiful animal,' Baldwin said.

'He's a dog, Baldwin. A *dog*. If he's a good guard he may have a use, but that's all. Dear Christ in Heaven, man, haven't you enough hounds already?'

'Simon, I fear when it comes to matters of canine interest, you are indeed a peasant,' Baldwin said loftily.

'Aye. And peasants know when knights talk ballocks,' Simon said unperturbably.

In her room nearby, Queen Isabella sipped wine.

She should, perhaps, have gone down to wish them all a good journey, but she did not feel it entirely suitable. No, perhaps were she to do so, others might comment. Not immediately, perhaps, but later, and that was a risk she need not take, so she would not. Instead, she stood at her window in the castle and peered down, sipping from her goblet of wine as she prayed for their safety, and especially for the protection of the Bishop of Orange.

'Godspeed, Bishop,' she whispered.

For she knew that the Bishop had a most important message to take to England for her. A message to her son.

# Chapter Four

**Christ Church**

'Are you *sure*?' Prior Henry demanded. He could feel himself sagging in his seat as he took in this new disaster.

The sub-prior, James, nodded grimly. 'At least the relics themselves are safe, Prior.'

'What on earth would someone have wanted to do that for? What is the world coming to, eh?'

It was a *disgrace*! If he weren't a man of God, he would choose more select language for this abomination. That a man could kill another, that was appalling, but men would do so. It was ever the part of man to kill others: for money, for jealousy, for pride, for anger, for lust . . . the reasons were all known even to a Benedictine, and had been since the age of Adam, when one son killed another. Well, so be it. If men wished to harm each other, there was little a man like Henry Eastry, Prior of the great Christ Church of Canterbury, could do about it, but that a man would dare to break into the church itself and try to steal the relics upon which the future of the Church depended, that was an entirely different affair.

'So, clearly, this fellow attempted to break in, found his way to the reliquary, and there was accosted by poor Gilbert. Gilbert gave chase, and the man slew him, and escaped.'

'Yes, Prior. But what was Gilbert doing there?'

'He was assistant to the—'

'But yet he should not have been in there so late at night, Prior. This was the middle watch of the night, surely.'

'What of it? That is the time that criminals will attack. Even churches are not immune.'

'No – what was Gilbert doing there? Why was he awake?'

'He heard something. He was woken.'

'Perhaps.' His flat tone betrayed his disbelief.

'And at least nothing was stolen from the feretory.'

'Not from there, no.'

The prior turned slowly to stare. 'What do you mean?'

'The man who escaped appears to have taken the oil, Prior.'

'Eh? What do you mean? You told me that nothing had been stolen from the church. You looked carefully, you said, and nothing was missing.'

The sub-prior looked about himself nervously, and when he spoke his voice was lower and quieter. 'Prior, the *bones* are all there. I counted them. But the oil from the crypt is gone. *The oil of St Thomas is stolen!*'

## *Friday following Easter*[1]

### *Beaulieu Abbey*

The sound could be heard all along the passageways – a roar of anger that made monks blench. But none would dare to remonstrate.

It was eight days now since the King and his entourage had arrived, and the whole place had been turned upside down in that time. The sedate life of the abbey had degenerated into an unholy mess, with the King's servants rushing hither and thither, knights swaggering, flustered clerks hurrying from one

---

[1] Friday, 12 April 1325

room to another, and over all, rendering any excitement to naught, there was the malevolent spirit who controlled everything.

It was he who was bellowing with anger now.

'You mean to tell me that the mother-swyving son of a churl won't even return all my lands to me? He means to keep the Agenais until his own judges pronounce on it? And I suppose that won't mean that they'll try to please their own master, does it? It is not as though a French judge wouldn't know which decision would best satisfy their liege lord, is it? And you thought that was a "good" deal, did you? Tell me, *what would a bad deal look like*?'

'Your royal highness, this is hardly the—'

'This is exactly the right time, my Lord Bishop! That bastard is stealing my inheritance from me, from the Crown! Christ's Pain, would you have me give him the whole of my realm? He is stealing the revenues from Guyenne, from Ponthieu and Montreuil while you "negotiate" with him, and for what result? The result I can see here, is that you have successfully given away the Agenais for ever, while giving up a year's revenue from all our other possessions over there – and you call this a "good" deal for me? You must think me a *fool*!'

John Stratford, the Bishop of Winchester, bowed his head a moment and waited again until the blast of raw fury was spent. He had grown accustomed to this over the last months. He knew, dear God, he knew all too well, that he was one of the few men whom the King would trust to negotiate on his behalf, but that did not make the King's moods any easier to bear. Every time he returned to the King, he was struck with the feeling that he was about to be penalised yet again. The cost of buying back his lands and stock before had been ruinous, and he could ill afford to do so again. All because the King had promised the bishopric to another. It was hardly Stratford's fault if he had been able to subtly persuade the Pope that he was the more deserving man. However, the suggestion that he was oblivious to the possibility that he might be given the see was enough to give the King the vapours. Not without reason. Stratford was already known to be a master tactician in the use of words and arguments, after all. Anyone, even a purblind fool, must see that he'd so contrived matters to give himself the best opportunity to take the post himself. And although there were many words which could be used to describe the King, 'fool' was not one of them.

But these tantrums of his were growing more and more petulant. It was alarming for a man like the Bishop, for he knew perfectly well how even some of the most powerful men in the land had been executed in recent years. Dear God, the King had even seen his own cousin, the Earl of Lancaster, most shamefully executed. That was a very new departure for an English King. But it was only the beginning of this king's irrationality. Since the French confiscation of Guyenne, his temper had grown ever more irascible.

'I was persuaded to allow my *dear* wife to go to King Charles and negotiate with him because her persuasion, together with your skills, my Lord Bishop, were supposed to be infallible, and what have you both managed so far? You've passed over half my kingdom! You've given up all my French territories without a murmur, haven't you? Sweet Jesus, I should have you gaoled in the Tower for bloody *treason*!'

'The Queen and I have done as much as is possible, my Lord. However, a man may not make bricks without straw. If you wish to negotiate with a man like your brother-in-law, you would be better placed to have some power behind you. He respects might.'

'Oh, yes! Power! And how would a little land like ours be able to confront the greatest host of knights and men-at-arms in all Christendom? Do you know how many men I have under my banner? Eh? Maybe two thousand knights. And King Charles? Ten thousand, maybe twenty. You suggest I threaten him? With what? War? That would destroy us. Ach! Christ's bones, you know all this. What are you trying to do, torment me with my bloody weakness?'

And that was it. His rage was done for a moment, and when the Bishop cautiously glanced in his direction again, he saw that the King was slumped in his chair. Behind it stood Despenser, that little sneer of a smile on his face once more, the evil bastard.

There were few men in the land who were so whole-heartedly detested as Sir Hugh le Despenser, the architect of so much misery. The King's best friend, and most fabulously rewarded adviser. Reputedly, he was the King's lover. He was an avaricious thief of all he desired. All who tried to thwart him found themselves confronted with the full might of the King's host, no matter that they were defending their ancient rights or property against the Despenser.

But this was not the time to wax bitter about him.

'My Lord,' Bishop Stratford began, 'perhaps this is not so dreadful as you think on first sight. The fact is, the French have already taken your possessions in France. The French hold them. What we are attempting is to *recover* them. You know that King Charles is perfectly within his rights to ask that you go to him to pay homage for all the lands under his crown which you possess. You have a duty under the law to pay fealty to him. This is no more than you would expect from

any of the lords in your kingdom. You would expect them to
come to you, their liege lord, to pay their respects and make
their vows to you.'

'But he took my lands by force.'

'Because his man was murdered.'

'Pathetic! Is that an excuse? This is ridiculous!'

'But we have to try to resolve it, my Lord. The best we can
agree at present is to go to France and make the necessary
oaths. When you do, King Charles says he will return to you
Guyenne, Ponthieu, Montreuil, and the Agenais will be
resolved by his courts.'

'I cannot go! How can I go to France when the King
supports and gives sanctuary to those who plot my death?'

All in the room knew whom he meant. His most detested
and feared enemy: Sir Roger Mortimer of Wigmore. Sir Roger
had been his most respected marshal, not only for his tactical
skills in England whenever the King sent him into battle, but
also for his Irish campaigns, pacifying that turbulent and
troublesome country. But even the King's most honoured
friends could find themselves threatened in this topsy-turvy
court. Mortimer had always been the enemy of Despenser,
even from before their births. Mortimer's grandsire slew
Despenser's at the battle of Evesham, and Despenser had
sworn to uphold the feud. Thus it was that when Mortimer and
other Lords Marcher lifted their flags against Despenser's
rapacity, they found themselves accused of treason against the
King. Mortimer surrendered to the King's standard, and was
held in the Tower for some while, but when news came to him
that Despenser had successfully persuaded the King to execute
him, Mortimer was helped to escape from the Tower by some
companions, and now he lived in comfort at the French King's
court – or had done until the King's delegation arrived to

negotiate this peace. It was a thorn in the King's side that the man was still alive, let alone that he was protected by his own brother-in-law.

'If there is no agreement on this, then there may be no peace,' the Bishop said heavily. 'It is clear that King Charles has every right under feudal law to demand that you go to him, and—'

'There can be no agreement,' Despenser interrupted rudely, stepping forward until he was almost between the Bishop and the King. 'It is clear that King Charles is demanding this because either he knows that it's impossible for him to retain all our Lord's assets in France without a struggle, or because he plots the capture and downfall of the King. If our King were to travel to Paris, would he even arrive? With Mortimer planning the King's murder from within the French court, could there be even a vestige of hope of reconciliation? The French know full well that we cannot even consider travelling there while Mortimer walks abroad under the protection of the French Crown.'

'Mortimer was evicted from the court before the Queen arrived, my Lord,' the Bishop said directly to the King, ignoring Despenser. 'If he wished you harm, it is not with the connivance of the French. It is his own solitary plan.'

'You say so? Yet I have heard that Mortimer is still in Paris, and still meets with the King's enemies there,' Despenser said coolly, staring at him with those unsettling eyes of his. He had eyes with all the humanity, sympathy and human sensitivity of a snake, the Bishop thought.

The Bishop shook his head, but he said nothing. There was little to say against a man with the spying resources of Despenser.

'What say you, William?' the King asked.

William Ayrminne was behind the Bishop. He had remained quiet while the others bickered, but now he looked up. In contrast to the ascetic-looking Bishop, Ayrminne was solidly built, and had the clear grey eyes of a man who was philosophical in outlook. He shook his head gently. 'My Lord Bishop is absolutely correct, my Lord. There is no resolution without your travelling to France. The French are adamant.'

'Then there is no resolution,' the Despenser said heavily, and the King slammed his fist on the table.

'*Damn* that son of a whore!'

## *Second Monday following Easter* [1]

### *Sandwich*

They had made good time, Simon thought to himself as he splashed ashore, uncaring about the water that soaked his thighs and feet. He held his sword high at his chest to protect it from the salt spray, but his attention was more fixed on the shore and the sand, gleeful at the sensation of solid, safe ground beneath his feet once more.

He had been on ships too often for him to count now, and he held a firm and unswerving hatred of his experiences. Each occasion he had been thoroughly sick, and so demoralised that he had actively wished for death. On one journey, while returning from pilgrimage, he had been attacked by Breton pirates and shipwrecked, only narrowly escaping with his life. Ships were for sailors, so far as he was concerned, and if he never so much as saw a ship again in his life, it would be all the same to him. He disliked the feeling of wobbling about on the water more than any other.

---

[1] Monday, 15 April 1325

They had been blown north. Oh, Baldwin had said that it didn't matter, that they were still heading more or less westwards, but Simon knew better than that. They'd ended up on the Isle of Ennor when they were heading for Cornwall last time he'd crossed the Channel, and now they were going *up* the English Channel. Knowing Simon's luck they'd end up in some ungodly damned country like the Norwegian lands, or even Scotland!

But instead, here they were. He wriggled his toes in his boots. Sand! Sand! Glorious, firm, solid, sound sand! He could have bent and kissed the ground, it was so wonderful to feel the shore under his sodden boots. Instead, he took the more acceptable opportunity to close his eyes and utter a prayer of thanks.

'Pleased to see you're rightly grateful,' Baldwin said drily.

'It's all right for men like you to be cynical,' Simon said righteously, 'but for those of us who actually suffer, there is nothing quite so wonderful as feeling the earth again.'

'You were hardly even sick this time.'

'Perhaps to you it looked like that,' Simon growled. '"Hardly" does not cover the feelings I had whilst in that bucket.'

'Well, with any luck you'll never have to see a ship again,' Baldwin said soothingly.

'No.'

There was a shortness to Simon's response which made Baldwin shoot a look at him. 'You're not missing your position at Dartmouth?'

'No. No, I couldn't say that. I disliked that job more than any I've ever had. I only really want to get back to Tavistock and return to my old duties on the moor. I'm a moorman by nature. The idea of sitting in a room and agreeing bills of lading with shipmasters, or more likely arguing over the customs due, is ideally suited to some blasted clerk, but not me. I don't like it.'

'It is sad that our old friend promoted you.'

Simon nodded. He had been a contented man before, riding out over the moors and wasteland of Dartmoor, maintaining the peace however he may, and making his way homewards each night whenever he could to see his wife and family. But then he had provided a service to his master, Abbot Robert of Tavistock, who owned the revenue from the moors. That kindly old man had been so pleased with Simon's efforts that he had given him a new post, that of his chief official in Dartmouth, responsible to him for all customs. Abbot Robert had been an enthusiastic gatherer-up of positions that might bring in precious treasure to his abbey, and he had paid many pounds to the King for the rights to the port.

But it was not a job to Simon's taste. He had felt divorced from his family, as though cast adrift on an unpleasant sea. Perhaps not all sailors were disreputable thieves who looked upon life at sea as a form of legalised piracy, but there were few who did not appear to do so. They all looked upon war as a wonderful excuse for them to break the heads of any foreign sailor and steal his whole cargo, ideally taking his ship as well.

He had quite liked some of the sea-farers. Most, however, were simply rough, violent men who were little better than outlaws. They would never have made a living on land. Although he held little sympathy for men like those of Brittany, who raided the English ships unmercifully, he had little, too, for those from Devon who waged war on the Bretons. And the men of Lyme. And those from the Cinque Ports . . . and those from any other town in England whose ships they felt they could steal without being seen. The law of the land only held force while a ship was in view of the land, after all. Beyond that, a man had to see to his own protection.

'Ah, there's the dog,' Baldwin said. 'He's a beautiful animal!'

Simon glanced back to see that the great beast Baldwin had so admired before had launched himself into the water from the rowing boat that was bringing the Bishop to shore with all the other dogs. Baldwin's favourite paddled through the waves with nose upward, as waves crashed over his head and smothered him, reappearing a moment or two later, blinking and straining determinedly for the land.

'I think he likes ships as much as you, Simon,' Baldwin said.

'No one can appreciate the depth of my detestation for ships,' Simon countered.

His grimness made Baldwin look at him. 'Not long now, and we'll be home,' Baldwin said quietly.

'Cannot be soon enough for me,' Simon said.

# Chapter Five

***Christ Church Priory***

Prior Henry eyed the coroner as he approached. 'Have you any news?'

'Little enough.'

Coroner Robert grimaced as he pulled off his thick riding gloves and wiped his brow. It was unseasonably hot today, and he had ridden fast from the last inquest.

'Sir Robert, please, I am forgetting my manners. Would you like refreshment? Wine?'

'Ale if you have it, Prior. It is a little warm for exercise.'

The prior watched while one of his servants ran for the drink. The coroner appeared almost uneasy, avoiding the Prior's eye as he stood, tapping his foot and waiting.

Soon the ale arrived, a large pewter jug and a silver goblet that looked ridiculously small in comparison. It took five refills of the goblet before the knight looked comforted and could nod to the Prior with a look of resolution on his face.

'Very well. Can we speak here in privacy?'

'Of course,' the prior said.

'Your dead man, Brother Gilbert, was undoubtedly murdered by the man who took the oil, but I am not sure that he was entirely blameless.'

'What do you mean by that?'

'Just this: the man who killed Gilbert was seen. Or, at least a man who appeared to have been trying to escape attention was seen on that night, running away from the convent. There is a peasant outside the city wall who's prepared to swear that he saw a man with what looked like a damp tunic running away from the postern. He said nothing at the time because it didn't occur to the cloth-headed fool. I daresay he was drunk and just thought that it was someone else who had been drinking. Now he has heard of the murder, he's had fresh thoughts, though.'

'He should have come forward sooner,' the Prior said bitterly.

'Perhaps. Maybe he knew something else, though, and chose not to.'

'That sounds a little strange, Sir Robert. What do you mean by it?'

'In the days before his death, you had guests, did you not?'

'Yes, you know that we had the embassy for the King pass by. They were asking where the King was, and I was able to direct them to Beaulieu. They stayed one night only.'

'In that night did you notice any of the monks speaking with the men in the embassy?'

'Yes. Of course they did. The monks here may be devoted to God, but that doesn't mean that they take no interest in affairs outside the convent.'

'Clearly that's true.'

'What are you inferring, Sir Robert?' Prior Henry challenged testily. He was growing uneasy at the coroner's apparent grimness.

'Did Gilbert have a dispute with any of the men from the party?'

'No, he did not. Coroner, I do not like your tone.'

'And I don't like what I've been hearing. The man who saw

the fellow running from here said that he was running away from the priory and heading westwards.'

'After them? But that is ridiculous! You're telling me that the men in the embassy could have stolen the oil? That is impossible. They were all gone the afternoon before the theft.'

'How many King's heralds were there in the party?'

'With the two bishops? I don't know ... there was that chubby one, and the shorter, stocky fellow. What of it?'

'I've asked about. Apparently the party rode on to an inn at Ashford. There was only one herald with the party there.'

'I am sure there were two.'

'I am sure you are right. One stayed behind and killed your Gilbert.'

'What possible reason could there be for him to do that?'

'I do not know.'

'I think you must be mistaken, Coroner. The party riding on would have noticed if they had lost a man.'

'In a group of how many? Fifty? A hundred? They would all believe that the man was in another part of the cavalcade. But there is another thing: the man said that the fellow's tunic was all wet. He also said that it almost obscured the fellow's tabard. It was the tabard of a royal herald.'

Baldwin was glad when they saw the first lights in the distance and could smell the faint tang of woodsmoke on the air.

There were few signs of civilisation so welcome to a traveller as these. The first thing he always sought out was a gibbet when abroad, because at least in a land such as Galicia or Navarre, when a man found a proof of punishment, there was also proof of law, and law enforcement. Terrifying to him was a land in which there was no respect for laws. That was dangerous indeed.

Here, though, they were approaching the city of Canterbury, and Baldwin was hopeful that they might soon be at the priory, where they might beg a room for the night before it grew dark. He was unwilling to stay in the open out here. There had been too much devastation during the terrible famine years. He had heard rumours of cannibalism here in Kent, and doubted that matters were any safer yet away from the cities.

There was little conversation with other members of their party. Their companions were a mixed group. The Bishop of Orange clearly thought himself too superior to Simon to speak with him, although he did condescend to talk to Baldwin on occasion. For the most part of their hurried journey he had maintained a stiff haughtiness, patronising the guards when he spoke to them, and irritating all who travelled with him.

The men-at-arms ranged from one scruffy churl, Pons, whom Baldwin would happily have seen fall from the ship just to see him washed, he was so foul, to one fellow who looked as though he might have been the son of an earl, because he was always immaculately dressed. This man, Jack, took one look at Baldwin early on in their travels, and appeared to wince at the sight of his old threadbare red tunic and torn linen shirt. He almost made Baldwin defensive about his style of dress. This one appeared to view the world with an eye that could discern a joke in any situation. Yet he reminded Baldwin of others, especially those who had lost their livelihoods and were forced to hire themselves out to whoever seemed to be the best new master. There were many of them since the famine of ten years ago.

Of the others he formed little opinion. There were two Flemings and a Frenchman, but they tended to keep to themselves and messed together. They were not rude to Baldwin and Simon, but Baldwin gained the impression that they were used to their master and tended to heed his moods. When he was quiet, so were they. Still, Baldwin noticed that the Frenchman in particular appeared to possess an ill humour. André appeared to lose his temper swiftly when he felt himself thwarted. Baldwin saw this when they stopped at one inn and the man-at-arms felt that his horse was not attended to speedily enough. André almost set hand to sword until a companion, the foul little one, calmed him.

Still, he had not felt as though he was in danger from any of them during their fast ride from Paris. They had not been forced to gallop, but the lightness of their loads had meant that they had been able to go at almost the speed of a King's Messenger, some thirty to forty miles each day, depending upon the land and roads. However, although messengers were entitled to take their ease on the Sunday, the Bishop had not suggested that. After Mass, he insisted they should continue. His view was that 'Travelling itself is not a sinful occupation on a Sunday. I look upon it as a necessary duty; the more so since we have a need to hurry in order to try to prevent another war breaking out between the English and the French.'

Baldwin was happy with this attitude. There were all too many men who'd delight in a day's rest when they had duties to perform. He was content that while the Bishop might well be a hard man to like, an arrogant, pig-headed, stalwart noble who looked down on any man who was not worth at least two hundred pounds a year, he was also dedicated. And no Christian could ask for more than that.

They were clattering along the road into Canterbury as the light began to fade, and Simon and Baldwin, who were riding in the vanguard, could hear the sound of bells tolling.

'My Lord Bishop, they are ringing the bells,' Baldwin called back urgently. 'With your permission, we shall ride on.'

'I will send my own men. You may remain,' came the firm response.

Baldwin took a deep breath, but decided to make no objection as two of the guards were sent on. It was the two Frenchmen: André and the scruffy little fellow, Pons.

It was a decision which he would later rue.

### *Beaulieu*

The King motioned sulkily as he completed his meal, and his servants hurried to do his bidding.

His men swiftly finished their food and bowed their way from his presence, each carefully walking backwards so as never to show him the insult of turning their backs upon him, and while one group of young servants set about removing all the mess bowls and clutter from the tables, another set to removing and folding all the table linen. As soon as that was put away, the table tops were taken from the trestles, and all cleared away, leaving a broad, empty space in front of him.

'It is always thus, Hugh. Always. In every detail of my life, I have been thwarted. At first it was my father, refusing to understand the depth of my love for poor Piers; then the earls took his place after his death and refused to countenance my friendship with him, even going so far as to murder him. Murder him! My poor Piers. All I have ever wanted was to be a good king, but I am prevented at every turn by fools and malcontents. Not satisfied with ruining my happiness by murdering poor Piers, they tried to make me cast you aside too.'

Despenser nodded with a serious expression on his face. Piers Gaveston was a man who had been universally detested throughout the country. Greedy, vain, ambitious and arrogant, he had finally been captured by barons and murdered, to the King's horror. 'They didn't succeed, my Lord, did they?'

'But they shouldn't have *tried*! I am their King, in God's name. I am the man anointed by God, chosen by Him to be their ruler on earth. Do they dare set their faces against Him through me? Are they that mad?'

'Only a fool would attempt such a crime,' Despenser said, clenching his jaw to stifle a yawn.

'But they do. Then there is the felon Robert Bruce and his rebellion in Scotland, and the arch-traitor, Mortimer. How has my reign become so mired with treachery and distrust? I only ever wanted to be a *good* king.'

'You *are* a good king. The actions of a few fools and criminals cannot alter that.'

'It all went wrong from that first moment. Do you remember that knight who died at my coronation?'

'Come, my Lord, we have—'

'Do not contradict me, Sir Hugh. I was delayed for a week because of that intolerable old fool Winchelsea, and all said it was because of disputes between me and the barons. Then there was a genuine argument about which earl should carry which item of the regalia, and the death of the knight when the mob pushed forward. Dear Christ, I can see it all now!'

And he could, in his mind's eye. The press had been so forceful that a wall had collapsed, bringing down with it the royal staging and knocking down the high altar. Sir John de Bakewell was the unfortunate man who happened to be standing at the other side of the wall, and he was crushed to death. The most devastatingly unpropitious beginning to any reign.

'It was an accident, my Lord,' Despenser said smoothly.

'An *accident*? It set off my reign perfectly,' the King said petulantly. 'A man dies at my coronation, and within a day, there are rumours of my displeasing my French wife's family, and stories about my association with my best friend. How much worse could the omens have been?'

'Yes.'

'And it could all have been prevented.'

'You mustn't let yourself dwell on such matters, my Lord.'

'*Silence!*' The sudden, snapped command held the power of a man who could inflict death in a moment with complete impunity. 'Do not presume to tell me what I may and may not consider, Sir Hugh. I am the *King*. Sir Thomas, Earl of Lancaster, tried to tell me what I may and may not do, and I saw him executed. Do not forget that!'

Sir Hugh bowed his head repentantly, but in his heart he laughed to himself. Just now he was the King's sole friend, and the King would not dare to remove him. Indeed, a large consideration that swayed the King against travelling to France to pay homage for the French estates was the knowledge that to do so would almost certainly result in a rebellion against Despenser. Without the King's protection, he was as secure as Gaveston had been on that lonely road when he was slain. And the only man who hated Despenser more than a natural-born English Lord was the French King. He detested Sir Hugh.

It all stemmed from the dreadful days after the war of the Lords Marcher. The bastards had imposed demands upon the King, first of which was that Sir Hugh should be exiled from England. That was not something he would accept. Instead, he based himself in Kent, at the coast, and set about a life of piracy. One ship he took was French, and ever since then the French King had said he was a felon. Were Sir Hugh ever to set foot on French soil, so King Charles IV had said, he would be executed immediately.

He could not travel to France with King Edward. Yet without him, King Edward was reluctant to go to France. He trusted no other man to act in his stead, but if Despenser were left, there would be a rising against him in moments, and he would be killed. That was why the King remained here in England – it was in order to protect his companion. His irritation stemmed from the knowledge that he would lose his French possessions in his attempt to protect his lover.

'If only I had been anointed with the oil . . .'

'It is over, my Lord. What is done is done, and there is little we can do to alter our destiny now we are set upon our roads.'

'You speak like a man who has knowledge of such matters. You were not so damned sanguine when you thought your life was threatened by the possible attack of a necromancer, were you?'

Sir Hugh shrugged. He had got over it once he'd ensured that the necromancer had been killed in gaol.

'St Thomas's oil,' King Edward muttered. 'If only I'd had it then. But no. Even then the earls were plotting my downfall, weren't they?'

'I am sure that—'

'Oh, *silence*! I am the most unfortunate monarch this land has ever seen. My reign was cursed from the first. And you know it!'

# Chapter Six

***Eltham***

The Earl of Chester was never happier than when on horseback. Riding out like this, his hounds and raches at his feet, he was perfectly content. There was surely no pleasure greater than that of a man who was exhausted after a day's hunting, he reckoned.

This deer park was a wonderful testing place for a man, too. The trees were thick, and often the hounds would have to chase into the undergrowth to spring the elusive deer, which made it still more challenging for the huntsmen to see where the beasts would burst forth.

Today they had found a good stag, and he'd given them an excellent ride, all over the park and then out, when the wily old devil found a weakness in the wall, and managed to clamber over a partly collapsed section. And then the men had to hurtle over it and across three vills' fields to catch him. A marvellous ride.

He had always been fond of this part of the country. The land was glorious, excellent for orchards and grain, and providing lush pasture for horses and cattle. And at the edges, perfectly maintained woods and copses. It was a fine example of a modern agricultural business.

Of course, it had been his mother's until recently. She had been given it by his father as a mark of his respect for her, and she had quickly altered it to suit herself and the needs of her household, which meant making it suitable for children. John, Edward's younger brother, was born here, and the girls always loved it too. Which was the sad thing now, with all of them away. It made the palace quiet. Quieter than it should have been. If he could, Edward would have had them all back – but his father had decreed that the others should all be looked after elsewhere, and Edward missed them.

Not too much, however. He was almost thirteen, an earl in his own right, and he didn't need to rely on *girls* and his mother to keep him happy. He was a man.

It would be good to see them all again. To hear their laughter in the solar, his mother's happy voice with that very French laughter in it as she played with them. He missed her too.

But he was a royal earl, and he had responsibilities that others wouldn't understand. For one thing, he was born to the prophecy, and he must live with that. The prophecy said that he would be another Arthur, the Boar from Cornwall, and it was a very daunting prospect, to follow in the footsteps of the greatest King England had ever known.

## Canterbury

Baldwin's first indication of danger was the sudden movement at the gate.

The traffic entering a city was always predictable. There were streams of men and women entering by the main gates all through the day, while another roughly similar number left. Those entering in the morning were pedlars, tranters and other traders who had goods to sell, or carters bringing produce in from the lush countryside all about. Those leaving were the men and women who had work in the suburban areas, or travellers who had rested a night in the safety of the city's walls. Later in the day the streams reversed themselves. The tradespeople, carters and sumptermen all making their way home, in various degrees of drunkenness, while those who had been at work outside made their way back to security. And travellers like Baldwin hurried to get in before the gates closed.

Yes. It was all predictable and regular, like the ebb and flow of the tide. But tonight there was something wrong. The stream of people walking to the gates had snarled up, and there was a tangle of men and women crying out. As Baldwin watched, he saw a flash, and knew in an instant that it was an unsheathed blade.

'My Lord Bishop, there is danger ahead,' he called quickly. 'Simon, there's a fight. I'll wager those two pushed all from their path and the locals have set on them!'

'Fight there may be, but I do not relish a rest in the open all night,' the Bishop grunted. 'We may, possibly, press on and meet with the people at the gate? *Viens! Allons-y!*'

Baldwin looked at Simon, who muttered a heartfelt, '*Shite!*' and then the two clapped spurs to their mounts and hurried off, trying to avoid the hounds who, seeing the horses beginning to race, joined in with gusto.

The road here was a dog-leg. A stand of trees at the wayside blocked their view for a moment. They rode past a great abbey – St Augustine's, Simon was later to learn – and after this, the road took a sharp turn to the right, following the abbey's outer wall. Now they could see the mess at the gate, and hear the shouting. Two men were plainly fighting. Simon could see one of their mounts rearing, while the fellow beat down with his sword, although whether he was slashing at an attacker, or merely knocking a fool on the pate with his pommel, Simon couldn't tell.

Now they were taking an equally sharp left turn, and making a straight line for the city's eastern gate, the Burgate. It was a run of only maybe a hundred yards, but now it was crammed with people shouting and screaming, and in the midst of it were the Bishop's two men-at-arms, their arms flailing, and as Simon came closer, he could see that their blades were red with blood.

'Christ!' Simon swore. 'Do you see them?'

Baldwin had no need to answer. There were three people on the ground at the feet of the two horses, two with bloody heads, and both the Bishop's men were retreating towards the edge of the road, where a fence prevented their escape, and were looking about them with angry nervousness, as well they may, for there was a ring of rough-looking men about them, four carrying pole-arms as though they knew how to use them, two more with ash staffs, and more rushing to their side with knives and clubs.

'Come, Simon!' he called, and galloped to them.

It was almost too late. He saw a whirling flash of silver, and one of the Bishop's men was lucky not to have his throat slashed wide by the razor-sharp weapon. It was only by clashing his sword against the staff's length that Pons managed to save himself, deflecting the bill's blade up and over his head as he ducked. His companion was less fortunate, and as Baldwin reached them, the lance held by one of his opponents tore a deep gash along from behind André's temple to the back of his head, behind his ear. He gave a loud bellow of pain, and would have ridden the lance-man down, but bill and lance were too well paired. Even as he crouched to spur his mount, the bill came down to point at his breast. Were he to move, he would skewer himself on the point.

'Stop this! Stop in the name of the King!' Baldwin roared as he approached.

It was enough to distract one pole-arm. A man turned and faced Baldwin with his lance pointing dangerously towards him. 'Halt!'

Before the others could turn, the mass of hounds and dogs was on them, barking and bouncing all about. The men with pole-arms could do little but beat at them with the butts of their staves, trying to push them away or club them. One or two blows connected – one in particular aiming a kick at Baldwin's favourite dog which made him spur his horse onward.

'Stop!' Baldwin bellowed over the row of howling and shouting. 'These two men are on the King's business and carry letters of safe-conduct. If you harm them, the King will have your heads! Stand aside.'

'Who are you?'

He was a short, pugnacious-looking man of about five-and-twenty. Dark, suspicious eyes met Baldwin's, and the set of his thin mouth was determined.

'I am Sir Baldwin de Furnshill, Keeper of the King's Peace and member of the King's Parliament,' he said. 'I am here to help protect a papal legate on an embassy to the King. An insult to the Pope's own official is an insult to the King who gave letters of safe-conduct.'

'That's all pretty well, Sir Knight, but as you can see, your friends here have knocked three people down.'

'This is not true!' It was the injured guard. He held a hand to the flap of scalp which had been sliced wide. 'We were trotting down here, when some arse threw something at us for riding past their line. I was struck by dung, and so was Pons here.'

'We were both hit.' Pons nodded, and turned his shoulder to demonstrate. On his flank there was a large mess of horse dung clinging to his tunic. 'These *fils de merde* insulted us, and we retaliated. *C'est tout.*'

'I saw these two wheel and ride down three people,' the gate man said firmly. 'That makes them felons unless the court decides that they were acting in self-defence.'

'This was no premeditated attack,' Baldwin said. 'They were attacked and defended themselves. Did you see the initial attack?'

'No.' The man met Baldwin's eye for a moment, then slid away.

Baldwin had seen that look in a man's face before. It was not outright dishonesty, but a wariness caused by knowing a little too much, a little more than a man should have to.

'Very well,' he said after a moment. 'I suggest this. Your name?'

'I am Adam Cook to my friends.'

'Very well, friend Cook. We are going to the Priory. I will wait for you there in the Prior's guest rooms. We shall discuss this matter there. For now, it is more urgent that you and your friends see to the locking of the gates than that we argue the matter here in the open.'

Cook nodded slowly, ignoring the angry cries of the men and women queuing behind him. 'Very well. Come along, get inside, all those who want to. We lock the gates as soon as it is dusk.'

Baldwin nodded, and trotted forward as the Bishop reached them, gazing down and studying the three bodies on the ground as he went. His dog sniffed at them with apparent confusion, as though not understanding what they were doing lying in the road, until a stone was thrown at him. He yelped, glancing about him as though hurt, before following his master, who absently made the sign of the cross as he rode past the bodies.

It was another festering English city, the Bishop thought as he rode under the gates.

If only the Pope had managed to persuade another to come here and take on this mission, but it was not possible. There was no one else with such a good command of the barbaric language these peasants spoke. Other ambassadors had suffered from that. The English would tend to go into huddles and discuss matters in their own tongue, which often left the Pope's men at a disadvantage. With such important affairs to negotiate, it was important that the best emissary was sent.

And there was the Queen, too. There was no one else who could be sent to speak for her. She was, as the Pope had said, 'an angel of Peace'. She knew how to deal with her brother, and appeared to have some influence with her appalling husband. It must have been a terrible existence for her, in this miserable, grey, country, acting as bed-mate to a king who showed her scant regard. Poor woman.

It was a great pity that she was not the ruler of this land. The people were ferocious, unruly, disobedient, and entirely without dignity. They would brawl at the slightest insult, the lot of them, churls, peasants, farmers, whores, lords and earls. There was no sense in any of them. Obstinate and foolish. And cold.

The knight in his guard-party was one of the worst, too. Cold, unsmiling, taciturn . . . he clearly had no liking for the Bishop, as though the Bishop had done something to deserve his enmity. But the Bishop had never met the man before, so far as he could remember. No, this Sir Baldwin was just another typical example of an English 'gentleman'.

The worst of them, naturally, was the one from whom all the ridiculous behaviour stemmed. A king who sought the companionship of peasants, who tested himself against hedgers and ditchers, who preferred the company of play-actors, dear Heaven, and who preferred to avoid the barons of his own land. He was intolerable!

It was fortunate indeed that no man thought him to be competent in his role as King. His failures in battle, his failure as a husband, his failure as a human, made him the laughing stock of all other lands. If he were to lose any more respect, he may even lose his crown among such a turbulent people.

That was a possibility to be desired. And it was why he was really here, of course.

'Sir Baldwin.'

Baldwin turned to see Cook, the city porter, at the door.

They had been here in the priory long enough to divest themselves of their dirtier clothing, time to see that their horses were well treated, to grab a flagon of wine and drain it, and to choose the best area for sleeping on the rough floor.

'Master Porter.'

'No, no porter. Just an honest cook who'd prefer to be in his kitchen than defending the city against miscreants.'

'The men you stood against were indeed rash, but not miscreants. If a man were to throw ordure at me, I, too, would deprecate his behaviour.'

'Enough to murder three? Who are those men? They didn't sound English.'

'There was no murder here, Porter. Only a chance

affray. But to answer you, the pair of them are Frenchmen, I think.'

'Will they be here long?'

'If you will permit us, we shall ride from here tomorrow early. We have to ride to the King.'

'Well, I'll do what I can, but I promise nothing. Those who died will hardly be missed, they were just peasants,' Cook said with a dry smile that held no humour. He was not amused, but trying to explain to a knight how the land lay. If Baldwin was truly in the party of an emissary of the King, it was best he was not delayed or provoked. 'But there are some hotheads who'd prefer to see some semblance of justice, even if they were all unimportant.'

'No man's life is unimportant,' Baldwin said. 'If I could, I would deliver the fools to you, but I have need of them to continue to defend my Lord Bishop. Without them, we are too few.'

'The city could present you with some replacements?'

'What would happen to these two?'

'They'd be held for the coroner. That will have to happen whatever may pass. You know the law. This was a slaughter on the road. We have a duty to hold an inquest and see what the jury says.'

'Very well. I shall inform the Bishop and see what he desires,' Baldwin said.

Cook nodded, then gave a short grin before leaving. It was enough to make Baldwin feel a little unsettled as he walked over the floor to the door on the opposite side. He had clearly failed to overawe Cook.

Beyond the door was a little chamber which had been set aside for the Bishop's men. The Bishop of Orange was himself in the prior's hall. Baldwin had only been seated a short while when an anxious-looking monk arrived with the message, asking Baldwin and Simon to go with him to the abbot's lodgings.

'What does he want with us?' Simon grumbled, regretfully eyeing his jug of wine as he stood.

'He wishes to discuss the murder, I think,' the monk said.

It didn't make Simon feel any better about leaving his wine.

# Chapter Seven

Coroner Robert was waiting in the Prior's hall. The Bishop sat at table, noisily dismembering a chicken and paying the prior and coroner no attention while the prior introduced them. As Simon said to himself, though, the man hardly spoke any English. It was no surprise that he was silent.

The Coroner of Canterbury had met enough knights and King's officers in his time. It was his firm belief that there were only a few different types. They all fell into one of three categories, and he was perfectly capable of recognising them all. There were those who were set upon personal aggrandisement, seeking money at the expense of all others; those whose sole ambition was to have power; and those, a form of reptile like the repellent Despenser, who wanted both at the same time. Coroner Robert had no time for any of them. Yes, in his experience all men fell into one of the three, and he wondered idly into which category these two fell.

'You are a keeper?' he asked of Baldwin. Hearing the response, he nodded to himself. If he had to bet, this was one of those who sought power. Clearly the other one, the former bailiff, was after money. You could see that by looking at the two of them. The better dressed, albeit with the stains and mess of the roads on his clothing, was the former bailiff, while the knight was quite shabby-looking. He clearly didn't have any care for fashion. Presumably, the former bailiff was looking to improve his treasure so he could maintain himself in the style he enjoyed, while the knight was merely power-hungry.

Satisfied with his conclusions, the coroner felt a vague disappointment. It was a common experience for him nowadays. Everyone could be slotted into one of the three sheaths he had seen. The King was not powerful enough to control the rampant ambitions of his nobles, and in the free-for-all that was modern politics, everyone was out to grab what they could. Even when the coroner had, generously, given someone the benefit of the doubt, hoping that the fellow would not fit into the sheath of greed or power, he had, unfailingly, been disillusioned later. Now he preferred to see the worst from the first moment. It saved trouble later.

'You are investigating the three?' Baldwin said. 'I am glad to see you take your job so seriously as to come here this late to investigate, Sir Robert.'

'We are not so populous that we can afford to lose three men without noticing,' Sir Robert said sharply.

'I would not have thought so,' Baldwin said with a smile. 'I respect you for your diligence, though.'

'Thank you. Now, these two who killed them. They are here in the priory?'

'They will go nowhere.'

The Bishop of Orange's words were the first the coroner had heard him speak, and he was startled for a moment. Then he bowed stiffly and thanked him. 'I am glad to hear it.'

'But I will have them with me in the morning when I leave.'

'My Lord Bishop, that is difficult. I have a duty to investigate the deaths of the three outside the city gate, and—'

'They are my guards. They must leave with me. I am on an urgent embassy to your King, and the guards fall under the protection of your King. They were set upon and attacked by a small mob. They defended themselves. That is all you need to know.'

'With respect, my Lord Bishop, the law of *my* country says that I have to investigate and record the facts. And if I discover that the men were guilty of murder, I have a duty to have them held until the next court is held to hear their case.'

'That is not possible. My men answer to me, and I will not have them left behind.'

The coroner's hackles were rising. 'My Lord, they must be kept here until my inquest. After that you may – *may* – be permitted to take them with you.'

Baldwin interjected. 'Coroner, I think that the only issue here is the urgency of our mission to the King. If there is any means of speeding the inquest, so that it could be held in the morning, would that satisfy your need for justice and the Bishop's need for haste? After all, it is to be hoped that the two will not be found guilty of deliberate murder. There was clearly no premeditation here, nor was it some secretive assault under cover of darkness. It was two nervous men who were assaulted, just because they were riding to the gate on the orders of the Bishop. The locals deprecated their temerity at hurrying past, and they tried to defend themselves against apparent attack.'

'So you say. I do not know until the jury meets.'

'But it would be possible to hurry the matter along?'

'Not if there is any risk of an injustice.'

'If there were,' Baldwin said gravely, 'I assure you, I would take a dim view of it.'

Of course you would! Coroner Robert thought to himself. Aloud, he said silkily, 'And, naturally, you would want to see them punished if they were found guilty?'

'Yes. I am Keeper of the King's Peace in Devon, and I spend my life seeking the fair punishment of those who deserve it.'

Coroner Robert nodded, but he was not persuaded. Sir Baldwin was clearly a man who enjoyed power and the trappings of power. 'You have been keeper for long?'

'It will be ten years next year, I think. Is that right, Simon?'

The bailiff nodded.

To the coroner's eye, the bailiff looked the grimmer, less trustworthy of the two. He had a bleak expression in his sunburned face, like a man who was constantly waiting to hear an insult so that he may avenge it. There was a bleakness about him that made the coroner feel wary.

Ten years. There were few keepers who had held their positions for that length of time. Usually their corruption was discovered much sooner.

'And you, Coroner? How long have you been in post?'

'I've been here for some six years now.'

Baldwin's eyebrows rose a little. Then he nodded slowly.

To the coroner's acute annoyance, it felt as though Sir Baldwin was having the same kind of thoughts about the coroner as the coroner was having about him. Admittedly, there were some coroners who were venal and unfaithful, but that was no reason to lump Coroner Robert into the same group. He was an honourable man.

'What of you, Bailiff?'

'Me? Well, I'm not really a bailiff any more.'

'No?' Ah. No doubt the man had been taking bribes or—

'I was made the Abbot of Tavistock's personal representative to the Port of Dartmouth. Now I only hope to become bailiff once more.'

'You *hope*? You have lost your post at the port?'

'It did not suit me. I'm happier away from the sea.'

'But it must have been a rewarding position.'

'Fairly, yes.' His expression darkened as though he resented the coroner's assumption that this could have had any bearing on his decision to leave his post.

The prior was clearly growing irritable. 'Coroner, are you going to discuss the matter or not? If you will not broach it, I shall.'

'What subject is that?' Baldwin demanded.

'Can I have some wine first, please?' Simon asked plaintively.

In the guest chamber, the guards ate their food and for the most part did not speak. Why would they? They were not comrades by friendship, but merely associates who had been thrown together by their service to the Bishop. It did not make for the refreshing sharing of confidences or the offer of sympathy, Jack of Oxford told himself.

He glanced across at the others as they ate, and winced inwardly. It was very difficult to have any feelings other than contempt for such fellows – and it was a mark of his own disgrace that he was here in their company.

Those two, André, his head swathed in linen after his wound had been stitched, and Pons, were both sitting a little apart. They were no different from any of the others, although today they were more reserved. The others were avoiding direct contact with them, as though they already had the ropes about their necks for their murders.

It was unfair, of course. If he had been there, Jack would have reacted in the same manner, drawing his sword in order to defend himself, especially if he'd seen someone throwing dung at him. The peasants in a city like this had no respect for their betters! Still, the pair of them were quiet now, fearing that here in this strange town their bishop might not be able to protect them. Now, without even the friendship of their peers, they sat solitary and grim-faced, contemplating their fate, should their master fail to defend them.

These fellows had nothing in common other than their master, and there was nothing to bind them either to him or to each other, really, except the money which he offered. For his own part, Jack felt no bond to the Bishop. He was not a warm-hearted man who inspired devotion. He was too lawyerly in his manner, looking at anybody as though he was peering at an interesting specimen, rather than a human.

Most of the men here had been in the service of the Bishop for some years. It was a large household, and life with the Bishop had great advantages. No man would go hungry living with a bishop. And that was an important consideration – especially after the dreadful years of famine.

Jack remembered them, all right. All too clearly.

He had been barely eighteen when the rain began in that awful year of 1315, and he had watched as the fields flooded and the grain rotted on the stems. All the food which they had expected to farm that year was lost, and there wasn't enough to feed the people, let alone the animals. Within two years, the herds and flocks had been all but wiped out, and the grain stored went rotten each winter. Although that was not what Jack remembered most of all. What he remembered most clearly was the sight of the bodies lying at the side of the road, the peasants who tried to work their lands, only to collapse and die, thin and racked with hunger, where they fell. It had been a time of misery, of grim, unremitting hell. The devil himself could not have imagined such scenes.

Jack's family had been moderately well-to-do at the time.

They had been small farmers, but they were at least free men. His older brother Peter was to inherit their farm on the death of their father, but when his father died, Peter was already two months dead. And by then Jack had decided that there was nothing for him there. He packed his bags and left the homestead which had grown hateful to him.

Those days had been appalling. People were dying all over the land, and he had been fortunate to find a fisherman who wanted help. He had lost his own son, and took Jack on, teaching him how to use the wind and the sea. It was only when the old man had himself died that Jack had taken his vessel and crossed to France, where he had hoped to find work. But so many were seeking food, that all were forced at one time or another, to find food in the oldest manner possible. Jack had, too, first by robbing, and then by killing.

He had never tried to count the dead. In his time he had waylaid and cut the throats of many, he guessed, but at last he had found salvation. He had been with a small band, trailing after some merchants travelling to a great fair, when he had seen a woman. She had been walking tiredly by the side of the road, and for some reason he had not indulged his whim with her as he had so often before, but instead had spoken to her, and learned a little about her. She was a maid to a lord, a kindly man, in a small manor nearby, he learned. He had stayed there with Anne-Marie for some little while, and when her priest came to talk to him, Jack had remained, out of affection for her. The few days became a couple of weeks, and then some months, and gradually he found himself slipping into the old ways of life, helping with the harvest, then with the ploughing and the sowing, until he suddenly realised he had been there a year.

This and his growing love for Anne-Marie, his love of the vill and the affection he felt for the area, made him offer his heart to her, and it was only then, when the people realised he wanted to take her for his wife, that the atmosphere changed. Suddenly he was ostracised, and his lovely little woman would not speak to him. He was foreign. He came from England. They would not let him have their girl, and she felt the same. She had never meant to lead him to believe that she could love him, she said. No. Of course not, he told himself cynically. He didn't believe her, of course. He reckoned she was just saying what the others in the vill wanted her to say, and so he did what he felt any man might.

He left the same day, bitter, and disillusioned. When he saw a man being attacked in Tours shortly afterwards, he, a natural fighter, entered the fray himself. It was more than trying to aid a man in need, though. He was seeking the peace that would come from battle. He allowed his rage to overwhelm him.

It was fortunate that the scruffy, foul little man whom he leapt to help had been the Bishop's own servant, and soon he was hired by the Bishop to join his bodyguards. At least, so he reasoned, it was safer for him to be there than to be out in the open where his rape could be punished.

'What do you say?' Prior Henry asked.

Baldwin glanced at Simon. Now that the bailiff had been able to quench his thirst again with a jug of wine, he was feeling a shade more lively, and the change showed in his face.

It was Simon who shrugged. 'We would need to see the place where it happened; the body, where he died, anyone who could have been about at the time, and we'd need to see where the stolen things were kept, of course.'

'What was stolen?' Baldwin asked.

Prior Henry looked at the coroner, then sighed. 'It was a phial of oil A very valuable oil indeed.'

'Just some oil?' Simon repeated disbelievingly. 'You say your monk died for some *oil*?'

'This was no ordinary oil. You see, many years ago, while St Thomas Becket was in exile in France, he had a vision. He saw the Virgin Mary come to him. She gave him this oil, and told him to hold on to it until the time of the sixth king after his own. That would be Edward, our King. But although the oil was there for his coronation, it was not thought . . . er . . . necessary to use it. There were disputes, I believe, about its authenticity. So it was not used for the anointing of the King. Instead, it was returned here, and placed in the reliquary with St Thomas's bones. And there it should still be.'

'If someone had not taken it.' Baldwin nodded.

'Quite so. And then killed our poor monk, too.'

'This Gilbert – he was trying to guard it, you think?'

'Of course.'

Baldwin could not help but notice the quick glance from the coroner. He wondered about that for a moment, but he continued without mentioning it. To him it looked as though the coroner was somewhat less convinced of Gilbert's innocence than the Prior.

He cleared his throat. 'Prior, how well did you know this Gilbert?'

The Prior had been studying the floor as he considered the matter yet again, but now he looked up sharply. 'If you are going to cast any malicious rumours against this poor, dead fellow, I will be—'

'Prior, the lad was up and about at a time when he should have been asleep, just like all his brother monks, from what you tell us. He alone rose in the middle watches, while all his brethren lay sleeping. Was he a uniquely light sleeper?'

'Well, not—'

'So we can exclude the idea that he alone of all the brothers might have heard something, then. Which leads us to the next question: what would have made him wake? Perhaps it was a call of nature. He needed the reredorter. Where is it?'

The prior wordlessly pointed.

'Fine. So, if he had sought that relief, he would have walked even further from the scene of the theft, and further from the barn where he was to meet his death. It is inconceivable that he might have seen something from the reredorter, so that is easy to dismiss. If not a call of nature, perhaps there was something he realised he had omitted to do the night before. Was there any such omission on his part?'

'No.'

'So that too, we can exclude. And we are left with any number of other possibilities: that he had a nightmare and woke – but commonly a dream so painful as to force a man to wake will also cause others to be disturbed. None other woke? No. Perhaps he was tormented with a pain – a tooth that ached, a twisted ankle, a blocked ear . . . did he make any mention of such an affliction?'

The Prior shook his head.

'So we come again back to the most obvious possibility – no more than that, it is just a possibility – that he may himself have been involved in the theft.'

Prior Henry shook his head, unconvinced and unconvincing. He wanted to respond waspishly to this accusation, but the conviction in Baldwin's voice kept returning to him. 'You are very certain of your reasoning, sir.'

'Pray, do not be offended. I seek the truth. It is all any man can do. I never seek to judge a man unless I am sure. I would prefer to allow ten guilty men to go free than convict even one innocent who was undeserving. I do not wish to malign

Brother Gilbert post-mortem, Prior. All I seek is the truth, so that we can attempt to recover your treasure.'

'He was an easy fellow to like,' Prior Henry said. Now that the barrier had weakened, his determination to protect the boy's memory was undermined. 'We bring many boys here from about the diocese, for without their education here at the priory, many of them, boys with good brains and hearts, would otherwise be lost to the Church. It is one thing for the world to lose another merchant, butcher or baker, but another thing for the world to lose a man capable of inspiring love for the Word of God. Gilbert was one of those.

'I think he had been a novice for only a matter of weeks, when I saw his potential. He had a purity of thought, and an astonishing facility with a brush or reed. His depictions of scenes from the Gospels were marvels of the art, truly astonishing from a lad of such tender years. And yet there was always something at the edge of his work, a certain humour on occasions, and when the subject deserved it, a bleakness to show that some men could be truly evil.'

'How long was he here as a monk?'

'Only a matter of some seven months. Before that he was still a novice. I called him into the chapter when I thought he was ready. The brothers all agreed with my judgement.'

He was sounding quite defensive, Baldwin thought, and he could see that Simon felt it too. It surprised him. 'It is not your fault if a brother decides to steal from the priory. You should not blame yourself, Prior.'

Now the prior and the coroner exchanged a look, and Baldwin understood that there was another point at issue. What it might be, though, he had no idea. 'Prior?'

'I think you should tell him,' Coroner Robert said.

# Chapter Eight

***Beaulieu***

The King was growing irrational, Sir Hugh le Despenser said to himself. It was not the sort of comment he would dare to make aloud, but when the man was raving about things like this, it was enough to make a man want to weep. There were the troubles with the French, the ever-present risk of another incursion from the damned Scots, not to mention the rabble in the country who seemed always to be seeking the next miracle and saviour.

First it had been the body of Thomas of Lancaster. Dear Christ! If there was ever a man who was more suited to the devil than him, Sir Hugh had yet to meet him. Lancaster was a grasping, mean, cretin. Most nobles were happy enough to seek to improve their lot, and there was nothing wrong with that. It was a natural inclination to win greater rewards, and sometimes a man would stretch the law a little to do so. If a fellow had ballocks, he'd ignore the laws, like Sir Hugh, or preferably have the King change them to suit him. But Lancaster was a fool to himself. He persuaded himself that he had a brain and could win against Despenser and the King; he was wrong.

Still, after his death a cult built up around him. It was said that he had died a saint, and some men were prepared to countenance his canonisation. Sweet Christ, they even started visiting the little plaque which he had painted and hung on the wall in St Paul's, celebrating the ordinances which had been forced upon the King. It had grown to such a nuisance that the King himself had ordered the damn plaque to be removed.

Intolerable! The man was a fool and a traitor.

Still, there was now the added problem that the King's mind was turning to the matter of the oil of St Thomas. That was something which could not be brought up again.

Originally, the oil had been hidden. Some said it had been given by St Thomas to a monk in a monastery in some Godforsaken part of France, and buried securely with a gold plate that said what it was, and explained that it should be used to save the King. The King anointed with this special oil would become a lion, raging against the heathens who had overrun the Holy Land. Eventually, the King would reconquer Jerusalem. He would become the most praised King in Christendom.

But the oil had been the target of an attempted robbery, and the Duke of Brabant had instead taken it for protection. When Edward was to be crowned, the Duke brought it with him, but for some reason it was not used. Instead, it was kept safe – originally in the Tower, and more recently in Christ Church Priory, for that was where it belonged, so some thought, with St Thomas who had first received this marvellous oil in a dream.

Why it hadn't been used, Sir Hugh did not know. He wasn't a close companion of the King in those days, he was merely one of the knights in the household. However, he did know one thing, and that was that were the King to be known now to be so desperate for any assistance that he was turning to an old tale like this, he could become a laughing stock – and it would not be long before he was evicted from his throne.

And Sir Hugh could not allow that. His own future depended upon the King's authority. Without King Edward II, Sir Hugh would lose all – including his life.

He could not permit the King to acquire that oil again. Not unless he could ensure that the King's reputation wouldn't suffer. There would have to be some means of guaranteeing that the King would remain secure even if he decided to use the oil, and until Sir Hugh found such a means, he could not permit the oil to be found again.

The question was, *how*?

### Christ Church Priory

Leaving the Bishop of Orange in the Prior's chamber, Baldwin walked down into the crypt with the Prior and coroner, Simon bringing up the rear.

'And that is it, really.'

'So the Queen deposited her hounds here because she knew you were supportive of her?' Baldwin said.

'Who could not be? I argued strongly that her embassy should be strengthened were she to be given some finances. How the King could propose to send her off with nothing, I do not know.'

'Which is very good, and redounds to your honour,' Baldwin said. 'But you feel that if the oil is not recovered, the King will take it ill?'

'He thinks I am disloyal because I was loyal to the Queen. We live in a strange land, Sir Baldwin, when a man can be thought of as a traitor to his King, just because he is known to support the King's wife.'

'Yes. Although I do not know what I may do to help you in this.'

'All I ask is that you look into the matter for me.'

'I must leave tomorrow with the Bishop.'

'Then please do what you can tonight to convince yourself that we have not omitted to seek the killer, so that if the King asks you, you can tell him we have done our best.'

'In one night? Do you know how long an inquest would usually take?'

'All I ask is that you satisfy yourself I have not been remiss,' the prior pleaded. 'Please.'

The crypt was a large space, filled with boxes and barrels, and strongboxes made of thick oak with steel bands, and Baldwin stood in the middle gazing about him, while Simon leaned against a wall near the doorway, watching him.

'This is where the oil was kept?' Baldwin said.

'It seemed safe enough down here,' the Prior said mournfully.

He was staring down into a heavy, iron-bound chest. One enormous key inserted into the middle of the lid unlocked the bolts on each face of the chest, and then the chest could be opened. The Prior opened it and showed them the inside. It was part-filled with documents and leather wallets containing scrolls.

'You're sure it's gone?' was Baldwin's first question.

'We have emptied it three times to make quite sure.'

'Would this monk normally have had the key?' Simon asked.

'No. There was no reason for Gilbert to have it,' the prior admitted. 'But sometimes a man may acquire such things. He had a close companion in the monastery, a man called James, who was responsible for the relics. James remembers having the key the day before. I suppose . . .'

'Gilbert must have taken it from him at some point,' the coroner said.

'I still find it incomprehensible that a king's man could have come and taken it from us,' Prior Henry said. He gazed down at the open chest with near despair. 'Why would the King order that?'

'There is nothing to suggest that the King knew anything about it,' Baldwin said hurriedly. 'It is perfectly likely that the man who saw this supposedly blood-sodden herald was simply mistaken. He saw a tabard and assumed it must be royalty. It was dark, you say, and you think he had been drinking?'

'Quite so,' the coroner said.

'There, then. It was as likely a merchant wearing a shield on his breast as a genuine herald.'

'Yes. I see,' Prior Henry said, uncertainly.

'The other thing to bear in mind is that the King could have no need to steal what is rightfully his. I understand the Duke of Brabant gave it to him?'

'That is what I understand,' the Prior said.

'Well, then. Clearly, it is nothing to do with the King.'

'Then who?' the coroner asked.

Baldwin looked at him, considering. 'The interesting feature in all this is Gilbert's own part. Why was he there helping in the theft?'

'People will assist thieves for many reasons. Perhaps he was simply evil? I suppose we could have been misled,' the Prior attempted.

Baldwin smiled ironically. 'A monk? Surely not. No, there must have been a reason.' It was good to see the Prior's relief at his words. And yet, why not, he thought. Maybe there was another man? Perhaps Gilbert was more innocent than he gave the dead man credit for. Was it possible that another monk had gone to take the oil to this 'herald' and Gilbert saw him, and so was killed? Possible, certainly. But not likely. 'Still, it is an interesting problem.'

The Prior looked at him sideways. 'Does it pique your interest?'

'Well, naturally. It is a fascinating little conundrum.'

'Then you will look into it for me?'

Baldwin smiled. So that was why the prior was telling him this tale. 'I wish I could, but as you know, I have to be on my way in the morning with the Bishop of Orange. We go to the King.'

'Yes. And I must inform the King of the theft,' Prior Henry said.

He looked at Baldwin. Baldwin looked back. Then Baldwin glanced at the coroner, and a slight frown passed over his features. 'Oh! Oh, no. No, I don't think that this is a matter for me to—'

'All I ask is that you inform him of the loss of the oil,' Prior Henry said. 'I shall write a note for you to take to him. What, would you ask that a special messenger be asked to do it when you are to be going to him anyway?'

Baldwin glared at the Prior, then peered down at the chest. 'No. You may well find the oil over the next few days. Telling the King would be a bad error, I think.'

'But we do not know how to seek it! You, you are the expert, won't you—'

'Oh, show us where his body was found. Perhaps I can help there, if only a little.'

Simon and Baldwin spent the next couple of hours studying the barn where Gilbert's body had lain, but there was nothing there which seemed to help with an inquiry. Too many boots had already gone over this ground for there to be any hope that they might discover something new.

'I didn't expect you to be able to help,' the coroner admitted as they walked back towards the prior's chambers over the grass.

'What do you believe happened?' Baldwin asked.

'Same as you. This Gilbert entered into some sort of agreement with another man, someone probably wearing a tabard similar to that of a king's herald, and then when he passed over the oil, he was slain to silence him.'

'Like a king's herald, as you say,' Baldwin agreed. 'And yet, what purpose could a man like that have for stealing what was already the King's?'

'You tell me.'

Baldwin eyed him. The coroner was one of those who kept his own judgement, a man who was silent much of the time, watching and assessing rather than opening his mouth. He reminded Baldwin of a Devon farmer. They were often happier to keep their peace, judging quietly rather than speaking. One had said to him once that: ''Tiz better to keep gurt zilence an' be thought a fule, raither'n open yure mouth and prove 'un.'

The coroner was a man in a similar mould. He would observe, note, and measure. And the reason was not hard to appreciate: all too many coroners had been shown to be corrupt, but so had keepers like Baldwin. He could understand the reluctance of a king's coroner to speak in front of a keeper when the matter under consideration related to a king's herald potentially being shown to be a murderer.

'Coroner, a quiet word?' he said.

'Yes?'

'We are both on the side of justice, friend. Let me hypothesise for a moment. Let us suppose that your peasant was no fool and knew the King's badge when he saw it. That could mean that a king's herald was here, and perhaps slew Brother

Gilbert. That would mean that we would have to wonder what that herald was doing. He must have had a reason to want the oil, after all.'

'Yes.'

'So, either he committed this act on the King's orders or he acted for himself, or another. It is unlikely that he would do this on the King's behalf. Do you agree?'

'Yes, on the basis of why would the King steal his own oil from the priory.'

'Precisely. All he would need to do would be to speak to the prior and ask for it to be sent to him. There would be no need for a clandestine theft. So unless new evidence comes to light, that possibility can be set to one side. Which leaves either a herald acting on his own behalf or on the commands of another, or a man clad in herald's tabard coming here and taking the oil.'

The coroner peered at him narrowly. They had no torches, and there was no light here in the court, other than the thin light from the stars overhead. 'Well?'

'We have little more to say, I think. Why should a herald wish to steal the oil? What possible use could he put it to? To have himself anointed with it and set himself up as King? Some fools could think that, once they were anointed with such a marvellous fluid, they automatically became God's chosen, I suppose, but not many living in the King's household would consider it likely.'

'So someone else put him up to it?'

'That is more likely.'

Simon was frowning. 'Who would have a motive to do that?'

'It is the King's oil. Someone who wanted to withhold it from the King, perhaps to ransom it to the King later? Or someone who wished to withhold it from the King to cause him distress? I do not know.'

'But you guess?' the coroner asked shrewdly.

'There are some who would not stop from any action. Those who are so proud and convinced of their own power that they would dare anything. However, my friend, they are genuinely dangerous. Unless you have a firm resolution, I should not personally seek to delve too deeply into this matter.'

'I thank you for your warning,' the coroner said, but there was a trace of sarcasm in his tone.

Baldwin shrugged. 'You will act as you see fit, of course. But one thing: did anyone note the names of the King's heralds who were here with the party before our own?'

'There were two, I think, but I don't know their names. You see a man like that, in uniform, and they are little more than the furniture in a room. Like a servant.'

'True enough. Someone must, though. Could you enquire for me? The other thing is, in which direction did the man say this herald was riding?'

'Away south and west. On the main Ashford road, so he could have been heading almost anywhere.'

'But that would be the road that we would take, I think?' Baldwin said. 'It is the road that heads towards the King at Beaulieu?'

'I haven't been there, but yes, I think so. It's the road the rest of his party took.'

'So, hypothetically, it is possible that the man was indeed a king's herald. And the King himself commands the heralds of his household.'

'So you think the King ordered a man to come here, and to murder a monk in the priory where St Thomas was killed by King Henry II?'

'The King has a friend who is capable of ordering a herald to do his bidding,' Baldwin said dangerously. Before the coroner could comment, he continued, 'Another thing, though, why should a young monk steal the key and take the oil to this herald?'

'Money? Some other reward?'

'Perhaps.'

'More likely that, than the King or the King's friend ordering the robbery of his own property,' the coroner stated flatly.

'Yes. Perhaps so,' Baldwin said, but Simon could tell that his mind was running along a different lane just now. He was looking about him in that distracted manner which Simon knew so well.

The coroner gave them a Godspeed, and stalked across the court.

Baldwin sighed. 'Simon, I think that man is destined for high office – or an early grave.'

### Beaulieu Abbey

The messengers were always with the King. Many of them had worn their uniforms with the parti-coloured blue patterns with stripes for more years than the King had been on the throne. Some had been used so widely that their shoes had been replaced more times than they could remember. Those who set off on foot would cover the same distance as those who went on horseback, for a man was more resilient than a horse, when all was said and done, but such cursores were still rather beneath a man like Joseph of Faversham.

Pulling his coat about him again, he felt his shoulders fill the tunic. It was a magnificent uniform, if he said so himself. Buttons drew the cloth tight over his breast all the way to this throat, while more ran from the wrist to the elbow of his sleeves. It was as blue as all the other messengers' tunics, but his was newer than any of theirs, and much smarter. He knew that because he'd deliberately bribed the man who had supplied it, paying over the odds to have the best.

There were good reasons for it, too. A man needed to stand out when he was one of a large company. And a king's *nuncius* should look good. It was all a part of his duty to the King. And since he had been honoured when the King sent him to the Pope earlier this year, there were good reasons for him to look as good as he felt.

Not that he'd been feeling exactly perfect when he first got back. It had been a very long journey, and one fraught with dangers along the way. It was fortunate that the route was fairly well-defined, and other *nuncii* had told him the best places to rest and those which he should avoid. With good fortune, and a certain amount of his own natural cunning and skill, of course, he had made the journey in only a little over the time it would have taken a man vastly more experienced.

But that was the advantage of being so much younger than the others. Most of them were close to being retired.

'Faversham, where are you?'

'Here, my Lord,' he responded, hurriedly climbing to his feet. The man calling was known to him, of course. He was the King's own bottler.

The bottler stood in the doorway now, a serious expression on his face as he studied Joseph for a moment with pursed lips. Then he gave a brief shake of his head as though in disgust, and jerked his head towards the abbot's hall, where the King was presently installed. 'The King wants you. Personal message.'

Joseph did not hesitate. A messenger was always ready to

be called on at a moment's notice. He had his little purse with the King's insignia embossed on it hanging from his belt, and now he pushed past the bottler, full of fire and excitement to be off again.

He only hoped it wasn't to be another foreign trip. The food played havoc with his belly.

# Chapter Nine

### *Christ Church Priory*

Baldwin and Simon were up early the next morning and, with relief, witnessed Cook bringing the jury to order before the coroner. The bodies were viewed, stripped naked before the jury, and then rolled over and over to show all the injuries sustained.

Witnesses were called to describe the events of the previous day, first Cook, then other guards from the gate, then the two bishop's men who had struck the three down, and lastly others who had seen the blows. There was little real evidence of intentional murder, Baldwin felt, once the fact of men hurling ordure at the two was noted. It was plain enough that the three had been angry to see foreigners ignoring the queue at the gate and showed their displeasure by flinging muck. The jury accepted that the men had felt threatened, and in justice to them, it was agreed that their swords had been bloodied because they had feared that they might be in danger of their lives.

Simon was not watching the matter as closely as Baldwin. Simon's attention was fixed on the coroner himself. The coroner

---

[1] Tuesday, 16 April 1325

was observing the two accused keenly, Simon noticed, and he was surprised enough to nudge Baldwin and point. Baldwin nodded, but then shrugged. He appeared to be saying it was nothing to do with him what the coroner thought of them.

At last the coroner summed up the evidence as his clerk recorded the facts, and he declared that the three had been killed by a chance medley. It was better than a decision that there had been murder done, a deliberate and premeditated slaughter, for that would have meant an argument about whether the men would be allowed to continue on their journey with the Bishop, but, with the official recording of the verdict, both of the men were relieved. A killing '*par chaude melle*', or in hot blood, with the implication of deliberation, would have prevented the two from accompanying the Bishop.

'A good result for the Bishop,' Baldwin commented as the jury began to disperse.

'Where are you going?' Simon asked.

'I want a word with that gatekeeper,' Baldwin said over his shoulder as he hurried after Cook.

'You got the decision you wanted, then,' Cook said as Baldwin approached.

'I think it was just. But close. I don't know those two men, but I can easily believe that they acted from fear, not maliciousness.'

'Can you really?' the gatekeeper said. He turned his back and would have walked away, but Baldwin asked him to halt for a moment. 'Why?'

'This monk killed in the priory barn. Do you know anything about it?'

'Only what you say, that he was slain in a barn and left there.'

'Hmm.'

'That tone carries a great deal of meaning, Sir Baldwin.'

'I was reflecting that the priory has solid gates, my friend. Do you suppose another monk, or perhaps a lay brother, killed the lad?'

To his surprise, the gatekeeper grinned. 'Do you? No. I think almost anyone would have learned where the weaknesses in the priory wall lay. There are plenty of men in the city who have seen brothers in the town after curfew. Any convent with intelligent young men will occasionally learn that young men are young men, and where there are a few lodged together, some will find the means to escape and find a tavern which will sell them wine or ale. I would bet I could find a way in within an hour, if I wished to.'

'So the priory is not so secure as your gate, then?'

'No. Not at all.'

'Which means that the killer was already in the city – unless you think he bribed a gatekeeper to open a postern and let him in.'

'No. None of the keepers would do a thing like that,' Cook said with certainty.

'I accuse no one. But if you were me, would there be any gate you would look to first, thinking a man might get through?'

'There are none,' Cook said, and he looked like a man who was now in a hurry. 'I must be off.'

'I thank you for your aid, friend Cook,' Baldwin said.

Cook looked at him, then over to the prior and a number of brothers who ambled along the way. 'There is one thing,' he said suddenly, lowering his voice and not meeting Baldwin's eye. He ducked his head to pick up his pack and swiftly spoke in an undertone. 'Look at the castle. There is a small postern near the castle wall. If I had to bet on a corrupt man . . .'

*  *  *

After the inquest and his talk with Cook, Baldwin and Simon went to break their fast with biscuits and cold meats and cool ale from the priory's stocks.

'Well?' Simon asked when he had eaten his fill.

'What?'

'The gatekeeper. What will you do now?'

'I seriously do not think that there is anything I can do to help the prior. I have a realistic explanation of how the man got into the priory. He had a corrupt monk, I think, who was prepared to sell the priory's valuables for money. The monk was killed, and his murderer made his escape over a section of easily scaleable wall, before making his way to a postern in the city wall, from where he escaped. There is no mystery. Which means that the prior and coroner are correct in their assumptions. There is nothing for me to do or say.'

'What will you do?'

'Tell the prior. There's nothing for me here. It's for the coroner and local officers to seek out the man.'

Once he had spoken to the prior, telling him what he had told Simon, Baldwin rejoined Simon near the stables. The friends stood watching while their mounts were prepared by the prior's stablemen.

'Did you learn anything to advantage last night?' the Bishop asked, although not with any real apparent interest.

'The prior has his own concerns,' Baldwin said evasively. He did not wish to blurt out his conclusions of the previous evening. A man of authority like this bishop was not to be trusted as a confidant.

'The good prior is a very harassed man,' the Bishop said, cocking his head as the Queen's hounds began to bay.

It was a sound which disconcerted his own, and apart from the calm dog which Baldwin coveted, his animals began to bark, one pair even beginning to fight. As Baldwin watched, the dog seemed to hunch his shoulders and try to walk from the fighting pair.

'Bishop, that beast of yours over there. He is a wonderfully handsome fellow. Where did you find him?'

For the first time Baldwin saw the Bishop animated. He curled his lips with disdain. 'That thing? It is useless. A man from the wild mountains gave him to me. I think he was just glad to be rid of a useless mouth, for the animal is singularly pointless. It barks when anyone walks nearby, but it won't fight, it won't fetch, it won't do anything. It just meanders along behind a man. And then it will come so near as to stub his nose on your foot as you walk. Useless.'

'But very handsome.'

'He has looks, I grant you, but there is no point to him. As I say, will he hunt? No. Will he chase? No. All he does is eat and drink my food. Look at him – he avoids a fight. He has no soul, no pride.'

Baldwin was about to respond when there was a slight commotion from the gates, and when he looked across, he saw a tall man in uniform marching towards him.

The fellow had the look of a man-at-arms. His hair was cut short, in a military fashion that left a cap of hair that sat over his ears and passed high over the nape of his neck, as though a large cup had been placed over his skull, and all hair below it had been removed. He was tall, with the bearing of a warrior, but with laughing blue eyes and smiling mouth. 'Sir Baldwin? I have heard of you from my friend, Coroner Robert.'

'Good day,' Baldwin said, unsure of the man and his effusive manner.

'I am here to help you, Sir Baldwin. You have need of haste to travel to the King? Well, it is not an arduous journey, but it is still more than twenty leagues, I believe, to Beaulieu. You will want men who are quick.'

'I thank you, of course,' Baldwin said, 'but we already have enough men, I think. With five men-at-arms, myself and my companion here, we shall be fine.'

'With five, I am sure you will,' the man said emphatically. 'That is why I am to boost your guard to five once more. I have some younger men in the castle who will be keen to go with you, but I—'

'But why? What do you mean by "boost my guard"? We have the men already.'

'Didn't you know, Sir Baldwin? The two who were accused of attacking and killing those peasants yesterday have fled.'

'What?'

Too late, Baldwin looked all about him in the court. He had spent too much time looking at the great dog, and not enough concentrating on the men about him. Now he saw that the castellan was telling the truth. His entourage was reduced. A flare of suspicion kindled in his breast. 'How did you know that they were missing? They were at the inquest, and all seemed well.'

'Oh, the coroner spoke to them afterwards about some details, and the two of them ran.'

'I see,' Baldwin said. His eyes were ranging over the people milling in the court, seeking out the coroner.

'But I have two men who'll be ideal for you, I'm sure.'

Baldwin eyed him ungraciously, then gestured towards the Bishop. 'It is up to the Bishop, my friend. *I* have no authority here. I am a mere guard myself.'

* * *

The Bishop heard his words, but they were nothing to him. He had more important business to consider: the message he had for the King, how he should phrase it, and how he must respond to the King's reaction.

While the message itself was simple and direct, the underlying message was not. Trying to make sure that the King understood it would be a problem. And if the King understood, perhaps there would be more aid for him, although it was not so desirable. The Pope and the Bishop both desired the end of this King's reign. He was that dreadful.

There had been many kings over the centuries who had believed that they were more powerful than they really were. Some had died heretics, of course, while others fought to maintain the feeble fiction of their authority. It had taken one English King, the fool, to demonstrate once and for all the folly of that attitude. Henry II had poor St Thomas murdered here in Canterbury, and as a result the Pope had been able to impose a dreadful public penance on the King. It was a shameful period and, in reality, had little effect beyond showing that the Bishop could be as pious as any, and that the King must bend to the will of the Church. That, really, was the important factor.

Kings were responsible for the law of the secular folk on earth. The Church, though, had the duty of care to all souls, and in addition there was a duty to look after the King. The Church was there to help direct the whole of Christendom towards Heaven, after all. And she must make any arrangements necessary to help the world on that path. Thus bishops could and would guide kings. It was why the Church anointed kings – to demonstrate their authority.

It was why the Bishop must undertake this irritating journey, to go and see the King and try to help him see that he must do anything in his power to prevent an escalation of the disputes between England and France. It was the King's duty to support the Pope's fight to unite Christendom.

The King was expendable. Soon he might well disappear. His reign was collapsing about him, his treatment of his wife was an international scandal; rumours of his homosexuality and affair with Sir Hugh le Despenser were rife; his bellicose behaviour towards his brother-in-law, Charles IV of France was creating a rift between the two leading Christian states in Europe. It was unacceptable. Now was the time for him to finally do some good.

And if he wouldn't, the Pope would make the remaining years of his reign still more difficult.

Jack of Oxford was interested to see how quickly the two had taken the hint from the coroner and fled the city.

He hadn't realised what they were doing at first, of course. All he saw was the coroner leaving his inquest and speaking with them. As he turned to march away, the two stood a moment before exchanging a glance, then sidled away. A little while later, he saw them both near the stables, although at the time he didn't make the connection. It was only when the others were told to fetch their mounts that he saw their two beasts were already gone. They had ridden off.

Well, they were hardly going to be missed. They were not the most reliable of servants to the Bishop, not in Jack's opinion. Personally, Jack wouldn't have trusted them as far as he could throw them. They were only heavies, brutes who'd attack anyone. He'd seen enough men like them to recognise their type. Even so, the Bishop had seemed to like them. He often gave them easier tasks, as though trying to reward them.

The Bishop would have need of protection in the dangerous roads between Canterbury and Beaulieu. Jack had some knowledge of the lands between, and they were invariably fraught with dangers of many types. There were forests, rivers, and the ever-present risk from outlaws.

No man could wander about the countryside with impunity in the King's England. All who wished to could attack and steal what they wanted. The rule of law often broke down irretrievably only a few miles from a town. There were all too many knights and barons who deprecated the rights of others to use the King's highways, and who would stop merchants and other travellers to demand payment of 'tolls'. Others would simply knock a man on the head and take his purse.

The two men who were to join them in replacement of the two men-at-arms who had fled were interesting characters. Both were tallish for men of Kent, and they were quite fair-haired, too. There the similarities ended, though.

Peter, the first, was a rugged-faced man of some forty or more summers, with the lines and sunburn to show that he was used to living out in the open much of the year. His eyes were a surprisingly bright blue colour, which gleamed with intelligence as he took in the sights all around, but from the wrinkles at either side and the furrows in his brow, he was more used to peering at his surroundings from narrowed eyes. He had a square face with a strong jaw, and a nose that had been badly set some while ago. There was also a series of scars along his forearms, which were bared. He obviously reckoned that the weather would remain clement.

His companion was a younger man, with narrower features, but a heavier build. Where Peter was quite wiry, like a labourer, John had the appearance of a knight, in the padding of muscle at his shoulders and arms. His eyes were darker, a deep grey-blue, and there were fewer laughter lines at the corners. Instead of his friend's alertness, this man's eyes moved with a noticeable deliberation, and he appeared to concentrate on one object or person at a time with great intensity.

Jack watched him, the still, serious man, and then turned and eyed the older man with the smiling face. He had been a felon for too long. He knew how to recognise men, to see which would be most dangerous, which he could pick on easily.

He wouldn't try anything with either of these, he decided – but of the two, he would leave the older, cheerful man well alone by choice. He looked much the more dangerous of the pair.

# Chapter Ten

After the excitement of the previous day and the morning, Baldwin was glad to be in the saddle once more, ready to leave Canterbury. As he and Simon sat on their mounts, waiting for all the other men to collect about the Bishop, Baldwin saw the coroner at the gate to the priory close. On a whim, he spurred his rounsey and crossed the court to Sir Robert's side.

'I thank you for your help today,' he said.

'What do you mean?'

'Scaring off our two guards. What did you say to them? That you'd be seeking their heads as soon as they left the good bishop's service?'

The coroner looked him up and down. He was leaning with his back at the gate itself, while his thumbs remained tucked into his sword belt. Jerking his chin at the Bishop, he said, 'What do you think of him? He worth protecting?'

'Of course he is. He may be able to save some lives, if he persuades the King to prevent war with France,' Baldwin said.

'Hmm. How would you like him to have only outlaws for his guards?'

Baldwin cast a look over his shoulder at the men, before sighing, 'Coroner, I and my friend may be the only two in his entourage who have *not* been outlawed at one time or another!'

'Ha! Yes, you could be speaking the truth there. And yet one of the two last night was recognised by men here in the city. The short, smelly one? At the inquest, he said his name was "Pons", didn't he? He has gone under the name of Stephen the Frank. I knew of him in Ashford as Stephen the Sailor, and others knew him under other names. He is rumoured to have killed his own master. The other I didn't know, but from his appearance I would think him formed from the same mould.'

'So you think you have helped to save the Bishop by persuading the two least reliable men from his party to go? Perhaps he was well aware of their unreliability,' Baldwin said. It was true enough. Often a baron or knight would gladly hire a man who was dangerous and known as a killer, because such a man would appreciate his safety in a larger household, as well as feeling a debt to his new master.

'Perhaps he was. But with the two replacements, you'll have a better party to travel all the way to Beaulieu. These two are known to me . . . They are safe.'

'Well, for that I thank you, at least,' Baldwin said. 'Do you know where the worst parts of the journey are likely to be?'

'The forests of Kent are moderately safe, I think. It's when you cross into Sussex and Hampshire that you'll find your progress endangered. That is what I have heard, in any case. Keep to the road past Ashford, through Cranbrook and Crowborough, and you should be all right. Watch your bishop, and watch your own back, Sir Knight. I wouldn't want you to learn that your companions are dangerous by their attacking you.'

'I am grateful for your words, Coroner,' Baldwin said. And then he bowed and saluted the man. 'Sincerely.'

Coroner Robert grunted. 'Get off with you, Sir Knight. I hope next time we meet it may be under a more auspicious light. Go with God and be cautious on the road. Farewell and Godspeed!'

*Second Wednesday after Easter*[1]

## St Mary in the Marsh

They were cold and tired by the time they saw the little cross in the distance. There had been plenty of other little settlements on their way here, but they had been keeping quiet, hiding up in woods last night. They were happy to be away from Canterbury, but now they had run out of food, and this prosperous little vill looked good to them.

Pons took a careful look about. It was the countryside he really liked. The marshes here were all flat pastureland, the grasses sliced apart by a number of little streams and rivulets, each dully grey, like rivers of lead in the verdant green. As they rode, the sheep on either side rose, startled, and occasionally they saw a shepherd in the distance, leaning on a crook and watching them – although whether suspiciously or merely from a spirit of mild enquiry, they couldn't tell.

So far as André was concerned, it was hard to imagine quite such a desolate landscape. It looked as though God had decided to eradicate everything from the place. There were no trees nearby, no hills, nothing. Just this lengthening grassy plain that had been slashed by water. It made him enormously nostalgic for his homelands, with the view of mountains in the distance.

'Where are we?' Pons said, looking about him with a frown of disdain.

'If God wanted to give the world a kick up the arse, he'd do

---

[1] Wednesday, 17 April 1325

it here,' André summarised. 'This is the shit-hole of the world. I've never seen a place its equal.'

'*Oui*. So what do we do?'

'We ride to that vill there, and see whether the road rides us out to the west. And if it does, we wait a while, and then visit the church.'

'And then?'

'Take what we may, and ride on. I will not try to kill myself by riding onwards with no money in my pocket. There must be something in there we can use.'

And as a plan, it was good. There was nobody about in the vill when they rode in. Everybody was out in the fields.

'Come!' André said, and trotted to the church door.

It was only a small churchyard, here, and the animals had kept the grass down, sheep and horses grazing it to a one-inch-long stubble. The little hummocks and stones showed where the older members of the vill had been buried, while one or two smaller lumps demonstrated that demise was not the prerogative of the ancient.

The door was new, but creaked like an abbey's. André walked, conscious of the noise his spurs made as he went, the cheap chain under the sole of his riding boots clattering on the flagstone floor.

'Where is everyone?' Pons demanded behind him.

'Do we care?' André said. His eyes were fixed upon the prize in front of him. There was a cheap cross made of wood sitting on the altar, and a box lay behind it. He smiled to himself and hurried to it, testing the lid, but it was securely fastened. Eyeing it, he reckoned he couldn't lift it, let alone rest it on his horse for him to carry it. No, the blasted thing was far too heavy. The metal straps ran about it, and it had two great locks at the front of it.

'Well?' Pons said. 'Can you open the thing?'

'Of course I can . . .' He felt the locks, and knew he had no chance. They were made by a good blacksmith. 'Where is the priest?'

All vills like this had a small lodging near the church, if not a lean-to beside it, for the priest to live in. Both men knew that – but they also knew that the priest was usually a man like any other in the vill. If they wanted to find him, he would almost certainly be out in the fields with the men and women, working the land or catching birds.

They tried the house next to the church, and inside they found the paraphernalia of a vicar, but no sign of the man himself.

'Do we wait?' Pons said.

'No. If we try that, people will see our horses as they come back to the vill. No, there's nowhere to hide or conceal the beasts here. We'll have to ride on,' André said regretfully.

It was the only sensible conclusion. The sight of their horses would set all the tongues wagging, and when news of the attack came to be known, the villagers would know exactly who to blame. They would be able to describe the two men on horses who had come to their vill and stole from the church.

With a leaden sensation in his belly, André turned from the little house and was about to walk back to his horse, when he heard the voice.

'My son, can I help you?'

'Holy Christ!' Pons muttered.

'Thank you, Father,' André said, ignoring his companion. 'May we have a word?'

### *Château du Bois*

The Queen lifted her arms as her maids stood about and slipped them into the sleeves of her dress.

'*Dieu!*'

The weight of it was astonishing! All the jewels which she had demanded, sewn into the fabric, made it extraordinarily heavy, and she looked down with some perplexity. 'Alicia?'

Alicia was her most trusted companion. It was not a position she had sought, but it was inevitable amongst the present ladies-in-waiting that she should win it. The others had all been selected by the King and Despenser to join her, and the Queen and Alicia knew perfectly well why that was: they were here to spy upon her.

There were two main agents of the King: Lady Alice de Toeni, the Dowager Countess of Warwick, and Joan of Bar, King Edward's niece. But the Queen was not so foolish as to believe that these were the only two who were watching her. Her husband was mistrustful of everyone recently, and the fact that his Isabella had been loyal to him through all the trials of the last ten years, that she had supported him when he most needed her aid, counted now for nothing. All the King would see when he looked at her was the woman who was sister to the French King. Nothing else.

Of course it was not spies of the King of whom she must be most on her guard. No, it was any man or woman who could be considered a friend or ally of that evil demon, Despenser. Evil demon. She rather liked that. The fact that the son of a peasant was now the most powerful man in the realm was entirely monstrous, but her husband had allowed him to take that position. It was his foolhardiness which had seeded the fruitful fields of Despenser's ambition. And his spies would be all about her. She knew that.

Interestingly, she was beginning to feel that Lady Joan of Bar was growing more and more sympathetic towards her. Perhaps it was not surprising, for Lady Joan had suffered from a brute of a husband.

'It pinches about my waist. I want it to be let out a little. I wish to be glorious, not suffocated!' she stated, and the dress was taken away to be reworked.

The wedding was not until July, but she must look her best. She had a duty to England, to her husband – whether he expected or cared about it or not – and to her cousin, Jeanne d'Evreux, the King's fiancée.

She was a lovely little thing, Jeanne. Already Isabella felt a certain understanding between them, which she hoped would only continue once Jeanne had married her brother.

He, of course, was more circumspect. As the King of France, he could not demonstrate too much compassion for her, but he had succeeded in making his feelings plain about some aspects. The fact that Despenser was gaining in wealth and treasure while Isabella's estates were confiscated was deeply insulting to the French crown; worse, the fact that her children had been taken from her was shameful. That seemed to imply that the King viewed her as a *traitor*! To suggest such a thing was an affront to the French monarchy.

It was one thing to say that something was an insult, but another to live with the effects, though. Isabella missed her children so much . . . her little John, only eight years old, and her little darling; Eleanor, two years younger, and Joan, little more than a baby at three years. Her first-born, Edward, was almost thirteen, of course, and he would not be so dreadfully worried. He had seen his father's irrationality before, and had seen it dissipate. She hoped he would be strong enough. But the others . . . to have been dragged from their mother, and still not to know their own father's love, they must be in misery.

She refused to think of such things. To do so in front of the ladies-in-waiting would only lead to rumours of her misery becoming widely disseminated. She would not give such solace to Despenser, nor to her husband. Instead, she would keep cheerful during the day, and only relieve herself in tears in the depths of the night.

At least some people were kind enough to support her. Henry Eastry at Canterbury had been very good to her; William Ayrminne was a solid friend; even the Bishop of Orange relayed messages of encouragement from the Pope which were generous to a fault. With fortune, all those with good wishes for her would be able to make their mark.

The Bishop was an interesting man, of course. Tall, urbane, shrewd as a farmer eyeing the cattle at market, he rarely allowed anyone a glimpse of what was going on inside his head, but he was the Pope's own ambassador just now, and that meant he was one of the most powerful men in the world.

Well, she deserved to have a man like him visit her and take up her cause. She was the daughter of Philippe the Fair, King of France, and wife to the King of England, whether he liked it or not. Isabella was a woman of standing. A noblewoman of the highest rank.

And she was deprived even of the companionship of her *children*.

### St Mary in the Marsh

The priest was a youngish man, with mousy hair and a slightly peering stance, head leaning forward, his eyes squinting slightly.

'Father, we're very glad to meet you,' André said.

'Ah, you are foreign?'

'From Hainault, Father. We are lost, trying to find our way to London.'

'You are a long way from there, my son,' the priest said, and André heard the sudden reticence, the suspicion in his voice.

Ach, it was an obvious error. He mentioned the first town that came to his mind in this strange land, and should have realised that the main city was some distance. But how could he know? It was many years since he was last in this country, and then he hadn't made it to London.

He smiled. 'Oh? And we thought it was so near,' he said as he put his hand about the man's neck and shoved his dagger into the priest's belly.

The man just gave a quiet gasp, nothing more. He stared in horror as André carefully ripped the blade upwards, using the sawing motion he was so experienced in, the priest goggle-eyed, mouth open, as though he hated to interrupt the fellow about his business, and then André smiled at him, nodding calmly as he saw the life fade from the priest's eyes, in a way hoping that his gentleness would ease the man's passing. In any case, it was fast, and there was not a great deal more any man could do than that for someone.

As the priest slumped, André allowed him to slide from the blade, and watched as the fellow began to jerk and twist in his death throes. One foot beat so hard against the floor, it ended up leaving a smear of blood, but that was nothing compared with the mess about his belly and the ground about him.

He had keys at his belt, though. While Pons took the ring from his forefinger, André went to the box in the church. The second key was clearly the only one that was the right size to fit the hole in the lid, and he thrust it in and turned it. The noise of the levers being shifted was music to his ears, and he opened the lid with a tingling anticipation in his belly.

Inside, he saw with a gasp of joy, was a gold cross with jewels set into it. The church here had a marvellous patron. Ach, he would have been glad to meet the man himself, and take advantage of the fellow's hospitality! Whoever he was, he had a goodly purse.

Back in the priest's house, he looked for spare clothing in the man's boxes. In his little bedchamber there was a chest, and inside it was a shirt and a thick robe. It was good enough. André ripped off his bloody and messed tunic, and replaced it. It was made of good, soft wool, and he was glad to have made the exchange.

The cross was soon installed in his shirt, next to his stomach, under his belt. He gave a low whistle, and Pons came running. The two of them walked out to their horses, and mounted, both still watching carefully. Perhaps a mile away, there was a huddle of men and women walking back from the fields, and André smiled, then turned his horse's head to the west and clapped spurs to the beast's flanks.

There was no need to worry about buying food now. This venture would make them both a fine profit.

# Chapter Eleven

*Second Thursday after Easter*[1]

### On the road near Crowborough, Kent

The Bishop grunted when their concerns were raised, but he did at least allow them a few moments of rest while they studied the land and rested their mounts.

Simon was impressed with the single-minded determination of the fellow. The Bishop of Orange was a heavy-set man, with a great round face, and an oddly square shape to his skull, visible when he removed his thick woollen hat. Commonly his eyes had only a distant absentness, unless there was food in the vicinity, in which case they suddenly held an almost feral concentration. Yet all the while, whether bumping along on his palfrey or sitting as his men lighted a fire and began to warm food and drink, he appeared to ignore any hardship, and focussed entirely on the mission.

Not today, though.

'I will not be delayed by the irrational and foolhardy concerns of a small number of peasants!'

'We would be foolish to rush blindly into a lair of outlaws,' Baldwin said.

'There is no evidence that a single fellow lies in that forest,

---

[1] Thursday, 18 April 1325

and if one did, what of it? We have many men amongst us, we do not need to fear being waylaid, do we? In God's name, man, I say I am determined.'

Baldwin grunted and threw a harassed glance over his shoulder at the trees behind him. 'The peasants in the farm told us to be wary. There have been many sheep stolen recently.'

'Probably a neighbour's dog.'

'There are strangers who've been seen, the fellows said.'

'There are strangers seen every day in the country. It is not cause to divert our route and delay our embassy. When the horses are rested we shall follow this road.'

It was not the first time that they had held this debate. The past few times they had passed under woods, Baldwin had been anxious, and cautiously cast about him for the threat of ambush, but each time his anxiety had come to naught. His warnings had been overruled by the Bishop – suavely and reassuringly, but definitely. However, this time Baldwin was more concerned.

They had paused at a small farmstead a mile or more back, and there the peasant woman had warned them of more footpads and felons who were hiding deep in amongst the trees. There was no doubt that the men in the woods were dangerous, she said as she poured them ale from an ancient, cracked earthenware jug, and Baldwin tried to soothe her with his gentlest of voices and manners, seeing that she was so anxious.

No one could doubt her sincerity. When they arrived, they saw her whirl in terror to see so many horses. For a moment or two, Baldwin had thought that she was about to flee, but something reassured her. Perhaps it was just the fact that she could see that these were no footpads or drawlatches. Outlaws would have worn shabbier clothing, or clothing that wouldn't fit at all.

There were many outlaws near here, they learned. From the way that she looked about her, she expected them to appear at any moment. And Baldwin knew that she must be petrified that one of the outlaws might learn that she had entertained a large party. An outlaw might well assume that she had been paid in cash for her hospitality, and would soon come to rob and rape her. She had a husband, she said, and that in a way was still more worrying. All had heard tales of outlaws slowly torturing a man in front of his wife, or a wife being raped before her man, he being bound and impotent to help her, just for a few pennies.

'Is your man here?' he asked.

'Working,' she said, and although she smiled, her eyes were nervous the whole time. As she spoke, the reason for her fear became clear. 'He has a coppice in the woods.'

She explained that having a man about the place would not protect her or the homestead. Will Fletcher and his Mabilla were both killed a month or so ago, although Will had tried to defend them both. Old Adam, the tranter who saw to the needs of so many about this way, had been set upon and slaughtered just inside the woods. Then a boy, one of Roger Hogward's lads, was seen down near the road's ditch, knocked down, although not killed, by a mercy.

His tale was one of misery. The lad had seen his father slain by a gang of men all armed with bills and long knives. Two had bows, and with them they used him for their practice after tying Hogward to an oak.

'They ravage the whole area,' she concluded.

'Have you raised it with the Keeper of the King's Peace?' Baldwin asked kindly.

'They do nothing for us. The keeper's a busy man,' she said curtly. 'What does he care if a peasant woman and her husband are harassed or killed by these felons?'

He didn't have an answer for her. He wanted to tell her that if she had complained to him, he would have raised a posse and ridden the outlaws down, for no man ought to be afraid of travelling about on his own business within the King's realm, but that would only serve to leave her more distraught. In the end, he hurried to drink his cup, and was soon back upon his mount.

'The woman said the boy was found only a matter of days ago, my Lord Bishop. His father's body was still bound to the tree where he died,' Baldwin said.

'Sir Baldwin, your concern does you credit, but my need will brook no delay. I trust that is clear enough? We have need of speed. To circle about this immense wood will take a great deal of time, time I do not have.'

'I am charged with others for your safety,' Baldwin said stiffly. 'She said that no one from this vicinity would enter those woods willingly until the outlaws have been captured and killed.'

'Your anxiety is noted.'

Baldwin nodded and marched away before his anger could burst forth.

'Well?' Simon asked as he approached.

Baldwin went to his rounsey and cinched the saddle strap tighter. 'Take my advice and make sure your mount is rested and that your saddle is tight,' he muttered. 'And then test your blade in the sheath. The thing may be needed soon.'

It was almost noon when the party prepared to make their way through the woods, and Simon was aware of a growing unease as the men climbed into the saddle again. The only ones who appeared entirely unconcerned were the two more recent guards from Canterbury. The older man, Peter, and the younger, who might have been his son, the one called John.

Simon had been content at first, but now he felt a little nervous at the sight of the two of them. They looked so stolid and resilient, they were Simon's vision of a pair of outlaws. True, they were moderately clean, but that meant nothing. So far as he was concerned, they were large, bold men, just like any other felon. And they were travelling with the Bishop's party as though they were entirely trustworthy.

Well, maybe they were. At least they hadn't slaughtered any innocents trying to reach a city, unlike the Bishop's original two men. Simon still reckoned that their flight was peculiar. They had been involved in the inquest and declared innocent, so what could the coroner have said to them that would have made them run away so swiftly?

More to the point, why would he have wanted to scare them away? Just so that he could have these two added to the Bishop's entourage, perhaps? Why would he want to do that, though? Unless he wanted to have the men wander this way, and he could have them help outlaws waylay the Bishop's party . . .

'You've been travelling too long with strangers,' he rebuked himself, and kicked his horse onwards.

There was nothing said, but all the men were wary and eyeing the trees with some trepidation. Nothing rustled or moved, there was no indication that there could be danger in there, but all knew the risks of walking under the trees. Woods gave too many opportunities for concealment, and a man hidden from view could do much damage with a bow. Two could halt a large force like this. They would only need to drop three or four men, and the Bishop's party would be halved.

Baldwin edged his mount nearer to the Bishop as they walked down the slight incline to the path through the trees, and drew his sword, lifting the cross to his mouth and kissing it as he offered up a short prayer for their safety.

At first they were moving through pools of sunlight that dappled the grass. But soon they were into truly old woods, with trees standing in some places so close together that there was scarce space for the brambles to take hold. It grew dark, a darkness that was filled with the odour of dampness and mulch. The air seemed thick with the scent of decay, a sweet, pleasant smell, while it grew cooler under the shadows.

'What do you think, Baldwin?' Simon asked, drawing level with his friend.

'I think that this would be an ideal place for a felon to launch an attack on a party such as this . . . but I can see no sign of such men,' Baldwin admitted.

Yet even as he spoke, he felt sure that he heard a shout. A bellow of fear, a shrill scream, and then the rumble of hooves.

'Simon – the Bishop!' he called, drawing his sword and spurring his mount.

The two men cantered forwards, past the Bishop himself, and then paused, blocking the path. And now, as his mount jerked his head up and down, pulling at the bridle, Simon heard it too. The far-off thunder of a horse at full gallop. He glanced at Baldwin, and the knight slowly nodded. They could only see a matter of twenty yards from here. After that the roadway curved gently to their left. Baldwin motioned, and the pair trotted onwards to the bend. And now Simon caught sight of the man on the horse. He was already a mere eighty yards from them.

'Stop!' Baldwin shouted.

'Sweet Christ, Baldwin – he's a King's messenger!' Simon

breathed, seeing the uniform as the man galloped towards them.

'Let me pass in the King's name!'

'Wait!' Baldwin said, and the fellow was forced to rein in his horse, drawing to a halt only a few yards from them. 'We are riding to the King. What is your name, messenger?'

'Let me past! Let me through, I need to get out!'

'You will wait, man! Are you all right?'

'I am Joseph of Faversham, Cursor to the King, and I am carrying messages for him. Let me through!'

'What is the reason for your haste? You were riding like a man with the devil behind him.'

'I have urgent messages!' Joseph looked about him at the men. He could see that one of the men was clad in the dress of a bishop, and the sight was some reassurance, but even a bishop looked suspicious to him today. 'Who are you?'

'I am Sir Baldwin de Furnshill, Keeper of the King's Peace, and this is Bailiff to the Abbot of Tavistock, Master Simon Puttock. We are here watching over the Bishop of Orange on his way to the King. So speak! What has so frightened you?'

Joseph glanced again at the Bishop, and then made his decision. 'A king's herald – he's been murdered.'

It took little time for him to guide them to the body. It lay a scant two hundred yards from them, further on into the woods.

Baldwin felt no thrill of excitement as he approached the body. In the past he had been aware of that *frisson* as he found a corpse, knowing that the dead could always tell how he had died, and sometimes point to the murderer. Not today, though. This body was certainly over a week old, from the look of it. Decomposition had set in, and there were the marks of wild creatures all about it. The eyes were gone, pecked out, and fingers and belly had been gnawed, while ants had set up a trail to the wound in the stomach.

'There is little we may learn from this,' he said heavily, gazing down at the body.

The man had been left at the side of the road, bundled into a small ditch. There was a thin covering afforded by some branches from nearby saplings, whose pale leaves washed with sunlight were so bright against the dead man's dark tabard, stained filthy with blood, that they concealed him all the more effectively. The tabard was disturbed where animals had foraged, and Baldwin doubted anyone would ever be able to tell how the man had died, there were so many signs of animal attack.

'I doubt his own mother would recognise him now,' Simon said from some yards away. He had a reluctance to view older bodies that had always rankled with Baldwin. To the knight, any corpse was a challenge intellectually, to tell how the man had died, to evaluate clues; for Simon, a corpse was merely repugnant, a foul reminder of a man's mortality. The scents and sights could always turn his stomach.

Simon continued, his voice muffled by his sleeve, which he held over his nose to avert the odours, 'Anyway, we know he must be about ten days dead. He was found by the outlaws who live here in the woods, perhaps, and they killed him for his purse.'

'Perhaps, yes,' Baldwin agreed. 'Poor fellow – to be set upon and killed all this way from any help.'

'Baldwin. His tabard is very filthy. Was that from a wound of his?' Simon said. 'Because if not, it could be the man who killed Gilbert.'

'We know Gilbert was murdered on the night of the

Monday after Easter ... this is Thursday, so Gilbert died a week ago last Tuesday. It took us two days to arrive here, and one man on his own might have made the same distance a little more swiftly,' Baldwin mused. 'It's possible, yes.'

'That would be justice of a sort.'

Baldwin nodded. 'Away, dog!'

His favourite dog from the Bishop's stable had intruded its nose and was sniffing with some interest at the corpse at Baldwin's feet. He gently pushed the animal away with his foot. 'Perhaps we should seek for the oil here, then.'

The Bishop called out, 'Are you done? We may report this man's body to the nearest vill so that they might call the coroner, but for now we must hasten.'

Joseph nodded on hearing that. 'I should be gone, too. I have urgent messages from the King to the prior at Canterbury. I have tarried long enough already.'

'You may go, then. And when you see the good prior, please inform him that we have found this body, thanks to your help. It is possible that the thief and murderer is himself dead,' Baldwin said.

Joseph nodded, but with a confused expression. 'This man's a murderer?'

'Yes. How did you see him, though, Joseph?'

'I saw a glint of some sort as I rode past. And, well, I have seen money discarded in the woods before. I suppose sometimes a man is beset by outlaws and seeks to prevent them winning his money, so throws it away. Well, I hoped it was that. And then found him, instead.'

'Do you recognise him?' Baldwin asked.

'Your companion's just said, Sir, that his own mother wouldn't know him now. I certainly wouldn't.'

Baldwin nodded, but insisted that the messenger lean

closer. 'You are in the King's service too. This is probably a man you have met.'

Joseph obediently wrapped a cloth about his nose and leaned down closer, wincing, and then shook his head. 'No, I cannot say. His hair is unfamiliar, and so is his face. But that is a genuine King's tabard for a herald. I do know that much.'

Baldwin thanked him, and Joseph climbed into the saddle, whirled about, and then cantered off eastwards.

'Should we mark the body?' Simon said.

Baldwin was still gazing down at the dead man. 'Yes. Yes, of course.'

'What is it?'

Baldwin leaned down and peered more closely. To Simon's disgust, he took a hold of the body by the shoulder. A cluster of flies rose immediately, but Baldwin simply waved them away from his face as he stared at the body. 'Just that it seems odd. His tabard is rucked up at the back, where he fell. And look: there is no hole in the tabard itself. Nor a mark on his throat.'

'What of it?'

'It is peculiar, that the man is dead, but his tabard is undamaged,' Baldwin said with a frown.

'Perhaps he was knocked on the head? Or struck by an arrow in his flank?'

'There is no arrow,' Baldwin pointed out. 'And as for knocked on the head – perhaps, but if that was the case, surely if he was struck hard enough to kill, his head would show some sign of it. His skull would be broken.' As he spoke, his fingers were moving over the man's head. 'No. No broken bones there.'

'Then, what?'

'I think he was killed, and then the tabard thrown over him.'

'That is a large inference from so little, Baldwin.'

'True enough. But it does at least suit the facts here,' he responded.

'What is the delay, Sir Baldwin?' the Bishop shouted from the main roadway. 'We have need of speed!'

'I have a need to ensure that this body is marked well so that the coroner can find it, my Lord Bishop. Do you continue with the rest of the men and I and my friend here shall see to it and catch you up in a moment or two.'

'Make haste, then, Sir Knight. Your duty is to me, do not forget. Not to a churl murdered at the wayside.'

His tone was sharp. The Bishop was irritated to be thus held up, and he held Baldwin responsible. Baldwin nodded, but said nothing.

As the two from Canterbury passed by, though, Simon saw John, the younger guard, grin and sneer at them, as though the death of one little man so far from anywhere was amusing. It chilled Simon's blood.

# Chapter Twelve

Jack watched the knight and bailiff with the body as he rode on past them. It was plain enough that the bailiff was less than comfortable in the presence of the corpse, but that the knight was relishing his task. He was a sick kind of fellow, in Jack's eye.

He had known a felon in France when he was first there, a short, ill-favoured man, marked with the pox, and who had a cast in his eye that made him appear still more foul. This man, Guillaume, took inordinate delight in torturing men slowly to learn whether they had more money or treasure hidden about them, or nearby. His favourite method was to slice open a man's foot, and fill it with butter before setting it over a fire to roast. The screams of those who suffered under his care Jack could still hear in his dreams.

However, there was at least good reason for that: the men all wanted to learn where wealth could have been secreted. No, it was the other damage inflicted which set Jack's belly roiling: once his victim had died, little Guillaume would set about mutilating the body for fun. Once he had emulated the Scottish leader, Wallace, and flayed a man so that he could use the skin as a sword-belt. It hadn't worked, though. The leather was poorly tanned, and soon rotted.

Those days were black indeed. At the time Jack had been certain that his life would end soon enough. The effect of the famine and the death of all his family had served to destroy his faith in the world and in God. God couldn't care for men if he could seek to destroy them in this manner. The loss of the Holy Land at the time of his birth showed that God had grown to despise His creation. Why else would He have given the Holy Land to pagans? No, God had decided that it was time to end the world, that was what Jack had believed back in those grim days, and Jack was content to watch it happen. He had little enough to live for. All he sought was a means of feeding himself each day, and without work, often the only way meant capturing a man and making him give up all he owned. He would die, but at least Jack and the others would live for a little longer.

Until he met his Anne-Marie. He had truly felt that with her, he could at last find some peace. The famine appeared to have ended, the cattle and the sheep began to wax fat on the grasses, and the people who had survived suddenly found that there was a superfluity of food for all. Men like Jack could return to little villages where their labour was desired and work for the good of others again, and in time perhaps forget that in harsher times they had been prepared to throw away their humanity and lower themselves to the level of beasts. But no matter how hard they tried, they would always find that the nightmares would return to them in sleep, and they would be forced to relive their past crimes and confront their victims once more.

At least his old companion, Guillaume, was dead. Jack had seen his head removed. But this knight could have been his student, pulling and shoving at the body with enthusiasm. From this distance, it looked as though he was enjoying the exercise.

Jack turned to the road ahead with his belly feeling uncomfortably hot, as though the acid was boiling and about to rise into his throat. He would watch out for this knight, too.

As he turned away, he noticed John was staring at him fixedly.

Jack truly did not like that man.

Baldwin set the man back down. 'This is very curious.'

'What?' Simon demanded waspishly. Watching his friend pulling the corpse about like that was deeply unpleasant. He kept expecting a decomposing arm to be pulled from the sack of pus and gas that was the torso.

'There is no obvious mark on his head or throat. Nothing that could have killed him.'

'So?'

'So, then, the wound must have been inflicted upon his torso to kill him. But in that case, you would expect him to have been marked through his tabard. Yet there is no such damage.'

'Perhaps it was flying away in the wind? He was shot by an arrow *underneath* it while he was on a horse, and fell down here.'

'Where is the arrow?'

'The killer came here to get it, and in the process he found the man's purse and other valuables. There! No wound on the tabard, a deadly blow that killed him, and it explains also why there is nothing of value about him.'

'True enough. But if he was shot, surely the arrow would be broken as he fell,' Baldwin wondered aloud. He broke off and studied the man's hands for a moment. 'Nothing to see there. He has been a man who has used his hands, but who hasn't?'

'When I've shot a deer, often it has fallen away from the direction of the arrow, as though punched by it,' Simon tried. 'The arrow remains uppermost.'

'Yes. You are probably correct. Yes,' Baldwin agreed. He strode to a nearby branch which had broken from its tree and lay on the ground nearby. Baldwin eyed it thoughtfully, then picked it up and set it over the body. He took the man's tabard off, and fixed it to the branch with a leather thong he took from his pack, and then set the makeshift flag over the body, bound to the limb of a nearby ash.

'That will do it,' he said. Then he began to cast about him, studying the ground, carefully parting the grasses and weeds at the same time as prodding with a small stick into any deeper patches.

'Do you think anyone will actually find his murderer?' Simon said, gazing at the body.

'The coroner will do his best to make a record, I've no doubt. When I found a dead king's messenger in Exeter, I moved heaven and earth to find his killer and succeeded – but that was in a city. People are close, there. Here, in the wilds, anyone could have done this. That is the great fear of the countryside. A man may commit homicide with impunity, when he would be fearful of doing so in the town. In a town his offence will be more speedily noticed, and the perpetrator can be uncovered. In the countryside, his crimes may never be noticed. Finding this body was more by luck than good judgement. He said he saw something metal, didn't he? I wonder what that was.'

'So – what now, Baldwin? Shouldn't we hurry to get back to the Bishop?'

'Yes – in a while. But first I want to check about here and ensure that there is no sign of the oil. This fellow has been killed in some manner, but there is something odd about the manner of his death. It is not . . . *right*!'

Simon grunted. 'In what way is it not "right"?'

'Do not use that tone with me, Simon,' Baldwin said with a grin. 'I know that long-suffering pitch too well. But since you ask, it's as I said earlier; he does not look like a man who has simply fallen here.'

'The tabard?'

'That is one thing.'

'If he fell, and then a dog or hog found him and hauled him along a short way by the leg, his tabard would ruck up, wouldn't it? There is nothing necessarily suspicious about it.'

'True,' Baldwin said thoughtfully. 'Except then his tabard would have dragged some leaves and twigs and soil under it, surely. There is little evidence of that. And the tabard would have brushed a swathe of the ground clearer, too. There is no sign of that either. No, I think that's not right.'

'Then what is your suggestion, Baldwin?'

'It is almost as though this fellow was killed, and then the tabard thrown over him to show he was the king's herald. It makes sense, after all. If he got here, he would hardly have ridden all the way from Canterbury with a bloodsoaked tabard, would he? No, he would have taken it off. So I *think* someone killed him, found the tabard, and then put it over him to show who he was.'

'Why?'

'I've no idea! Perhaps I'm wrong – a man could have come along later, found the body, and wanted to show that it was a man of some position, in case someone else came along who didn't mind finding the body.'

There was no need to explain why. All too often, a man who discovered a body would do nothing. The 'first finder' was required to appear at the subsequent inquiries, on pain of a fine. So many preferred to walk past.

Oddly, it led to a small market in discovering bodies. Once a man had found one body, he would have to turn up to describe what he found to the justices. He would not be amerced again for the second body, so many took the pragmatic approach and would tell the man in the area who had already found one body, so that he could 'discover' any subsequent ones. First finders often had a monopoly in their areas.

Clearly this man had not been found by anyone who knew a first finder.

Simon eyed the body again. 'You seriously suggest that someone killed him and threw his tabard over him before riding off?'

Baldwin had conducted a careful examination of the ground immediately near the body. Now he stood and wiped his hands on his old tunic. 'There is one thing for certain, old friend: whoever this was, whoever killed him, the oil is nowhere near. So the killer, or someone else, took it.'

'Unless, of course, this fellow had nothing to do with the matter at all,' Simon pointed out.

'Yes.'

'Fine. Now, let's get back to the Bishop. This place makes me uncomfortable.'

'Very well.'

Baldwin was about to set off with Simon when something on the dead body caught his attention. Stuck in the fold of his shirt, hard by his neck, there was a gleam, and Baldwin bent to peer closer. He could see something shining there, and when he moved the head to the side, he could pull it free. 'Aha! So this is what Joseph saw!'

'What is it?'

'A necklace formed of pilgrim badges,' Baldwin said,

handling the lead badges with care. 'They may help find the dead man's identity.'

'If we can find someone who knew a man who carried a string of badges about his neck like beads,' Simon said as they started to walk to where their horses were tethered, but then Baldwin stopped and glanced back.

'When you said "uncomfortable", you were right, Simon. And you saw how that messenger was affected by the woods. They are fearful, aren't they? Just imagine how that poor man must have felt, riding in here, all alone, and then feeling the blow that killed him. All alone, and the one man in the world whom he didn't want near him was there, and he killed him.'

'And you call *me* fanciful and superstitious!' Simon said.

Joseph trotted much of the way through the trees, his eyes flitting nervously from one side to the other as he rode along, until he was close to the outside of the woods. There, a blackbird squawked at his horse's hooves, and made the beast shy, while the blackbird pelted along an inch from the ground, calling out his warning song.

It was enough for him. Joseph set spurs to his mount and burst from the woods and into the open in a flurry of dirt and dust, crouching low as though thinking that all the French host was after him.

He hurried on for a long way, hardly taking any note of the distance, but when he reigned in, he found he was a long way from the edge of the trees. They stood some half-mile distant, looking like a ruffled green blanket, with the swirls of the treetops. They were almost beautiful.

His heart was still thrilling, though. The thought of the dead man lying in there . . . that was enough to make his belly try to empty again. Those hideous eye sockets, the trail of ants to the wounds . . . he had to think of something else.

There was smoke ahead. He was cautious, but it was possible that there was a cott up there through the trees. If there was a small house, a pot of ale would help him feel a little more normal.

He could see it through the trees, a small, low, thatched property, built of crucks and with wattle and daub to fill the spaces. It would be warm, in the winter, and with all the wood about here, plentifully supplied with heating. There was a man, a shortish, thickset peasant, who was using his bill to split saplings for firewood. For an instant, Joseph thought he knew the man: something about the cast of his head, the way he swung his arms while chopping the wood . . .

'Who are you?'

The woman appeared from nowhere, staring at him with fear.

'Good wife, I'm just looking for some ale. I found a body in there in the woods, and it made me feel unwell. I'm a king's messenger, and I'd be glad of something to help settle my belly, if that is all right.'

He glanced back to where the man had been, but he was gone now.

She looked behind him, along the way he had come. 'A man?'

'A King's man. A herald.'

It didn't strike him at the time, but afterwards, he was quite sure that she was relieved to hear it. She probably just didn't want to think that a neighbour had died, he thought.

*Second Friday after Easter*[1]

## *Beaulieu*

It was all to no avail. As the sun gradually began to sink in the west, the friar was forced to accept that his mission had failed, and there was little point in extending his stay here. The King would not see him.

Nicholas of Wisbech was about to leave the precinct when he saw a bench, and overwhelmed with a sudden lassitude, he sank gratefully on to it and rested his legs.

As a friar he was perfectly well used to walking up and down the country, but these last days of standing about, waiting and hoping to be able to see the King, had been not merely tiresome but also enormously exhausting. It was fortunate that a kindly clerk had found him a berth in the great tithe barn, for without that, with the rain of three days ago, he might have died of cold and exposure. All the friars were aware of the dangers of lying out in the damp and cold of an English night. For others, for peasants with thick jerkins and warm hosen, it was less of a trial, but for a friar who was never overly well-fed on his diet of begged bread and pottage, it was indeed a hazard. He had seen his own companions catch chills and hasten their souls away to heaven in that manner.

Yes, he was safe from that gloomy ending, being discovered one morning under a hedge hard and cold as ice, like his old friend Walt. It was discovering Walt that had made Nicholas seek a more reliable occupation than mere preaching.

It had not been an easy transition, but he had ever been fortunate. Nicholas had been sent to college when he was still young, and had proved a shrewd academic and philosopher

---

[1] Friday, 19 April 1325

already. It took little persuasion of his prior to win a place at Oxford when he had shown his abilities, and once there his intellect made him rise above so many of his peers. There was no point concealing the fact that he was remarkably fast to understand complex concepts, and the fact that the masters and tutors were occasionally behind his own reasoning was enough to prove that he was possessed of an unnatural brilliance. And so he was elevated, and found himself soon employed in researches of some arcane material. Such as the oil of St Thomas.

Now he could curse the day he found that reference, for it had led to so much hardship for him, even this present disaster, in truth, but at the time he had instantly comprehended the potential of the marvellous fluid.

The King, Edward II, had been widely respected and adored when first he came to his throne almost twenty years ago, but that had instantly changed when the character of his friend, Piers Gaveston, was better understood. Suddenly the barons began to withhold their favour, and tried to impose restrictions on the King himself that would control his rule. He could not comply with those who sought to clip his wings – and why should he? He was King, anointed by God. If God chose him, Nicholas was content with God's choice.

But his reign went from bad to worse. While the Scots destroyed the Royal Host in some foul backwater called Bannockburn, while they invaded his Irish colony and imposed the reign of Edward Bruce on an unwilling population, his own barons grew more fractious. And then it was that Nicholas found the reference to the oil. St Thomas's oil.

Such a simple solution to all the King's problems. That was how it appeared to Nicholas that day when he learned the whole story. A frayed and worn parchment told of the gift, the wondrous gift, passed to St Thomas in exile. The man must have been almost an angel to have been granted such a vision and so magnificent a treasure from the Holy Virgin herself! No one else would have been vouchsafed a vision of her, let alone a gift. But St Thomas took it, and straightway obeyed her injunction, delivering it to a monastery where it could be buried for safekeeping until it was needed.

And here it was in London, brought especially for the King. And when brought, it *remained unused*!

Dear Christ in Heaven, the fools who had withheld it must have rued the day they were born. If only they had delivered it to the King on the day of his coronation, his reign would have been blessed, and all the catalogue of disasters, from his choice of advisers, to his inept war-leadership and failures over his French territories, would have been reversed. But no, some baron or other must have decided that the King had no need of such a great boon, and had rejected the oil. For preference, they made use of the normal holy oil used for his predecessors. That baron must be kicking himself now, Nicholas thought to himself as he scurried to the King to tell him all about the wondrous discovery he had made.

The King had appreciated the importance in an instant. And under Nicholas's prompt urging, had agreed to send Nicholas to the Pope with a request for his aid.

It had taken an age, that journey. All the way to Avignon to the Pope's palace, and then returning with the sad response which had ruined Nicholas's life.

The unfairness of it was shocking. Truly shocking. All Nicholas had tried to do was help others, and yet here he was, sent on his way home with the Pope's message: 'If you wish to be anointed, pray be so. It can do no harm. But I cannot spare my cardinals at present to do it for you.' That was the gist of the courtly Latin which Nicholas had to read out to a dumbfounded King on his return.

Dear God, it was as close as he had ever been to being murdered, from the look on the monarch's face. Nicholas had already heard of the King's tempers, even though this was before the terrible revenge which he visited upon his enemies after Boroughbridge, and the fact that the Pope had elevated Nicholas to papal penitentiary, as well as giving him a licence to allow him to take Cambridge University clerks and install them in vacant benefices, did not affect the King. No, he would have nothing to do with Nicholas of Wisbech. His career was ended.

It had taken him all his courage to come here to Beaulieu to visit the King and to try to persuade him to look upon him more favourably. After all, it *was not* his fault that the Pope chose not to comply with the King's request. The Pope had made it plain that he wouldn't help by sending one of his own cardinals, but he did give permission to the King to have any of his bishops in the land conduct the ceremony and anoint him. So the mission was not a complete disaster. Nicholas had secured that. And all the King need do was arrange for a bishop to visit him with the oil, and all would be well. Surely, if he was touched by the holy oil of St Thomas, his reign would be cured of malignancy and treachery, and King Edward could reign contentedly from then on.

But he wouldn't so much as meet with the friar. To the King, Friar Nicholas was dead. It was so unjust that he could burst from simple indignation.

# Chapter Thirteen

*Third Monday after Easter*[1]

### *Eltham Palace*

Earl Edward strode along the passageway and burst in through the door to his tutor's chamber without ceremony. 'Richard?'

Seated behind his desk, the clerk made little impact, the Earl thought. There were many others who had tried to teach him in the past, but none had managed to affect him in the same way as this man from Bury.

There was a seriousness about him that was reassuring. Most of the others by whom the Earl had been tutored had been more frivolous. They sought to win his friendship, rather than his respect. Perhaps, he considered, they already respected his own position too much to be able to treat their own with any great devotion. They were mere servants, and could not see themselves attain any higher ambition or post.

Richard was different, though. For one thing, he clearly viewed the Earl as malleable. He did not seek to bow to the Earl's will at every opportunity: to his mind, the Earl was a bright, intelligent twelve-year-old, and as such was demanding of instruction. And for that, Bury sought to ensure that the

---

[1] Monday, 22 April 1325

Earl's mind was filled with material suitable to his station. And to the prophecy.

There was so much bound to his name, the Earl knew. He respected the prophecies, naturally, but at the same time he was a calculating realist. It was his calculation that the fact of the prophecies would make people regard him in a subtly different light than that by which they viewed others, and that, for a man who was to become King, was a very useful point. Certainly, he had already heard men whisper comments about him which showed that they were alive to the differences between him and his father. 'A dragon, then a goat,' they said. All knew what that meant. There was an inevitable sequence in life: after a strong, virile King there tended to follow an unfortunate one. Perhaps the successor would be incompetent, or more likely badly served by his advisers, but that made little difference. The fact was, that there was a recurring fluctuation in the fortunes of succeeding kings. And Earl Edward's father was not a fortunate ruler.

Such prophecies affected some men more than others, and Richard of Bury was exceedingly susceptible to their allure. He lived and breathed the magnificent stories which were already weaving themselves about his earl. Earl Edward would become King, he would unite the Scottish within his realm, bring all the lost lands back under the Crown, win over the French territories once more, renewing the fabulous Angevin Empire, take for himself the crown of the Holy Roman Empire, and reconquer the Holy Land . . . Truly, Earl Edward would become a king to rival King Arthur.

But that was not to say that Richard of Bury was lax in his teaching of the Earl. That was not his way. He believed that God gave men an innate ability, a skill, but that the perfection of that skill was the duty of the man who possessed it. Thus, if Earl Edward was capable of being a new paladin, he must be shown the correct ways in which he must improve himself so as to bring out his own best qualities.

This determination had already led to some arguments, for on occasion when the Earl awoke with a mild hangover, the last thing he desired was a serious contemplation of the life of King Arthur, or Alexander of Macedon. And yet that is what he was forced to study, no matter the tiredness of which he complained. Richard was indefatigable in his resolve: the Earl would become a great world ruler, and must not waste a moment in striving to learn all he could that would make him a good King.

'Today, my Lord Chester, I should like to talk about the marvellous leader, Julius Caesar, the man who conquered Rome itself, and the world. He was the foremost leader in warfare, and in the arts, too. A strong man, who was finally betrayed by those whom he had trusted.'

'Is it true that he conquered England too?'

'He conducted two excursions on to your soil, my Lord. It was Claudius who actually added England to the Roman Empire, though, not him.'

Earl Edward nodded, but he was considering other matters as he opened the book passed to him by Bury.

'You seem distracted, My Lord?'

'I was reflecting, Master Bury, that all the leaders you have shown me have all been both devout *and* literate.'

'That is *exactly* the case I was going to make to you, my Lord! Hah! It is difficult to teach you some things! You pick them up naturally!'

Richard's fulsome praise would once have rankled, so similar was it to the subservience of other members of the court. If there was one fault which annoyed the Earl more than any other, it was fawning insincerity. But with Richard, it was not obsequiousness – it was a reflection of his immense excitement and exuberance. He fairly bounced about the room when the Earl showed comprehension of a difficult concept. In the last nine months or so since Bury had arrived here as his tutor, the Earl had quickly realised that whatever else Bury might be, he was no slave.

Now Bury was flicking through the pages of another great book until, reaching the passage he sought, he turned it triumphantly to the Earl. 'See? Read this.'

As the Earl of Chester began to read, slowly, his finger tracing the lines of the words, Bury continued seriously.

'You see, no great ruler can achieve anything without learning. And the greatest proofs of learning are an appreciation of the importance of the written word, first and foremost. Because whether you or I know anything at all is unimportant, so long as we have the *sense* to own the books which already preserve that which we need to know. So long as we have our books, we have all knowledge at our fingertips.

'That passage says that the Greeks had no ruler of stature who was not literate. I would extend that to include all the great Romans. All were intelligent men who appreciated the written word and the arts. And, more than that, all were entirely convinced of the help of God. True, the Greeks and Romans did not understand about God for they lived in heathen times before the birth of Christ, but can you doubt that a man of the strength of purpose of Alexander, would not have offered thanks and praise to Our Lord for his achievements, had he but known of our God? Of course he would. And Our Lord must also have felt that he had a purpose in elevating Alexander over all others in the world.'

'A heathen?' asked Earl Edward.

'A great man, though! Look at him! A man who could do so much, and then, as they say, who could weep, seeing that there were no more great lands for him to conquer. He died young, and yet he achieved so much more than any other man before or since.'

'No man can emulate him,' Earl Edward said with some sadness.

'You think so? You want to give up your crown now, my Lord? You want to surrender your future? Then do not say such a thing!' Bury said with asperity. 'In the Lord's name, I declare, I believe you shall be a king to rival Alexander or Caesar! I swear that your name shall ring down the ages and lead Englishmen to sing your praise with admiration for as long as England survives!'

Earl Edward looked up at him. 'Bury, keep a firm grip on yourself. You are growing overly choleric.'

'How can a mere clerk not be passionate when he has such a great duty, so enormous a charge as I?'

## Christ Church Priory, Canterbury

He was exhausted as he clattered under the city's gate, but Joseph felt only gratitude and relief for the safety that the city walls promised. He saw the man at the gates, and nodded, but hurried on his way as soon as possible towards the priory, determined to reach it before the final bell and the closing of the gates.

It was little time before he was led upstairs to the prior's chamber.

'My lord Prior. Messages from the King.'

'And what are these?'

He opened his little wallet and removed the tiny scrolls, passing them to the Prior, then he stood back, waiting.

'He wants the oil?' the Prior muttered. 'This is wonderful! Just what I need now!' To the messenger, he cast a sombre look. 'Anything else?'

'Only a short message from Sir Baldwin de Furnshill, Prior. He told me to say, that "The thief and murderer may be dead."'

'Why? What has he found?'

Joseph told of the discovery of the herald's body, and the prior listened carefully, but then frowned hopefully. 'And the oil? Was there any sign of the oil he stole from me?'

'I know nothing about that, my Lord, but I do not think that there was anything on the body. Perhaps it was something in a saddle-bag? The man did not have it about his person, so far as I saw.'

'And he was definitely dead?'

'Oh, he had been dead for some days,' Joseph confirmed. He swallowed uncomfortably at the memory. Poor fellow. It was one of those nightmares which he suffered from occasionally. The idea of being stabbed and left for dead in the middle of nowhere, perhaps never being discovered.

'That is good. Good. But the loss of the oil makes my task difficult.'

Joseph knew when he should keep silent. While the prior stood and walked about his chamber, glancing every so often at the papers in his hand, Joseph held his tongue, waiting to hear what he might have to say.

'Very well,' the Prior said at last with a sigh. He looked at the note for a last time, and then admitted defeat. 'Um. I have a note for you to take back with you.'

How to explain to this prickly monarch that the one salvation which he had counted upon had, in fact, already been stolen.

*Third Tuesday after Easter*[1]

## *Beaulieu*

Baldwin felt only a lightening of his spirits as he rode into the grounds of the great abbey at Beaulieu. This, hopefully, was to be the end of his journeying in the King's service. From here he and Simon could throw down their commitments to the King and return homewards to Devon, where Jeanne was waiting for him, as well as his little Richalda and baby Baldwin, his first-born son.

It had been too long since he had seen them. He was longing to hold his children, but still more keen to grasp his wife. The last time he had been apart from her, he had been sorely tested. Shipwrecked, lost, thinking himself the prisoner of pirates, he had taken the comfort and compassion of an island woman, and his treachery to his own wife, the betrayal of her trust, had marred their relationship for some time thereafter. It had taken a little while for them to recover that delicate balance which marks a successful and generally happy marriage, but at last they had achieved it, and now here he was, still a hundred miles away. He wanted to be with her again, lying with her in their great bed in his manor.

And soon, soon he would be!

The great estate of Beaulieu was entirely enclosed. Some five and fifty acres or more, Baldwin guessed as he entered through the huge gatehouse. From here, he could see the church clearly, a magnificent construction, all built of a plain white, clean-looking stone. The other buildings were set about to the south of the abbey church, as was normal for a Cistercian monastery. From the road leading up to the abbey,

---

[1] Tuesday, 23 April 1325

Baldwin could see the frater in the south wall, the lay-brothers' living quarters to the west of it. The abbot's house lay east, of course, but today the little gardens beyond, which would usually be so neatly set out, were a mess of tents and wagons.

'The King is still here, then,' Simon breathed, looking at the flags hanging limp at the poles.

'Yes. He hasn't denuded the area of food yet,' Baldwin said, but not sadly. He couldn't be unhappy today. Perhaps later this afternoon he would be able to leave Beaulieu and make his way homewards. He set to calculating. It must be some thirty leagues to Devon and his home, so at ten leagues a day, roughly thirty miles, he must ride for about three and a bit days to get home. Well, it wasn't as fast as he would have liked, but it was a great deal better than riding back from Scotland. And since much of the land hereabouts, from memory, was quite good riding land, he might make better time, so long as he didn't wear out his rounsey.

The Bishop gave a peremptory command, and Baldwin and Simon pulled aside so that he might lead the way, glancing about him with that absent expression on his face again, seeing much, but apparently noticing little.

'How did a man like him ever manage to achieve the position of bishop?' Simon wondered aloud.

'Don't underestimate the fellow,' Baldwin warned. 'We have seen him at his worst, when he has been uncomfortable, with a difficult mission to achieve, and many miles of journey ahead of him. Yet he is highly respected by the Pope, by the Queen, and, for him to be here, presumably by the King as well. He is no fool.'

'You may think so,' Simon said, 'but all I know is, he appears to look down on anyone who is lower than a knight.

It's all right for you, old friend, but he has ignored me all the way here as though I was a churl – or a felon.'

'And the good part about it is, he won't want you to continue with him anywhere. He looks down upon you, you think? In that case, Beaulieu is the end of our official travelling, Simon. We can return home!'

'Aha. Yes. He is not so bad, when you look upon him in that sort of light,' Simon agreed amiably.

A guard at the inner gatehouse stood in front of the Bishop. He was clad in the King's colours. 'Who are you and what do you want?'

'I am the Bishop of Orange, and I have urgent messages for the King from the Pope, and his wife in France.'

And suddenly Simon saw the Bishop change. He lost his absent appearance, and now he bent, glowering at the guard, fully alert and boldly seated in his saddle.

'Open the gates and allow me to pass.'

In the corner of a room high overhead, he watched them closely. The Bishop he had seen before, although the man's name wouldn't come to mind just yet. He'd have to remind himself who it was later.

Thomas of Bakewell pushed himself away from the wall where he had been whittling at a stick, and used it to pick at a scrap of pork in his teeth. His wisdom teeth had been giving him hell for some time, but the pain had reduced now and, instead, he found that they were a storehouse for every shred of meat and vegetable after a meal. Not ideal. And irritating when a man was sitting on a horse. Sucking never seemed to work. It just hurt his tongue.

He swept a little dust from his tabard. Wherever you went in this place, the walls were freshly limewashed, which was nice to look at, but played merry hell with a man's clothing. Especially when it was this dark. A king's herald was always on show, and woe betide the man who allowed himself to look scruffy in the King's presence.

Not that Tom wanted to. He was proud of his position. After his brother died, it was the Queen herself who spoke to him so kindly, so understandingly. She was a mere child, almost, then, only just old enough to have married, so some twelve years old, and yet she displayed more generosity of spirit than the monks in the abbey or any of the knights. They all looked on Tom as a nuisance to be removed urgently so as not to disrupt their great day.

It was because of the Queen that Tom had a job now. Taken in by her, into her household, he was given the job of learning the job of a kitchen boy at first, then page, and finally she permitted him to enter her service as a messenger. Which was fine until the King saw fit to destroy her household and exile all her French staff. At least the English were taken into his own household so that they could work for him direct.

The royal family had been good to him. Yes, very good. But he would have traded every suit of clothing, every free drink, every wonderful meal, just to have had another week with his dear brother John.

# Chapter Fourteen

The King watched narrowly as the Bishop entered. There were a few men about the room, and he looked at Despenser as he ordered the others to leave.

The King and the Bishop made some polite comments at first, both edging closer to the moment when they would have to come to business. It was the King who broke the peaceful nature of their conversation, irritable at the long-winded introduction and keen to get on with the important matter in hand.

'My Lord Bishop. You have a message for me, I believe?'

'It is from your good lady, Queen Isabella, my Lord.'

'And?'

'She instructs me to say, you will already have heard from the good Bishop Stratford and William Ayrminne.'

'Yes. They would have me accept the loss of my lands,' the King growled.

'This is a matter you have doubtless considered already,' the Bishop said, and then summarised: 'If you do not go to France, you will lose all. You cannot hope to return at the head of a host. There are not sufficient men-at-arms in England, Scotland, Wales and Ireland to permit that. The territories are too vast. Even if you could afford mercenaries, even the pikemen of Morgarten could not avail you. The French King has the mightiest host in Christendom.'

'I know all this.'

'So the conclusion is, you must go to France unless you wish to surrender all. If you go, you should recover most of your lands apart from the Agenais. I would think that you will lose that, because the fate of that area rests upon a French court whose composition has been arranged by the French King. You cannot win that back.'

'So what is my Queen's suggestion?'

'That you distract the French King. Accept his terms, and agree to go there at the earliest opportunity. You cannot hope to deflect him from his purpose with any action of yours: you go, or you stay. If you go, you will retain your lands – most of them, in any case.'

'This is most interesting. I shall need to consider. Do you have any other message for me?'

'Only this, that the Pope himself has heard of this proposal, and he views it as commendable. He wishes me to make clear to you that it would be a most desirable means of resolving the foolish state of friction that exists between France and England.'

'I thank you,' the King said more coolly. He had no need of that popinjay's thoughts. So far as he was concerned, the Pope had let him down too often. He had not helped when King Edward asked to be re-anointed with St Thomas's oil, and nor had he helped poor Hugh when the Despenser had heard that Mortimer had enlisted the help of a necromancer to bring about his death by use of magic. Instead, he had sent a terse reply suggesting that if Hugh were to embrace God, live more honourably and kindly, and stop seeking to advance his own position at the expense of others, he may find himself with fewer enemies. As if that was likely to help him, just when a necromancer had been paid to kill him!

It was a vicious response to a man who was fearful of his life, and the King felt sure that it demonstrated a papal contempt for his own position. The Pope knew how close Hugh Despenser and he were. It was a simple rebuff of the rudest kind. The Pope was arrogant, swollen up with his own importance and pride. He had installed himself as the most powerful man in Christendom, and felt he could even command kings. Yet kings were selected by God, not by popes. If God thought Edward should be King, then no man, neither cardinal nor pope, could have any right to gainsay him.

Not that such arguments held any sway with the Pope himself.

'You may leave me now.' He waited while the Bishop respectfully reversed from the chamber, showing the correct deference by not turning his back, before motioning to a servant. 'Fetch me Ayrminne and Bishop Stratford. Tell them I would have the benefit of their advice.'


Baldwin was happily repacking his satchel of clothing when the servant arrived for him.

'Sir Baldwin, I have been asked to conduct you to Sir Hugh Despenser.'

'What does he want?' Baldwin asked. There was a slight tension in his back at the name. No one could hear the name of the King's chief adviser and friend without trepidation.

There was no answer, though, and Baldwin finished his packing before joining the servant and walking along behind him to the Prior's lodgings. Here, he was ushered into a small chamber.

'Sir Baldwin. I am glad to see you once more. You enjoyed your little journey to Paris?'

'Yes, Sir Hugh. It was pleasant.'

'I would imagine it must have been. Perhaps you would enjoy a life of more privilege.'

'I fear not. I am keen to leave behind all affairs of such great importance and find some peace in my little manor once more. So much more restful than all this travel and high living. As soon as my latest task is done, I shall be happy to return to my home.'

'What is that latest task?'

'I have personal messages for the King.'

'You may give them to me.'

'I was asked to give them to the King.'

'I am the King's adviser.'

'I know who you are, Sir Hugh,' Baldwin said firmly.

'I am not a good man to make your enemy, Sir Baldwin.' Sir Hugh eyed him without any obvious emotion for a moment.

'So I have heard – and seen.'

'You have been an irritant to me.'

'I have not intended to be.'

'You say that? Do you take me for a fool?' Despenser's voice grew colder. 'I say this: do not thwart me, Sir Knight, else I shall crush you.'

'You have tried already,' Baldwin said. 'But I shall oppose injustice while I may.'

Sir Hugh le Despenser nodded, although whether agreeing with this sentiment or merely accepting that this was Baldwin's view, the knight couldn't tell. Despenser said, 'I have heard that you conducted yourself well while out there.'

'Some perhaps did not expect me to return,' Baldwin said.

'I cannot think who.'

It was Baldwin's turn to be silent. A short while before leaving England for France, Sir Hugh had become aware that he had once been a *Poor Fellow Soldier of Christ and the*

*Temple of Solomon*, a Knight Templar. He had then intentionally told the French King of Baldwin's past affiliation,
expecting the French King to capture and possibly execute
him. But the French King had shown himself more honourable
and generous than Despenser, and had warned Baldwin that he
knew of Baldwin's past.

'So you have come back with Queen Isabella's ambassador
to her husband?'

There was a wealth of cynicism in those few words. The
man was certain of himself, that much was obvious. He knew
that Baldwin had been involved in some of the discussions.
Perhaps he wanted Baldwin to give him some insights into the
way that the Queen had conducted herself, or was looking for
some juicy snippet of another sort?

Whatever his wish, Baldwin was not prepared to aid him. 'I
am merely a guard to the Pope's emissary, who has been asked
to bring some messages.'

'Oh, a humble guard, Sir Baldwin? And you had no idea of
anything curious whilst on your travels?'

'I do not know what you mean, nor what you wish me to
say.'

'I would have thought I was clear enough. Did anything
unusual strike you during your travels, Sir Baldwin?'

Baldwin was about to respond sharply that there was
nothing, when he suddenly wondered what the man was asking
about. At first, Baldwin thought Despenser was enquiring
about the Queen or the Bishop of Orange – but now, he
wondered.

The theft of the oil from Canterbury was certainly curious
enough, and the discovery of the man in the woods, a filthy
royal tabard thrown hurriedly over him, that was curious in the
extreme – but Despenser could not have known of either of

them. Could he? If Despenser was responsible for the theft of the oil, he might certainly know. His man could have returned here already and given Despenser the oil. But what on earth could Despenser have wanted with a phial of oil for anointing the King?

Nothing, unless the King desperately desired it, and Despenser sought to enhance his position by providing it. Especially if he could keep concealed the fact that he had stolen it originally.

'Sir Hugh, what do you mean by "unusual"?'

He contemplated for a moment or two. 'I mean, you were in France. Among our enemies. Was Mortimer there? Was there anyone who could be a threat to the Queen or the King?'

'I do not involve myself in matters of—'

'In God's name, Knight! Do you not realise we are on the precipice of war again?'

'The strangest thing I encountered was here in England. I found a dead man on my way,' Baldwin said, watching him closely. 'It was a man who was clad in a king's tabard, but it would not be easy to identify him.'

'Why?'

'You have seen dead bodies after being left in the open for a week or more.'

Sir Hugh nodded. All had. 'We shall have to enquire as to whether any of the King's men have disappeared, then.'

'I should be grateful if you would. He was dressed as a herald.'

'A herald? A king's man?' Despenser said with a frown.

'Yes. I think it likely he was waylaid by outlaws. There are many in those woods, apparently. He had no money or belongings on him, except one. And that makes me think he was most religious.'

'Why do you say that?'

In answer, Baldwin brought out the necklace of pilgrim badges. 'He went to Canterbury, to St Thomas, to Santiago de Compostela, to Our Lady of . . . he has been all over. So it would be good to learn if any religious heralds are missing, wouldn't it?'

The friar walked from the hall where he had been waiting as soon as he heard the tumult of the new entourage appear.

Nicholas of Wisbech watched as the men dropped from their saddles and dogs milled at their feet. This was clearly a senior man's party, from the look of them. He could see the Bishop's horse, but there was no sign of the man himself. Only some guards. Struck with a vague inquisitiveness, he left the building and wandered down to see who had arrived, but by the time he reached the yard, there were only a couple of men remaining.

'Good day, Friar.'

'God bless you. Whose party is this?'

'The Bishop of Orange, Friar. He's come with messages for the King.'

'And you are with him?'

'I am, Friar. I am called Jack.'

'A good name, my friend.'

'Aye, well,' Jack said, embarrassed. If only the friar knew his background.

'Where have you come from?'

'Paris. We stopped at many places, though. And I was glad to see Canterbury,' Jack said, trying to curry a little favour from this accommodating man of God. 'I had wanted to visit the place for many years on pilgrimage.' Which was true, although he saw no need to explain that he felt that there was a desperate need for him to beg forgiveness for some of the murders, rapes and robberies he had been involved in.

'It is many months since I was last there. I adored it. It is a shining example of the goodness of God, and the power of St Thomas.'

'Yes,' Jack said. And then, because the friar was so interested in the place, he told of the theft of the oil of St Thomas.

He had never seen a man's face fall so swiftly.

Baldwin left the Despenser in a pensive mood. He had not given much thought to the dead herald during the journey here, because he had spent his time looking forward to leaving Beaulieu and hurrying on with all speed to Devon and his family – but now, having seen the expression on the Despenser's face, he wondered whether the Despenser could himself have had anything to do with the man's sudden death.

The Despenser was no stranger to plots and murders. It was all too common for him to seek to destroy those whom he felt stood between him and a prize. Man or woman, it mattered not a whit. Sex was no barrier to his rapacious greed. There were rumours that he had even captured the widow of one of the King's knights and tortured her until her mind was broken. All for a relatively minor profit.

But it was surely too much to think that the Despenser could have been responsible for a herald's murder. From the first moment, Baldwin had been suspicious of the death, it was true, but he still remained confident that the killer was almost certainly the gang of felons who inhabited the woods. It had not occurred to him before that the murder could have been part of a larger conspiracy.

It was plain enough that the Despenser was himself anxious

about something, too. The man was exceedingly on edge. Not at all like the man whom Baldwin remembered from before his trip to France. The pressure of the realm's uncertainty was getting to him as well. Probably because of the number of his enemies who had been exiled and now lived safely in France, he reflected. A man could not continue to make enemies without one day reaping what he had sowed.

'Baldwin? Are you all right?'

'Simon, I need to think,' Baldwin said with frowning concentration. 'I need to think very carefully.'

It was just then that the servant came to ask Baldwin to join the King in his hall.

Nicholas was tempted to run straight to the King and demand to know what in Christ's name had happened to the oil, but a moment's reflection told him that this was not necessarily a good idea.

The King was no longer his friend. If Nicholas were to go to the King and demand to know what had happened to his oil, he may find himself in an unpleasant position. However, he need not be so blunt. And maybe he need not go to the King himself? There must be another man to whom he could speak in this great abbey. Someone who could assist him. A man who could speak for him, present his case and beg on his behalf.

All he needed to do was to find the man.

# Chapter Fifteen

Simon and Baldwin had met the King before when they had been to Thorney Island, where the palace of Westminster stood. There the King had been a forceful character, strong-willed and cunning. But then, too, he had had his wife nearby, and he was the undisputed commander of all England. Now his wife was away in France, he was distracted, and petulant at the thought of the price the King of France would levy for the return of any of his estates in France. That was a thorn in his side, a thorn that twisted and stabbed no matter what he plotted.

He was still remarkably handsome, though. His longish face was strong and deceptively masculine, his eyes clear blue, his hair clean and blond, his beard smartly trimmed. About his powerful frame was a tight-fitting blue cotte, and there was a fur-trimmed cloak over his shoulders.

All this Baldwin took in as he entered and made an elaborate bow. It was the rule that common men and those of lower classes should bow and remain bent, eyes downcast, in the King's presence. Only those who merited some regard were permitted to stand.

Clearly, Baldwin did not deserve such respect, then, for the King made no suggestion that he and Simon should stand straight.

His tone was peremptory. 'Sir Baldwin. I am told by the

good bishop that you have a personal message for me from my good lady wife. I would be most grateful to hear it.'

Baldwin closed his eyes, wondering for an instant whether he should be blunt or persuasive, but then the little speech which she had given him came back to him, and he began to speak.

'Your royal highness, I was called to the Queen and asked to bring you this message. She said that her brother King Charles would not be content to allow you to keep your French possessions without formally paying homage to him as your liege-lord for those territories. She has attempted to propose alternatives to him, but her sole victory so far has been to extend the length of the truce. She finds this deeply shaming, and would return at once to your side, were it not possible that there could be another solution.

'Your lady, her Majesty Queen Isabella, is fully seized of your feelings of disgust for the suggestion that you should travel abroad to show subservience to your equal. For this reason she would like to propose that another take your place in paying homage.'

'Yes? And who would she suggest? My falconer? My fewterer? My chief steward?' the King demanded sarcastically.

'Your lady the Queen suggests that because you are reluctant, rightly, to travel to France, perhaps you could create another who would be more fitting.'

The King frowned. '"Create" another? What is that supposed to mean?'

'Queen Isabella begs that you consider a different route. If you elect to rest all your French assets upon your son Edward, you can then send him to France in order to pay homage for his lands held under the French King. If you settle your French territories on your son, he could then go in your place, my Lord,' Baldwin persevered. 'Earl Edward could have the

Agenais, Montreuil and the other lands given to him, and then he could go to France to pay homage for them to the French King.'

'Let my son go there?' the King wondered with a frown of incomprehension. 'How will that help me, or the Crown?'

'You will have divested yourself of responsibility in that regard, so the French King, your brother-in-law, will have no recourse against you. If he withholds the lands from their new master, the Earl of Chester, your son, he will be reviled throughout Christendom for such unwarranted cruelty. The French King naturally looks upon you as his equal and rival. That is surely one reason why he wishes you to go to him. It would humiliate you to do so, and it would only serve to enhance his position in the world to have you bend your knee to him. Both must be attractive to him,' Baldwin said. 'But if he were unkind to his own nephew, your son, he would squander any advantage. Treating an English earl in such a manner would not win him any friends.'

The King was tempted to gape. He had an almost unbearable urge to turn to Hugh and ask his thoughts, but he knew that to turn to Hugh at this moment would be to appear weak.

'There is more, my Lord,' Baldwin said. 'The Earl is also the King's godson, I believe? If he were to mistreat his own godson, he would be despised throughout Christendom for his lack of chivalry. He cannot be so base to your son.'

King Edward had a fluttering in his breast, and he could feel the muscles of his belly growing taut with expectation, but he made no sign. That she could have thought up this! The woman whom he had treated with such little regard recently, was yet capable of a stroke of genius like this!

Genius, he had called it, and genius it was. The boy could go over to France as a duke in his own right, give up his homage, and, by so doing, leave Edward more perfectly secure than ever. If he disliked it, as Baldwin had said so clearly, King Charles could do nothing without embarrassing himself and showing that he was acting in bad faith.

'Are these your words or the Queen's?'

Baldwin allowed himself a smile. 'My Liege, I would not dare become embroiled in such matters of state. This is something so far beyond my capabilities, I would not wish to speak my own mind.'

'You have been to Paris. You have met my brother-in-law, King Charles?'

'Yes, my Liege.'

'So what is your opinion?'

'In my opinion, I think the lady is quite right. Her brother would be most content to see you embarrassed, and to have you taken to him to pay homage would enhance his own standing. Others would look and see a king paying him homage. That can only serve to benefit him.'

'But?'

'But if you were to send your son, having just made him Duke of all the French territories, that would confirm your independence, retain the French territories under the English crown, and protect the revenues from those lands. I feel sure that King Charles would feel entirely unable to embarrass your son, his nephew and godson. Would he wish the world to see him take advantage of a lad little more than a boy? That would indeed shame him.'

'Perhaps. Bishop? Do you have anything to add to this?'

'I would only say that this knight is an astute observer of human nature, King Edward. I would commend his advice to you.'

The King nodded, and then glanced at Simon. 'What of

you, Bailiff? You have a good mind, I think. What do you make of this suggestion?'

'Me?' Simon said. He felt his face colouring as he spoke, and resisted an urge to babble. He kept his eyes fixed on the ground, desperately thinking. 'I believe your wife has your best interests at heart, my Lord. I'm sure that my friend Sir Baldwin speaks his mind, too – but I'm only a simple countryman. I don't understand matters of this—'

'Bailiff, you have met the French King, and you have judged his character. Do you think I could trust my son to his care?'

Simon considered carefully, and then said, 'If he were my son, and I was asked to send him to the French king, I would fear my son's exploitation, Your Highness. But if the French king was his uncle, I think my lad would be safe. The French King is a king. He is surely a man of honour.'

'As are all kings, eh? My good bailiff, you have much to learn about kings and the quality of their ambitions!' the King chuckled. Taking a small purse from his belt, he continued, 'but you must have been fearful to come to me and say such things. The last thing in the world a bailiff from the wilds would expect would be to be asked to advise on affairs of national importance like this. So here – take a reward! And now,' he said, having tossed the purse at Simon's feet, 'leave me to consider this matter in full. I must consult with Sir Hugh, I have need of his thoughts.'

Jack had finished with his horse when he saw them.

It was an ancient rule that a man who relied on his mount must see to it before attending to his own needs, but for Jack it was more than a principle of kindness to the beast – it was the careful assessment of a man who was accustomed to being chased, in the past, by those who wanted to try to kill him.

There were too many who wanted to see him dead for him ever to leave his horse without checking him over, grooming him, and seeing that he was well-watered and comfortable.

He had stowed his brush away, and slapped the fellow's rump in farewell for the day, when the men at the gates showed an unwarranted energy, and he peered in that direction with some interest. There stood Pons and André, glaring about them as they were questioned.

'Where did you two run to?' he asked, once he had persuaded the guards that these two were indeed with the Bishop of Orange's party.

Pons ducked his head and gave one of his little smiles. It always made Jack think of a monkey he had once seen in Paris, the way that Pons drew his upper lip over his teeth. 'It was that coroner, you see. He told us he would have us arrested for lying. Us! All the jury had already agreed that we were innocent, and said we should be permitted to go, but no! The grand coroner said we must remain and he would hold us there for so long as he wanted, stuck in the worst, nastiest gaol in the castle. He was a very nasty man, that coroner.'

'Really? He gave us two more men to look after us for the journey, so he was not so very unkind to us,' Jack said. 'I think the Bishop preferred them to you two.'

'Ah, you are joking, are you not? This is not kind.'

'Where have you been? You could have joined up with us at any time.'

André answered in his supercilious manner. 'You think so? Eh, we travelled urgently as soon as the coroner made those disagreeable suggestions, but we missed our road. Instead of turning, we managed to make our way south in our panic. Otherwise we would have been happy to come straight to the Bishop's entourage, naturally.'

Oh, yes, naturally, Jack thought. Except that, from the smell of these two, they had managed to find their way to a tavern. They had probably been sitting there inside it for the last few days.

'Where is the food? The buttery?' Pons asked, looking about him with that eagerness that spoke of the true warrior, always ensuring his next meal before any other matter.

'Follow me,' Jack said. He was not particularly keen on their company, but he had to admit, they were more appealing than John and Peter, the two men supplied by the castellan at Canterbury. At least these two looked less dangerous.

Baldwin was about to move backwards from the King's presence, when Simon nudged him sharply in the ribs. '*The oil*,' he whispered.

'What is that, Bailiff?' the King demanded.

Simon was appalled to have been noticed, and flushed violently this time, incapable of speech.

It was left to Baldwin to explain about the oil's theft, but that was not his duty. No. 'The Prior asked me to tell you of this monk's death, Your Highness. Brother Gilbert.'

'Brother Gilbert?' the King frowned. 'The name is familiar.'

'The second thing we discovered was, while travelling here, a body at the side of the road.'

'What of it?'

'We think that it was a man killed by outlaws.'

'Outlaws lie everywhere,' the King swore. 'Keepers of my peace should be more assiduous in seeking the perpetrators of such vile crimes. Was it anyone of significance?'

'I believe it may have been a man from your household, my Liege.'

'*What?*' The King gaped.

'He wore a herald's tabard, but there was nothing else upon him to show who he was. I think he had lain there for a week or more, and there was no distinguishing mark I could see on his body. Only some personal items.'

'The coroner will hopefully be able to make some sense of it. If not, the locals will have a large fine to pay. Will he be able to find the body?'

'I marked the position of the body most carefully. I would have posted a guard, were it not for the urgency of my own mission here, and the need to protect the Bishop through what were clearly dangerous woods. Others before we reached the woods told us of the dangers. There have been several killings there.'

'Let us hope the coroner will find the body, then. You are fortunate that you were not harmed. I would have expected a man of your experience to avoid a wood when you had already been warned of the danger.'

'The Bishop is a man of strong views, Your Highness.'

The King was not amused. 'It hardly matters. I prefer live emissaries, not murdered ones. In future, you will act more cautiously. Was there anything else?'

'There was one thing that may have some significance,' Baldwin continued. 'The dead herald wore a necklace of pilgrim badges about his neck. He must have been a most devout Christian.'

'I will have my men ask whether such a man is missing. Can you tell me more about him?'

'I would say he was about five feet and ten inches high, not running to fat, probably young, with brown hair, worn rather long for fashion. He had a strong, square jaw, and good teeth.'

'Where is the necklace?'

'It is deposited with Sir Hugh, Your Highness. He has it so

he can learn who was the dead man. Do you know whether any of your heralds have disappeared?'

The King looked at him. 'You expect me to monitor the movements of all of my household? Now, leave me to consider my Queen's suggestions.'

Outside the hall, Baldwin sighed with some relief. There had been moments in that room when he had wondered how the King would react to his words, but, so far, the man had been entirely reasonable and sensible. It was fortunate, he felt, that he had avoided mention of the oil.

The Bishop of Orange was making his way across the court towards the rooms which had been allocated to him when Baldwin saw the dog again. The beast was sitting near a pillar, and as soon as he saw the Bishop approaching, the dog sprang to his feet, tail wagging. But the Bishop was uninterested, and instead of trying to stroke the head thrust towards him in a display of affection, he lifted a hand as though to strike it. Instantly the dog was cowed, and drew away, an expression of uncomprehending despair on his face.

Baldwin frowned. 'That poor beast . . .'

'Sweet Jesus, Baldwin, look at this!'

Simon had tentatively opened the purse so casually thrown to him by the King. Inside the velvet interior nestled a good handful of silver coins. 'It's a fortune! Ten pounds, I think!'

'Protect it well, then, old friend,' Baldwin chuckled. 'In God's name, don't flash it around here too much.' Looking up, he saw Pons and André. 'Yes, keep it hidden. That much money would tempt many men to knock you on the head – even me!'

# Chapter Sixteen

The Bishop of Orange was content now to see how the King would react. There was plenty for the man to consider, it was fair to say. He had sown the seeds of the ideas, hopefully. Now to see how King Edward turned.

It had been deeply interesting how the knight and his friend had not mentioned the stolen oil. He would have to consider that. When Sir Baldwin arrived, he assumed the fellow would tell all about it immediately. Perhaps he would prefer not to bear bad tidings. A messenger was often victim to his master's rage.

For the same reason he was keen to make no mention of it himself. It would be too easy to offend. Better by far to deny knowledge. In any case, it would be easier with the arrangement with the Queen to keep as far from discussion of that cursed liquor as possible.

In the meantime, it was interesting that Despenser had said little before him. The fool was perhaps beginning to realise the limitations of his abilities – and of his power. Either that or he had been instructed to hold his tongue while in the presence of the Bishop. Interesting, either way. Could it mean that the King didn't trust him so much any more?

He was walking across the court while silently considering the effects of his embassy here, and now the Bishop looked up to see Peter, the older guard from Canterbury. The man nodded briefly, and then the Bishop saw him give a little smile. It was enough to make a frown pass over his features.

The fool shouldn't make any signs that they knew each other. It was too dangerous, especially here, in the King's stronghold. Secrecy was all.

Baldwin was almost at the door of the little house where he and Simon were supposed to be lodged when he saw the figure of Ayrminne leaving the small church.

'I think that is William Ayrminne,' he said quietly to Simon, and then called to him. Soon he and Simon were at the side of the canon.

'I think we met earlier this year when I was in London with my Lord Stapledon of Exeter?' said Baldwin by way of introduction.

'Yes? Ah, yes, I think we did,' Ayrminne said. He nodded towards Simon affably enough when Baldwin gave his name. 'Do you wish for something?'

'It is possibly nothing,' Baldwin said, 'but on our way here, we passed by a body in the woods near Crowborough.'

'How sad.'

'Yes. And I was wondering whether you lost anyone from your party on the way here?'

'Why? What on earth would make you think this fellow could have come from our group?'

Baldwin considered for a beat, and then nodded. 'The man was dressed as a King's herald. I was wondering whether one of your heralds left your party?'

'It is true that we did have a herald with us, but he is still here. His name is Thomas, Thomas of Bakewell. A most reliable man, too. And perfectly alive, I assure you.'

'I am very grateful. You have put my mind at rest.'

'But there is something else? You didn't ask me just because a man was killed, did you?'

Baldwin smiled and shook his head. 'No. There was something which might have been stolen from Canterbury, from Christ Church itself, and some say that this man may have been the thief.'

'Truly? In God's name, what was stolen?'

'A valuable treasure of the King's,' Baldwin said evasively. 'It appears to have been mislaid.'

Ayrminne gave a low whistle. 'Really? But surely a herald wouldn't steal something from his master?'

'We do not know. All we can do is seek the truth,' Baldwin said.

'Then good hunting, Sir Baldwin.'

'Except we're not, are we?' Simon said pointedly as they walked away from Ayrminne.

'Hmm?'


Sir Hugh le Despenser acknowledged the demand for his presence with a curt nod, and as the messenger from the King turned to walk out, Sir Hugh was already following.

'Sir Hugh, come in. So, Sir Baldwin has already seen you about this dead herald?'

Despenser smiled without humour. 'Yes indeed.'

'And have you managed to discover anything about him? Sir Baldwin mentioned a necklace of pilgrim badges. Is that right?'

'Quite right. He was a well-travelled man. That should make it easier to find out who he was.'

'Good. Sir Hugh, do you know of a Brother Gilbert who was living in the Canterbury priory?'

'Yes, he's the son of my old friend Sir Berengar. Why?'

'Didn't you know? He has apparently been killed. In Christ Church Priory. Sir Baldwin told me just now.'

'Sir Baldwin did? How good of him.' Despenser nodded to himself. His face displayed none of his internal turmoil at this sudden revelation.

The King turned his back and was discussing some matter of his purchase of new horses from Spain, but Sir Hugh could barely concentrate.

That knight from Furnshill had known of the murder all the while he was in his room.

And forebore to mention it.

'I was thinking,' Baldwin said quietly, as he walked to their room with Simon, 'that the man killed in the roadway in those woods was probably the King's herald, and after stealing the oil and murdering Gilbert, he perhaps rushed on to bring the oil to the King, and was waylaid and killed. By sheer misfortune, he happened upon felons who slaughtered him, and he was left there.'

'You didn't mention the theft of the oil in front of the King!' Simon protested.

'No. A degree of caution struck me while I was speaking to him – it was Despenser's attitude. It was teasing at my mind. But so was the matter about the tabard. What if the man was, for example, involved in the theft of the oil? It seems a little remarkable as a coincidence that the King's herald was killed at about the same time as the theft. Could that mean that the thief passed along that same road?'

'That would be possible, except . . .'

'Yes?'

'It is a little unlikely, isn't it? The chances of a man coming along that road by chance? How many roads are there from

Canterbury? What on earth would be the reason for a man coming along exactly that route?'

'I think it is not so unlikely. King's messengers and heralds will know the same paths, and they always tend to use these ones. One messenger will pass on his knowledge to the next to take his path, and thereby the roads used tend to be the same. The interesting possibility of this, though, is that the herald stole the oil and then was robbed of it in this area. Could that mean that the theft of the oil came to be more common knowledge, or that the herald had an accomplice who killed him to steal the oil?'

'That is hardly likely. That presupposes two killings by accomplices. One, the monk, I could believe; two, I cannot. An escalation of violence isn't credible. Not to me, at any rate.'

'An excellent point, Simon. And another is the fact that we are told that the dead man was not from the good William Ayrminne's party. You remember, the coroner told us that he thought that a herald had been seen on the night of Gilbert's death. He appeared to assume that this herald was from the men with Ayrminne. But not so, according to Ayrminne himself. So this thief was not one of the men who came back from France with the ambassadors.'

'No.'

'So let us consider it from another angle. A thief took the oil. Perhaps he rode to the woods, and was there waylaid by felons, then; felons who live in the wood. They killed this false herald, and stole the oil. Yet why would they take the oil? I cannot believe that. I doubt they needed oil for their meal that night! And I doubt whether ordinary outlaws would have killed a churl and thrown his body aside like that. It was merely left by the side of the roadway. Surely an outlaw would have hidden the body a little so that the murder would not be brought to his door?'

'Outlaws can be astonishingly dim, Baldwin. I have seen it on the moors.'

'Perhaps, but concealment would surely be more likely. And especially given the rank of the dead man. Murder of a herald is not common, and more to the point, it is astonishing that such a thing might happen to the very man who had just stolen a phial of inconceivably valuable oil. What is the likelihood that the thief, clad in a King's tabard, would then come across a felon set on murder?'

'So what do you think happened?'

'I have no idea. Perhaps the man was already dead, and when the man with the tabard happened along with the stolen oil, he saw the corpse, and chose to conceal his own identity by shoving the corpse's head through his tabard. That is possible . . . also possible is that the killer of Gilbert came by the same route – there are only a few through those woods and that one may have been commonly used by messengers, for example – and killed the first man he encountered, throwing his tabard over the dead body to conceal his own identity.'

Simon considered. 'That would involve a lot of boldness on the part of the killer.'

'Yes.'

'It would also surely imply a purpose. The King would not steal the oil – it was his own, stored where he had ordered it – so it was someone else, if you are right.'

'Yes. Someone who had something to gain by removing the oil. Either that was someone who wanted the oil for his own purposes, or it was someone who sought to ransom it to the King.'

'And your guess would be?'

'What would the King do to someone who thought he could ransom the King's own property back to him? He would have the fellow in his gaol in no time. A blink of an eye. No, this was no simple theft for swift gain. This was a carefully plotted theft with a longer-term benefit in mind.'

'Who could think in those terms?' Simon asked. And then he thought a moment, and added, 'Oh.'

Baldwin nodded. They had both had enough experience of Sir Hugh le Despenser to know what he was capable of. 'Yes.'

Simon's face hardened. 'Well, in that case, the best thing we can do is leave well alone and return home as soon as possible.'

'Simon, he could well have been responsible for the murder of that monk – and the man in the woods.'

'Yes, Baldwin. And I don't want him responsible for our murders. Baldwin, if he were guilty, what could we do about it? Accuse him in front of the King? The man who is his best friend? You think we'd achieve anything by doing that? Who are you trying to fool, Baldwin? There is no possibility of our getting anywhere. Me? I'm for leaving him alone. He's the most powerful baron in the country after the King himself. If you accuse him or irritate him, you will be signing your own death warrant. Do you want that?'

'I am a keeper of the King's Peace. I have a duty to justice.'

'No, Baldwin,' Simon said, and this time his voice was more gentle. He stepped forward and rested a hand on his friend's shoulder. 'You have an honourable duty to finding the truth in your own lands, back in Devon, and you have a duty to protect and serve your *wife*. You and I have to look to our families, Baldwin. If you go chasing Despenser, you will die. You know that. And when you die, he will not stop from persecuting Jeanne and your children. You know Despenser.

He is relentless and ruthless. He will destroy you, then your family, and he will steal your lands and property to leave your widow utterly penniless. You will have nothing at all to leave to Jeanne and your children. Think of them, Baldwin.'

'But if he was guilty of that murder . . .'

'He is guilty of other killings, Baldwin. We both know that. We've seen the results of his jealousy at Iddesleigh and at Westminster. Remember that innkeeper? What would it serve justice for us to die too?'

'You won't help me, then?'

'Yes, I will. I'll help you all the way home, Baldwin. But I won't help you to see yourself destroyed. That will serve no useful purpose.'

Baldwin had been looking at the ground. Now he looked up, and Simon was relieved to see that the veil of grim determination which had harshened his features was now gone. In its place a shamefaced smile appeared. 'Yes. You're right. It's time to give up any ideas I may have had of a great destiny, and to return to my quiet life in Devon. I was forced into the limelight by Stapledon, and we have done our part by escorting the Queen to France. Surely that is enough. We'll go home.'

'Good,' Simon said with a grin. And then he slapped Baldwin on the back and laughed aloud. 'I cannot wait to see my wife's face when I appear!'

'Nor I mine,' Baldwin said. And as he spoke, his eyes took on a faraway look. The Bishop's dog lay asleep a few yards away. 'But before I go, there is one purchase I should like to make.'

*Third Thursday After Easter*[1]

The summons came a little after his midday meal. Sir Hugh le Despenser had elected for a quiet lunch with his steward and two clerks to discuss the income of his Welsh estates, and the messenger received a cold stare when he demanded Despenser join the King.

Matters of state came before his own estates, though. At least it was nothing more that the slimy turd Furnshill had slipped into conversation. He had been glad to see that prickle riding off a couple of days ago with his friend the bailiff. At least they were two problems fewer for him to deal with here in Beaulieu.

'If His Highness desires it,' he said, rising.

The King was in an even more explosive frame of mind than usual. 'Did you know? Did you?'

'Know what, my Liege?' Despenser responded mildly. He observed the King's mannerisms with interest. The man appeared to be losing control of his mind.

'Look! This messenger has just brought news from Prior Eastry. You remember him? The wretch who was so persuasive on behalf of my wife, and insisted that she should have large funds to draw on while she was over there in France. Him! You remember? I told you that one of his brothers had died, didn't I? That young fool Gilbert.'

'Yes. What has happened now? Sir Baldwin told me most of this.'

'Did he also mention that my coronation oil has been stolen!'

'Your . . . what?'

---

[1] Thursday, 26 April 1325

'St Thomas's oil is gone!' the King snapped. In an instant his face had blackened with anger. 'How would someone dare try such a thing?' His fist slammed down on the table, making the jug and goblets jump. 'My oil! *Taken!* I want you to instigate a full inquiry into how this was done, Sir Hugh. Seek for it, and find it, and when you do, I want the men responsible to be punished for this. Punished so that no one will even think of stealing such a thing again!'

'My Liege, surely—'

'Find it, find the oil, and find me the man who took it, Sir Hugh! The last man who stole from my father was skinned, and his pelt still adorns the door to the crypt at Westminster Abbey as a sign to all the monks never to try their King's patience again. Well, someone *has* dared to try my patience, and I want *his skin for it*!'

# Chapter Seventeen

'The oil is gone,' Despenser repeated quietly to himself.

It was a bad piece of news, certainly, although not a catastrophe – yet – and he would have to ensure that it never grew to be one. True, the King should not have been told so quickly; Despenser should have been told first, so he himself could have told him, but Despenser could rectify that. It was better to seek the oil and find it first. And hang the man who stole it, by the cods from the highest beam in the ceiling at Westminster Palace! Any man who dared to steal from the King was dangerous, but someone who was bold enough to take something that was useless to any *but* the King, he was a dangerous opponent. Or mad. Either way, he was a threat to Despenser. And Sir Hugh did not like to leave threats go unheeded.

The King shouldn't have been told yet. There was no need for him to know. He had that damned knight from Furnshill to blame for this.

This was not the first time he had come across Sir Baldwin de Furnshill. Sir Baldwin, the meddler who had stood in his path in Devon, in that outlandish vill called Iddesleigh, and who then had gone to France with the Queen. Somehow, whenever Sir Baldwin was about, Sir Hugh le Despenser's plans went awry. Not only him, either. Sir Hugh was reminded of the little embarrassment at Dartmouth, when he had lost one of his better allies. At the time the name of the Keeper of the Port had meant nothing to him, but now the name 'Puttock' took on a certain significance.

Well, no more! Furnshill had deliberately kept both these pieces of information from him. First that his own friend's son had died, and then that the King's oil was stolen.

Sir Hugh le Despenser had many more important fishes to fry, but these two were treating him with contempt. The knight was withholding information from him. From *him*! The King's most favoured adviser, in Christ's name! Shit, the bastard deserved to be grabbed and hauled off to the Tower!

But he had some powerful friends, from Bishop Stapledon downwards. Even the King appeared immoderately fond of him. That was one of the strange things about King Edward. He would sometimes pick a man and decide that he was an honourable, decent fellow. It didn't matter what the man had done before, the King could forgive almost anything, unless it was disloyalty or treachery to him. Now he appeared to have chosen Sir Baldwin. That was why the knight was sent to France in the first place. King Edward actually *trusted* him about his wife.

Well, swyve him. Swyve them both! They'd learn that it was not a good idea to twitch the tail of Sir Hugh le Despenser.

Sir Baldwin and Bailiff Puttock. Stannary Bailiff, he was. Or had been until the Abbot of Tavistock died . . . *he* could be intimidated. He could be taught an object lesson in civility. Sir Hugh had not formed a very strong opinion of Simon Puttock. He was a churl, a serf in the pay of the Abbot of Tavistock, and nothing more. Being made Keeper of the Port of Dartmouth may have inflated his self-importance, and he had a few brains, no doubt, but little capacity to defend himself intelligently against an astute man. Or a powerful one.

Sir Hugh had just such a man. A man who would teach the pathetic little Bailiff to be more careful with his betters, and who would thus show Sir Baldwin that when he picked an enemy, he should be more wary. Sir Hugh was not a man to make bitter.

With his jaw set, he walked through to the door at the rear of his chamber. From there he passed through his solar block and out into the sunlight, where he cast about for a little while, before seeing his man at the far side.

He beckoned, waiting with composure.

'Sir Hugh?'

'William, I wish you to travel to Devon as fast as you can. There is a man there, a fellow called Simon Puttock. He is a bailiff, I believe, with a house in Lydford near the stannary gaol, as I understand it. Go there, and take his house.'

'It's yours.'

'He may be there. If he becomes angry, provoke him. He's not well trained in fighting. You know what to do.'

'Sir.'

'It is possible, if you ride hard, that you may reach his home before him, though. That would be amusing. You could enjoy yourself with the man's wife. You would like that?'

William Wattere smiled. He had an easygoing manner, and an ever-ready grin for the women, which concealed a lust for brutality that was unequalled in Despenser's experience.

Watching him swagger away bellowing for a horse and shouting at four or five others, Sir Hugh gave a thin smile himself. But then he shook himself. There was much else to do.

There was another of his men near the horse trough. He crossed to the fellow, then held up the necklace of pilgrim badges. 'You recognise this?'

'No.'

'They were found on the neck of a dead man in some woods. Apparently he was clad in a tabard of a King's herald. And now we have been set the task of learning who could have been responsible for the King's loss. And I want to know, too. Do you have any idea who was the most devout herald among the King's men?'

'There was that Richard de Yatton. He was very keen. I remember someone saying he travelled half as far as all the others in a day because he stopped at every chapel to pray. He would be the most religious.'

'Good. Now, I have something I need you to do for me.'

*Monday before Feast of the Apostles*[1]

### *Furnshill*

Jeanne de Furnshill, a tall, slender lady in her middle thirties, with a pale complexion and straying reddish hair, stood upright, hands resting in the small of her back as her daughter ran across the grassed pasture before her house.

'My Lady, you want some wine?'

'No, thank you, Edgar. I am fine just now.'

She had much to thank Edgar for. When her husband had left her to travel with Bishop Stapledon, it had appeared that there was no alternative. She had at the time only recently given birth to her son, and Edgar, her husband's sergeant from those far off days when he had been a Knight Templar, had been a sturdy support for her. He was reliable, constant, and although often all but invisible, she had only to raise her voice and he would materialise at her side like some faithful hound, or so she always thought.

---

[1] Monday, 29 April 1325

His wife, too, had been a great companion to her. Petronilla had more experience in childbirth than Jeanne, and just as her own Baldwin was born, Petronilla was weaning her own little boy. It was all too easy for her to become nursemaid to Jeanne's child, to the comfort of both women. Jeanne found breastfeeding her boy a trial, and Petronilla was very glad to be able to help. She adored Jeanne's boy almost as much as she did her own.

There came a pattering of feet, and Jeanne had to brace herself to absorb the impact as her daughter pelted into her, arms clinging to her thighs beneath her skirts. 'Richalda!'

'Daddy! Daddy! Daddy!'

Jeanne looked down at her for a moment, and then across at Edgar, who gazed back blankly, and then grinned broadly. A large dog had appeared about the corner of the house: a black dog, with brown eyebrows and cheeks, with a white muzzle and paws, a white tip to his tail, and a white cross on his breast. 'I think she is probably right, my Lady.'

'What? I—' and then Jeanne heard the steady trotting gait, and glanced up at the trail that wound past their door, and saw him. And without realising that Edgar had taken her daughter, she was already running up the track to her husband, skirts billowing, her coif flying from her head.

*Fourth Tuesday after Easter*[1]
Baldwin woke with a panic, dreaming he was in a field, in a tent, Simon at his side, and the screaming was from a man murdered outside in the fine snow . . . cold . . . it was so cold, especially at his armpit . . .

And then he opened his eyes with a jolt, drawing away from

---

[1] Tuesday, 30 April 1325

the dog's wet nose, and found himself in familiar surroundings. He knew that ceiling, those rafters, the feel of this bed . . . *Home!*

Pushing his newest dog away, he muttered, 'You'll be sleeping outside if you keep shoving your nose there, dog. Go on, piss off!'

Still, waking him every morning was the least of bad behaviour he would have expected. 'Wolf' was in almost every way a perfect companion. Handsome, obedient (when he understood what Baldwin was saying) and ever-present. Baldwin was sure he would become an excellent guard.

Yawning voluptuously, he scratched his beard. It was strange to be here again, he thought contentedly. There was a loud whining from the door, and he rose on both elbows to look. The beast needed to go out. At least the thing was house-trained. He stood, let Wolf outside, and then slapped bare-footed across the planks to his bed, flopping down. He grunted, stretched, and threw his arms over his head, causing his wife to mumble and complain in her sleep. She rolled over to enfold herself into his body again, her cheek against his breast, hands clasped as though in prayer under her chin, one soft thigh placed gently over his own. He ignored the cries from his daughter, in the room beneath, and let his arm fall over his wife, cradling her closer.

'What now?' she murmured as his hand slid along her flank.

'I was enjoying the peace before dawn,' he said. 'I do not suppose you . . . ?'

'It will not last,' she said with confidence. Already there was the sound of small feet downstairs, and Baldwin was sure that in a moment the door would be thrown wide open and Richalda would be upon him.

'I missed you,' she said quietly.

'And I you.'

'It was hard, not knowing when you would be returning.'

'It was as hard for me, Jeanne. I had no idea when I might be permitted to return from the Queen. Still, I am back now.'

'And hopefully you will not have to leave us again?'

'Jeanne, if there was any such need, I would take you with me.'

'What, even to France? You know that they have clothes and material in Paris that a woman would sell her children to buy?'

He chuckled. 'Then it is fortunate that we won't be going, maid. We can stay here and live the gentle life of rural knighthood. I shall be Keeper of the King's Peace again, you shall be my wife, and the King and the Queen may sort out their own problems.'

'You think so? There are terrible rumours, Baldwin.'

'Of what nature?'

'People talk of traitors gathering hosts abroad, Baldwin. They say that we could be invaded by the French, that they will come and pillage and kill all who stand before them—'

'No. I saw no desire to try to overcome our lands while I was there. The French are angry that our King will not go to pay homage to their King for the lands he holds from King Charles, but there is not desire for war. They will absorb the King's possessions, that is all.'

'They say that the traitors will come, though.'

'There is one traitor, Roger Mortimer, who would be able to collect some mercenaries about him, but even the French King knows what sort of man he is, I think. He sent Mortimer from his court. The man's without friends even there.' He did not say that Mortimer had warned Baldwin of the threat posed to him by Despenser.

'That relieves me, husband.'

'Good,' Baldwin said. There was no need to worry her. She need not hear that he had met Mortimer. It was the kind of information that could serve no useful purpose.

'Will you remain here now?'

There was a small tone of doubt in her voice, a note that tore at his heart. Only a short while before, Baldwin had been unfaithful to her. Oh, there were plenty of excuses to justify his behaviour, but he had found when he came home again afterwards, that his relationship with Jeanne had been affected. He felt his guilt, and it put a pall over their love. It was only recently that he had felt the shame and remorse lift, and their lives had returned to – if not the same tenor as before – a new balance.

'I will remain here, woman. Unless the King calls me away. And if he does, you may journey with me, as I said, even if it means I must take you to Paris and buy every item in every haberdashery shop!'

She mumbled at that, and by the regularity of her breathing, he knew she had fallen asleep again.

He wished to sleep like his wife, but try as he might, he was left with a sour flavour in his mouth whenever he thought once more of the man left dead at the side of the road in those woods. He felt a certain guilt at not seeking the killer more relentlessly. It was the first time he had not. There was no comfort in the reflection that it was not his responsibility while on the road – that was only a sop to his own conscience. If he could return, he would spend more time on seeking the man's murderer.

And learning who it was who had taken the King's oil.

### Beaulieu

Sir Hugh le Despenser was already in his chamber, his clerks at their table, running through the expenses for his stay here at Beaulieu so far, and keeping an eye on his ready money, when the knock came at his door.

His man was a hard-faced fellow with the thick hair and grey eyes of a southern Welshman. He was slight, with a gentle gait that concealed his strength. Although his limbs looked thin, they were immensely wiry and powerful.

He looked at Despenser. 'I've checked.'

'And?'

'The herald you mentioned, Richard de Yatton, has been missing for some days. He was sent off to see the Castellan at Leeds Castle, but he never came back.'

'How long ago did he leave?'

'About the end of the Lenten period. Not sooner.'

'He left in Lent? Before Easter? You're sure?'

'He was sent away while we were still in Westminster, and hasn't been seen since. He never came back.'

'Good. I think we know who the dead herald at the side of the road was, then,' Despenser said with a cold frown at the ground. 'But who killed him, and why? What would be the point of killing a King's herald? It's not as though he was carrying a lot of money about him. Or was he?'

'It'd be sure to bring down a painful load of trouble on the man's head, Sir Hugh.'

'Yes. I think you're right there. We need to do the same.'

# Chapter Eighteen

*Vigil of the Feast of the Apostles*[1]

### *Near Lydford*

It took Simon an extra day to cover the distance to his own home, and it was the excitement at seeing his wife again that caused him to rise before the dawn on that Wednesday and set off on the last few miles of his journey after spending the night on the moors.

He had stopped at the little inn that nestled on the southern side of the road from Mortonhampstead, perhaps one third of the way over the moors. From here he could turn up, past the little dwarf trees at Wistman's Wood, and head westwards, towards his home. It was a route he had taken often enough, and it would give him a clear view on how the moors were. After his travels to London and thence to France, it felt like an age since he had last been here, on the moors where he had been happiest. There was nowhere better for a man to live, he reckoned.

All appeared normal. There were occasional plumes of smoke from the tin works, where the miners tried to smelt their ore into black ingots of semi-pure metal, and the constant sound of water from leats, hammering, and the slow, rumbling

---
[1] Wednesday, 1 May 1325

of mill-wheels. On the early morning air, all these sounds carried so clearly, the workings might have been right at his side, rather than perhaps a mile distant. Not that he cared. The main thing was, that the moors were being farmed, so there was still work for him, provided he had a job.

Some months past, he had been given a new post as Keeper of the Port of Dartmouth, a great honour and promotion which his master, the Abbot of Tavistock, had given him as reward for his service over the past years. The sad truth was, however, that he didn't want it, and neither did his wife. Meg would have been happy to remain as the wife of a bailiff on the moors. She had no desire for more money or the authority that came from a senior position. All she craved was that their lives might continue comfortably, that their children might grow strong and healthy, and that she and her husband might enjoy their time together. The idea that they should be uprooted and dropped some tens of miles to the south, devoid of friends, without even the companionship of the animals on their small farms, threw her into a despondency. And the alternative was to see her husband go to do his duty while she remained here at their home.

It had been a wrench, but that was the only resolution at first. But now all had changed, because the good abbot had died, and the two men who desired his abbacy were fighting over it tooth and nail. Simon had no idea who would eventually succeed to the post, whether it be John de Courtenay, whom Simon considered a fool, or the more urbane, calm, Roger Busse, whom Simon thought much brighter, and possibly more corrupt. There were rumours, which Simon had confirmed to his own satisfaction, that Busse made use of a necromancer in Exeter. That was itself enough to disqualify the man from the abbacy, so far as Simon was concerned.

Still, at least he should soon know which was to become the abbot, and when he knew that, Simon would be able to confirm what his own position would be – whether he would be entitled to return to his work here on the moor, or whether he would have no position within the abbey at all. If that was the case, he was not sure what he would do.

At last he found himself dropping down the hill at Brat Tor, a long, gentle incline that halted at the road which headed northwards from Tavistock, and here Simon had to turn a little north himself, to meet the long road that took him along the ridge towards Lydford itself.

So many of the roads here in Devon wound about the long scarps at the top of hills. The alternative paths were precipitous lanes that sometimes dropped vertiginously into valleys, and then climbed alarmingly – and exhaustingly – back to the next. Simon had spent much of his youth swearing at such hills, but now that he was older, he minded them not at all. Especially since his rides to London and beyond. Those journeys had shown him how tedious travelling could be. There were whole plains in which a man could ride for days seeing scarcely a tree, and the only alteration was in the quality of the soil. Few places had the rich, black soil of the peat-filled moors of his homeland, or the deep red of the lands about Crediton, the earth that shouted to him of vegetables and cattle pasture. Nowhere he had seen could bear comparison with his own lands, he felt. Simon was a Devonian through and through.

The road brought him straight into the old stannary town of Lydford, and just as the great square, black block of the prison came into view, he turned left into his yard, and sat there a moment looking about him contentedly. He knew that the pride and happiness he felt now could not be improved upon.

It was as though he had been a soul travelling for a thousand years in purgatory, only to suddenly find his way to the gates of heaven itself. He sighed with a gentle moan of contentment, and then took a deep breath.

'Hey! *Hoi!* Is there anyone at home?' he roared.

'Simon? Simon? *Oh, Simon!*' his wife called, and suddenly he was standing on the ground and Meg was in his arms.

He knew only delight at the feel of her breasts at his chest, her hips at his, her arms about him, her lips on his, and then she pulled back a little, hands on his shoulders, and he saw the tears in her eyes and smiled. 'I'm home, Meg.'

But her words made his soft smile dissipate like fog in the sun.

'Oh, Simon, what can we do?'

## *Beaulieu*

There was no solution, Nicholas of Wisbech told himself. He needed one man to make his case for him, just one man, and in a week of searching it seemed plain that there was no one here.

He knew most of them. He should do after so many years working first with the King, and latterly trailing after him and his household, trying to see how to work his way back into the King's favour, but of all of them, none appeared to desire to help him. There was nothing they could do, they said. Nothing they wanted to do, more like.

At least one or two had been happy enough to tell him the story of what had happened to the oil. A monk slain, the oil taken. That was bad, truly bad – but others said that a king's herald had been killed, too, a man had been found by the side of the road, and that might mean that he had been killed by the same murderer and thief. Perhaps. There was no proof, of course, but in the King's household, proof was rarely necessary to provide a good tale.

So the oil was gone. It was galling, and dreadfully soul-destroying. To think that, after all his efforts, the monks of Christ Church had failed so miserably, allowing the King's property to be stolen like that ... well! They might as well have left it on the roadside for anyone to pick up.

And meanwhile, he was stuck here, wondering what he might do to win a little favour. Oh, perhaps he ought to give up on all this and make his way back into the Church. He could join the Bishop of Orange, perhaps. The men who professed to know said that he was going to be returning to the Pope soon with a letter from the King. Perhaps Nicholas should volunteer to go and help. That might be a good idea. At least it would get him away from this blasted land with all the misery and failure he had experienced.

So long as the Pope didn't look on him as unfavourably as the King, of course.

His feet had taken him on a circuit about the abbey gardens, and now he had made his way back to where he had started. He felt like some beggar at the door, walking about like this, trying to think his way through the problem. It was deeply shaming. But he could see no way round it. There had to be a means of . . .

And then he saw him. A man in the uniform of a king's herald. A strong-looking man, tall, quite striking, really, and oddly familiar. Where had Nicholas seen him before, though?

### Lydford

'They came early in the morning,' Meg said. 'Five men, all of them armed, and they said that they were to take over our lands here.'

'No one can take away our lands,' Simon said. 'These are mine!'

'They said that the farm was owned by Sir Hugh le Despenser, Simon. They told me I had a week to leave, and then they'd come and formally take the place.'

'A week? When was this?'

'Sunday. Oh, Simon, it's been driving me mad to think of it!'

'What was the name of the man who said this?'

'He was a man-at-arms, a man called William atte Wattere, he said.'

'And did he have any kind of warrant?'

'Nothing, husband. Simon, what can this mean?'

'It means that someone has made an error, Meg. Don't you worry yourself.'

'But our farm – all our lands, everything we've built in the last ten years, we'd lose everything if he succeeds!'

'No one is taking my farm from me, Meg. In the worst case, I'll speak with the new Abbot of Tavistock. My service there is enough to make sure I have the support of the new abbot. Uh – who *is* the abbot?'

'You hadn't heard?'

'In France? No. Who is it?'

'There isn't one. The monks all elected Robert Busse to take the abbacy, but John de Courtenay contested it, and so the Pope has appointed the Cardinal de Fargis to adjudicate between them. It's all in uproar in Tavistock, they say. All the monks are arguing and fighting, and the two men at the centre will not talk to each other. It's horrible.'

'Oh,' Simon said, but his mild tone belied his racing thoughts because he did not truly *own* this place. He held it on a lease. Still, that meant Despenser could not simply take it from Simon. However, without an abbot to give him support, he was in a weaker position. There was no man whom he could petition in his defence. Although he had lived on these lands for almost ten years, that did not mean he was secure. If Despenser had it in his mind to take them, it would be enormously difficult for Simon to fight so strong a protagonist.

Baldwin was his friend, of course, and if there was a fight, Simon knew he could count on him. But this was not an ordinary problem. It was a matter of politics, too. He had no idea what the man Wattere thought of it, but if Despenser was involved, that meant that it was a situation where national politics could hold sway. Despenser would make sure of it. And if Despenser wanted, he could force Simon from the land by use of his men. He had so many people he could use to make life impossible for men like Simon, men without hosts of servants and men-at-arms, men without political influence . . .

Except he did have a friend with political influence. He was friends with Bishop Walter II, the Bishop of Exeter. Bishop Walter would know what to do. And with luck, he would be prepared to help Simon.

### Beaulieu

Sir Hugh le Despenser was not known for dilatoriness. Rather, he was likely to make a swift decision and stick to it. It was always his belief that, generally, the first decision made was the best, and in any case, he had enough men at his command to be able to rectify any occasional little embarrassment.

He had no need to worry about Simon or the course upon which he had launched William Wattere. That was one decision that had been taken. The bailiff would soon be neutralised as an effective tool of any enemy, and his friend the Knight of Furnshill would either learn from his friend's discomfiture, or would overreach himself to get back at Sir Hugh. More than likely, he would bow down and hope to avoid Despenser's rage. That was what most men did. No matter how often they espoused their convictions and declared their loyalty to a man or a cause, at the first sign of personal risk they were silenced.

Yes. That was one problem which was hopefully to be cured very soon.

But there were other issues which beset him. Times when he stood and stared out through the windows here and wondered, desperately, what his enemy was doing at that moment. There was only one man who deserved that title: Sir Roger Mortimer of Wigmore.

'Sir Roger,' he muttered with a swift curse. The hogswyving son of a mongrel was the biggest thorn in his side. Of course it was possible, quite possible, that Sir Roger Mortimer was enjoying his time in France so much that he had had no time to even consider Despenser. And sows might fly. No, Sir Roger was still the most dangerous threat to England, to the King, and to Despenser himself, naturally.

He had been an enemy of Despenser even before they had been born. It was three-and-forty years since Roger Mortimer had slain Hugh Despenser. The two, grandsires of Sir Hugh and Sir Roger, were opponents at the Battle of Evesham, and ever since he had heard of his grandsire's death at Mortimer's hand, Sir Hugh le Despenser had wanted revenge for that bloodletting. His family was humiliated by it.

But there had been no possibility during the long years of Mortimer's ascendancy. It was only when Sir Hugh became the King's closest friend and adviser that he had been able to begin to scheme the end of Mortimer. And he had managed much, even precipitating a war with Roger and the other Marcher Lords – although that was not intentional, and at the time Sir Hugh had been petrified, thinking he would lose everything. After the brief war, Roger Mortimer was locked away in the Tower of London, where he festered for eighteen months.

And then he managed a dramatic break out and escaped! The bastard was incredibly lucky all his damned life. The warrant for his execution had finally been signed by the King, and Sir Hugh was going to ensure that it was swiftly carried out, but then the crazed *shite* got clean away. And somehow to France.

It was this which occupied his mind so much of the time. Mortimer had been the King's most competent, experienced general. All through the King's reign, it was Mortimer who had been sent off to Scotland, Ireland, anywhere. And he was astonishingly lucky even then. Now, though, since he was ensconced in France, he was still more dangerous than ever before.

The first intimation of danger had been when the plot to have Sir Hugh and some others murdered by means of that damned magician had been uncovered. Well, Despenser had seen to it that as soon as the man was captured, his life and prospects were reduced to precisely nothing. But that wasn't all. There were stories of men being sent here to England by Mortimer and his friends, spies, ill-contents, rumour-mongers, all trying their best to destabilise the realm.

Well, Sir Hugh le Despenser wouldn't stand by and let them have their way. The most important thing to him was to protect the realm from all these scum. And that was what he'd do, right up until the day he found Roger Mortimer in front of him and he could kill the bastard, nice and slowly, and as painfully as possible.

Of course, Sir Roger had an incentive to unsettle the King, and he knew the King well enough, too. He would know just how much the theft of the oil would affect the King. The King would be bound to think it unbearable that a man would dare to take something quite so valuable from him; still more so now, while his reign was being looked upon with contempt by so many in the land. Perhaps it was all an affair of Sir Roger Mortimer's making. He had sent a man to find the oil and take it to France for him. It wouldn't matter whether it would serve any useful purpose, the mere fact that he had deprived the King of it would be enough.

Yes, he nodded, it was sure to be him. Sir Roger had taken the oil. So the question now was how to retrieve it for the King?

### Lydford

At his house, Simon looked through all his business and especially the state of the farm itself. His other affairs were in good repair, fortunately. All his finances were strong, and that was fortunate because he had the expense of the impending nuptials for his daughter to cover.

'How is she?' Simon asked his wife.

Meg looked at him seriously. 'How would you have felt when we decided to marry, if you had heard that my father had left the country and no one knew when he would return so that the marriage could go ahead?'

'I'd have grabbed you and given you my oath and hoped you'd have done the same.'

'Just because the Church accepts that you don't have to wed in a church, doesn't mean that it's right,' Meg said pointedly.

'Your daughter is a good child, who wouldn't marry until her father was here to join in.'

'I suppose her boy doesn't have enough money to be able to support her without the dowry, then?' Simon demanded grumpily.

'Nonsense!'

'And you haven't answered me yet. Wouldn't you have made your oath to me if I swore mine to you?'

'If you think, you great lummox, that you can evade the issue by asking silly questions like that,' Meg said, tossing her blond hair severely, 'you don't know me very well. Now, what will we do about this wedding?'

'Arrange it urgently and save her any more damned torture, I suppose,' he said heavily. He had no desire to see her married. She was his little girl still. Allowing her to marry would be like admitting to himself that he was an old man now.

'Very well. Where is she?'

'In the field, I think.'

'Get her here. I will need to discuss this with her. If I'm to give away my daughter, I'll need to see the man who's getting her, too.'

'Simon, you've already met him.'

'I know. And I'll meet him again, and make sure he's going to be a good husband to her.'

Little Edith marrying. Leaving him and Meg. It hurt him just to think it.

It hurt more than the idea of losing his farm.

# Chapter Nineteen

**Beaulieu**

The Bishop of Orange was sitting in the chamber given to him when the gentle knock came on the door. He felt quickly for the dagger which he always carried strapped to his calf before calling, '*Entrez!*' A man who knocked so quietly was often a man who was set upon violence. A quiet knock meant no one else would hear.

'What do you want?' he asked as Peter walked in.

Peter smiled. 'Don't worry, Bishop. My son is in the corridor out there. He'll let me know if anyone comes.'

'What do you want, I said?'

'Well, now. Only this: we were asked to come here to help guard you on the way, but now it looks like our work is more or less done, so we'd like to get back home again.'

'You are to remain with me all the while I am in England.'

'Yes, but there is little point. You've already got your old two back.'

'Pons and André? Those two? I do not think that they are reliable men. No, I need you two, still.'

'I don't think so. We should return to our master.'

'Your master? And what do you think he would say about you deserting me here before my long return journey? If any harm comes to me, he will be most displeased.'

Peter grinned. 'Ah, well, I think I can take that risk.'

'He is perhaps little more than a boy, but make no mistake, my friend. The Earl of Chester is yet the heir to a realm. He will be your king one day, if you live long enough to witness it.'

'My master would want us back with him.'

'Then go. But I will tell him you deserted me.'

'Hardly deserted.' Peter's grin and expansive wave of his hand took in the whole abbey, indicating that there were many others nearby to protect the Bishop.

'In any case, it would seem likely that we shall meet him shortly.'

'How so?'

'We shall move to London, nearer him, before long. The King wishes to discuss the treaty provisions with his barons. He is calling all his barons to Westminster. I am myself to go there to take any further instructions from your king.'

Peter nodded, still grinning, but there was little humour in his voice. 'Very well. We'll remain with you a little longer. But only a little. We owe our service to him, and no one else.'

*Feast of the Apostles*[1]

### Lydford

Waiting for his daughter and her husband-to-be, Simon was fretful and on edge. He had already sent his wife off out, and his manservant, Hugh, away to speak to Sir Baldwin, so that he could speak with his prospective son-in-law in private, but he was not looking forward to the interview. The idea of losing his daughter was as painful as the idea of losing a limb. She was a part of him. But, as Meg would keep pointing out, Edith

---

[1] Thursday, 2 May 1325

was over seventeen now. She was old enough to know her mind.

When he heard the horses arriving, he went slowly across the floor of his hall, and stood by the fire, now smoking gently, and waited there, his back to the flames, arms folded, legs firmly planted. The boy would have to enter and confront him like that, a challenging father. Perhaps a fearsome one.

The man who entered was not Edith's Peter, though.

'Who are you?' Simon demanded.

'You are whom?' the man asked.

'I am the owner of this farm, friend. Who are you?' Simon grated.

'My name is known to you already, I think. I am called William atte Wattere. And you are, I suppose, Simon Puttock, one time Bailiff of Lydford for Abbot Robert?'

'That is correct.'

'Ah, good. Then I have the right place.'

'I do not think so.'

'You are wrong.' Wattere smiled.

'By what right do you claim to be able to take my land?'

'It is not your land, friend. It belongs to my Lord Hugh Despenser. He owns it now, and wants it for his own, so I have been sent to remove any obstructions.'

He did not look like the brutal enforcer of an illegal act of theft. Rather, he was a mild-looking man with a slight squint. He had the narrow features of an ascetic, but without any appearance of a rat. He had gleaming eyes, which seemed to be bright with pleasure and fun, and Simon had the distinct impression that he would be enormously enjoyable as a drinking companion, if the circumstance of their meeting was different.

'Such as the true owner?'

'Such as any squatter, yes.'

Simon looked about him. His hall was as familiar to him as his own hand, and yet as he stood here, it looked to him slightly different, as though it was already taken from him, and he was, in fact, a trespasser here.

And then a flood of pure anger washed through his veins.

He was no petitioner! He was no humble *churl* who could be forced to submit to the rape of his property and treasure. No man, none, could take from *him* what was his own. The bastard who tried it would have his head broken!

'You must have your things out of here within the week,' Wattere said. 'I gave your wife a week, but in your absence, so I suppose a little compassion is in order. Unless you make it difficult, of course.' His mild grin grew wider. 'I'd like that.'

'Make it difficult?' Simon snarled. 'I'll be damned to hell before I agree to being robbed by a felon like you!'

'If you take that attitude, I will ensure that you are out of here in days, and your eviction will be as unpleasant as I can contrive.' And now the eyes changed. The humour and pleasantness left them, and in their place was an icy calmness. A calculating expression that was almost desire.

Simon felt a red curtain of rage fall over his eyes. He grasped his sword-hilt and moved towards the man, sweeping out the blade.

Wattere had seen Simon's sudden movement, and he stepped back and to the side in the same instant. His sword was out, and the two swords clashed, ringing. 'It will make things worse for you if you try to thwart Sir Hugh's official,' he grated, all amiability gone from his voice.

'You dare threaten me for defending my own?' Simon roared, and sprang forward, sword up.

There was a scream, and he shot a look over his shoulder. There, in the doorway, was his daughter Edith and her fiancé. Simon felt a swift burning over his left shoulder, and knew he had been struck. Then he lifted his own sword and felt Wattere's slide down its edge. The two were watching each other, their eyes firmly locked. Simon could remember once being taught that it was a mistake to watch the man's sword. Better by far to keep an eye on the man's face. 'Watch his eyes, boy. Watch his eyes. You'll see his intention there, and when he wants to attack, he'll betray it.'

And he saw it now. A momentary narrowing of the eyes, and suddenly the blade was lancing forward to his breast. A slash of his own, and the blade was swept aside, an upward flick, and Simon's point raked along the man's inner forearm. He felt it strike the elbow with a soft sucking, and yanked it free. Wattere's arm was oozing blood, a thick mess, and his sword was already on the ground when Simon took a pace forward and rested his sword-point on Wattere's throat. 'Yield.'

'Why? What will you do?'

'You attack me in my own house, my own hall, and you ask what I shall do? This is my home, *churl*. You desecrate it with your presence. Yield, or I'll destroy you.'

Wattere looked up at him and curled his lip. 'You? Kill me?' he sneered. He knew enough about Simon Puttock. He had checked on him before threatening him, for a man was a fool who tried to bully another without being aware of his strengths, and he had been told that this man was a mere clerk at best. He'd been a bailiff on the moor, but that was an easy job, and then he'd got an even softer position as Keeper of Dartmouth. That, Wattere had been told, was more or less a clerical post, and the man was a lightweight. He hadn't drawn sword in many years. Anyway, these Devon boys were mere children when they were set against a man like Wattere, with years of fighting and enforcement for Despenser. There was nothing to fear here.

Now, though, he saw something different in Simon's eye, and was prey to a sudden doubt. Wattere recognised pure, blind rage when he saw it, and the expression in Simon Puttock's eyes just now was not that of a gentle, bovine creature. If this was a soft-hearted animal, it was one which had contracted rabies. His eyes were more like those of a terrier when put in a sty with a sackload of rats. The red mist had fallen over him, and he was perfectly capable of killing, especially now, in hot blood.

'*Shit!* I yield! I yield!' he snapped quickly as he saw Simon's sword move.

'Get up, and go. If I see you here again, I will have you arrested and held at Lydford.'

'Lydford, Puttock? You forget yourself. You have no authority to hold me there or anywhere. You are no bailiff any more. And you've lost your job at Dartmouth, I hear? You are *nothing*. Me, I represent Sir Hugh Despenser. You have made him your own personal enemy. I should leave quickly now, before you earn more of his just ire.'

He bent to pick up his sword, but Simon put his boot on it. 'You will leave that. You draw steel on me in my hall, you prickle, and you lose it.'

William Wattere nodded, his eyes lidded, and then he cast a long, slow look about the hall. 'I shall tell my Lord what you have done. I'll show him this injury. I hope you enjoyed your time here, Bailiff, because it's coming to a swift conclusion. My respects to your wife.'

### *Beaulieu*

Peter found his son outside and said nothing as he came level with him; he just nodded to John and continued on his way.

'So we leave here and go back?'

'Our master will have to cope without us for a little longer. We are to stay here with the Bishop. He tells me that the King's going to have a meeting of his advisers in Westminster before long, so we can travel there with the Bishop. All the members of the King's council will be there. That means all the Bishops and earls will be present for it.'

'So if we stay with the Bishop, we'll get up there anyway? Good.'

'Yes. The sooner we can return the happier I'll be.'

### *Lydford*

Simon had a hurried conversation with his daughter and her man before sending Edith from the room.

'Right, Master Peter,' Simon said grimly, walking back to the fire with the two swords in his hands. He sheathed his own, and peered at the one he had retrieved from William Wattere. 'Hmm. Not bad.'

Peter was a young apprentice who lived not far from Lydford. He had been the cause of Simon's unhappiness ever since he had been given the post of Keeper at Dartmouth, and he held the lad in little regard as a result.

It wasn't his fault, though. He had fallen in love with Edith, and she with him. That was why Edith had complained so bitterly at the thought of going with Simon and Meg to Dartmouth: she had no wish to be further away from her Peter than necessary. That was why she'd wailed and moaned and complained about the idea of being sent into 'exile' so far from her home. Peter couldn't go with them – he was apprenticed to a successful merchant, Master Harold – so that was that. Edith did not wish to go, and they could not leave her behind. So Margaret, his Meg, remained here in Lydford with Edith and their son Perkin, and Simon travelled on alone.

Peter was staring at him with unabashed astonishment. Perhaps mingled with fear. It was that realisation that made Simon grunt an apology. If he had attempted to beg the hand of his own wife in marriage at a tender age from a man whom he had just witnessed fighting with another, Simon might have been reticent, too.

'What, boy?' Simon demanded.

'Do you want a cloth? A towel?'

Simon frowned, and looked down at his hand. His sword hand had blood all over the palm where Wattere's blood had run along the blade and down to the hilt. With a gesture of irritation, Simon wiped it on his breast. 'It's nothing. Not mine,' he added. 'Now, you are still determined to take my daughter?'

'Yes, sir.' Peter was staring at his other shoulder.

Simon eyed him a moment in silence, then realised that the boy was gazing at the wound Wattere had inflicted on him. With a quick glance at it, he convinced himself that it was a very minor scratch, and marched across the room to his little sideboard. There was a small pewter jug on it, and a couple of goblets which he had asked Meg to set out earlier. Now he poured from the jug a little of that wonderful, potent, burned wine[1]. Passing one to Peter, he contemplated the lad once more.

'You are apprenticed to Harold the Merchant?'

---

[1] A medieval term for brandy

'I was. I am not now. I have finished my apprenticeship, and I work with him.'

'What of your father?'

Peter was embarrassingly keen to tell Simon all he needed to know, and as the sun passed slowly around, the pool of light from the southern window moving two feet across the floor, Peter told all about his youth, his father's business as a merchant in the city of Exeter, and his own hopes to become a freeman of the City himself.

'Enough!' Simon said, pouring the last of their drink. 'You will look after her?'

'Of course. I love her, Master.'

'You can call me Simon,' he said, and with those words, he felt an emptiness as deep as a well in his heart.

With those few words he had agreed to give away his daughter.

*Morrow of Feast of the Apostles*[2]

### Furnshill

Baldwin had finished a leisurely breakfast of cold meats and a hunk of bread when he heard the clattering of hooves outside on the cobbles, soon followed by a deep bark from Wolf. He turned his head to one side to listen, glancing at his wife as he did so. 'Who can that be?'

He did not have long to wait to find out. The man who entered was a grim-faced, glowering man who gazed about him with the natural suspicion of a shepherd in an inn full of rustlers. Baldwin knew him as Hugh, Simon's oldest and most trusted servant. Hugh had no great affection for dogs other

---

[2] Friday, 3 May 1325

than the native sheepdogs he had grown up with as a shepherd out near Drewsteignton.

'Hugh, please come and take some wine or ale. What are you doing here?'

'Have a note.'

Baldwin smiled as he took the scrap from the taciturn man, and read slowly. Gradually, his smile faded, to be replaced with a cold scowl. 'How is Simon now?'

'Angry.'

'And Meg?'

'My lady is very anxious.'

'She is right to be.'

'Husband? What is it?' Jeanne asked.

Quickly Baldwin explained what had happened to Simon. 'He asks me to send for help from Stapledon.'

'Is he in Exeter? The Bishop is so often away in London and elsewhere.'

'I think he should be there,' Baldwin said. 'I will send Edgar to seek him out.'

Hugh nodded, then turned and would have gone, but Baldwin called him back.

'Wait, man! Where are you going?'

'Back to Lydford. Don't know what the man'll do next, but my master needs me. I was the only man he could send to you, but he'll be in danger without me.'

'Wait, Hugh. I will be with you in the time it takes to have a horse prepared. Jeanne, do not worry about me. I shall be back in a day or two, but this matter must be resolved. The idea that Simon and Margaret could have their house stolen from over them is appalling.'

Jeanne smiled, although with a trace of fear. 'That is fine, Baldwin. But why should Despenser seek to hurt Simon?'

'That, my love, I hope to learn before long,' Baldwin said. 'Sadly, I expect it is only a vengeful, brutish sport for him. Nothing more. Still, we shall inquire as best we may.'

# Chapter Twenty

## Beaulieu

The King threw down the notes and swore again. It was enough to make Sir Hugh le Despenser want to hit him. This temperamental display was growing tedious. Christ's teeth, he had better things to be doing than listening to the regular complaints of the King.

'The shits! They think they can scare me into this pathetic peace! I should be negotiating with—'

'There is no one with whom you may negotiate. Not now. If you wish to keep your territories in France, you have to remain constant to the French King, my Liege.'

'Constant to him? The base-born bastard wants all my lands. Mark my words, Sir Hugh, he won't be content until he holds the keys to the Tower itself! He complains of *my* behaviour, but he would scarcely dare to do so to my face! In God's name, the man steals from me and then demands I pay him for his efforts!'

'Your reply will be sent once you have consulted?' Despenser said with a mild yawn.

'Yes. Ayrminne and Stratford must do their best as soon as

---

[1] Monday, 6 May 1325

I know the council is behind me. But it's so unreasonable. I think I may write to the Pope and beg his assistance. Perhaps if he were to consider the matter . . .'

'What good could he do?'

The King snapped, 'The Pope could instruct the French to be more bloody *reasonable*! I'm expected to surrender my territories to the French Crown, perform homage, and hope that they'll be restored to me, and all in so short a breadth of time as to make it next to impossible! Is that fair?'

'Of course not,' Despenser said smoothly. It was not the first time the King had made this speech, and he knew it would not be the last. However, it was dull to have the same arguments regurgitated so often in the space of only a few days, and Despenser was heartily bored with it.

'And what of the other matter?'

'I do not know what you mean.'

The King span to face him. 'You were investigating the theft of my oil, Sir Hugh! I want that oil back – I *must* have it back! It could be my salvation.'

'Why now? What does it really matter?'

The King shivered. 'Build up that fire!' he commanded a servant, and then he eyed Despenser. 'What does it really matter, you say? I tell you this, Sir Hugh, that oil may just protect me and the Crown. Have you not paused to think what it may be worth to me? If the French do take my lands in France, what then could I do, other than retire in shame? But if I could make use of the oil, then I may become revered again. People would look upon me and think, "Yes, he has been anointed with the oil blessed by the Holy Virgin and St Thomas!" That would mean people would respect me again, and then, perhaps I could take a host to France, even win back my lands again, and all . . .'

Despenser listened with a rapt expression on his face. To listen to the King, it was almost possible to believe that he was rational. Could he seriously believe that the mere presence of a cardinal or bishop with a pottle of oil could change the attitude of his barons and people? Perhaps he did. In Christ's name, Despenser thought, it is fortunate that I am here to protect the King, because if I weren't, he would lose his crown, realm and probably head in an instant.

'So I *need* that oil, Sir Hugh,' the King finished. He held out a hand, and Despenser was ashamed to see that the King had tears in his eyes. Not tears of shame or embarrassment, though, only those of a man who saw salvation. 'You understand me, don't you? I must have it so that the people can renew their faith in me.'

Despenser studied him a moment, then nodded. 'I have issued instructions to the Sheriff of Kent to eradicate the outlaws who are living in those woods. There is as yet no sign of them. It is quite possible that they have moved somewhere else. In the meantime, I did not worry you about this when you had so many other concerns,' this was as close to irony as he dared sail, 'but I am fairly content that the dead man was Richard de Yatton. You remember him?'

The King shook his head.

'He was with you when you were last in York, and I think he served you when you were at Castle Rising.'

'I think I vaguely remember him ... a strong jaw, square face?'

'That was him, yes. He left here to take a message to your son, and never returned, so far as I know.'

'What else?'

'I have had my own men visit the Christ Church Priory, and they have told me that the oil was stolen from a monk there, who was himself slain. The man who committed the murder ran off into the night. But it is said that he was seen, and that he was a man just like Richard de Yatton. He was described even down to his tabard.'

'Christ Jesus! You say this seriously? The man went there and stole my oil? But why? Who would dare such a thing?'

'Maybe the man sought to blackmail you? Some people are aware how much the oil means to you.'

'He would understand that I would never know peace until I had seen him skinned and gibbeted if I knew he had done so!' the King growled.

'Yes, but perhaps he hoped to keep his identity secret from you.'

'How would he do that after robbing and then blackmailing me?'

'I cannot tell, Your Highness. But either way, it would seem that he has paid already for his crime.'

'A good thing – and bad that you do not say where the oil went. And is there something you have missed?'

'I do not think so.'

'You point out that many know how high a value I place on that oil, Sir Hugh. Who would be most alert to that value?'

'I . . . I don't think I . . .' he stammered, trying hard not to allow his face to register the fact that he, of all those in the realm, knew better than any other the value the King put on this damned oil.

'The *French*, Sir Hugh. The French know how important that oil is to me. Who better? Is it not likely that this whole matter was thought up by my brother-in-law?'

'Ah!' Despenser said, trying not to sag with relief. 'I had thought it might be Sir Roger, Your Highness.'

'Mortimer?'

'He has much to gain by harming you and me, and he is a vindictive, cruel man, isn't he? It is entirely in keeping with his devious cunning that he might try this terrible theft.'

'Yes. The evil devil! So, in that case, does he have it already?'

'I should think that when the felons in the wood killed your herald, they would have taken everything of value. That is why I am seeking them. Perhaps they recognised the value of the ampulla in which the oil was stored, and have kept it by in case they can sell it.'

'It is weeks now, since my oil was stolen. I want it back!'

'And I hope you shall have it back as soon as the Sheriff tracks down and executes all the outlaws from those woods, my Liege.'

The chamber which Despenser had appropriated for his own use was a fair-sized one only a short way along a narrow corridor near the King's own, and Despenser went there now. He had plenty of work to occupy him, but today he wished to concentrate on his own affairs. His estates were so extensive that running them was a full-time job for several stewards, and there were some matters that called for his personal involvement.

'Ah,' he said as he found the message from Devon. He took it up and read it carefully, then set it down and frowned to himself a little while.

It validated his reasoning before. The affair of the friar in Iddesleigh had been at the back of his mind for a while now, ever since he had first met Sir Baldwin, and now his feeling had been confirmed. The two who had made his acquisition down there in Devon so difficult were this knight and his friend the bailiff.

The bailiff, of course, was nothing. The man was little more than a peasant. Nothing except a focus for Sir Hugh's anger and bile. The knight, though, Sir Baldwin, he was different. Especially since Despenser had learned that he had once been a Templar.

Sir Baldwin had some credibility, it was true. Many appeared to like him, to trust him, and to court his advice and judgement. The King was one, although of course it would only take a determined assault by Despenser to force him to change his mind. Still, there were others who were less easily swayed, such as Bishop Stapledon and others. The Bishops were growing hot under the collar again, because of Despenser taking over lands. True, he was taking territory which was not necessarily his own, but that did not matter. It was the way of English rulers to take what they wished. It was the rule of the strongest. England was a powerful land, with peasants and barons who were never slow to assert their rights, and in return England found herself ruled by still more powerful lords and kings. Naturally. And their advisers, too. Like Sir Hugh le Despenser.

If a man wished to make a mark, then he had to take a firm grip on the various controls which maintained government. And Sir Hugh le Despenser was clutching hold of all he could.

If Sir Baldwin de Furnshill was a fly in his food, he would scoop out that little fly, and crush it. That was what he would do now. He would control the knight by the use of an attack upon his best friend. Simon Puttock could be ruined, entirely destroyed, if Sir Baldwin did not come to see reason. Perhaps he would, in which case Sir Hugh could make up his mind whether to appear magnanimous in victory, or perhaps just prove to all that setting one's face against him was a recipe for disaster. Either way, the bailiff would find life more difficult shortly, he told himself with satisfaction.

No one had ever managed to mark Wattere and live before, and Sir Hugh le Despenser seriously doubted that a peasant bailiff from the bogs of Devon would achieve what so many had died in attempting.

### Lydford

Simon felt the wariness again as he peered through his window.

'There is no one there, Simon,' Baldwin said. He was standing at the side of Simon's large table, spearing a slab of meat and putting it upon his plate. At his side the ever-expectant Wolf watched hopefully. 'He won't come this early.'

'Why?' Simon demanded, rolling his injured shoulder. It stung badly. Margaret had treated it with some foul-smelling concoction of her own devising, which hurt more than the original wound. Well, he told himself, often the cure was a lot worse than the injury. He only hoped that was correct.

'Because he'll have formed a regard for your hardiness, since you scratched him. He'll either come at some unearthly hour of the morning to intimidate you, or perhaps late at night, in the dark, when you'll be unsettled.'

'Not during the day?'

'An all-out assault during the day? I doubt it greatly. That would be most foolhardy.'

'What can we do, Sir Baldwin?' Margaret asked quietly. She was pale with anxiety.

Baldwin smiled at her. He had never seen her look more

concerned, and the sight of her paleness was enough to stir his own anger. 'My dear, we shall wait for Edgar to arrive here with help from the good Bishop Stapledon, and then we shall take our fight to the man who has caused all this upset. This William atte Wattere. You know where he can be found?' he asked, turning back to Simon.

'Hugh has tracked him down to an inn at Mary Tavy.'

'Good. Then we can take a ride there later, when Edgar arrives.'

### *Eltham Palace*

Richard of Bury left his table and walked the short distance from his room to the great hall, where he walked through to the buttery and drew off a jug of ale.

Walking back to his chamber, he saw the Earl. 'Your Highness, are you to come to study soon?'

'I have other matters to occupy me just now,' Earl Edward said.

Bury nodded, standing aside for the Earl. He was clearly very busy just now. From the look of his hosen, he had been riding through some very muddy fields, and knowing the Earl as he did, Bury guessed that he had been hunting or hawking for most of the morning. Now, however, there was something else in his eyes, too. 'Is there anything with which I can help you?'

The Earl stopped a moment and peered at him. Bury almost had the feeling that he was going to speak, but then the moment passed, and the Earl shook his head briefly, before walking off.

It left Bury with the odd feeling that, not only was the Earl keeping something back from him, but he was also keeping something back in order to protect Bury himself.

That, Bury told himself, was not comforting. Because if the Earl knew of something that was so dangerous to Bury that Bury himself must have it hidden from him, it was a deeply alarming secret indeed.

# Chapter Twenty-One

***The Golden Cock, Mary Tavy***

Late in the afternoon, they reached the inn and stopped, their horses resting and cropping the scrubby grass, while they studied the land about here.

In happier times Simon had been here fairly often. It was a useful stopping point when he was on his way to or from Tavistock. Not absolutely direct, it was true, and to come here he had to divert a little from his usual path, but the landlord had always been accommodating, and the ale refreshing after a ride in the sun. Many were the evenings he had rested here after a long day's ride.

The old inn was a long, narrow building, with the low thatch that was so common of the older long-houses. The windows were small, unglazed, and all but concealed by the thatch itself. A small hole in the thatch let out a thin mist of smoke from the fire, but more seemed to be oozing from the window and door.

Baldwin and Simon rode to the front of the place, and sat there a while, peering at it before swinging from their saddles. Wolf stood with head lowered, eyeing the place with a frown on his great head. While they waited, Baldwin's man Edgar slipped down from the trees beside the inn and ran noiselessly to the inn's wall. Hugh was already at the other corner of the building.

When Baldwin had been a Templar, Edgar had been his man-at-arms. The two had trained together as a unit, fighting on horseback, riding with lances, then practising with swords and axes on foot, but although Simon had seen Baldwin become enraged and fight with ruthless efficiency, it was Edgar whom he viewed with the greater respect. Edgar was that little bit younger, he was slightly faster, and he had the mind of a born killer: he could kill without compunction. Not because he enjoyed inflicting pain, but because he was perfectly honed as a weapon. Simon was a good fighter, in an untrained way. He was quick and competent, his skills built up over the years, but Edgar had been taught by the Knights Templar. A man who was originally competent, he had become thoroughly professional. Simon knew that Baldwin regretted having killed men; he was not sure that Edgar ever suffered from the same feelings.

However, he was not to kill today. Baldwin had made that perfectly clear. Today was to be bloodless. They were here to speak with the man who was attempting to persecute Simon.

Gripping a long staff, Edgar moved along the wall of the inn with all the noise of a shadow, while Simon and Baldwin made a meal of tying their reins to a pair of saplings. The two of them looked at each other, and then marched side-by-side to the doorway.

Then, just as they reached the threshold, before they could enter, the door slammed wide open, and William and three men hurtled out, coming to a halt a few paces before them. William had his sword out already, and it was pointing at Simon.

'You thought you could jump me, Master Bailiff? I am surprised at you. Attacking a man in a tavern could be thought of as an attempt at murder. You know what that means, don't you? A premeditated homicide carries the same penalty as a successful one: death. Looks like I'll have to arrest you and take you in. And then your nice little wife can entertain me when I go to take over the house.'

'What is your reason for trying to steal this man's house?' Baldwin asked harshly.

'He is a squatter. My master owns the land outright. And your friend there will be happy enough to agree to that when we ask him.'

'What does that mean?'

William Wattere smiled thinly. 'We can put things to you in a way you understand. Perhaps we'll string you up and rape your women in front of you until you sign it all over to us, eh? Or we could take a hammer to your fingers, one by one. You have made me angry, you see. I was happy to be reasonable, but when you found out you were dealing with Sir Hugh le Despenser's man, you should have expected someone a bit more competent than you. You aren't bright enough to take me, Bailiff. And it's stupid, anyway. You try to hurt a man who is Despenser's own, and he will always seek you out. You'll always pay.'

'So what do you intend now?' Simon demanded.

'Oh, you're arrested, Bailiff, so keep your hands away from your sword, there, Master. And you too, Knight. You try to fight, and we'll be happy to kill you. It'll save all that trouble later. We'll just bring round the documents to your wife and have her agree them right now, while you stay here. Women are always so much more . . . helpful.'

Simon was about to respond when two more men appeared in the doorway, both with swords in their hands. One had eyes only for the men before the door, but one happened to glance to his side. He saw Edgar there.

Edgar smiled at him, raised a finger to his lips in the universal gesture of silence, and then looked thoroughly disappointed when the man shouted, 'Will!'

Wattere was about to turn and look when there was a sudden crack from the doorway. A cry, a shout, and Edgar swung his iron-shod staff at the man to Wattere's left. He fell like a stunned hog, landing partly over Wattere's feet.

Realising he had been fooled, Wattere's eyes widened with horror and anger, and even as the third of his men crashed to the ground, Wattere made a quick choice and sprang over the body of his man, flying towards Simon. Simon had no time to grab his sword. With the flat of his hand, he tried to bat the blade away, down to his left, and he grunted as he felt the scrape of the blade on his palm, cutting deeper towards his wrist. It hurt more than his shoulder, and he bared his teeth in a snarl as the blade slid away. He was close enough to grip the man's wrist with his right hand, and as he did so he turned, swivelling on both feet, hauling at the same time, using Wattere's momentum to pull him off balance, and then he gripped Wattere's sword wrist in his left and slammed back savagely with his right elbow.

He had meant to hit the man's nose, but his elbow missed slightly, and he raked over the nose and into his eye and temple. There was a satisfying sensation of pain in his arm as he did so, and a still more pleasing feeling of heaviness in Wattere's body as he collapsed unconscious at Simon's feet.

Pulling his sword free of the scabbard, Simon watched while Baldwin and Edgar pushed the last man standing back until he was at the inn's wall. Then he looked about him wildly, before throwing his sword down and holding his hands away from his dagger. Edgar looked at Baldwin, who was returning his own sword to its sheath, and then hit the man very deliberately in the middle of his belly with the iron tip of his staff. The man doubled over, retching, trying to gulp in some air. Edgar imperturbably grasped his hands and yanked them round behind his back, and then bound them with a rawhide thong.

'Simon,' Baldwin said, peering about them affably, 'would you care for an ale?'

## Beaulieu

Nicholas of Wisbech had endured a thoroughly depressing few days. He had done all he could to try to advance his case, but no matter what he did, he could not find anyone who could help him. All the knights and lords about the King here seemed to be those who had no knowledge of Nicholas and his difficult mission. There was no one who could speak out for him.

There was a grim expression on his face as he walked about the cloister. He had been here ages, and yet had found no means of defending himself. Perhaps he should simply leave the place and see if he might find a berth in a little monastery somewhere.

He had tried to write to the Pope for his support, but the Pope's response had been most discouraging. If he had to guess, he would think that the King's own letter had arrived before his, and the Pope was wondering now whether the King's assertion was true. Nicholas had heard this already: the King had told people that Nicholas of Wisbech had invented the whole matter of the Oil of St Thomas, and the oil itself was not genuine.

Dear God, how could anybody think that, when the oil he had found had been brought to England by the Duke of Brabant especially for King Edward II's coronation? It was hardly in Nicholas's hands for him to be able to manipulate the phial and place false oil in it. But the King could be most persuasive, and he was, after all, a king. People would *tend* to believe him – or, at least, they would say they did.

But it did leave Nicholas feeling strangely abandoned and deserted. He might have been a sailor, wandering the seas, desperate for a return home, only to be shipwrecked. And here he was, on this unfriendly shore, wishing for a little help, only to find that there was nothing for him. Nobody would aid him.

He was morosely kicking at a pebble when he happened to glance up and see a face he recognised immediately.

A man had ridden in, and he reined to a halt before swiftly dismounting. He had a shock of thick brown hair, brown eyes, and a laughing face that instantly sent a shock of fire into Nicholas's belly. The last time Nicholas had seen that face, it had been twisted with horror and grief.

'I know you!' he breathed, his eyes narrowing with recollection. Where had he seen the man – not here, not recently . . . and then he had a startling memory, of a face whitened with lime, eyes staring and dulled, a trickle of blood from the shattered skull.

And a boy, reaching to touch his face while the burnished steel of another knight gleamed in the sunlight. And he saw again Despenser's face, twisted with disgust as he cuffed the boy about the head and then spat at the floor, spinning on his heel and storming off back into the church.

## *Mary Tavy*

William Wattere found himself confined. His breath was loud in his ears, and there was a roughness on his cheek. Then he noticed the smell: there was a strange, cloying, musty odour about him. His cheek was sore, and so was his left shoulder. For some reason he was lying on the floor, his legs curled up, arms behind him. He tried to move the constriction about his face, but all he could do was swear when he felt the pain in his wrists. His arm was only vaguely healed, he recalled . . . but that didn't explain the pain in the other wrist. What was that stuff on his cheek: rough, smelly . . . sacking? Yes. It was hessian or something. He tried to move his arms, and that was when he realised he was bound hand and foot.

That *mother-swyving churl*, Puttock! He'd knocked William down, hadn't he? William could just remember the sight of that elbow coming back and the sensation of it hitting him, club-like, in the eye was all too fresh. Sweet Mother of Christ, the bastard had hit him hard enough to shatter his cheek! When he was free of this, Wattere would see to it that the bailiff recognised how foolish he was to attempt such an assault on a Despenser man. He would cut the man's ballocks off, he'd skin his arse, he'd pull out his liver with his bare hands . . .

'Awake, are you?'

William Wattere rolled, and by pushing up with his face, managed to lift himself to a kneeling position, gazing about him within the darkness of his sacking hood. 'Get me out of this, Bailiff. If you don't, I swear I'll have your family destroyed! I'll burn that hovel you call a house and salt the land so that no one will live there for a hundred years! When I tell my master what you've done, he'll have your legs broken, then your arms, and leave you to crawl on your belly for all your days! He'll have your wife taken for the amusement of his garrison, he'll have—'

'When you've finished shouting, Wattere, would you like to know what I've done while you've been dozing?'

'I don't care what you've done, you hog-shit! When I'm finished with you, you'll regret the day you were born!'

'Oh. Oh, well. Just so you know, Wattere, I've brought you into our shed, so I can hang you up here – where the pigs are hung for the blood to be collected. I'll lift you by your hands until you lose all feeling, and then let you rest so all the pain comes back to your hands. You like that? I can do that fifteen or twenty times, but I'm told that if I do it too much, you'll become unconscious again, and I don't really want that. No, I'm happier knowing you're feeling every fragment of pain I can give you, after your threats to my wife.'

'If you don't cut me free right now, I'll see your *whole* family entirely destroyed. You know what I mean? I will kill your wife, your children, your parents, all of them! And I'll do it in front of you, you miserable—'

'Why did you threaten to take my house?'

'Go and swyve a chicken!'

'Not now, Wattere. Perhaps later. Who told you to threaten us?'

'You know who did it. My master, Despenser.'

'Do you mean Sir Hugh, the younger Despenser, not his father?'

'You know who.'

'Why?'

'Because of what you and your friend did to my master at Iddesleigh, of course.'[1]

'What do you mean, what *we* did? It was his men who tried to murder others, and . . . well, no matter. So that's why you were sent? To force us from our home, to forcibly remove us

---

[1] See *A Friar's Bloodfeud*, also published by Headline.

even though you had no reason to? Because you have no case in law, do you?'

'Why should I care? You are dead, now. Dead. My Lord takes what he wants. If you get in his way, he will kill you. And all your family. Feel proud, do you? You've signed the death warrants of your whole family, little bailiff.'

'Cut him down, Edgar. I have heard enough.'

This was a different voice, and William stopped and cocked his head. 'Who's that?'

His hands were released at last, and he pulled at the sacking, hauling it over his head like a linen shirt, and then he felt a terrible sinking feeling as he took in the sight about him. This wasn't a pig-slaughterhouse. It was the inn at Mary Tavy. Dear Christ, they'd taken him nowhere. They'd only pulled him inside. And that man . . .

'My name, my friend, is Bishop Walter of Exeter. And you, my friend, are arrested for attacking a servant of the Church and threatening him, and his family.'

## *Beaulieu*

Jack sat back easily. Resting came naturally to him, and since the hurried ride here, he had been keen to take his ease as much as he possibly could. Any seasoned traveller, like a veteran at arms, would understand his enthusiasm for any snatched moment of peace.

They had been here some time now, and if he was honest, Jack was growing a little bored. Beaulieu was a lively little palace for monks, no doubt, but there was little entertainment for men like him. He had noticed that even the two, Peter and John, from Canterbury, had been showing signs of restlessness recently. It made him wonder about them again.

Thing was, they'd been perfectly amiable during the ride

here. Oh, they still had that odd way of looking at a man as though wondering whether to knock him down immediately, or to first let him open his mouth. Just once. There was nothing that inspired a man to trust them. But to their credit, they appeared to be cautiously watching everyone else, too, as though they were themselves nervous. Not surprising. They didn't really know anyone.

Which was what was so odd about their coming here in the first place.

He was sipping a large mazer of wine as he considered them, and then he heard a shout. Idly standing, he wandered to the corner of the barn, a good few tens of yards from his bench, and then gaped.

Some of the King's men had encircled Peter and John.

'Look at them! A pair of complete whores, aren't they? Cock-queans, the pair of them,' one was shouting exultantly. 'Come on, let's take their ballocks. They don't need 'em!'

'You sad, little man? You want a kiss?'

'Ah, look, he's going to cry, if you're not careful!'

The ribald comments grew more lewd and less subtle as the courage of the men grew. There was no sign from Peter and John, no evidence of fear, no reaction whatever. And yet Jack was struck again with that sense of immense power and authority in the two. It made him mutter to himself, 'No, don't pick on these two.' He even winced, as though he knew what was about to happen.

And then one of them, the smallest of the six taunters, stepped forward. Jack wasn't sure what he was going to do, other than tease and torment, but he had no chance to do anything. As soon as he was within range, he was suddenly snatched up, and heaved over Peter's shoulder. Peter eyed the men watching, while the little man on his back squeaked and threatened, and then Peter hefted the fellow high, and allowed him to fall, flat on his back to the hard, packed earth. The squeak became a squeal.

'Oh, shit,' Jack murmured. He had witnessed wrestling before, and he feared that this heavy man might jump at the body on the ground, but then he saw his error. The little body was an obstacle for any others to surmount. It was plain enough the two had fought together before, and now they stood shoulder to shoulder, Peter again with that oddly unsettling smile on his face, almost as though he was a little sad, but if the others wanted to play like this, he would join in. The other just scowled about him as usual.

A pair of men exchanged a glance, and then rushed forward. One drew a dagger. That was an error. In some kind of swift manoeuvre, Peter took his hand with his left, pushed it away from him, and hooked his own right through at the man's elbow. A jerk towards his chest with his right fist, and Jack could hear the elbow shatter over the man's shriek of agony. He fell.

John had done nothing, merely waited for the second. He hurtled forwards, swinging a punch at John's face, feinting, and then snapping his left into John's belly.

It had no discernible impact. John caught the right fist in his left hand, and merely gripped it. Very tightly. Then he peered down with an expression of near-perplexity at the man as he whimpered, gazing up at him, slowly sinking to his knees, not even attempting to strike John again. That would have been as painful as it would have been futile. When he was down, John looked across at Peter, who gave a short moue of considera-tion, and then shook his head. John released the man, who fell on to his rump, and then stood with Peter, both blank-faced, and watched the last three.

There was no more fight left in them. The sight of their friends being so swiftly beaten was shocking to men used to bullying others. They took up their fallen friends and helped them to hobble away, the man with the broken arm weeping in a high-pitched tone. If Jack was any judge, that man would never wield a dagger again in that hand. He was ruined.

Jack whistled. He had known that the pair of them were dangerous.

He had no idea who they were, nor what they wanted, but suddenly he was glad that he would before long be leaving this country with the Bishop, to return to the Pope.

# Chapter Twenty-Two

*Lydford*

Bishop Stapledon was not a man who undertook journeys lightly. He was a tall, slightly stooped man, with fading hair and a perpetual peering manner because of his failing eyesight. When reading, he was forced to use spectacles, a fact which never failed to irritate him immensely. As a younger man, he had been possessed of exceptional sight, as he never tired of mentioning. He could read the very smallest script without any aid whatever. No longer, sadly.

He looked up as Edgar bowed at his side, proffering a goblet of Baldwin's best wine. Taking it, the Bishop eyed Baldwin and Simon carefully over the rim. 'This is a very serious matter, of course.'

'I think we were aware of that,' Baldwin said drily. 'It is Simon's house and farm that is at stake, after all.'

'A little more than only that, now. The man you have captured and placed in my care is Sir Hugh le Despenser's henchman. Despenser will be furious when he hears that you have had him incarcerated in my gaol. *Get off, dog!*'

'Come here, Wolf,' Baldwin said quickly. Wolf, seeking an affectionate stroke, had nudged the Bishop's elbow as he lifted his wine to his lips, almost spilling it over his breast. Baldwin absentmindedly patted Wolf's head as the dog sat at his side.

'He was trying to steal my house!' Simon protested.

'It has happened before. For some reason, this time Despenser did not use his normal approach,' Stapledon said, warily eyeing Baldwin's newest dog.

'What would that have been?' Baldwin asked.

'He would bring a large number of men and attack in main force, or, failing that, he would have no men appear at all, but instead would proceed through the courts. I would think that he wouldn't dare try that because he knows that the King trusts you, and that I and many other senior members of the Church do too, so any fraudulent claim would be set aside. Usually, if he couldn't do that, he would turn to overwhelming force. I wonder why on this occasion he did not.'

'Because he was not serious in intent,' Baldwin said thoughtfully.

'How so?'

'He knew that I would react if he attacked my friend here. But there can be no basis for his assault on Simon. Simon leases his own property. So any legal matter would fail, but so would an all-out attack. This was a little show, a threat. To show what he could do, were he to choose to.'

'But he failed,' Bishop Walter said.

'Did he? He cost Simon many hours of lost sleep, I would guess, and his wife plenty of distress, too.'

'It's true,' Simon admitted. 'I didn't know what to do.'

'You have at least gained a pleasing sword,' Baldwin said. The sword which Simon had taken from Wattere was leaning against the wall, and Baldwin went and took it up. 'It has a good balance.'

'It is the second sword I have taken from him,' Simon said with a grin of shy satisfaction. 'The first was when he came here. Not that I have a sheath for it, sadly. I didn't take that from him. Still, I have the sheath for this one.'

'He appears to be providing you with all the weaponry you could wish for,' Baldwin said with a chuckle.

'It will infuriate the Despenser, the fact that you have prevented him,' Bishop Stapledon said. 'He is used to having his way.'

'Not this time,' Baldwin said. 'He will not take Simon's lands. Nor mine. Not while we have friends such as you, Bishop.'

'No,' Bishop Walter said.

He smiled at Baldwin, and Baldwin gave a brief grin in return, but not with ease.

At any time in the last eight years or so since he had first met the Bishop, Baldwin would have said that he was a close friend. All over Devon and Cornwall, Bishop Walter II of Exeter was popular and held in high regard for his stalwart defence of the diocese. He visited all the churches and convents, and was a keen supporter of education. In Ashburton he had built a small school, and together with his brother he had founded Stapledon College at Oxford, as well as aiding many poor boys by giving them education if they appeared to merit the investment. All in all, his good works had benefited most of Devon.

But there was another side to his nature which Baldwin had discovered only recently. Stapledon had been involved in national politics for some years, indeed, he had been Lord High Treasurer and reformed much of the administration of the treasury. In the last year, he had taken the side of Despenser and the King against the Queen. It was said, and believably, that it was Stapledon who had argued for the confiscation of her property in Devon and Cornwall, on the basis that this would remove a potential threat to the realm, for if her brother, the King of France, were to try to invade the country, he would undoubtedly try to land there, where his sister held so many assets and had loyal servants.

For whatever the reason, Bishop Walter had seen to the sequestration of her estates, and then he supported Despenser in the eviction and exile of much of her household and in the removal even of her small children, having them taken into protective custody, as though the poor woman would have tried to poison their minds against their father, her husband. All this had left a very sour taste in Baldwin's mouth. He was still convinced of the Bishop's good will towards him and towards Simon, but he was not so certain that the Bishop was an ally in the greater political battles that raged in Westminster – and less sure that he could remain friendly with a man who could actively seek to have a woman's children taken from her. That, to him as a father and husband, was cruelty beyond his comprehension.

However, although Stapledon was an unenthusiastic supporter of Despenser, perhaps because Despenser gave him a means of acquiring much in the way of financial rewards, he was still not allied entirely. If there was a matter that affected the Church, Stapledon would immediately oppose Despenser, and to his credit, if there was an issue of state, he would more than likely be independent. But money was a strong lure to him. Some of the wealth he won went straight to the cathedral – a great deal, in fact – but much also went into the Bishop's pockets, Baldwin guessed.

It was his long-standing friendship with Simon that had counted in Baldwin's mind when he sent Hugh on to the Bishop at Exeter and asked him for his aid. At that time, though, he had not expected the Bishop himself to come all the way to Lydford. That was a surprise and great relief, for with Stapledon having heard Wattere's words, it made the defence of Simon against the Despenser much easier.

'Tell me, Simon. What is your status?' the Bishop asked, leaning forward to peer intently at the bailiff.

'Me? I'm not free, I'm a serf in the service of Sir Hugh de Courtenay.'

'Not free?'

'No. But I own this farm and my house on a lease. I have been successful. And I still own my old house outside Sandford.'

'That is good,' the Bishop said, but Baldwin saw his gaze slide over to him with a considering look in his eyes. He was not happy about something.

'Have you told the Bishop about your daughter?' Baldwin asked, by way of filling the sudden silence.

It was successful. Suddenly Simon grew animated, and the Bishop and he discussed the wedding in detail, emptying their jugs of wine, so that when Meg walked in again, Baldwin was pleased to see that she soon wore a soft smile that eased the lines of worry and smoothed her forehead of fear.

He only wished he could feel confident that Simon's problems were truly over. The trouble was, he feared that they weren't.

### Beaulieu

Sir Hugh le Despenser was sitting at his table when the friar entered. 'Friar. How can I help you?'

Nicholas swallowed anxiously. 'It is this matter of the oil that was stolen from Christ Church, Sir Hugh.'

'What of it?'

'I think I know who has taken it.'

Despenser was silent for a moment. He leaned back in his

chair and studied the friar doubtfully. 'And who was it, then?'

Nicholas grinned without humour. 'You think I'm a fool? First, I want to be able to speak to the King. You arrange for that, and then I shall tell you who it is, and how I know it.'

'What do you want to speak to the King about?'

'We must find his oil! The holy oil given by St Thomas for him to be saved, because . . .'

Sir Hugh was peering at him like a judge who heard a beggar deny taking alms. 'You think the King will trust anything you have to say about his oil? You know what the King thinks about that oil? He thinks it is all a part of a conspiracy to upset him. Nobody believes that the oil is genuine. That is nothing. Now, who was it?'

'You say he doesn't believe in the oil, and then you ask to know who took it! You think I am stupid but I am not!'

'Oh, I think you are,' Despenser said. He had risen from his seat and now he walked around his table. In a moment he had grasped Nicholas's throat, and now he pulled the friar towards him and snarled malevolently. 'You are very stupid, Friar. You think that because of your ragged robes you can come into my chamber here, and still be protected. You are not protected, and nor will you be if you speak to the King. I don't care about some oil that has a fictional story appended to it. I do care about the murder of a monk at Christ Church, though, and about a king's herald slaughtered by the roadside and left to rot. I care about them very much, and if you don't tell me all you know in the next moments, I shall have you carried down to where the King's executioner plies his trade, and we'll see how castration can loosen your tongue!'

*Wednesday before the Feast of Gordianus et Epimachus*[1]

## *Beaulieu*

It had sounded too bizarre to Sir Hugh le Despenser when the friar blurted out his story, but there was a crazy ring of truth to it. There are some tales which are too peculiar for any man to have thought of inventing them, and this had all the hallmarks of one.

He had spoken with one of his Welshmen as soon as Nicholas of Wisbech had concluded, and then had him repeat his story. The Welshman understood what was needed of him, and went about the abbey to confirm the story.

In truth, there wasn't much to validate. Sir Hugh remembered vaguely the knight who had died on the coronation day, not that it was that much of a problem at the time. No, much more important was the obscene behaviour of Gaveston, the arrogant prickle, prancing about like some earl from a bad dream, all purple and bejewelled, as though the day was *his* and not the King's.

It was appalling, his conduct so repugnant that there were many there that day at the feast who were convinced from that moment that Gaveston would have to be killed. Despenser was one of them. Not that he actually had any part in the murder. A shame. He would have liked to have participated.

But his man had been able to come back and fill in the gaps. Yes, the herald called Thomas was the brother of John of Bakewell, the knight who had been crushed to death in Westminster Abbey when the wall behind him collapsed. Thomas of Bakewell had been looked upon sympathetically

---

[1] Wednesday, 8 May 1325

by the Queen, and she had taken him into her household, and from there he had migrated to the King's.

He had been a reliable member of the household, by all accounts, and had been sent to Christ Church to tell the Prior that the King had been travelling to Beaulieu, so that when the ambassadors arrived there, they would know where to go to speak with the King. As soon as they arrived, Thomas was supposed to have hurried back to tell the King that they were on their way.

Oddly, he had arrived only a day before the others. While they should have been travelling more slowly than he, for some reason Thomas was much more late than the journey could explain. And meanwhile, Richard de Yatton had been killed and left at the side of the road.

'I want you to find out where this man Thomas sleeps. Go through all his belongings, in case there's a phial of oil there. If there is, bring it to me.'

'What about him, Sir Hugh? Do you want us to do anything to him?'

'Not yet. If you find the oil, you can kill him.'

# Chapter Twenty-Three

*Feast Day of Gordianus et Epimachus*[1]

## *Eltham Palace*

Earl Edward was back early from hunting, and he marched heavily across the court from his stables while the grooms cleaned and brushed his horse.

There had been a good morning's ride, with the hounds taking the scent of a fine stag early on. They had nearly lost the beast, but it was Earl Edward himself who saw him crashing off through some bracken and young trees over on the hillside east, and he'd himself drawn the hounds back to it, leading them initially with a whoop of encouragement, until they all saw his direction and the lead bitch caught the scent.

A marvellous ride, though, fast and furious, even through a tangle of briars, before the sudden death, with the deer brought down swiftly and despatched with a knife at the throat, while the hounds bayed and whined, kept back by the fewterer.

It was the sort of life he was born for. A man like him was fitted for this sort of life. It was all he knew, in truth. His training for when his father was dead.

Strange, to think of his life in those terms, but it was true. All his life was a lengthy training. He must learn to be quick-

---

[1] Friday, 10 May 1325

witted, to judge men and their character, to see opportunities, to listen out for deceit in any man's words . . . all these were the key foundations of a king's safety, because his would be an entirely solitary existence.

He knew that. Who better? He had seen his own father at work. No sooner had Earl Edward been born, than his father had made him an earl, the highest position to which a man might aspire, unless he sought the Crown itself. As Earl of Chester, he had his own household to look after him, and he was already to be seen as a member of Parliament at the age of seven. Great things were expected of him, as he knew. As the nation knew.

But the reward took a heavy toll. It was expensive being an earl, expensive not only in treasure. He had not known a happy family existence. The relationship between his parents was always fraught with tension. From the earliest moment, he could remember them, he shouting, she shrieking, and no calm, no peace. He was more dedicated to his friend, '*That* man Despenser', as she always called him. And the King would assert that she was happier in the company of all her French maids and servants than in his, her husband's.

For the Earl, it was clear that both were telling the truth. She did not love the King any more. She tried to, she was an absolutely devoted wife and mother, and Earl Edward adored her, but he could not deny that she could, on occasion, be a little hard to deal with. While the King, generous, loving, affectionate as he was, was also occasionally childish, tyrannical, petulant, and prone to displays of vicious brutality. Of course, a lot of it was deserved. If a man proved himself a traitor, he should expect the full penalty of the law to strip him of his property and livelihood, and see him executed. There were enough men who demonstrated the King's desire for justice in those cases. All the men who had raised a sword against his standard, they had all been killed. There was no use for mercy in such matters. The Earl understood that perfectly well. Mercy was a sign of weakness. The King was right to be ruthless.

But there were times when the Earl wondered whether such extremes of violence were actually justified. Not often, no, because his father had a clearer understanding of life as a king . . . and yet, Earl Edward already knew from his learning with Richard of Bury that a king must be prepared to be utterly ruthless with enemies, but that was not the same as some of the men whom the King had seen executed. It was plain enough that the Earl of Lancaster, even if he was King Edward II's cousin, had attempted to dethrone the King. He'd tried to stop the King from ruling in the manner which he had chosen for his own. And that was unforgivable. The Earl had even attempted to put constraints on the King. That was . . . well, it was *wrong*.

There were others, though, whose crimes were not so clear and deserving of punishment. In the past, men who happened to be knights attached to a lord's household wouldn't have been executed out of hand, their heads sent to London, or hung in chains for the crows and rooks to feast on. Yet these were. There were no towns in the country, so the Earl had heard, which didn't have a corpse gibbeted on public display. He could believe it, too. In his own travels up and down the country, he had seen the gibbets at the town walls.

The Queen had finally managed to persuade him to show a little mercy. The bodies had been cut down, but Sir Hugh le Despenser said it was an act of weakness. Those corpses were perfect, he reckoned, because they demonstrated the King's authority. Earl Edward wasn't sure. He thought they proved only jealous cruelty. A man so jealous of his own power that he would exterminate any other who attempted to encroach was no leader. Alexander wouldn't have done that. He would have had no need to – he would have been leading by example, keeping his men busy, leading them from one glorious victory to another.

Not his father, sadly. The shame had been felt by all England when the Scots destroyed his army at Bannockburn. It may have been while he was only a brat, a baby mewling and puking in the arms of Margaret, his wet nurse, but the reverberation of that catastrophe rang through every year since. Not even the mauling the King gave the Lancastrians three years ago had wiped out the memory of that disaster, nor of the other shameful losses as the Scots riders ravaged the whole of the North.

That was why he hated his father's 'friend' so much. Despenser, he knew, was in truth a friend to no man. A fellow might rely on Despenser while he was of use to him, but more than that, no. Despenser was too much a creature of his own. He looked after himself and no one else.

The proof had come when Earl Edward was almost ten – nearly three years ago. After Boroughbridge, the King had been wonderfully exuberant. It was a great, a magnificent victory, and he was justified in feeling a fresh confidence. Full of his martial prowess, he launched another offensive towards Scotland.

This was to be one of the most ignominious defeats ever inflicted upon English arms. In God's name, the memory still rankled with Earl Edward. It was enough to make any man smart, to think of it. The army marched on into Scotland, and found nothing. Only one scabby cow was left behind. The Scots were too adept at gathering all their folk and goods, and retreating before the King's host. And that meant that there was no food. Demoralised, starving, racked with scurvy and dysentery, the King's forces were forced to retreat. Many died. Even the King's own bastard, Adam, whom the King had taken on his first campaign, succumbed.

Worse was awaiting them. As the King passed into Yorkshire, intent on raising more forces, the Bruce circled around them, almost cutting off the King himself. King Edward panicked and was forced to flee – but not before asking others to rescue his wife, up in Tynemouth. He was at Rievaulx, with Despenser, but Despenser refused to go and rescue the Queen. Oh, the King and he escaped, at the expense of losing all the baggage, a load of treasure and many of the state's official documents, but they left the Queen to the mercy of the Bruce – this a man who had seen his own mother and sister tormented by Edward II's father. Oh, the Bruce would have been happy to capture the English Queen. He would have made great sport with her, if he'd taken her. As it was, she had been forced to flee by ship, and in the dreadful journey, two of her ladies-in-waiting died.

Yes, she blamed Despenser for that, and so did Earl Edward. Despenser was a coward, who persuaded his father to run to safety while leaving his mother to the mercies of their enemies.

He wouldn't forgive Despenser for that. Never.

## Morrow of Feast of Gordianus et Epimachus[1]

### *Lydford*

It had come as a great surprise to him that the wedding had been so far prepared that there was little to do other than confirm the orders for ale, wine and food.

'Edith, my child, what has happened to you?' Simon breathed when he saw her for the first time in her wedding dress.

She was wearing a simple white woollen tunic, embroidered with a pattern of plain flowers, also in white. It trailed on the ground, concealing her feet, and was loose in the skirt, but tight over her bust, with a daring, scooped neck that showed a little of the top of her breasts, though not indecorous quantities; her forearms, too, were exposed, the sleeves ending at the elbow, with long dangling strips that reached to her knees. Her hair was plaited, and partly concealed beneath a loose veil, that was little more than a square of filmy cloth sitting over her head, leaving her face free.

'My little girl, you're beautiful!' Simon breathed, and in a moment he felt curiously giddy. The sadness of losing his lovely daughter was mixed with an immense pride to see that she had turned out so wonderfully. He gazed at her for such a long time that she coloured prettily and bent her head in embarrassment, but he gently lifted her head for her, a finger under her chin, and smiled at her. And then he felt the flood of tears threatening.

'Don't cry, Father,' she whispered, a trace of real panic in her voice.

'I won't cry over this, maid. You've a good man here, and you'll make him proud of you.'

---

[1] Saturday, 11 May 1325

She smiled, and walked beside him along the grassed pathway to the church door where everyone waited for them.

And that, in truth, was much of his memory of the day. The priest stood and portentously intoned the words, while the two children – he hoped he would grow to remember that they were adults now – smiled shyly at each other and the crowds waiting, putting on the ring on her fourth finger, swearing their vows to each other . . . Simon knew all this happened, but it was all he could do to keep a grip on his wife's hand as it all progressed. He remembered to announce the dowry, which stunned the audience when they saw the King's purse and his money, but after that, when Baldwin clapped him on the back, and Jeanne came to him and congratulated him on acquiring a stolid, stable son-in-law who would be a credit to his family, all he could do was mumble. It was only later, when he sampled the brides-ale, that he began to feel a little more normal.

'She looks lovely, doesn't she?' Margaret said as the shadows lengthened and the crowds grew rowdier, the priest bellowing at a small group of men gambling on a cockfight, while others drank themselves to a stupor on a grave nearby.

Simon took a deep breath and let his eyes range over all the people in the yard. 'She looks almost as lovely as you did, Meg, on the day I married you,' he said, and encircled her waist with his arm. He could see his son Peterkin running about with three friends from the town, all playing tag, and as he looked over at Edith, he saw that she was wearing two little crowns, one of primroses, one of cowslips, and a necklace of violets. And suddenly he felt an enormity of sadness welling up in his breast, as though his life was all but ended.

'Simon? Are you well?' Margaret asked.

'Of course I am. Are you?'

She turned a little away. 'I feel so happy, I almost feel sad.'

'He has a good wife, there. He'd best look after her.'

'With that dowry, he'll be able to afford to,' Margaret said.

'I hope so,' Simon responded. 'I wish them both all the happiness in the world.'

Baldwin had approached with Jeanne, who had arrived the day before, fetched by Edgar, and heard his last words. 'So do we all, Simon. So do we all.'

## Beaulieu

Despenser sat back in his seat as the two men entered. 'Well?'

'We've not been able to look until today, Sir Hugh,' the first, Ivor, said. 'We looked through all his belongings, but there was no sign of anything there.'

'You are quite sure? The phial could be very small, perhaps only the size of a sword's pommel?'

'There was nothing there that could hold oil. We've been through everything.'

Despenser ground his teeth with frustration. It wasn't as if he had all the time in the world. There were reports coming to him of possible invasion plans for the conquering of England. Joseph had just returned from the prior of Christ Church with another story of shipping off the coast of Holland, and here he was, trying to find the oil that could provide salvation. Oh, he'd told that fool of a friar that he didn't believe in the oil, but that was less than honest. He didn't know whether the oil was St Thomas's or not, but that didn't matter. Not now.

Before he had wanted it for himself, just to prove to the King that Despenser had his best interests at heart. However, now he was beginning to change his mind.

If he could find it and let it be known that the Abbot of Westminster, perhaps, had used it to renew the King's vows and have him anointed again, then men throughout the realm would listen and perhaps have faith in him once more.

That was the main issue now. Despenser had picked up rumours from spies that Roger Mortimer was in Hainault. And the men there were notoriously keen on taking up arms for any man who could afford them. They were skilled, and numerous. If Mortimer succeeded in persuading Guillaume, the Count of Hainault, he would have a large army at his disposal. Only last year Despenser had learned of a plot to invade, and ships had gathered off Zeeland. He'd ordered the admiral of the eastern fleet to keep his eyes open, but fortunately nothing had come of it then. That didn't mean Mortimer wasn't attempting something equally audacious now.

If he was successful, the King would need as many men as possible for when the invasion force arrived. There were few enough who had shown any interest in fighting for him so far. The oil could be the last little grain of sand that tilted men back into his camp and prepared them to fight for the King again, rather than leave all to fate. Fate would be a painful experience for Despenser, he felt sure.

He had to find that oil. It may be just enough to put a little fire in the bellies of the men who needed it, and Despenser must find it to prove once again that he was the one man in the kingdom upon whom the King could rely.

'You want us to catch the man, Sir Hugh?' Ivor said hesitantly. 'I could tickle him up a little with my knife, see if that loosens his tongue?'

It was tempting. But . . . 'No. Not yet. We will be leaving in a couple of days. The King must return to Westminster, ready for a meeting of his barons to discuss France. He is to persuade the Bishop of Orange to join him. The king's heralds will all be on the journey with us. It will be easier to find the oil then, on the road. He will have to bring it with him, unless he's planning to leave it down here. It's too valuable for that. No, leave him for now. We'll take him and have our sport later.'

The Bishop of Orange was content to be leaving this place, but it was a source of great annoyance that he was to travel up to London. The city was no doubt diverting enough for most men, but for him it was merely an additional journey which entailed going still further out of his way. His path should take him back to the Pope, not up to London. It was almost the opposite direction, in God's name!

When he heard the knock at his door, it made him glance quickly at his table to ensure that any indiscreet documents were hidden before he called out, '*Entrez!*'

Nicholas walked in slowly, downcast. This was no time for pride. He had to show how humble he was. At other times he could show a little pride in his habit, but not today. Today he was a mere supplicant, begging some assistance from another man of God.

'What do you want, Friar?'

The tone was not welcoming. 'My Lord Bishop, I am a deeply miserable friar. I have been here at Beaulieu for some weeks, trying to see the King to plead my case, but he will not see me.'

'What is your case?'

'The oil of St Thomas,' Nicholas said, and felt sure that the Bishop understood. Immediately, the Bishop seemed to give him his full attention, and even as Nicholas told his story, he gained the impression that the Bishop already knew, or guessed much. Perhaps it was not so surprising, though. The Pope knew about the oil, and surely some of his closer advisers would also have been told of it.

'This is most interesting,' the Bishop said. 'But what do you want me to do? Raise the matter with the King? I do not think he would be grateful for a foreigner to bring it up.'

'No. I was hoping to be able to travel with you, my Lord. If you would allow me to join your party on the way to the Pope, I would be very grateful.'

'Your gratitude is no doubt a fine thing,' the Bishop said without enthusiasm. 'However, I have a large entourage already. If you wish us to carry food and drink for you too, it will add a great deal to my baggage.'

'I can walk, and I have little need of food, my Lord. We friars are used to the ascetic life and little nourishment.'

'True enough.' The Bishop studied him thoughtfully for a while, and at last nodded. 'Very well. I will allow you to join my men on the journey to the Pope. However, I cannot guarantee the reception you will receive.'

'I am very glad to hear it! I will make my peace with him as best I may.'

'Yes. I am sure that he will be most interested to hear more about this marvellous oil,' the Bishop said.

# Chapter Twenty-Four

*Lydford*

It was a very exhausted Bailiff Puttock who was assisted by his wife to his bedchamber that night. Peterkin had already fallen into his truckle bed, and Simon and Margaret stood undressing, both watching their remaining child.

'For all the arguing and troubles over the years, the house will seem quiet without her,' Margaret said ruminatively.

'That little devil will make up for any lack of noise on her part,' Simon said with a mild belch. 'He's already taken it upon himself to talk more than all the rest of us put together.'

Margaret smiled, then lifted her tunic over and off. She only wore a linen shirt beneath, and this she now removed as well, before climbing into bed. Sitting up, she watched her man undress.

He was still firm in the body. Every so often he would put on weight, but then the rigours of his work on the moors would wear it away again. That was the case in the past, anyway. The last months, living away from her, while he was working in Dartmouth, had made him lose more weight than before, and as she looked at him, she saw how the lines had become more deeply graven into his forehead. He was a good man, she knew. All through the dreadful times when she had been trying to give him another son, he had been sympathetic, calm, generous . . . and all the while he was desperate for a little boy to replace the one they lost.

It was some years since that appalling disease had struck. Poor little boy, he had died slowly, and Simon had never forgiven himself. Whereas usually he was the calmest, kindest father and husband, the one thing he could never abide was witnessing one whom he loved suffering pain. And their little boy had died so miserably, vomiting, screaming, with diarrhoea, and unable to eat or drink anything at all. It had torn at both of them to see him fade away, but Simon found it harder. He had once admitted to her that he blamed himself because he had wished the child to die at the end. He was so exhausted by the three days of sitting up and trying to comfort the boy, that the end was almost a blessing. And Simon never forgave himself for that.

It was sad, too, that Edith had always been 'his' child. They had an unholy alliance, Margaret sometimes felt, against any form of order in the house. And now he had lost her. She was in love with another man. It must be terrible, she felt, to be a parent and see the love which once had been specifically reserved for you to be passed over to another. It was something she feared herself, because she knew that Peterkin, her little Peterkin, would always be closer to her than to Simon, and she knew that when Peterkin was old enough, she would be desolate to see him leave the home and start his own family.

Ah, well. All mothers have to accept that. Once they have given life, they have to keep on giving, until they've given so much that their son can leave. And the mother must hope there's enough life left within her to keep herself alive for a little longer.

'Feeling lecherous, wench?' her husband leered.

She looked up and smiled. In truth, she had hardly ever felt less lecherous in her life. Yet Simon had been a good husband to her, and if she were being truthful, the loss of her daughter made her ache with sadness. She was an old woman now. Soon she might hear that she would be a grandam. She was unsure how she could cope with that.

Margaret was filled with a warm sense of love for him. This was no duty, it was a proof of her affection for him. Moving aside, she made space for him, opening her legs to ease his entry. She had the marriage debt still to pay, after all. As did her daughter now, she thought with a twinge. She hoped Edith would take as much pleasure from the debt as she always did.

Simon grunted with pleasure, smiled down at her, belched, and then, resting his head on her bosom, began to snore.

*Monday before Ascension Day*[1]

### *Eltham*

Up as dawn was breaking, Richard of Bury found that his charge was already out of his bed and on a horse.

It was one more proof of his mental and physical fitness. The lad seemed determined always to show himself as capable as any other, no matter what the task. He was exactly the sort of fellow who would, when King, lead his hosts from the front rank. 'Never ask others to do what you would not dare yourself' appeared to be his motto. And since he believed that a strong man needed to make the most of every day, and a fit man would be first to rise in the morning so he could take advantage of every moment of sunshine, he was usually one of the earliest to be out of his bed. It made his guards deeply unhappy.

---

[1] Monday, 13 May 1325

The Earl had always been a strong-willed lad, Richard of Bury considered. Not only did he have a mental rigour when considering abstruse philosophical arguments, but he could also be quite ruthless in his reasoning when he thought about more practical matters of kingship. When a fellow took into account the fact that he was born of such a disastrous marriage, it was perhaps no great surprise, but the mental powers which he possessed were still impressive. They would have been in a much older man.

Some might have said that he was callous, that he was cold and unemotional when viewing other people and their needs, but to Richard of Bury that was essential. A king was first and foremost the supreme arbiter of justice, and any man who would be King must be entirely impartial – unless it was an issue that affected his own authority or the realm, of course. Then the two must override all other considerations, naturally.

That the lad had the ability, Richard did not doubt. He was a thoroughly effective student, and appeared to appreciate all that Richard told him of past kings, and his analysis of what had made them great.

They had held an interesting discussion this morning, for example, while walking outside in the court.

'So, my Earl, what do you think of the present disputes between your father and your uncle?'

The Earl had smiled slightly. 'The King my father has a fully legitimate claim to the lands which are the remnants of the lands which he inherited. My mother brought a great deal of France with her as her dower, and it would be shameful to deprive her of that. But my uncle also has his own realm to consider. He is the King of a great land, and it has to be his desire that he might one day bring all under his authority. While my father holds on to his lands and refuses to pay homage to my uncle, his loyalty is suspect. And if my father *does* go there, he is accepting the fact that he is subservient to my uncle. That would be a galling draught to swallow for any man.'

'Can there be a resolution?'

'Only if the two crowns are united, or if they are entirely separated. If my father had no lands in France, there would be no issue. Or if my father was King of both England and France, there would also be no difficulty. It is merely this intermediate stage, when both are King, and yet one should pay homage to the other, that creates all the trouble.'

'I see. So how would you resolve it?'

The boy looked up at the towering beech trees and for that moment looked just like any other young boy: innocent, guileless, but looking for the next mischief he could cause.

'Me? I would stake all on a great gamble. I would raise a host and go to France to conquer her. I would take her in a series of mighty battles, relying on my ability to move about the land at speed with a number of knights and men-at-arms all mounted on horses. Forget the idea of a series of long-drawn-out sieges of cities. We would ride out on *chevauchée* and devastate the countryside, eating all the foodstocks, burning what we could not eat. It would be a case of ravaging the country to prevent the people from ever living comfortably again. And I would force the French King to meet me in battle, and I would destroy his forces. And once I had him captured, I would treat him with great humility and generosity, as an equal. Because the war could only be won through the magnificence of chivalry. Like Arthur, I would be magnanimous in victory, but relentless in pursuit of it. All would hear my approach and tremble.'

'Interesting. And do you think you would be able to

command enough men to make such a prospect even remotely possible?' Richard said, half jesting. 'You do realise that for every English knight the French King has five or six? His is a greater land than all England.'

'I would do it.' There was an unsettling certainty in his tone. 'I would create more knights from the wealthy, and those who refused to accept knighthood would needs must pay a fine to permit me to fund two men-at-arms. A king must have the men he needs to fight his wars. Of course, my father cannot do this.'

'Why?'

'He has lost the respect of his men. When he succeeded at Boroughbridge, many were prepared to give him their respect, but that all ended when he treated his victims so shamefully. That caused others to fear him. And when the Despenser family took so many spoils, people grew to despise him. There is no respect for him. And since Boroughbridge, he has lost more battles, hasn't he? That is no way to inspire his men. So he cannot go to France. His barons would not trust his generalship, and his men would not have faith in his largesse.'

'You can reason very clearly. Although I should say that your father the King has the love and adoration of all his loyal subjects, of course.'

'Yes. You should say that. But do not pretend that you believe it, Bury. We both know the truth.'

'May I ask how you came to such a conclusion, then?'

'It is very easy, Master Bury. When I look at an issue, I try to think how one of your heroes would have viewed the same problem. And I try to emulate the greatest of them all, Arthur. How would Arthur have looked at an affair like the breakdown between England and France? How would he have resolved it? After that it becomes very simple. He was a man of honour, chivalry and enormous power. All I need do to succeed is copy him.'

'And you can be so rational about the present position?'

'You mean my father, don't you?' the boy said with a little sigh. 'Well, of course I know I ought to be more plainly loyal and devoted to him, but the truth is, it is difficult. I hardly ever see him now. He is always roving about the country, and I know he is very fearful of losing the Agenais and Guyenne for ever. He would be devastated by that, but it is really no worse than his loss of Scotland. And he appears to have accepted that.'

'You think so?'

The Earl turned to him with such an adult look on his face that Bury shrugged and apologised.

'I am sorry, my Lord. Yes, of course he has. He has negotiated, and a man with whom you negotiate, you assume has the power to do so. If the King will negotiate with the Bruce, he has demonstrated that he believes the Bruce to be the actual authority in Scotland.'

'Precisely. And the reason why he feels now more than ever he must resort to negotiating is nothing to do with the Bruce himself. It's not him my father fears.'

'Who, then? The French?'

'Master Richard, I seriously believe I may have to instruct you, my tutor! No, of course not. He fears his own mightiest and greatest general, Sir Roger Mortimer. The traitor who now lives in France or somewhere. That man is the real danger to our realm. Not the Bruce. The Bruce and Scotland are merely a distraction.'

'So what do you think King Arthur would do?' Bury asked with a smile.

'You mean if he were King? He would not have come to this pass.'

'So, if you were to become King, what would you do, bearing in mind how matters stand?'

'I would have to curry favour with my uncle, and betray my father.'

Now, back in his chamber, Bury could see the expression on the lad's face once more. There was no sign of irony there. Only a fixed, serious concentration. Bury was sure that the lad meant what he said. If he had been King at the time, the realm would not have come to this pass. And if he were to take over in the near future, he would be forced to become a traitor to his own father.

He also wondered . . . the boy looked as though he could easily plot to do just that . . . but no. No, that was stretching things too far. He was a lad of not yet thirteen years. There was no possibility of his planning anything at his age.

Still, he was plainly the right heir to Arthur, just as the prophecy foretold.

A series of shouts from outside made him look up, momentarily forgetting his disturbed thoughts. He went to the window and peered down into the courtyard, and saw a messenger dismounting and stretching.

'Message for the Earl of Chester.'

As Earl Edward's tutor, he was soon to hear that the message was a summons to Westminster. Usually that would be a cause of excitement for Richard of Bury, because any excuse to go to the centre of power was reason for rejoicing, as it also involved excellent food and drink. But not today. Today Bury had a cold sensation in his belly. He remembered that look on the boy's face the other day, a week ago, when he had seen Earl Edward. That day, the Earl had seemed on the verge of saying something. In God's name, he hoped the Earl hadn't done anything that could be regretted.

Perhaps his tutoring of the boy had been too rational, too worldly. Maybe he should stop the teaching of political and military achievement from ancient Greece to Rome, and instead, concentrate on less martial subjects.

But how could he deny the training Arthur's heir demanded?

### *Lydford*

Baldwin was already outside in the little garden when Simon rose that Monday morning. It was a lovely, fresh, late spring day. The clouds were few, and high in the sky, the sun casting long shadows this early, and there was a fine dew on the grass as Baldwin went through his exercises.

Simon sat on an upturned stump. Soon afterwards Wolf came and sat beside him, leaning against his thigh and resting his head on Simon's leg, staring up at him beseechingly, demanding his attention. Simon patted his chest, enjoying the peace of the morning. Both their wives were still in their beds, as was Simon's son. Baldwin's children were still at his house. Jeanne had left them with their nurses rather than make the journey too slow. She would not be here for long, after all.

As he watched, the knight span and whirled, sword in his right hand, now in his left, making the movements that had been taught to him as a Templar. His order had placed a great deal of emphasis on daily weapons practice, and now Baldwin's muscles were inured to the routine. He stood with his sword up, point angled downwards, right hand over his forehead, left hand flat like a blade, over his belly, where he could slap away an attack. Then he whirled, sword sweeping about, until he stopped with his right fist at his belt buckle, sword pointing upwards to block, left hand over his breast. Each manoeuvre carefully distinct, every time the blade glimmering with speed, only to halt firmly, unwavering. And as uncompromising as the movements of the steel was the expression on his face.

'You should train as well,' Baldwin said.

'At this time of day? I don't think so.'

'At any time, Simon,' Baldwin said.

Simon gave a twisted smile and nodded towards his shoulder and hand. 'With the wounds still this fresh? Meg would kill me if I opened them.'

'Aye, you may have a point there.' Baldwin grinned. He sheathed his sword before wiping a forearm over his sweaty brow. 'Let us not be fools. We both know that Despenser sent his man to you to make a threat. But the fact that we bested his man may lead Despenser to decide to try again, just to soothe his feelings of injured pride. He does not need your land or house, but the fact you stood up to him and prevented him from taking it makes it unbearably tempting for him.'

'What will William Wattere do about it?' Simon scoffed. 'He's in gaol.'

'For now. Do not forget that Bishop Walter is a close associate of Sir Hugh Despenser. Despenser is perfectly capable of demanding that his man be freed. He will twist the King's arm until he has a pardon, or perhaps he will simply deny that there is a case to answer and have his man released by threatening the Bishop.'

'How could he threaten the Bishop?'

'Simon, to my knowledge, he has stolen lands from ladies up and down the country. He has threatened and captured men, and taken all he wanted from them. He has deprived men and women of their treasure. He will stop at nothing to maintain his power and authority, and if he finds a man is in his way, he will do all he can to force him to move. Now if news of your success against his man was to become known, he would be in an intolerable position: he would be in a situation where others could see that he could be prevented. If men see that an outlaw can be stopped, they do not fear that outlaw again. It is only the ruthless exercise of might that keeps Despenser in power. Take away that might, and he becomes a nothing. That is what he fears.'

'So what do you propose that I do?'

'Keep a wary ear on any sounds of escape from the Bishop's gaol. So shall I. If Wattere is freed, we know that Despenser is tensing his muscles ready for some kind of demonstration. And beyond that, plan to defend your home.'

'You do not fill me with confidence.'

'I fear I have little enough of it,' Baldwin said heavily.

It was later that same day that they heard Wattere had been released.

# Chapter Twenty-Five

## *Beaulieu*

Jack set about his own packing early in the morning. There was little for him to worry about. A small parcel of clothes which was bound inside a linen sack, a goatskin for some wine, a leather wallet with some bread, smoked sausage and cheese, and a pair of thick fustian blankets, rolled tightly and bound with thongs, for the colder nights. He pulled his cloak about him, and he was ready.

Everyone else here appeared to be preparing to leave as well. The Bishop of Orange was watching carefully as men stored his papers in a cart, the King's steward and Despenser's bottler were stalking about among the wagons and sumpter horses ensuring that all was packed, while clerks of the various departments of state were hurrying about, squeaking at men who looked as though they might drop a chest or misstore a box in the wrong wagon, and generally getting in the way of everyone else while making themselves thoroughly miserable at the same time.

It was not the kind of sight a man like Jack would see often in a lifetime. Once, he would have stood here on the steps near a hall watching for very different reasons. Then he would have been here to assess the best method of stealing as much as possible. He would have kept an eye on the wagons so that he could see which was holding all the gold or coins. Treasure was best, of course, because a handful of rubies was lighter than its value in coin. Yes, there had been a time when he would have been eyeing all this with carefully concealed desire. But not today.

Strange to think that a man like him could change so much. Yet he had. What had he been? A farmer, a sailor, a fisherman, an outlaw, and now a guard. Honourable again, he knew he was a rarity. Most men, if they once turned out bad, were bad for life. That was what all said. A man who became a felon was as dangerous as a wolf. That's why they were called 'wolfshead', and the law entitled any man to strike off their head without fear of punishment.

It was just. A man who was determined to be evil, who wanted to make his living by stealing and taking the property of others deserved his end, he told himself – and then gave a wry grin. Strange how quickly a man's attitude would change to reflect his new reality.

The carts and wagons were for the most part filled by the middle of the morning. Clerks and men-at-arms stood about looking weary already before the last sumpter horse had been fully packed, and Jack took stock.

Over on the left the marshal of the horses stood frowning at a horse which was holding a hoof in the air, injured, while the yeoman of the horses berated two grooms for some infraction in the beast's treatment. Nearby were the wagons set aside for the King's favourite treasures. They were filled with the leather chests bound with iron, which, earlier, Jack had seen packed with cotton before having the more easily damaged goods installed, the expensive silver plates and bowls, the salt and mazers of gold. The buttery had been more or less squeezed into four different wagons, the barrels all chocked and held in place with ropes, while the other foodstuffs were kept in a pair of wagons behind. All in all, with the men milling about the place and the noise of the hounds, it was impossible to concentrate on anything.

This was an enormous household. Jack hadn't appreciated just how large before, because many of the men and most of the horses, the palfreys, sumpters and many dexters, had all been lodged elsewhere in the neighbourhood – there were too many to expect the good Abbot of Beaulieu to support on his own at one location. Of course, not everyone would travel together. The harbingers had already gone. One from the King's chamber, a clerk from his kitchen, a servant from his hall, and a pair of servants from his kitchen staff. They left very early, so as to make sure that the next stop would have food and drink waiting. Meanwhile, the second team to go was the party who had the clothsack. They had the King's personal items with them, all his clothing and basic articles, and would leave shortly. After them would come the King, once he had eaten his meal. With him would be the steward, his marshals of the hall and chamber, the sewer and other servants who would serve him, and all his men-at-arms and knights. Finally, all the other servants and main baggage would follow on behind.

Jack shook his head. He would be travelling with the Bishop in the main party with the King, so he had heard. It would be a slow business, though. On the way here, they had managed between thirty and forty miles each day, striving hard to make the journey as swiftly as possible, and now all was being delayed for the King's pleasure. The Bishop had hoped to be back at Avignon with the Pope by now, but instead here they were, waiting on the King's letter. He wanted to write to the Pope, he said, so the Bishop must hold up here, and hope to receive the letter before winter arrived. And in the meanwhile, their journeying would be far lengthier than necessary. The King would probably only make fifteen miles a day or so. Jack had heard a servant talking about the speed of the King's father, Edward I, who had managed twenty, but Jack seriously doubted that anyone could do that with so many wagons. The damned things were so slow and unmanoeuvrable, and every time they came to a hill, the dexters hauling would fail, and the grooms of the marshalsea would have to go and hire some oxen to pull them up. No, it would slow things down immeasurably.

All of which was frustrating. But there was nothing he could do about it, and besides, he was in no hurry personally. Jack idled the early morning away, watching the preparations with some amusement.

Until, that is, he saw the man in a herald's uniform.

### *Lydford*

'How could he have let the bastard loose?' Simon demanded. He clenched a fist and slammed it into his cupped hand. 'Sweet Jesus! Didn't he know the bastard would be a threat to us?'

The messenger from the Bishop stood, somewhat disconcerted by the reaction to his news, and immediately Wolf grumbled deep in his throat. The man looked at him, alarmed. 'I was only asked to come and tell—'

Baldwin shook his head at the man, and held out both hands soothingly. 'Simon, be calm! Wolf! Silent!'

'My love,' Margaret said, pale but calm, 'he is an old friend. I feel sure he would never knowingly put us in danger. He knows us all so well, and he is so kindly towards us. Can you imagine him willingly hurting us or our children? Of course not!'

'Whether he intended it or not is irrelevant, Meg,' Simon said harshly. 'That goat-swyving churl is a danger to us while he lives, if he remains with his master and in Despenser's service.'

She was silent as he stalked away and stared from the window.

'I begin to wonder whether the Bishop is truly our friend,' he said, and there was a cold tone to his voice she hadn't heard before.

She turned to the messenger. 'Was there anything else the good bishop wished us to know?'

'Like I say, he has released the man Wattere, but only because Sir Hugh le Despenser has asked for his man to be sent back to him so that his transgressions may be investigated.'

'I suppose Bishop Walter couldn't do that himself in Exeter?'

'Simon!' Margaret snapped. 'Let the man finish!'

'He has been taken by the Bishop with his entourage. The Bishop has been summoned to advise the King in Westminster. He told me to tell you that it is a matter of grave importance about the affairs in France. And he said to tell you that the man will not be likely to come here to trouble you. He will remain with the Bishop all the way to London.'

'How reassuring!'

She hated seeing her husband like this. It was unnecessary; pointless. She had been nervous, of course, when the horrible man had turned up and threatened her. It wasn't something she was used to, having been a bailiff's wife for so long. People usually tended to show her and her family respect. But perhaps this was just a sign of the troubles to come.

Simon and she had known that when the Abbot of Tavistock

died, it was possible that their lives could become more difficult, for Simon had already been sent to Dartmouth to work, ironically, as a kind gesture by Abbot Champeaux, who thought he was rewarding Simon for all his work in the past years. Sadly, though, it was the worst thing he could have done. It split their family, and made it extremely difficult for Simon to maintain contact with their children. Let alone the debilitating effect it had on his relationship with Meg herself. When she heard that poor Abbot Robert had died, she was slightly relieved to hear it. She knew that with Abbot Robert gone, there would be a change in power at the abbey which must inevitably lead to Simon being asked to give up his post on the coast.

As had happened. However, she had not been prepared for the fact that both of the protagonists seeking the abbacy might try to put someone in Simon's place on the moors as well. If he were not to have his old post as bailiff, when he had already lost his position at Dartmouth, then what would they do for money? It was hard to tell. Perhaps he would be forced to leave this area completely?

At least Simon was not a serf of the abbey. He was one of Sir Hugh de Courtenay's men, so he could leave here whenever he wanted, and they could return to their farm, if need be. The little farm near Sandford. It would be a shame to leave this house. She had been very happy here – but the farm was a good property, too. It had been a wrench when she had first been told that Simon had won the post at Lydford. With a sad little smile, she could now remind herself that she had not wanted to come here. It was odd how attitudes could change.

It was Jeanne who tried to placate him now. 'He tries to be your friend.'

'You don't understand,' Simon said.

'I think she understands better than you, Simon,' Baldwin said.

'What does that mean?' Simon demanded.

Margaret said, 'Surely if Despenser's demanded the release of his man, the Bishop can hardly refuse? The Despenser is the most powerful man in the country after the King, you keep telling me.'

'He is, yes, but the Bishop must be almost as powerful. The King listens to him, and—'

'There is no "and", Simon,' Baldwin said. 'You were in London with me. You saw how the King deferred to Despenser. The two are close. Very close. And the good bishop has little power compared with Sir Hugh.'

Simon turned to face him. His face showed his bitterness and concern. Margaret would almost have called it fear. 'You want me to just accept it, then? Should I give up my home here? Make a gift of it to Despenser? What is it to him, after all? The man has so much, so many houses, castles, entire provinces! What does he want with this little place?'

Margaret shook her head. 'He doesn't care about the size. From all you've said, he's like a hound who feeds until he cannot eat more. He won't stop eating because he's full, because he doesn't know when he can gorge again; in the same way Despenser won't stop stealing all he can because he doesn't know how to. While he is in a position to, he will seek to continue taking all he can.'

She stopped and looked about her. This little house had been her delight. She still loved it. That screen she had had built a while ago, a neat, wooden construction that kept their private chambers beyond warmer and less draughty.

She had had paintings on the wall, one of St Rumon, the patron saint of the Abbey at Tavistock, and one of St Boniface of Crediton, to remind them always where they had come from, where they had been so happy. This had been her home for almost ten years. It was a long time. Hard to give it all up. But better that than find a man like Wattere appearing again.

'No man just keeps stealing for the fun of making mischief, though,' her husband was saying.

'But, Husband, he isn't. He is doing this to upset you, as he has succeeded, and to upset Baldwin through you,' she said. 'Why else would he do this?'

Simon stopped and stared at her. It was Baldwin who responded, though.

'I think you are quite right, Margaret.'

'What can we do, then, Baldwin?' Simon said. 'If you two are correct, and the evil bastard son of a whore is trying to anger you and me, what should I do?'

'Well, there is little point arguing with his henchman,' Baldwin said. 'It is he alone who can prevent any further problems.'

'But would he? He hates us both, so he'll hardly want to help us, will he? He could deny all knowledge of Wattere's actions, and support Wattere in the background, and we'd not be able to do anything. We could take Wattere to court, and with his money, Despenser would be able to bribe any justice, any jury . . . I would be ruined in no time.'

'There is no point, Simon,' Margaret said sadly. She looked about her again. The picture of St Boniface had a lovely smile to the face, and she smiled with a weariness she hadn't known since her boy had been weaned. 'He has won the battle. There is no point in struggling against him. We should rent this house, and move back to Sandford. That way, we gain more time. And it won't matter, because you aren't Bailiff any more.'

'You want to give up all we have done here?'

She looked at Baldwin. 'How many men and women has he killed?'

'I don't know. Many, though.'

'Simon, I cannot lose you, and I cannot risk losing Peterkin. The house is just a house. We have another. Perhaps if we move back to Sandford, he will leave us alone.'

'Perhaps he will, at that,' Baldwin said, to her surprise. And then he continued, 'But I should feel happier if I had brought the whole matter to the attention of the King himself. And I think that he owes you and I a favour, Simon.'

## *Beaulieu*

Thomas of Bakewell never felt entirely right here among all the King's men. At heart, he was still the Queen's, heart and soul. He would never forget her lovely face, only a little older than his own, and the frown of compassion on it as she smoothed the hair from his brow that dreadful day of the King's coronation.

Not the only thing that went wrong, either. There were other problems. The barons all deprecated the fabulous riches worn by the King's past lover, Piers Gaveston, the smarmy son of an impoverished Breton knight, whom the old King had exiled. Gaveston was cocky and rude, and he seemed to set out to upset all the most powerful in the land, giving them insulting nicknames and then using them in front of others. And it wasn't helped that he was enormously competent in the lists. He beat all the older barons in a tournament.

But on that coronation day, he inspired more than jealousy

or contempt. He may have set the scene for the difficulties between the King and Queen – and France.

The Queen had arrived with a fabulous dowry, not only lands, but many jewels as well. And on the evening of the coronation, she saw that Gaveston was wearing them. This was a mortal insult to her, and to those members of her family who were also there. It was a miracle, so she said later, that no one had demanded to know how the primping fool had acquired them all. But then, no one needed to. They all saw perfectly clearly how the King fawned on his 'brother'. Sickening.

Yes, the Queen had the patience and kindness of a saint to have coped with her husband for so long. His infidelities, his deceits, his conceits, and his string of friends and advisers, on whom he lavished ever more inappropriate gifts – he could not help himself.

Thomas shook his head, hefted his little pack and blankets, and continued on his way out to his horse. He was to ride off with the King and his men, and had best hurry, for the King and his companions had almost finished their meal.

He walked from his room, down a narrow staircase, and along the passage at the side of the hall, until he came to the open air again – and was suddenly shouldered back inside.

'What in God's name—' he spluttered, reaching for his sword.

Immediately a knife was at his throat, just behind his chin, pointing upwards, making him lift his head and stop struggling. There was a man at his back, who said slyly, 'Didn't you hear me, Herald?'

A Welshman, Thomas noted, but that didn't mean anything for a moment. Then he heard footsteps, and he rolled his eyes to see who it might be. As he did so, he saw Sir Hugh le

Despenser appear. He was ready for the journey, cloaked and gloved, but as he approached Thomas, he tugged at the fingers of his left glove, gently easing it off. At last in front of Thomas, he gripped it in his right hand and slapped Thomas twice on each side of his face. The heavy leather made his cheeks smart, and there was a loose rivet, which slashed his cheek open near his jaw.

'That, Herald, is merely a beginning,' Despenser said. 'I want to know where the oil is. Where did you hide it?'

'What oil? I don't know what you mean, Sir Hugh.'

'I'm glad to see you know who I am. Now listen to me carefully, Herald.' Despenser approached closely and leaned near to Thomas, so that Thomas could see little other than his eyes, peering into his own with a look of mild enquiry. 'You were coming back that way, weren't you? You met with Richard de Yatton, and you killed him. Why do that? Just because he saw you there?'

Thomas frowned up at him. 'I don't know what you are talking about, Sir Hugh. I went up to—'

'Canterbury. I know. And while there, you stole oil from the monks and killed one. I don't know why, but I am not bothered about him. What is one monk, more or less? Nothing. But the oil you took, that is valuable, my friend. And murdering a king's herald, that is still more terrible. The King has a habit of not forgiving those who shame him, and he does, I fear, consider men who steal from him to be profoundly embarrassing to him personally. He will not be pleased with you, I fear.'

'Then take me to him now. I have done nothing.'

'I don't know if I believe you.'

Thomas shook his head. 'I don't know what you are talking about.'

'Open his bags,' Despenser commanded.

Thomas watched silently, keeping absolutely still as the knife under his jaw pressed upwards. He was sure he could feel the dribble of blood at the tip as the second man with Despenser took his dagger to the roll of blankets. He cut through the hempen string binding them, and unrolled them. There was nothing inside, but the man was nothing if not thorough. He ran his blade along the blankets until there was nothing but a shredded mess. Nothing useable.

The pack was a simple canvas one with a single strap. He took his knife to this too, opening the material and laying the lining bare. All the items inside were taken out and studied, before being crushed or ruined. There was nothing inside of real value, for Thomas had never owned anything of genuine worth, but the sight of the man merely ravaging his property for no reason was enough to set Thomas's blood racing.

'Not here, then, eh? We'll find it,' Despenser said coolly. 'And when we do, I'll take you to the King myself for judgement. You'd best be ready for that.'

'I do not have it.'

'What made you kill Richard? Eh? What had he done to you to deserve such ill-use? Or the monk, come to that? And after the poor devil had brought you the oil in the first place. It doesn't seem very kindly to accept his aid, and then cut his throat.'

Suddenly there was a shout, and Thomas felt the man behind him slowly release his hold, the knife blade running slowly to the line of his jaw-bone, then backwards to beneath his ear, where it remained a short while. Then it was gone. Meanwhile Despenser and his other man had retreated, and now were out of sight.

He was alone again. Gradually he sank to his knees, then

fell forwards to all fours, choking and retching with shame and rage, as another man hurried to him.

'Are you all right?' Jack demanded.

Thomas was so relieved, he could not speak, but instead closed his eyes and allowed his head to droop.

# Chapter Twenty-Six

*Lydford*

'Baldwin! Baldwin, stop, please,' Margaret called, running from the house to him. He was already astride his horse, his wife nearby; Edgar tightening the saddle a short distance away, while Wolf capered with one of Simon's hounds on the grass beside the road.

'Baldwin, don't, please. There's no need for you to do anything which might lead to more danger for you!'

'Margaret, do not worry about me, my dear. I am perfectly content that I am doing the correct thing.'

'You cannot go alone,' Margaret said.

Jeanne had heard their words, but was unsure of their import. 'What is this? Baldwin, tell me what is happening? Why do you want to leave so soon?'

'He has decided that he will go to the Despenser and fight him!' Margaret said.

'No, I have not,' Baldwin said reasonably. 'I have decided I need to return to speak with him, though, to try to ensure that there is no further risk to Simon and Margaret from his men. There is no point in his attacking people who have nothing whatever to do with his affairs. If that itself will not work, I shall petition the King himself.'

'When you say there's no point in his attacking someone, you mean yourself?'

'Jeanne, I have not picked a fight with the man. Not intentionally, at least. Yet he now appears to blame me for something which he is solely responsible for. If he proposed to hound us to death, I may as well ask why. And if I can deflect a little of his ire from Simon and Margaret, that is worth attempting.'

'You are going again, then? How long will you be gone this time?'

'In honesty, I do not know. All I can say is, I shall be home again as soon as I may be,' Baldwin said.

'Husband, I ask you not to go,' Jeanne said. Her face was pale, and she leaned towards him beseechingly. 'Please, Baldwin, don't do this. I have already missed you so much this year, and I do not want to have to live as your widow yet.'

'I will not be gone for too long. Hopefully only a week or so,' Baldwin said. 'Now, Margaret, do not fret, and don't think of moving from here yet. Leave it to me, and I shall let you know the best thing to do.'

'But I have already decided to leave Lydford and return to Sandford. It is more sensible. It is safer there, and nearer to you.'

'That itself does make sense,' Baldwin muttered.

Another horse clattered over the cobbles, and Simon crossed to Baldwin's side. 'I can't leave you to go alone, Baldwin.'

'In heaven's name,' Baldwin cried. 'Is there anybody else? Do you want to bring your chickens, too?'

'You are both determined?' Jeanne said, looking from one to the other. 'Is there nothing that your wives can say to you both that would cause you to reconsider? Not our sorrow, nor our fears? How safe will Margaret be here if you go away, Simon? How safe will I be, if Baldwin's gone from his home?'

That was also in Baldwin's mind. He sat on his horse a moment, considering. 'Simon, could you have Hugh travel? Good. Then let him accompany Margaret and Jeanne along with Edgar. Your Peterkin will go with them, as well as any valuables, and Edgar will deposit them at my house. They will be safe enough at Furnshill, won't they, Edgar?'

'Aye. Especially if I can recruit a couple of men from the vill.'

'Then it is settled. Margaret, you are to bring your boy to Furnshill, where you will have a peaceful time. Meanwhile, I should install someone else here in your house, someone who can defend it,' Baldwin continued.

Simon grinned. 'There is another bailiff from the moors who'd like the chance to live here: Ham Upcott. I'll ask him to come. He'd enjoy beating up a king's officer or a man from Despenser.'

'Make sure he realises the sort of men we're talking of, Simon,' Baldwin warned. 'These are harder men than many about here.'

'Christ's cods – do you really think so?' Simon asked. 'You've forgotten what sort of men they are who mine for tin on the moors. I'd have more sympathy for the next poor fool Despenser sends down here, than for a moorland bailiff.'

*Vigil of Ascension Day*[1]

### Guildford

Jack's worst fears were not realised.

To his amazement, the men who were with the King were so efficient and organised that every day, the majority of the

---

[1] Wednesday, 15 May 1325

men set off before dawn, and the next lodgings were always ready before they stopped travelling. This meant that they were outpacing Jack and the Bishop's journey from Canterbury to Beaulieu, which was only helped by the fact that the roads were much better here. The King was often about this part of his realm, Jack assumed, and the Keepers of the King's Peace maintained the roads and verges with more care than elsewhere in the country.

'Are you all right?'

Thomas was at his side, riding along with a fixed expression of distaste on his face every time he caught sight of the Despenser or his men. 'I am fine.'

It was fortunate that Jack had possessed two blankets, for having seen what Despenser had done to Thomas's own, he was able to share one of his. It did mean he grew a little chilly on some of the evenings, but for the most part he was fine, and it was good to feel that he had performed an act of kindness. A strange feeling, but curiously warming to the soul. 'You should try not to keep staring at him.'

'Despenser? Why not? He ravaged my belongings, accused me of murder, suggested I stole the King's possessions, and you think I should forgive and forget?'

'Neither. But I do recommend that you leave him alone. He's too powerful, too rich, for you to think of hurting him.'

'Perhaps so – but I can dream!'

'Save your dreams for the night. You don't want to fall from your horse.'

'No. And thank you.'

'What for?'

'For helping to keep me sane. Without you helping me, I daresay I would have tried to jump on him and kill him. And that wouldn't help me a great deal.'

'It would be one way of ending all your wordly problems,' Jack said with ponderous humour.

'I'd rather find another means of resolving them.'

'Good. Now, since he says you stole a possession from the King – can you tell me what this was supposed to be?'

'There is a phial of oil at Canterbury – or was. It was given by St Thomas, they say, to help our King.'

'So it was that? I heard about the robbery – it was the week before I got to Canterbury with the Bishop. Who would want to steal it?' Jack asked.

'Only someone who intends the King harm. Or someone who wants to do someone else good, I suppose.'

'If this is holy oil from St Thomas, then it must be marvellous indeed, and very potent.'

'I believe so. But since it's been stolen, we may never know.'

'Why does he say you stole it?'

'I happened to be there at the priory a few days before the theft.'

'So were many, I daresay. That's no reason to accuse you.'

'Yes. I don't know why he thinks I may have taken it. I can't see any reason to.'

'You don't hate the King, then?' Jack said lightly, but regretted his words as soon as he spoke them. 'Ignore my words. I sound like a cheap spy trying to have you confess to treason just so I can have you arrested.'

'It is all right. No, I don't hate the King. And I love our Queen. Those two I would do much for.'

'But not Despenser, eh?'

'Him, I would not piss on him if he was on fire,' Thomas said, and in his mind's eye he saw that cruel, arrogant face once more, spitting at the ground after he had cuffed Thomas for reaching to his dying brother during the coronation.

If he could, he would happily kill any number of Despenser's men – and Despenser himself, if he had the chance.

It was late that night, when Thomas had rolled himself up in his blanket and cloak to keep the night chill off, sharing some straw for his bedding with a number of other men and some rats, that he suddenly woke.

He was not usually good at waking up. To him early mornings were a form of unpleasant torture that must perforce be endured, rather than enjoyed. But this time he woke with a start as though suddenly hearing the last trumpet.

It was no trumpet, though. Perhaps a rat had scrabbled past, too close to ignore, too fast to see? Or was it a random thought, something which had sparked like flint and steel in his brain and made him wake?

He was aware of the talk he had had with Jack earlier in the day, and suddenly he felt a wariness. Jack had said that he sounded like a spy, and in truth, yes, he did. It was precisely the kind of conversation which a spy would have had with a man, letting his words ramble on until enough had been said and the spy could denounce him.

But it did not seem right with Jack. Jack had been so helpful, so friendly, that he surely couldn't be involved with Despenser.

He *couldn't* be.

### Near Sherborne, Dorset

Simon could not help but keep casting sidelong glances at Baldwin all the way as they rode, Wolf reluctantly loping along behind them.

They had made good time so far. Two days ago, after Baldwin had stated his desire to hurry, their little party had reached Okehampton by evening. Yesterday they had reached Furnshill fairly early, and then Simon and Baldwin carried on at a more urgent pace, and to Simon's surprise they reached the old town of Ilminster. With luck today they might get as far as Shaftsbury, and tomorrow, perhaps, they would get to Winchester, although Baldwin had already said that they would be best served by making sure that they reached Stockbridge and then letting their mounts have a good rest.

Baldwin had been a good friend for so long now that Simon could hardly remember a time when they had not been companions. It was nearly ten years ago when they first met, over the fire at the little vill. They had discovered a band of trail bastons, 'club men' who were ravaging the countryside and killing wantonly. There were so many men who took to violence in those terrible days. The famine was hitting everybody hard, and there were starving families all over the country. Although Devon was not so badly affected as some regions, that only meant that there was an incentive to foreigners from up-country – Somerset and Wiltshire and beyond – to travel to Devon to steal what they could. That was what it felt like at the time, anyway.

Simon had been new to his elevated position as bailiff. It had been largely due to Baldwin's help that he had caught the trail bastons and firmly secured himself to his post at Lydford. How ironic it would be if he was now to lose everything because of his friendship with Baldwin.

'I don't know that this is the best thing to do, Baldwin,' he said at last. 'Despenser is an irrational creature. He knows that you and I are thorns in his flesh. What if he decides that the best way to remove us both is to have us murdered?'

'If he were likely to reach that conclusion, and thought he might get away with it,' Baldwin said, 'he would already have done so. No, he is a shrewd and cunning man. If there was merit in killing us, he would have sent that man Wattere with more men and killed you as soon as possible. But he did not. All he did in truth was send you warning that he intended to deal with you at some time in the future.'

'True enough, but if he finds that we've followed him to London, won't he think that we're just growing too annoying to be supported? He'd rather just remove us.'

'So you think you'd be best served by remaining at home and hiding?'

Simon wanted to make a sharp rejoinder, but instead he looked away. The idea of running from any man was repugnant to him, but there were some situations which deserved caution, and this was one such. The man Despenser was the most dangerous in the whole country. He had money, men, and the ear of the King. 'Running away has never been part of my character.'

'Nor mine. You could run away from him, Simon, but if you do, you will be forced to run for ever. Yes, if you were to sell the house in Lydford and return to Sandford, he would be thwarted for a little while, but he'd soon find you. He has spies all over the country. But it's not you he wants, I don't think. I hope I do not suffer from unjustified arrogance when I say that I think he is more concerned about me.'

'So what do you intend to do?'

Baldwin gave a twisted grin. 'I *hope* to have a chance to have a frank talk with him. I have never sought to be thrown into politics. At every possible opportunity I have tried to avoid it. And he may not realise that, nor that I have done all in my power to keep away from him. It is not that I mean to harm his interests, only that I have barged into his affairs wherever I have gone. He is strangely ubiquitous.'

'And then, because you have always seen that his affairs tend to be unjust and unfair to the others who are affected, that is the only reason you have deliberately thwarted him?' Simon said. 'I don't think that is entirely the right way to convince him to leave you alone, Baldwin!'

'Perhaps not. But I would have an accommodation with him if it were possible. I do not wish to live with a permanent fear of him, dreading what he may do to Jeanne or the children; nor what he might do to you and your family. That is unbearable. So if I am forced, I will beg of him that he leaves me in peace.'

'Beg?'

'For the peace of my family and yours, yes I would beg,' Baldwin said firmly.

'Well, if we are to endure such an unpleasant experience, let's get it over with,' Simon said.

'Yes. If only we had something we could use against him,' Baldwin said. 'I would feel much happier entering negotiations with him knowing that I had something more than begging as a last resort.'

'I think you will have to wish for that.'

'Yes . . . and yet we did wonder about the oil, didn't we? The oil stolen from the King.'

'Yes. And we agreed to avoid Despenser.'

'We would be happy to do so, Simon, if only he had left us alone. But when we considered the murder and the theft of the oil, you were asking me about the dead man in the woods, weren't you? Do you remember, I said that perhaps the killer of that man was the same as the murderer of Gilbert at the priory? The man killed Gilbert, stole the oil, and took to horse through the woods towards the King. He met with a man in the woods, and sought to . . .'

'Sought to what?' Simon demanded irritably.

'I just had a most curious thought,' Baldwin said. 'What if he sought to conceal his identity by throwing his tabard on to the dead man he saw at the side of the road?'

'How would that work? Unless he was a herald himself, of course,' Simon scoffed, and then frowned.

'Yes, it would make sense, wouldn't it? A man who was dressed as a herald would know that a king's herald would be sought for the murder of Gilbert, so as soon as he could, he threw aside that uniform. From that moment he would be seen as an innocent when it came to the murder. People would seek a man in that tabard, and failing that, they would assume the murderer was dead. They wouldn't know who to seek.'

Simon frowned. 'But they would still search for the murderer of the herald.'

'Perhaps so. But it would be some local man, not a fellow from the King's household, wouldn't it? So they would hardly realise who it was they questioned. And in fact, so long as the *murdrum* fine was paid, there would be little need for them to investigate further. The coroner and King would be content so long as the money was in the King's coffers.'

'So the herald killed a stranger, and then ran into the woods with his oil?'

'It is one possibility. I say no more than that.'

'Then we need to consider who had a desire for the oil.'

Baldwin nodded. 'And we already considered that, didn't we? We both felt it was likely that only one man would have dared such a bold theft.'

'But why should Despenser want the oil?' Simon said. 'It

makes no sense. He could not hope to be crowned, so the oil would have no benefit to him.'

'The only advantage it might hold would lie in the properties of the oil itself. Perhaps he thought that such a blessed unguent might help him?' Baldwin guessed. 'Or the alternative would be that he sought to hold on to it until the King's need became overwhelming, and then intended to blackmail the King.'

'Would he dare?'

'There is little Despenser would not dare, given his appalling arrogance and greed,' Baldwin said flatly. 'But there is another possibility, of course. Perhaps he wanted it solely so that he could ask the King to have it used urgently now, to give him the sort of aid his reign requires.'

'And to do so, he was prepared to see a monk murdered. Hardly the way to ingratiate the King with God,' Simon said with contempt.

'Despenser's mind works in very strange ways,' Baldwin agreed.

# Chapter Twenty-Seven

*First Monday after Ascension Day*[1]

### *Thorney Island, Westminster*

William Wattere was not happy to be here in the Bishop's entourage. He had not actually been bound during the journey, but at all times the Bishop had two powerful men at his side, and it was clear enough that a severe bump on the head was the minimum he could expect, were he to try to escape.

The journey had been slow, too. That would not endear him to his master. Christ's cods, the last thing he needed just now was to upset Despenser, when he had failed in his main task at the bastard bailiff's house in Devon. Not much he could do about it, though. The bailiff had snatched him up with skill, and then having him confess while in front of the Bishop had been something he could almost admire, were it not for the fact that he could have happily cut out the bailiff's liver and eaten it raw for making him seem a fool. He'd have that bastard. His arm still smarted badly from the cut the man had given him. It had been washed extensively by the Bishop's men, but it still stung, and although it hadn't gone sour and sweet-smelling, it was painful while riding. The skin seemed

---

to have tightened, and gripping the reins made it stretch, which hurt like hell.

The pain was not helped by the reflection that he was daily coming closer to his master, to whom he would have to explain his failure. Approaching Westminster made him feel deeply uncomfortable.

At the entrance to the palace itself, he felt the weight of the gatehouse over his head like a threat, and just inside, when the Bishop ordered that he dismount, he was tempted to disobey and bolt for it, but he knew that it would not save him even if he tried it.

No, he would have to accept what fate had in store.

Simon and Baldwin had been here for over a day already. They had managed to make excellent time from Stockbridge, and were here in Westminster late on the Saturday. However, both were very tired, and now they sat outside the tavern by the gate, watching Wattere and the Bishop.

'Come, Simon. Let us go and reintroduce ourselves to our friend,' Baldwin said.

Simon flexed the muscles of his hand, feeling the stinging where Wattere's blade had cut into his palm. 'I'd like to do that.'

They stood and began to make their way over the great court, but before they could reach the Bishop's party, another group arrived. A man rode out in front, a knight, from the look of him. Then came several others, all well-mounted on dexters, and a man on a palfrey who looked considerably less martial.

As Baldwin and Simon stood back hurriedly, the party swept past them in a rush of dust and hot air. The horses puffed and blew, one neighing, while carts and a wagon clattered in through the gates, and it was only when all was still, the horses stamping, that Simon saw the flag.

'The King's son,' he said.

Richard of Bury eased himself from the saddle with some care, feeling the hideous soreness, and settled himself on the ground with that caution that only men who have experienced piles while needing to ride a horse could possibly understand.

'Thanks to Christ!' he murmured as he sighed with relief. The pain of that journey had been hideous, although, if he had to be honest, it could have been worse. Fortunately, his young charge was kind to him, and had not forced the pace at all. And there was plenty of time before they had to be here, so it wasn't as though there was a need for urgency. No, but for all that, the saddle did mean that his backside felt as though someone had taken to rubbing sand and salt into his arse, and that was not a happy sensation.

The Earl himself, of course, had the constitution of an ox, while his arse was as solid as a block of oak. As much sense in it as in most men's heads, too, he added to himself bitterly. But there was no need to be foolish. He was just a young lad who was perfectly used to travel, and to riding his horses. He took the damn things out every day. At least he was comfortable just now. It would mean that Richard would have an easier evening. Which was good, because Bury intended an early night, involving something along the lines of three jugs of good wine . . .

'Master?'

'What? Who are you, and what do you want?'

'I am called Sir Baldwin de Furnshill, Master. And what are you called?'

'Don't be impertinent, Sir Knight. I am the tutor to the Earl of Chester, by the grace of God. I asked you what your business was?'

'And I, in return, ask politely that you stop being such a rude person and instead treat your betters with the respect which they are due,' Baldwin said, and his smile held that strange quality which Simon had seen before, of being a smile with the bottom teeth only. It reminded him of a story he had once heard of a beast abroad, a great reptile, with an enormous jaw studded with many teeth, and which appeared to smile all the time – until a man approached too close and realised his error.

'Um, Baldwin, perhaps you should—'

'I wish to pass on a message to the Earl of Chester,' Baldwin said.

'You can speak to me. You are Sir Baldwin, you say?'

Simon felt his heart plummet. Behind him came the clear voice, as yet unbroken, of a boy of tender years. Boys of that age could be capricious, dangerous, and when as powerful as this Earl of Chester, the first in line to the throne, they were still more lethal. Simon glowered at his friend, but Baldwin appeared oblivious.

'I am honoured to meet you, my Lord,' he said, bowing low as he would to the King. 'I have a message for you from Her Royal Highness, your mother.'

'You have seen my mother?' The Earl's excitement was unfeigned and so eager was he, that Simon forgot his fear of upsetting the boy. He sounded so much like other lads he had heard in his home town when they had news of long-departed fathers.

The Earl of Chester was an extraordinarily good-looking boy, he saw. Fair-haired, with his hair held long, much like his father, he had the ease in the saddle of a man who spent much of his time hunting. He was quite powerfully built, too, with the shoulders and neck of a lad much older. It must be due to all his practising with sword and lance, Simon told himself. It had paid off well. Already, although the lad was very young, Simon could see that he would be a dangerous opponent.

Now, though, his blue eyes were fixed on Baldwin with a strange intensity. He was much like an older man in that, too. Simon would get to realise that this fellow would concentrate on a man like a philosopher on an abstruse concept, reading and rereading the person until he felt he understood him. Perhaps living in a household with two strong, powerful, but sadly out of love and opposed parents would do that to a boy. He would feel a great urge to understand people.

'Speak, sir!'

Baldwin nodded. 'Your mother asked us to say that she hopes you are strong and healthy, that you remember your lessons, and that you pray for her with as much affection and love as she uses when praying for you. She said to say that she misses you sorely, and that she is desperate to see you again. She said to send you her love.'

The Earl smiled and the tension seemed to leave him in an instant. 'I knew that she would not have forgotten me. When you return to her, please tell her from me that—'

'My Lord, I fear we are not returning to Paris,' Baldwin said hurriedly. 'We have spent too much time away from our lands already. We have wives, and cannot leave them any longer.'

'Lands? Do you not have stewards? And wives? My retainers all have to leave them behind. It is a part of service. No, when you return to her, I shall have a message for you to take. For now, though, you may leave me.'

And thus dismissed by the haughty Earl, Baldwin and Simon bowed and retreated before he could issue any more commands.

* * *

'That was a happy experience,' Simon said sarcastically.

'Simon, what would you have had me do? Pretend that there was no message? What, then, when she returns and asks why he did not reply? We should have been in serious trouble, wouldn't we?'

'In God's name, though . . . you don't think he will send us back, do you?'

'There is every possibility of it, I fear.'

'Dear God! How can we escape it?'

Baldwin looked at him with slow deliberation as they paused at the door to the tavern at the gate once more. There was an enormity of shock in his eyes, like a man who bent to stroke a small lap-dog, only to be bitten by the mastiff behind. 'All I did was pass on her message.'

'You had best start thinking about how we can avoid this, Baldwin. We cannot run from our wives again,' Simon said seriously, as he thought of the man released from the Bishop's gaol. 'Let's have a quick drink to stiffen the sinews, and then find the Bishop and ask his advice.'

'Advice?' Baldwin said doubtfully.

'He knows politics and he knows Despenser. Who else can we turn to?'

Wattere had seen the two approaching, and had hurriedly slipped away, leaving the Bishop's horse with a groom and moving swiftly along the courtyard to the gate which took him past the great hall, and down to the side door. Outside it, he found a guard who recognised him and was able to point him in the direction of the small chamber where Sir Hugh le Despenser was working.

Despenser was standing at his table, barking questions at

his clerks. He did not turn as Wattere opened the door, plainly assuming that whoever could have entered his chamber was little threat to him. However, one of the clerks did make a gesture towards him, and suddenly his master turned to face him. An eyebrow rose in sardonic amusement at the sight of him.

'So you didn't enjoy your stay at the Bishop's pleasure?'

'He kept me in his gaol! Like a common thief!'

'When you are nothing of the sort, are you? There is little common about you, my friend. You are a very special form of thief.'

Wattere said nothing, but watched Despenser coolly.

'Did you manage to evict that bailiff? No. Did you upset the knight? No again. You do not strike me as a particularly successful functionary.'

'I did do well at first, but I didn't expect the knight to arrive with the bailiff, and both with other men too. I had expected the man to back down quickly. Men usually do when they know that they are against you, my Lord.'

'Yes. They do. But it's dangerous to make assumptions about men like them. They can be fairly ruthless. What have you done to your hand?'

'It was the bailiff. He caught me. A lucky strike.'

'Heavens, he has been fortunate, hasn't he? What a lucky fellow,' Despenser said. Then he took a swift pace forward and leaned in close. 'And you are not, are you? Once you were lucky, but now, clearly, you are not. I think I have no need for fools who can't obey a simple order and then get themselves caught. Jesus, you even gave them your ballocks, didn't you? You let them bring in my Lord Bishop Walter to hear your confession!'

'That means nothing now, though.'

'Doesn't it? Oh, so you think that you can fight them here, and outwit them? When the good bishop is here too, and can vouch for them and denounce you? Do you think that would be a good idea?'

'I think—'

'I don't *care* what you *think*!' Despenser spat. 'Get out of my sight. I may find a use for you, but for now, you had best avoid me, fool. I'll call you when the privy needs to be emptied.'

William Wattere nodded and left the room quietly. He felt entirely crushed. In the past he had always been highly regarded as efficient and now he was close to losing his post in his master's household.

And his forearm was still stinging.

Despenser was often accused by the King of being a marvellous actor, of being able to feign almost any emotion at will, but he was not acting today. He was consumed with anger at the way the fool Wattere had let himself be captured, especially since his gaoler was the Bishop upon whom he most depended just now. The state required that he and Stapledon work together effectively.

'Get out!' he snapped at the two clerks, and aimed a kick at the slower of the two as they hurriedly scurried from the room.

He walked to the table again and leaned on both hands, his elbows locked, staring down at the boards.

'Too many problems, too many problems,' he told himself quietly, still simmering gently after his meeting with Wattere.

It was not only that bailiff Puttock and the knight. He had too much to consider, what with the issue of the Queen and what she might be doing abroad, the rebel Mortimer and what he was up to, the Scots, and now this matter about the oil. He still had no idea what had happened to it, but he needed it for the King and the bolstering of the King's reign.

Sweet Jesus! He had to clear his brain and resolve one issue at a time! There was no time for this prevarication. Complaining about the perils of his position was pointless. And pathetic. It was not the action of a man. Resolve the problems one by one, he told himself.

Arriving here, he had been passed a message from one of his men. The outlaws had been tracked down in the woods near where the body of the herald had been found. On the local keeper's command, they had been cut down, almost to a man, and even though the survivors were questioned carefully before they were hanged, none knew anything at all about a man in king's tunic who had been killed. Two had been able to walk, and had been taken to the spot where the body still lay, in the hope that they might recognise the location if not the corpse, but both denied all knowledge. There were some who would do that in the hope of life, but these two had no such false expectations. They knew that they would soon die.

No, if he had to guess, he would say that neither was involved in the death of Richard de Yatton. In which case, who was? And where was the King's oil?

Despenser clenched his fists and slammed both down on the table. 'Damn the bastard!'

He would find this thief, and when he did, he'd have the man paunched like a rabbit for putting him to all this trouble. Soon the King would be demanding to know what he had discovered, and being forced to admit that he had learned little was not good for his reputation nor his temper.

# Chapter Twenty-Eight

Jack was content with his own actions. There were some men whom he could not like, no matter what happened. It was irrational, certainly, but there were just some fellows who made him angry. And just as ridiculously, there were some who appeared not to deserve any interest at all, with whom he suddenly found himself fascinated.

This fellow Thomas was a perfect example. All he knew of Tom when he left Beaulieu was that the man was the brother of John of Bakewell, who had died in the abbey over there during the King's coronation. Jack had heard that from the man himself. He was not concealing the fact, nor anything else, as far as Jack could tell. And yet Despenser had decided that Tom was interesting in some way. That could only mean that Despenser had some notion that the man had something of value. All knew Despenser's reputation, and he wouldn't put himself out unless there was something in it.

Not that Jack had any more idea what it might be than Tom. Both had discussed Despenser and his attack on Tom over evenings beside the fire, and yet they could not reach a conclusion. Jack wondered whether it could be something to do with the murder of the monk and the theft of the King's oil. According to the herald, Despenser had asked about the oil and Canterbury. It made Jack interested.

What business such affairs were of Despenser's, Jack didn't

know. Such things weren't really any concern of his, and he preferred to keep out of the way of the rich and powerful like the Despenser. Still, he didn't want to see a man like Tom die just because the fellow had been unlucky enough to be distrusted by Despenser. That was just plain unfair.

But life was unfair, of course.

Baldwin and Simon walked the short distance to the Exchequer, where they could see Bishop Stapledon chatting with a clerk.

'Ah, Sir Baldwin, and Simon,' he said. 'I am glad you arrived safely.'

'It is a journey we are growing accustomed to,' Simon said, adding, 'Sadly.'

'Simon means, we're not happy to be parted from our wives again,' Baldwin said.

'But you weren't called to be a part of the council, were you? It's not a parliament,' the Bishop said.

'No. We're here because we were keen to avoid any more unpleasantness with Despenser,' Simon said.

Stapledon gave a quick frown and shot a look at Baldwin, before walking from the hall and motioning to them both to follow him. 'Simon, you must realise that language like that is exceedingly dangerous. Especially here, where you are effectively in his power base. You must not challenge a man like Despenser. And language like that is bound to be viewed by him as a challenge.'

'He has tried to force me from my own house, Walter,' Simon pointed out. 'He petrified my wife, and then sent his henchman to my hall to threaten me!'

'That is so, and I have already spoken to him and made it clear that I do not expect to hear of any more attempts on your property or life. I think he appreciates that it would be counter to his wishes to do it again.'

'You think he'd back off that easily?' Baldwin said.

'I think that he did what he did to upset *you*, Baldwin. He doesn't care about one property in Lydford. If he thought he could take over the whole town, that would be different. He would devote hours and many men to an adventure like that. He stole swathes of land from other lords to consolidate his Welsh lands, didn't he? He rules the whole of the south of Wales now as a private fiefdom. But one house? No. He did that to annoy you, Baldwin, more than anything else.'

'But why?' Baldwin said, genuinely puzzled. 'I have done little to him, in truth. If he wanted to harm me, I could perhaps understand that, but why try to distract me with Simon?'

'As punishment for something you have done to him? I don't know. In any case, while you both live within my see, I think he will leave you alone. If for no other reason than that he has other matters to concern him. As have we all,' he added almost as an afterthought.

'We just saw the King's son,' Simon said.

'Oh, the Earl of Chester is here? That is good. Then we may begin to plan matters from here.'

'What is in the offing?' Baldwin asked.

'The King is waiting to hear back from France on the state of negotiations. After the meetings here, he intends to send another embassy to the French with some suggestions. I think the French will insist, since they have the upper hand, but you never know. We won't, anyway, until we receive a response. And then the King also wants to send a message to the Pope by the Bishop of Orange, pointing out the unfairness of this situation. He is justified, certainly.'

'Will it work?' Simon asked. 'Would the Pope actually take his side in an argument against the French?'

'No,' the Bishop said bluntly. 'But that won't stop him trying. Meanwhile, we are forced to rely on the King's wife.'

There was an eloquent pause after that. Baldwin himself wanted to wince to hear the Queen referred to in such a manner. From all he had seen of her, she was a perfectly responsible, dutiful wife. Certainly she had earned the love of her son, and Baldwin knew that many of her staff idolised her, and would hear no bad word against her. A woman who could inspire such adoration was not deserving of the Bishop's ire.

'She should be back before long, I suppose?' he said after a moment.

'Yes. Depending upon the negotiations over there, she could be home again within the month,' Stapledon said.

'Her son will be pleased to know that,' Simon said.

'Perhaps so. For the rest of us, her return will make matters more complicated, though. What is the King to do with her?'

'Live with his wife as a man should,' Baldwin said quietly. 'And throw Despenser to the dogs.'

'You think the King could govern on his own, while maintaining the peace of his realm?' Stapledon hissed. 'Baldwin, if Despenser goes, either the Queen will be controlling the government of the realm, assuming she and the King can make some kind of compact, or another baron like Despenser. Which would *you* trust to be in charge?'

'Bishop, you may be right. But if it is another baron, at least there is a chance that he will be better than Despenser, and the Queen would undoubtedly be a great improvement. Do not forget, this is the man who just last week sent a man to petrify Simon's wife. Do you honestly think that he could be better than *anyone* else?'

\*　\*　\*

Joseph arrived in Westminster late in the day, and the only thing on his mind, when he had at last delivered his messages to the King's clerks, was to find a goodly jug of wine and sink it quickly.

The court of the palace yard here was as full and loud as ever. There was something about Westminster and the King's palace which gave the place the air of a bear garden when the betting had been particularly high. It was always frenetic, there was the sound of women laughing, men shouting, calls offering food, quieter voices murmuring suggestively, and all over it, the noise of people making deals. Some making little bargains for drinks or sex, while others, the quieter ones, were trying to decide issues of law. There were many of them.

Joseph walked around to the inn at the gates and bought himself a pint of wine, which he didn't take long to drink. The second pint was a little slower going down, and he took himself off to a rough stool to watch the passers-by as he drank it.

The last time he had been to the palace, all the heralds and messengers had been here with the King. He had been holding a parliament, and the men were all being prepared to take the reports and commissions to every sheriff in the country. There had been some fun then! All the cursores and nuncii had held competitions to see who could sing the loudest, who could run fastest – all the way to the Temple Bar and back – while others merely gambled and played and drank.

That, he realised, was when he had last seen Richard de Yatton. Yatton and a few heralds had joined them for the fun, and afterwards there had been repercussions. He didn't know who it was now, but two of the lads had got into a dispute of some sort, and the upshot of it was that some damage had been done to the King's own property. Some hangings in a wagon or something. Anyway, Joseph and all the others had been called into a little chamber, where they were discussing what they would all say to each other.

'If you say that we were at the tavern but left early, I'll back you up,' one had whispered to Joseph.

'Yes. What we have to do is back each other up. We will all stick together,' another had told him.

'We can't be shaken. If we all stay together, we'll be all right.'

'We can all speak for each other,' the first had nodded.

'But we won't, will we?' Richard had said, smiling. 'As soon as we go in there, we're going to do anything we can to cover our own arses.'

It was the truth, of course. But after so much effort trying to convince each other that they would stand by their friends and even their enemies, it was Richard's honest simplicity that Joseph remembered. It was a shame he was gone. Joseph hadn't known him very well, but he thought Richard had a strangely appealing straightforwardness.

He was still enjoying the warmth which the harsh Guyennois wine spread from his fingers to his toes, when he saw the Bishop of Orange.

The Bishop was walking about with his usual expression of mild absent-minded enquiry, but Joseph was not fooled. The man had one of the brightest brains in the Church, he reckoned. The Bishop was one of those in whom the Pope himself placed a great deal of trust. He was intelligent, shrewd, and was effective as a collector of information. All of which made him a most useful tool for the Pope.

But not a friend for other men. And Joseph had no desire to see him. Not now. The last time he had seen the Bishop was at the body of poor Richard.

He would never forget that day, he reckoned. Seeing poor Richard lying there, and then the lovely woman who looked so nervous at the fringe of the wood, and her man with her . . .

Suddenly he felt his belly lurch with something akin to horror. The *woman*! Of course! She'd been so nervous. And her man had disappeared when he arrived!

Her man must have been the killer of Richard de Yatton.

Simon was about to sip again at his wine, when a man walked past him, and he idly looked the fellow over.

It was a routine thing for him. Every time he saw a new face, he would try to commit the face and any recognisable features to memory. Not because the man was a felon, but because he was keen to know all those who worked on his moors. And now he had no moors to patrol, the habit was so deeply entrenched that he could not help himself from doing it.

His eyes passed over the man's long hair, down to his parti-coloured blue and blue-striped hosen, over the tabard with the King's insignia, and on – and then back. He looked at the King's sign more closely, peering with a fixed frown on his face, before sitting back and considering.

'What is it, Simon?' Baldwin asked, noticing his pensiveness.

'I was wondering. When the King's herald was killed, he died on the road between Christ Church and Beaulieu.'

'Yes. And also in-between many other towns.'

'Aye, but it was still between those two. When we spoke to Prior Eastry at Canterbury, he said that the man who killed the monk and stole the oil was seen going west, too. Going in that same direction. So we assumed he was a genuine king's herald.'

'Yes.'

'But there are others who wear the tabard, aren't there? Not all are heralds.'

'True. So what?'

'Well,' Simon said, waving a hand expansively about the yard before them. 'Whoever he is, and whatever he is, if he's a King's man of any sort, the chances are, he's here somewhere.'

Baldwin gave a slow nod. It was a thought which should have already occurred to him, but he had so effectively erased that murder and robbery from his mind that he had not considered it for days. He looked about him now, and it struck him how out of place he and Simon were. They were country folk, unused to so much display and boastfulness. All about them men were talking about their prowess in one field or another, usually with little regard for the truth. To Baldwin, the scene was familiar, but somehow skewed. He was accustomed to the ways of great courts from his time in the Knights Templar. More recently, his experiences at the courts at Exeter had helped form his opinion that more good justice was handed down locally than at the King's courts, no matter what they were labelled. There was less posturing, less jockeying for position in the local courts.

Here, though, the place reeked of ambition. Men would trade their souls for a little of the power that resided here in the King's hands. It made Baldwin suddenly realise why it was that men would go to war. Oh, some no doubt actually believed in the causes espoused by their leaders, but more, he felt sure, were driven either by an immediate desire for money, or by an urge to show themselves to the King. So many would do foolish things in order to be noticed, in the hope of winning that coveted trophy of knighthood, or perhaps in the hope of a reward of lands or money later. All would risk much in order to achieve something that was in essence trivial. But they thought it worth dying for.

And men came here to serve the King from all over the country in the hope that he might see them and be impressed. Impressed enough to reward them.

A man might, just might, come here and present the King with a gift, he thought. That would be a knightly way to be noticed, arriving here with a small phial that contained holy oil from St Thomas.

'You're wanted,' the man said.

Baldwin eyed him with an expression of blank disapproval. The fellow was dressed like a Welsh shepherd, with long hosen under a rough tunic of some cheap material that looked almost like fustian. He wore a thick, quilted linen jack, with a leather cotte over the top, and a green cloak about his shoulders. Although quite tall for a Welshman, he was not so tall as Baldwin, not that it mattered. The fact that there were three of his companions behind him, two with staffs in their hands, was more than enough reason for Baldwin to avoid an altercation.

'By whom?'

'My Lord Despenser.'

'The Earl of Winchester?'

'His son.'

'Oh, so you mean *Sir* Hugh.'

'I mean my master.'

'And he told you we would be here?'

'Yes.'

'Fascinating, Simon. Sir Hugh takes such a keen interest in our well-being, that he sends his own men to guard us on the way to his side.'

The journey was only short. Earlier in the year, Simon had been mouth agape at the sight of the hall with its fabulously decorated ceilings, the richly coloured walls, the huge desks at which so many courts were sitting – but not now. He was here with very specific business, and he was nervous about the outcome. The idea that the whole of his life's safety depended upon the next half-hour or so had not escaped him. Even as he marched alongside Baldwin towards the Despenser's rooms, he felt a grim certainty settle upon his soul that there was nothing he could do against a man who was so recklessly powerful.

'In here,' the man said, pointing to a door.

'You first,' Baldwin said.

The Welshman sneered, as though the idea that he might try to capture the knight here in the King's palace was so laughable that only a man scared of his own shadow might succumb to it, but he walked inside nonetheless.

'Sir Baldwin's here, Sir Hugh.'

Baldwin walked inside, Simon wary at his back, and the door was closed quietly behind them.

Before them was a small chamber, richly decorated. On the wall were hangings of marvellous colour, depicting hunting scenes of various types. The floor had a thick layer of reeds, which added a rich aroma of hay to the room. At the further end was a long table, on which stood a chessboard, and Despenser stood over it, eyeing the board with an expression of extreme concentration.

'Welcome, Sir Baldwin. Bailiff. Come in and take a little wine with me.'

# Chapter Twenty-Nine

As he regarded Baldwin and Simon, Despenser decided that he must be cautious with these two. He turned back to the board.

It was plain enough that they were both intensely distrustful of him. The idea that he could mould them to his thinking was ridiculous, but there might be an angle which was exploitable, purely because of the assault by Wattere. It was worth a try, certainly, he thought.

'You badly hurt my man, Bailiff. He tells me you bested him twice.'

'He insulted my wife, and then tried to rob me. What would you have an Englishman do?'

'You have stood in my path once more.'

'I will stand in your path many times if you seek to despoil me,' Simon grated.

'Simon!' Baldwin said calmingly. 'Now, Sir Hugh, we do not take action against you lightly. However, clearly you anticipated just such a response to your man. You had a motive, and I do not believe that a man who spends so much time acquiring manors and estates would be interested in a small farm.'

'I do have rather more interesting lands already,' the Despenser said modestly.

'So what did you intend when you sent that man to Simon's house? Merely to upset him? Or was it to warn *me* away?'

'You have a high opinion of your importance,' Despenser said. He turned his attention from the board and gazed at Baldwin seriously.

'No, I do not. I do have a high opinion of your intelligence, though. You would not do something without good reason.'

'Perhaps. I feel honoured that you can be flattering, though.'

'It is not flattery. It is simple realism.'

'Very well, then. I shall be singularly honest in return. Yes, I had a motive. It was to persuade you that any further interference in my affairs would prove to be dangerous and painful to you. I did not, and do not, want you taking any further actions against me or my men.'

'That we can agree, Sir Hugh – provided that your actions do not have any bearing on members of our families or friends, and that you don't try to harm our own interests.'

Despenser tilted his head to one side. 'That does seem perfectly reasonable. Then we are agreed?'

'For my part, yes,' Baldwin said.

Simon remained standing, saying nothing.

'And you, good Bailiff?'

'I came here today thinking that I would be likely to be killed by your men for insulting you, and now I learn that you will leave us alone, so long as we do likewise. You'll excuse me, Sir Hugh, if I feel confused. Why would you agree to leave me alone so soon after attacking me in my own home?'

Despenser gave a slow smile. 'You are a shrewd man, Bailiff. Very well. Perhaps it is merely that, as adviser to the King, I have so many other matters to take up my time. There is much going on right now which makes demands on me. I cannot afford to waste it running around after impecunious bailiffs from the wilds of the West Country.'

'That is good.'

'However,' Despenser continued, strolling to the cupboard and filling himself a tankard, 'if you wanted to seal our new understanding, you could help me.'

'In what way?' Baldwin asked sharply.

'Nothing too stressful. I merely ask that you consider the matter of this stolen oil. You were at the priory shortly after the murder and robbery, I think. You perhaps spoke with some of the people involved there, so you would be well-placed to try to make some sense of it all. I confess, from the miles which lie between Beaulieu and Canterbury, I could make no sense of the affair.'

'You wish us to conduct an inquiry into the theft?' Baldwin said.

'Yes. And quickly. We need to have the oil back, if the King is to have any defence against the hordes which are arrayed against us.'

'What hordes?' Simon enquired.

'A host of men is being recruited even as we speak. I think that if the King doesn't get to France in the near future, the French will come to him.'

'But if we agree to hold an inquiry into the death of the monk and the oil which was taken, you will leave our homes and families in peace?' Baldwin said.

'Yes. Completely.'

'Then tell us everything you already know,' Baldwin said.

And so he did. After he had run through his investigations so far, he added, 'The man you found dead was called Richard de Yatton. He'd been up to Leeds Castle, near Maidstone, and should have been back at Beaulieu long before. I don't know what he was doing there on the road.'

'It is a question of whether or not he had anything to do with the murder,' Baldwin agreed.

'I heard that the killer was seen escaping, and that he wore a King's tabard,' Despenser said pointedly.

'Any man can pull on or take off a tabard,' Baldwin pointed out. 'And the body was so decomposed that it could have lain there a week or longer. A man may have killed him, knowing he was to pass by, taken his tabard, and then made his way to Canterbury. He killed the monk, then rode back and put the tabard on the dead herald, before making his escape. It is a possible explanation.'

'I see . . .'

'Another explanation, however, would be that the herald rode along that way, an outlaw saw him, slew him, dumped his body, and stole the little he possessed in ready money.'

'Yes,' Despenser grunted. He sighed. 'I suppose I should tell you that I believed the man Thomas had something to do with it. The friar, Nicholas, pointed him out to me, and I think he was acting oddly. But although I had my men search his belongings twice, there was no sign of the oil.'

'Is there anyone else you suspect?' Baldwin asked.

'My dear Knight – I suspect everyone. That is my job.'

Simon left the room in Baldwin's wake, feeling confused and angry.

The man had not apologised. He admitted that he was responsible for the violent threat against Margaret, that he had tried to evict Simon from the home he had possessed since he first took on the job as bailiff of the moors, and yet Despenser had the nerve to then demand Simon and Baldwin's aid.

'He would taunt the devil and then ask his advice,' he muttered.

Baldwin glanced at him, but continued on his way. 'Not here, Simon. There are too many men about here who would be keen to know your thoughts.'

It was not until they were outside again, that Baldwin stopped and looked about them carefully. 'You are unhappy with the arrangement?'

'The arrangement appears to be that we must work for him and hope that he will then prove trustworthy and honourable. When has he given that impression before?'

'Simon, he is not. However, there is another aspect to this which may have escaped you. He is asking us not to help him, but to help the King. If we question the King's men and investigate this affair, the King will get to learn of it. And then he is likely to ask us what success we have had. I am more of a fool than I realise if I do not manage to mention the fact of the persecution which you have endured. And if I then ask the King to help us, by refusing to allow Despenser to continue in his campaign against us, I am sure that he will do so. The King is an honourable man, and when he has given his word on a matter, he is likely to hold fast to it.'

Simon considered. 'I suppose that makes sense. However, it does not leave me any more content for now.'

'Of course it doesn't. But do not fret about it. We shall resolve the problem in one way or another. And now, Simon, we should think about how we may proceed.'

'Do you want to return to Christ Church?'

'I am not sure that it will be necessary,' Baldwin said with a frown as he began to wander slowly along the path to the main court.

'No,' Simon agreed. 'The man who killed the monk was probably wearing a tabard, and we know—'

'There are two factors we need to think about most deeply,

Simon,' Baldwin interrupted gently. 'We know as much as we are likely to about the matter of the dead monk, and we think that the killer may have passed by the woods and killed the man there.'

'The herald.'

'The man clad in a herald's tabard, yes. But what intrigues me about the whole matter is, who could have benefited from the theft of the oil? At first, I was happy to think that it was yet another scheme planned by Despenser himself, but that is clearly wrong, unless he is trying to confuse us entirely, because why should he ask us to look into it if he was himself responsible?'

'He may just be over-confident in his arrogance,' Simon said bitterly.

'I do not think so, Simon,' Baldwin said. 'I think that he has some healthy respect for our abilities as discoverers of unexpected secrets. No, I think we need to look elsewhere for motives.'

'Then who could have had a motive?'

'There is still the possibility that the affair was caused by a thief who knew the oil's value, and sought to use it to demand money from the King. However, I do not incline to it. No, I think it's more likely that it was someone who wanted to take it from the King to upset him.'

'Sir Roger Mortimer, then? He would surely be glad to do anything which would anger the King. They have such a loathing for each other now, I would have thought that the oil's disappearance would suit Mortimer very well.'

'Very true. Especially if Despenser is correct and there is a fleet massing ready to invade the country. Unsettling the King just at this moment would be ideal.'

'Who else?'

Baldwin shook his head. 'There must be someone, but I cannot . . . would the Queen wish to so irritate the King that she could instruct her allies to take the oil? It is possible . . .'

'But extremely unlikely. Would she appreciate the oil's importance?'

'Who would, Simon? I would not until a matter of a few weeks ago. I had heard of it; I vaguely recall someone telling me about it a long time ago, when it was first mentioned after the coronation, but that is all. I had thought that the King, like the barons, thought it was a fictitious oil.'

'It was brought for his coronation, though? Why wasn't it used?' Simon asked.

'No one truly believed in its provenance, I think. Nobody would have dared to withhold it otherwise. The barons would have wanted it to be used, and the King would have demanded it, naturally, if either had believed in it. The fact it went unused is proof enough that nobody thought it important. And that must mean no one believed in it.'

'Was no one interested enough to seek to validate the story?'

'I understand a friar sought to do just that a few years ago, but his attempt foundered. Even the Pope didn't trust the story.'

'So nobody believes in it. Apart from the King now.'

'And possibly Despenser,' Baldwin said.

'You think he does?'

'He certainly declares it.'

'I wouldn't take that as signifying anything,' Simon said. 'But Prior Eastry of Christ Church seems to believe in it too.'

'The Prior of Christ Church? I wonder. I believe he understands the danger of the stuff. Now it's been stolen from him it is more important to him than ever. The fact that he allowed it to be stolen is proof, I think, that he didn't value it terribly highly.'

'The French King would want to remove it.'

'Yes. He is another, with Mortimer, who could have a good motive to take it. And we know that he does have agents throughout England.'

'Why do you think he'd want it? What would he do with it?'

'Merely to deprive the King would be enough to make King Charles happy, I think. But then, perhaps, if he or another declared our King so feeble he couldn't even protect his oil, perhaps the French King would offer it to any man who would overthrow King Edward?'

Simon shrugged. 'So we have the French King and Mortimer.'

'Yes,' Baldwin said, but now his eyes held a faraway look in them.

'You are wondering about another?'

'I was merely reflecting on the great estates in the land,' Baldwin said. 'There are the barons, and many of them are extremely displeased with the way that the King submits to Despenser and allows the man great sway over the rule of the nation. Then there are the men of the Church, too. Some, like Walter, will support him, but his reign has been divisive. Many churchmen would be happy to see the King embarrassed.'

'Even at the expense of the nation?'

'This is all speculation,' Baldwin sighed. 'A man needs straw to make cob, but we have not even mud.'

'No. But at least we have one consolation,' Simon said. 'We do know that the King has a number of enemies. All we need to do is question those who could have been about when the monk and the herald were killed, and perhaps that will lead us to a motive too.'

It had better, he added to himself. The idea that they may fail was tearing at his mind. For if they failed to find out who had taken the oil, and where it was now, he was sure that no matter what Baldwin said about the King, Despenser would return to persecuting Simon and his wife.

*First Tuesday after Ascension Day*[1]

### Westminster Palace

Joseph was intrigued by the two men when he walked into the room, intrigued and nervous.

It was rare enough for any man to be offered the aid of Despenser, but these two had managed just that. This morning he had heard that Sir Hugh le Despenser had given a writ to this Keeper of the King's Peace and his companion, which gave them the right to question all the heralds and messengers urgently. That meant that they had considerable influence with Despenser, if not the King as well. And it meant that Joseph must be cautious. Any man close to Despenser was not a man who could be trusted. There was not a single King's messenger or herald who didn't know that.

But at least he felt he had some information he could give them which might help them.

'You wanted to see me?'

'Yes. You are a king's messenger, and you were sent to Christ Church, which is where we met you, in those woods?'

'I remember it,' he said quietly. 'The poor man.'

'Was that pathway very well known to all the messengers and heralds?'

'Well enough. When we pass along roads, we let others

---

[1] Tuesday, 21 May 1325

know if they have grown more dangerous recently, or if other trails have become safer and more swift. We have a duty to tell others if they can travel faster or more safely.'

'And that path was thought safe?'

'It was the last time I used it – which was that day when I met you on it. Now I use a different route.'

'So any of the messengers would know that a herald would have taken that path?' Simon said.

'Yes. We'd all have known Richard would have been there.'

'Richard?' Baldwin asked.

Joseph looked at him in surprise. 'He was Richard. de Yatton. Didn't you know? I heard you brought his necklace to Beaulieu.'

'I did.' Baldwin nodded. 'I think it was the metal you saw gleaming in among the leaves. You remember? You said you saw something glinting there, and that was what led you to discover the body there. But no one saw fit to tell me whose it was.'

'Oh, well, any man in the King's service should have recognised that necklace. Poor devil. His own mother wouldn't have recognised him as he lay there at the roadside. I certainly didn't.'

'Where was he going at the time?'

'I heard he was on his way from Leeds Castle back to Beaulieu.'

'He went to Leeds Castle straight from Beaulieu?'

'I don't know. I suppose so . . .'

'How would he have reacted to a stranger on the road?' Simon asked.

'Suspiciously, but not with fear. We tend to reckon that a man on the road will be less likely to affect us than some other poor traveller. No outlaw wants to court the enmity of the King, after all. It would make no sense.'

'So if he fell in with another traveller, he might well allow the man to get behind him?'

Joseph chuckled at the idea. 'No. I said he'd be suspicious, and I meant it. There are too many men who would like to get their hands on private correspondence. General outlaws are less of a threat, because no messenger or herald carries too much money with them, but that doesn't mean that there aren't enemies about. I doubt whether Richard would let anyone get too close to him. He'd be more keen to leave another traveller and go alone, than go with a man he didn't know.'

'Where were you in the week before we met you in those woods?' Baldwin asked bluntly.

'Me? Not far from there. I was sent to the King's son at Eltham, but had to deliver a note to the King's man in Rochester first, so I took the same route. He wasn't there then, so far as I know.'

'Was there anyone who had a dislike for Richard?' Baldwin wondered.

'No more so than any. He was very religious, so he tried to visit many shrines and chapels, which annoyed some of the men, but apart from that, he was a mild enough fellow. No, I don't think he irritated that many. There were more whom he'd have had reason to dislike, than could have formed a loathing for him.'

'Which means that he almost certainly did die as a result of some accidental meeting. Perhaps an outlaw?' Baldwin said.

'I think so,' Joseph said. And then he took a deep breath. 'Look, I had not thought of this before, but it occurred to me yesterday . . .' and he told them of his sudden suspicion of the peasant woman at the wood's edge.

'That could be the woman who told us about the outlaws in the area,' Baldwin said.

'She was very anxious, you thought?' Simon said.

'Yes.'

They questioned him in more detail, but there was little more for him to tell them. He left them soon afterwards, and Simon and Baldwin looked at each other once he was gone. Baldwin shrugged.

'He was there,' Simon noted. 'He felt no need to conceal the fact. He could have invented the story about the peasant woman.'

'But why would he kill Yatton? And how would he know Yatton had the oil on him?'

'Perhaps he didn't,' Simon guessed. 'The same goes for any other man who saw the herald and killed him, though.'

'That peasant woman. From the way he described her and her holding, it must have been the same place which we saw before entering the woods. And that woman was certainly worried, wasn't she?'

'Very worried.'

'But I just thought it was because she saw so large a mass of men entering her yard. If her tales were true, I thought she may have feared being set upon by outlaws.'

'Whereas Joseph thinks she knew who the killer was and reckoned we were the posse.'

'It would make more sense. I mean, the woman could hardly have thought a man like the Bishop was a drawlatch. Nor me.'

Simon studiously avoided glancing at his friend's threadbare clothing. 'And her man didn't appear while we were there. But when Joseph came upon the place alone, he was there. Until he heard Joseph talking, that is. Then he disappeared.'

'According to Joseph.'

'Perhaps he killed Yatton in error? If Yatton came upon the

holding at night, say, and he thought Yatton was an outlaw, couldn't he have killed the herald, and then realised his error, and so taken the body into the forest and left it? He discovered the oil, so set about . . .'

'What? Set about selling it? Didn't recognise what it was, so he threw it away?'

'I know. Cob without straw . . . I may as well suggest that Yatton himself was not the victim, that Yatton met someone on the road, killed him and set his tabard on the body to hide the fact that he was running away . . .'

Baldwin peered at him. 'Do you think that likely?'

Simon looked at him. 'What, that Yatton happened to meet a man on the road who was his size, killed him – I suppose he ran on to Canterbury, killed the monk as well, stole the oil, and returned there to the forest to live a life of indolence and mild insobriety? What would he live on? The hope that the oil would itself bring him some form of marvellous wealth?'

Baldwin eyed him. 'So you don't think it likely?'

# Chapter Thirty

They were able to speak with many of the King's messengers as the day passed, but when they saw that it was almost midday, they called a halt and made their way to the New Palace Yard, and the stalls selling everything from pies to honeyed larks. With their bellies filled, they felt prepared to return to their questioning, and they set at it until the middle of the afternoon, but by then both were growing despondent.

There had been five or six heralds and messengers passing by that roadway in the days between Richard de Yatton's disappearance and his body's discovery. Of them, some could be discounted, because they had remained in the company of others at all times, but there were some who didn't have witnesses to their actions, and these were the ones in whom Baldwin was most interested.

'So, there is this fellow Philip, one of the cursores,' Simon said. 'I didn't like his look.'

'He was the one with the slight squint?' Baldwin said with a grin. Simon was often suspicious of those who had any kind of mark which made them stand out or look different. Baldwin had often tried to explain to him that he shouldn't judge people on the basis of physical differences, but Simon was still of a mind to doubt the word of those who looked more villainous.

Baldwin continued, 'I felt his word sounded good enough. To be fair, he was with other people for almost all the time, except for a two-day period, and he said a man was with him in Maidstone. If we can confirm that, he must be innocent. He'd never make the journey to the woods in the time available.'

'What of the man called Thomas?'

'He was interesting. There was something about him that struck me as curious. Did you notice that?'

'Yes. He was oddly reluctant to speak about himself, wasn't he? There was something strange about him.'

'But if he was telling the truth, there was no need for him to be nervous. He said he was in the party with Ayrminne and the others, all the way homewards from the Queen to Beaulieu. Did you see him in France?'

Simon paused and considered. 'Not that I remember, no. But you know what it was like over there. We spent all our spare moments just talking to each other about how much we wanted to get home again, didn't we?'

'Let's go and ask Ayrminne about him.'

William Ayrminne was staying in rooms in the grounds of the abbey, and he received the two with a smile and motioned them to a bench seat.

'Sir Baldwin and Bailiff Puttock, it is very good to see you both again. And so soon, too.'

'We have been asking people about some of the messengers who could have been responsible for the death of this man de Yatton on the road,' Baldwin said. You had a man with you on your travels back from France, a fellow called Thomas, I think you told me. Thomas of Bakewell? What did you think of him?'

'You asked me before whether he had disappeared from my group, I think?'

Ayrminne was no fool, and he looked from one to the other shrewdly. This was an embarrassment, potentially, and he had no desire to be thrust into a difficult position because of these two and their investigation.

Until January, Ayrminne had been the Keeper of the Privy Seal and a canon of St Paul's Cathedral. He had lost those positions when he was elected to the see of Carlisle, but then he lost that when his election was quashed. It was a sore trial, seeing such a magnificent post go, but that was a part of life. Now, with the Queen's backing, he had hopes of the next senior position to come available. There were stories of John Salmon, Bishop of Norwich, being in an increasingly frail state, which made Ayrminne hopeful. But he would do or say nothing that could hurt the Queen.

'I would be most grateful for anything you can tell me,' Baldwin said firmly.

'Then first, you must know this: I am a very enthusiastic supporter of our Lady Queen Isabella. I make no bones about my affection for her. You understand? Good. Then I can tell you some things: first, the man Thomas was the brother of the poor fellow who was killed in the abbey church on the day of the King's crowning. Remember that?'

Baldwin tipped his head back as realisation hit. 'Sir John de Bakewell! Of course. I knew that the name of the town was familiar for some reason.'

'He died when the wall behind him collapsed. Poor old Westminster. It's not that long ago that the fire took much of the outbuildings, and then there was the jewels robbery in the early years of this century, which was a great embarrassment, and finally this fresh disaster. Just as they hoped to leave so much shame behind them and have a great coronation ceremony, the damned wall fell over and flattened poor John.'

'It was not an auspicious beginning to the King's reign,' Baldwin noted.

'Hardly. And that man was Thomas's brother. I understand he was found at his brother's side by the Queen. And it was she who went to Thomas and helped him up. She was only a little older than he at the time, I suppose, but she had Thomas taken into her household and gradually she elevated him until he became one of her most trusted messengers. Now, of course, he is back here with the King's men, since the Queen has seen her household taken from her.'

'So he would be entirely loyal to the Queen, then,' Simon noted.

'Yes. As are so many. Many of us have much to thank her for,' Ayrminne said coolly.

Baldwin and Simon walked hurriedly away from the canon's lodgings, up past the great Belfry, and back into the New Palace Yard.

There was a small chamber near to the main room where they found the messenger called Thomas sitting with the other, Jack, the guard from the Bishop of Orange's party.

'Masters! You want to speak with my friend here?' Jack said.

'This is Thomas? Brother of Sir John de Bakewell?'

'That I am.'

Baldwin stood leaning nearby. 'We have heard that you were the loyal servant of the Queen until only a short while ago.'

'That is right. I am still her man,' Thomas said. 'I don't change allegiance just because others seek to forget their own.'

Jack put a hand out to him as though to calm him, but Thomas looked at him in some surprise, as though he was only stating simple facts and not the clearest treason.

'You were with the Queen in France, but returned with William Ayrminne?' Baldwin asked.

'Yes. Why?'

'Why do you think, man?' Simon burst out. 'We're seeking the murderer of the man who was slain while in the King's service, and the oil which has been stolen from the King, and you were returning from that place just at the right time.'

'Me? You think I was responsible for that man's death? Are you mad?'

'I shall reserve my judgement on that,' Baldwin said.

'I returned with William Ayrminne and the others. All the way to Beaulieu. How could I have left them and hurried to Canterbury? It must have been someone else.'

'Somebody managed it,' Simon grated.

'Perhaps they did. Not I, though.'

Baldwin peered at him closely, but although he and Simon asked more questions with the hope of dislodging the man, there was nothing they could do to shake his apparent conviction of innocence.


Thomas was disturbed by the line that the questioning had taken.

'You shouldn't concern yourself. They ask the same questions of all of us,' Jack said soothingly.

'I know that!' All the heralds and messengers were being questioned, of course, but he was alarmed by the way that Sir Baldwin had asked about his own journeys in the weeks before Richard de Yatton's death. He had been in France, he told them. And yes, he'd come back with the entourage of the Bishop of Winchester.

'You weren't the only man coming back in the Bishop's party,' Jack said, as though he could read Thomas's mind.

'They know that well enough. They can't state that you left to return to Canterbury. It could have been anyone.'

'It was a very large party,' Thomas said uncertainly.

'So they cannot say it was definitely you, any more than they can say it was someone else.'

'You mean a man might have been able to leave it without being noticed? Not for long, though. An afternoon and early evening? Perhaps.'

Yes, Jack thought. And then, while riding back through the forest, perhaps a man would have been able to slip away for a moment or two – long enough to defecate, certainly – without causing comment. He had been with large parties like that one. And that same man might have been able to shove a herald's tabard over a corpse, say.

It was clear that Thomas did not like it. He felt that this questioning was beginning to point in a very unpleasant manner towards himself.

Jack was less sure. He reckoned that it was giving him a clue about others. About a conspiracy. He had heard enough. Someone had waited until Ayrminne's men had gone from Canterbury, and then wandered in and stolen the oil. It was easy. Then he had lain low in the city until the Bishop of Orange's men arrived, and perhaps passed the oil on to one of them. Pons and André ran off with the oil, and brought it with them to the Bishop again in Beaulieu. The matter of the herald murdered in the woods was a different affair entirely. Sad, but it had nothing to do with the main issue: the oil. Yes. He felt he had the strings of the story in his hand now, and he was tying them together neatly.

And information about something like this could be valuable.

\* \* \*

'That was a waste of time,' Simon said as they left the chamber. 'I need answers, but we're getting nowhere!'

'Yes,' Baldwin agreed. 'And I begin to see that we have a problem – if we consider men like Joseph or Thomas, they can declare that they are innocent, perfectly happy in the certainty that we will never be able to prove them liars.'

'What does that mean?' Simon demanded. 'All we need do is learn that one man or another was missing, and we have our killer.'

'And how do we prove a man wasn't there in the party from one day to the next? It is easy to prove a man *was* a part of a travelling group, but how do you prove he *wasn't*? If that fellow Thomas was with Ayrminne, and Ayrminne tells us he was with him almost all the way, we have a certainty. If he says he was there, but Ayrminne tells us Thomas was nowhere near him, does that mean he wasn't with Ayrminne's men, or simply that Ayrminne didn't notice him? There is no certainty, Simon. None. How can we make cob without straw or mud?'

'Well, we have to look for some rock on which to base our conclusions,' Simon said.

'How far do we dig for it?' Baldwin demanded sarcastically.

Simon looked at him coolly. 'I do not care how far I have to dig! I want Despenser satisfied so that I can know some peace in my home again.'

Jack was thoughtful after the questioning by Baldwin and Simon. Thomas was in no mind to discuss what he had said, but instead sat scowling at a far wall and made a bitter comment or two about the quality of modern knights. It was enough to make Jack think that he either knew, or had guessed, who was guilty of the killing.

This was the sort of affair which could easily lead to a man losing his head, Jack thought to himself, but he had no desire to do so. Still, there were problems for a man who wished for a quiet life. Sometimes he must risk a little in order to get it.

He was unpleasantly certain that he had not cut a dashing figure in the eyes of the knight and his friend the bailiff, but that was little concern to him. There were many others who regarded him in a more respectful light.

'You all right, Thomas?'

'Yes. Yes, I'm fine. I just wish I knew why so many people believe I have something that can help with this. I don't know anything!'

'Despenser hasn't tried to finger all your things again, has he?'

'No. Nothing's been touched so far as I can see. There's no need to, anyway! I don't have anything. I don't *know* anything! All I did was ride back from France with William Ayrminne. What is so wrong with that?'

'They obviously think you left Ayrminne's men to go off and rob the priory,' Jack said.

'It's ridiculous, though! How could I have had the chance?'

'True enough,' Jack said. 'Tell me, how was Ayrminne to travel with?'

'He was a good companion. He talked all the while to all of us, he was very friendly and cheerful. You'd never have guessed at his importance. He could talk to any man on his own level. Or woman. Even the highest.'

'You mean the Queen?'

'Oh, yes. He visited her a few times when I was there with her. She had many messages for me to bring for her – some for the King, others for Prior Eastry, making sure he was looking after her pack of hounds. There were loads of them.'

'And he was correctly deferential, then, even though he treated you and the others well?'

'Hah! Oh, yes. He was quite subservient to her and to the Bishop, too. But when he left the room, and the two behind, he was his usual self again. Much easier.'

Jack nodded, grinning. He'd known others who were like that. They tended to be the easiest for a man to deal with.

And then he almost gasped. Ayrminne had been with the Queen – and so had the Bishop. Then Ayrminne came to England and was at Canterbury, and the monk had died, the oil stolen that same night.

The Queen was estranged from her husband. Everyone knew that they got on as well as a fox and a chicken. Something she'd be keen on having would be some sort of lever over her husband, and to be able to take his oil, and threaten him that he'd never see it again – that could be a mighty threat.

This was a guess, but he reckoned he was in possession of important information, and it was a case of how best he could use it. The oil had been stolen, and he didn't know who'd done that, nor what they'd done with it. But the Queen was in contact with people in Canterbury, and Thomas had delivered her messages for her. So Ayrminne could easily have plotted with her to have it stolen for them.

Someone had killed the monk, taken the oil, and then passed it on to the Bishop of Orange's men when they arrived. André and Pons had disappeared in a hurry. They had returned to the Bishop's party when it was safe, when he was at Beaulieu, and there, no doubt, they gave him the oil so he could take it back to the Queen. There was no risk he'd be searched for it at Canterbury because the two already had taken it. And he could transport it all the way back to the

Queen in France. That way, the French bint would have a lever against her husband.

It was quite impressive, really, he thought. Now – the next problem was what to do with the information.

But there was no struggle there. He knew what to do. His years as an outlaw had made him keen on the acquisition of treasure, and this information should be worth a few pennies. The question that exercised him was, who he should sell it to?

He knew already.

The Bishop of Orange looked up when the tentative knock came on his door. 'Yes?'

Nicholas walked in with that reticence so typical of a friar who was unsure of his welcome, and less certain of his own position generally.

Since giving Despenser all he had wanted, Nicholas had been ignored by the magnate. Perhaps that was no bad thing. His throat was still bruised where Despenser had grabbed him. The man had the sensitivity of an ox. And it was Nicholas who'd pointed out the potential resolution to Despenser's problems. The man should have been grateful, curse his name.

At least the Bishop had given him some security, which was a huge relief.

'What do you want, friar?'

Nicholas smiled anxiously. 'I wanted to know when we were likely to return to France, my Lord?'

'I imagine that our business will be completed here within the week. I most certainly hope so. I am supposed to be going straight to the Pope, as you know.'

'I am most grateful, my Lord Bishop.'

'I do not imagine that you will be enormously popular with His Holiness, any more than you are here in England, though.'

'You are quite possibly correct there, my Lord. But I have to consider that my life will be safer in France with the Pope than here with the English King. He is so entirely devoted to his adviser that any man who seeks to help him but who is forced to speak the truth about the Despenser is inevitably harmed.'

'And you want to tell the Pontiff about this oil again?'

'When I brought news of it to him originally, I was hoping for his aid to validate the rumours about the oil, but no longer. Now I am convinced of it. And it is more important than I had realised. You see, it has been stolen and could fall into the wrong hands.'

'And whose hands would be so wrong?'

'I am coming to the conclusion,' Nicholas said, his voice dropping to a hushed tone, 'that the worst possible hands would be the King's. King Edward, were he to win the oil of St Thomas, could become successful. But look at him, my Lord! Were he to have the oil used on him, he could become invincible!'

'You think that the oil could have such a supernatural effect?' the Bishop asked. There was no sarcasm in his voice, he was genuinely seeking Nicholas's opinion.

'If St Thomas was right, and this was given to him by the Blessed Virgin Mary, then I think so, yes. The man who possesses this oil must be entirely safe from any enemy, surely.'

'Then to whom should the oil be given, if not to the King?'

'To his son. From all I have heard, Earl Edward is a bright, intelligent young man. And he is not prey to the same – um – unfortunate urges.'

'Interesting. So you think that we should seek out the oil and give it to the boy?'

Nicholas stared at him very straightly. 'I think we should do all in our power to prevent either the King or his adviser Despenser acquiring it. That is the most important thing.'

The Bishop leaned back and eyed him coldly. 'That is interesting.'

# Chapter Thirty-One

Earl Edward grunted to himself with relief as he sprawled on his bed, a large mazer of wine in his hand. When the knock came at his door, he winced and shouted, 'If that is you, Richard, I am going to sleep. I suggest you do the same!'

'Ah, my Lord, I would be so grateful for the opportunity, were I able to take it. Alas, I have to see to my young master's comforts before I can think of my own.'

'Yours is a terrible life, old friend,' the Earl said ironically.

'Aye, I think truly I suffer more than many would guess,' Richard said. 'And now, has my pupil managed to study the works I have submitted to him?'

'You seriously believe that I have had a spare moment to look at the books you sent me?'

'Master, I fear you have so little time to investigate the wisdom of the ancients, you should take advantage of each and every opportunity.'

'Perhaps you do at that, Richard. And what if I disagree?'

'Then you have every right to do so. And I will be forced to accept your word. However, that would mean that I would be unable to finish my work with you, so I would be forced to resign my post at your side, which is something I would deeply regret, but it would be absolutely necessary.'

'Oh, really,' the Earl replied without any conviction whatever.

'Yes. Truly.'

'What is it you want me to learn about today, then?'

'I had wondered about the story of Solomon, when he was anointed by Zadok the priest.'

'Why?'

'It seemed a suitable reference for you, my Lord.'

'You realise, do you, that my father's oil of St Thomas has been stolen?'

'Yes. I had heard. That was why I thought it might be a good time to consider the importance of anointing.'

'What is that supposed to mean?' the Earl demanded, rolling over on his bed until his feet were on the floor, and then lifting himself up to stand.

'It is nothing to upset you, my Lord. I was wondering whether you were aware of the different attitudes to anointing, that is all. And whether you realised that the anointing has little importance from the perspective of the oil itself.'

'I don't understand.'

'It is very simple. The oil is a carrier. It brings the blessing of God upon you when the priest makes the mark of God upon you, but the oil itself is nothing important. It is a means by which God's blessing arrives.'

'Are you trying to say that St Thomas's oil is worthless?'

'Hardly that, my Lord. No, but it is not of great value, either. The oil is less important than the standing of the priest. Now King Solomon had Zadok, but were you unworthy, the finest oil and the most revered priest would not avail you. If you went to your coronation with a light, uncaring heart, no matter what the ceremony, you would not win the support of God or Christ.'

'But if the oil was given to St Thomas by the Blessed Virgin herself?'

'That may have some impact, in terms of bringing the ceremony to the attention of God, but I would still hold that it is the conviction of the King and what lay in his heart that would carry most importance and, secondly, the purity and belief of the priest. The oil is relatively unimportant in the scheme of things.'

'Is this the teaching of Christ? Is it in the Bible?'

'I have seen nothing that says my assertion is untrue.'

'So it is not, then. Richard, what is your real aim here? You don't believe that this oil is a nonsense any more than I do.'

'If men are killing over it, their actions are perverting the oil itself. If this was given to St Thomas by the Blessed Virgin, do you think she would want to have men squabbling over it? Would she want to see blood spilled over it? Of course not. The men who commit such crimes deserve every punishment for their foul deeds.'

The Earl pulled a grimace. 'You try to scare me? Should I reject such an oil if it comes to me?'

'I do not mean to do that, my Lord. No, I only seek to show that if it is never found again, it will matter little to you.'

'And the prophecy?'

'If you want my honest opinion, my Lord, it matters not a whit.'

'What!'

'If the prophecy is valid, my Lord, it matters not at all what men attempt. If you are to be the "Boar from Windsor", then the presence of the oil will make little difference.'

'But the prophecy said that I must be anointed by the oil.'

'And if the oil is necessary, the Holy Mother Mary will bring it to you. Do you honestly think that *any* man could prevent her from ensuring you have it if it is her firm conviction that you *should* have it? Do you think Despenser could stand between her and you if she wished you to have it? Of course not! To think that would be blasphemy! If she intends you to have it, she will ensure that you do.'

Aye. Aye, she will, the Earl told himself, and aloud, he said, 'You are right, of course, old friend.'

Inside, he reminded himself that helping the Virgin to achieve her goals was not against her wishes. He would do all he could to ensure that her wishes were carried out.

Simon and Baldwin had been invited to stay with the Bishop of Exeter again in his house, and they made their way to his great hall on the banks of the Thames with a sense that they had achieved little.

'If only I had seen a man look nervous in front of me, I'd be happier,' Simon said. 'But of all the men we saw today, not a one looked as though he was anxious about our questioning. It leaves me wondering whether we have missed the correct man entirely.'

'That is always possible.' Baldwin wore a frown. 'Yet that would mean that the actual murderer is someone entirely divorced from the King's entourage, and surely the fact that someone knew where to find the herald means that the attacker must have had some information based upon time spent with the King's household. I can only assume that we are correct and it was a herald or messenger who killed de Yatton.'

'What if it was someone else, though? Is there someone else who'd have had the ability?'

'I daresay some men in Despenser's household would have had the ability; just as someone from the King's own household would have had. Then again, there are the others.'

'Who do you mean?'

'Well, the Queen's hounds were there and the body was found by her hounds – perhaps her master of hounds . . .'

'Baldwin, that could be a touch of brilliance.'

'Could it? I doubt it. What possible aim could *she* have had in taking it?'

'The discomfiture of the King?'

Baldwin stopped in the street and stared at the cobbles all about. 'But she is busy on her embassy. I never had the impression that she was capable of such dissembling. Did you?'

'No, but . . .' he was tempted to point out that she was both female and French, but Simon held his tongue. There was no need to cause an argument just now, he reasoned to himself. 'Look, it is not only her, is it? Perhaps others seek to cause our King some difficulty. From Despenser's attitude, it seems plain to me that the King is unhappy about losing his oil, so perhaps we should look for someone who sought to achieve that.'

'It would have to be someone with great knowledge of the King. Either that, or someone was merely fortunate in causing this effect.'

'If it was intended,' Simon agreed.

Baldwin shook his head. 'No. By that reasoning I merely return to Sir Roger Mortimer. He is surely the man with the most to repay. His debts to the King and Despenser are very deep. He has lost everything, even his wife and children.'

'So he would be delighted to irritate the King, then,' Simon pointed out.

They had reached the Bishop's house, and knocked upon the gate. The aged porter took one look at them and grunted before opening the door, and they crossed the main yard to the hall.

Simon shook his head. 'It's a shame we're sure that Yatton is dead. If he were alive, it would make the situation easier.'

'How so?'

'Well, it would be an elegant solution, wouldn't it, if Yatton had been the killer. He waited until a man appeared who was about his size, killed him, set his own clothing on him, and then ran away. Perhaps to a widow in the area. But how would a messenger get to know a woman in the vicinity, let alone . . .'

Baldwin shook his head slowly. 'It would be easy to see how a man might get to know a woman in the area – if he was travelling up and down the road regularly, he might well meet one. And then he was often late, Joseph said, because he had a religious attitude, so was often delayed. The delays may have been because of his assignations with the woman, rather than visits to a chapel.'

'But what of the oil?'

'Yes. It founders on the oil, as you say. The oil. What would be the point? What would he have done with the oil? There was no need to take it.'

Simon shrugged. 'Mind you, if he were still alive, perhaps he would only have been an agent for another. He could have . . . what's the point? We know he's dead.'

'Yes,' Baldwin agreed. 'He's dead. And yet that doesn't invalidate the inquiry. What could have happened was, he stole the oil himself, and was then killed in his place.'

'The likelihood of the murderer killing and then being killed in his place?' Simon said scoffingly. 'I thought we had discounted that theory.'

'There were ancient kings who would bury treasure and then kill all those who had worked there to keep the secret,' Baldwin mused. 'Men like Despenser would like that concept – maintaining rigid security.'

'Yes,' Simon said. Despenser was a threat he could not forget. The man was always in his mind now.

## Bishop of Exeter's House, Straunde

'Simon, Baldwin! Come in and sit with me.'

The Bishop appeared to be in a thoroughly good temper, and he insisted that they sit beside him, one on each side, while he had his servants bring in bowls for them to wash in, then strong wine for them to drink, and finally a good mess of thick soup with hunks of bread to dip in it. 'Fill your bellies.'

Baldwin sipped at his, while Simon dived in, his spoon working hard as he plied it from bowl to mouth.

'Tell me, Sir Baldwin, have you encountered any obstacles in your searches today?' the Bishop asked him.

Baldwin considered. 'No. No obstacles erected by those who sought to obstruct, in any case.'

'But there were others?'

'We are confused by the lack of witnesses and lack of genuine information. There is a story there, but I have not yet heard it.'

'I see. Well, perhaps there is nothing to learn, then. Maybe the monk was killed by another monk, there was no herald, and the man left at the roadside was killed in a chance encounter with felons.'

'But the oil is gone. That is what I keep returning to. The oil.'

'Well, perhaps the dead herald did have it, but it was taken by the felon who killed him. Stranger things have happened. Perhaps it was in a pretty bottle and he sought to have it.'

'No. I cannot believe that. An outlaw would look at it, sniff the contents, and discard it. How many beggars of your acquaintance would keep something like that? You distribute alms often enough – would they be glad of a little bottle with oil in it instead of money or food?'

'True!' the Bishop said. 'But where else could it lie?'

'I do not know,' Baldwin said. 'Despenser said he had searched the man Thomas's belongings, but perhaps . . .'

He wondered now, remembering the crypt. All those boxes and chests, so many places to conceal a small phial of oil. It would have been easy for a man to hide it. But then, why would the monk Gilbert have gone to the barn to meet with the thief? No, he must have provided the oil to the felon, his accomplice. Perhaps for no other reason than simple money. So often motive came down to the most basic of human urges. And then the felon took the oil and fled the city.

'Canterbury is a city!' he muttered.

'What of it?' the Bishop asked, startled.

'Walls. Walls and gates.'

'You are rambling, Sir Baldwin.'

'Does it seem so? No, I was reflecting on the fact that the city has walls, and the gates are locked each night. The man killed the monk, and then escaped, so we are led to believe. But it was night time, and that tells me much.'

'It does?' Bishop Walter asked bemusedly. 'What?'

'I need to speak to two guards of the Bishop of Orange tomorrow,' Baldwin said with conviction.

## First Wednesday after Ascension Day[1]

Ayrminne walked back to his chamber after Mass with his head bowed as he considered the day ahead. It was to be a long

---

[1] Wednesday, 22 May 1325

day, from the sound of all the business the King wished to conduct.

'Master Canon?'

He turned to see the scruffy fellow from the Bishop of Orange's entourage a matter of yards from him. 'Yes?'

'I was hoping you might help me, Canon.'

'In what way?' Ayrminne asked bemusedly.

'The King's oil.'

'The oil of St Thomas? What do you know of it?'

'I think I know where it is, Master.'

Ayrminne felt his belly lurch within his body. 'You do?'

'Don't you, too?'

The anger on Ayrminne's face was unfeigned. 'You dare to suggest I would keep back such knowledge from His Majesty, churl? I would rather have my hand cut from my arm than allow any treason! Damn your cods, if I knew anything about it, I'd have told the King immediately.'

'A man who could tell the King where it was might well be rewarded,' Jack said more quietly.

'What of it? If you know where it is, you should tell the authorities now, or suffer the consequences.'

Jack shook his head with a faint smile on his face. 'I think it'd be safer all around were I to buy it back. The man who provided the money to get it would be well rewarded by the King, and the finder could also benefit, eh?'

'What do you mean?'

'I mean this: I think I know where it may be, and I'm prepared to put my life to the hazard of recovering the stuff. But I'll need a lot of money, in case I need to bribe someone.'

'How much?'

'At least a pound. More, if it can be found.'

Ayrminne heard a bell tolling. 'There is no time now. That

is the bell to call everyone to the King's audience. Come to my chamber – it's that one up there – when the audience is finished. If you need money, I can provide it, but I'll need to know exactly what you think has happened.'

'Very good.'

'And, fellow, tell no one of this talk. Understand?'

# Chapter Thirty-Two

The morning was as grim as any on Dartmoor. Grey clouds loured overhead, blocking out all sight of the sun, while the rain drummed incessantly, turning the roads into quagmires, and pelting at the Thames, churning the surface into a pock-marked mess that looked astonishingly uninviting. Looking at it, Simon remembered journeys he had made by sea, and told himself that he would never again go aboard a ship. They were too hazardous.

He hurried with Baldwin along the roadway to the palace, both of them trying to keep their heads down, Simon wearing his hood up to try to keep his hair dry, while Baldwin wore a fashionable cap made from a thick but soft wool. It was a mess before they had reached the palace, but he didn't care. All who walked outside today would be in a similar position.

'Whom do you want to speak to?' Simon asked.

'I never thought of this before, but what if there was a conspiracy at the priory, Simon? The two fresh guards who were sent to replace the two fools from the Canterbury city gate who ran, might they have been sent to us for some ulterior motive?'

'I don't . . . you mean they were involved in the robbery, and were sent along with us in order to . . . what?'

'If you were seeking to conceal something, would it not be best to have a decoy? Someone who was probably above any investigation, someone who was unlikely to be searched, so that if somebody caught wind of the attempt, he could believably deny everything? And then you would send the thing with someone else in a similarly impregnable position. Perhaps you might send them with the oil in a second party, a party that didn't arrive until long after the murder and theft? But this is the clever part: you would ensure that you had your own men added, so that although it appeared that the party was all innocent, in fact your representatives were there for the robbery, they had the oil, and then they were added to the Bishop of Orange's party, let us suppose, where they were allowed to pass through any suspicions. No suspicions would adhere to these two, any more than they would to you or me.'

'If you are correct, that would make for a perfect scheme.'

'Yes. Sadly, it means that the coroner is probably guilty of being complicit in the robbery and murder.'

'Possibly. But think on this: he told you that someone else told him Pons or the other one was guilty of using aliases, didn't he? He could have been told that by someone in the castle, couldn't he? He may well be entirely innocent, Baldwin.'

'I hope so. I almost liked the man.'

'There is one issue, though,' Simon said musingly. 'If you are correct, it relies on the fact that the murderer was seen. What would be the point of having one man commit the crime, and then the other two take the oil a short while later?'

'I think that that would be cleared up by the monk himself, if he were alive. Possibly he knew his murderer, or the murderer knew something about him, enough to blackmail Gilbert? Or it was simply money. Gilbert wanted it, and the killer offered to pay him for the oil.'

'Perhaps,' Simon said shortly.

Baldwin looked at him. 'You are still worried about Margaret?'

'Everything worries me at the moment. Will Despenser let us have peace? Will my house still be there when I return? Is Margaret all right? Is Peterkin safe with her? There is so much to fear when a man like Despenser decides to make life difficult. How can such a man live with himself when he knows how much pain and worry he has inflicted on others?'

'With great ease. He settles back on to feather-filled pillows each night and pulls a soft woollen blanket over himself, and he is warm, cosy and safe. And he has no feeling or compunction about the way he treats others. There are men like that. Men who don't care at all for their fellow men. He is one such.'

'I couldn't behave in the way he does.'

'I am very glad to hear it. I don't think you and I would be companions, let alone friends, were you to treat others in the way that he has.'

'I suppose so,' Simon muttered.

There was a loud bell ringing, and the two of them began to follow the general movement towards the Great Hall. Soon after the hall had filled, the King himself entered, walking slowly and majestically towards the throne.

'It will be resolved, Simon. I am sure that we can dissuade Despenser from causing more trouble.'

'I wish I was so confident.'

William Ayrminne was relieved to hurry away from the scruffy little man-at-arms and find his way to the palace. It gave him a little time to reflect and consider.

And the Bishop of Orange knew what he must do as well. His path was perfectly clear. In the chats which Ayrminne had held with him, it was plain enough. He would report back to the Pope that the King of England was a spendthrift wastrel with the brain of a pigeon. His treatment of his wife was a disgrace to his crown. His behaviour towards his 'adviser', Despenser, was a scandal.

There was no point in further discussion. The man was an embarrassment to his people. It would be a terrible shame for the throne to lose the magnificent properties in France, but while this king was in place, they must be lost. They may just as well hand over all the . . .

But that was unthinkable. No, better by far that they were retained somehow, and there was only one person who could ensure that. The Queen. She must be supported, no matter what.

He found his eye being drawn to the austere figure of the Bishop of Orange even as he considered.

The meeting in the Great Hall was an odd occasion, Simon felt. The last time he had been here, earlier this year, the King had impressed him, and the hall itself had been glorious, the paintwork gleaming, the rich colours almost blinding the eyes. It had seemed almost fairy-tale-like in its richness and glory.

Today it felt very different. With the gloomy weather outside, it seemed as though the entire atmosphere had subtly altered. The colours inside were dim and murky in the dull light. The windows showed only the dirt that had settled upon them, and the clothes of all the nobles and prelates were steaming in the cool interior. There was a distinct odour of damp dogs about the place. It felt less like the great hall of the most important magnate in the land and more like a cattle-shed.

Despenser called them all to listen, and gave them all to understand that the King required them to respond to some issues of national importance. As he continued, it became obvious that he was talking about the state of affairs with the English territories in France.

It was not interesting enough for Simon. Not only was he uninterested in such matters of state, he was also repelled by the voice of the man reading them. The two conspired to make his attention wander, and he found his eyes ranging over the crowd until they settled upon the full figure of Richard of Bury.

He was a fortunate soul. The opportunity of helping to guide a young mind, especially one so important as that belonging to the young Earl, was daunting, but somehow thrilling at the same time. Simon would not have wanted the job, but he could comprehend the excitement of a man like Bury. What better pupil could a man have, after all, than the son of the King?

And the Earl was there at his side, Simon saw. He noticed, as he allowed his eyes to move on, that the man nearest the Earl was the Bishop of Orange. No doubt he was there as a witness of the events. As a foreigner he could not give advice to the King, of course.

He was clearly fascinated by the way that the King was given his advice, though. Every so often Simon saw him leaning down to Bury and speaking, then nodding. As Despenser began to outline the options available to the King, the Bishop bowed to the Earl and made his way off through the crowds. As Simon watched, he approached William Ayrminne, and stood beside him for some while, head bent, while Ayrminne spoke directly into his ear, as though whispering something deeply important.

And then Simon saw Ayrminne and the Bishop turn and stare directly at him.

\* \* \*

The King was bored with all this. It was tedious. He had already more or less made up his mind, and once it was made up, as any who knew him would be fully aware, his mind remained made up. He was not an indecisive fool like some.

His Queen wanted him to send his son to France. That was enough to set his teeth on edge. He would be *damned* before he'd give up all his French estates to his son. What, make his son the owner of Guyenne and the Agenais? Dear Christ in Heaven, that would make his son more wealthy than he, and if the lad decided to become a thorn in his side, as he himself had once been to his own father, how much more easy would it be from a position of such great wealth? It was a ludicrous proposal.

So the only true decision to be made was, when he should go to France to submit to that son of a diseased whore, Charles IV. It hurt, but not as much as the idea of the actual ceremony. The bastard would make the most of it. He could, as the feudal lord, but that didn't make it any easier to swallow. Having to bend the knee to a jumped-up little prickle like him was an insult to a man of greater birth and nobility. Charles said he came from Charlemagne in a direct line! So what! The English were descended from the heroes of Troy, as any man knew who was interested in history. That was why the English were so powerful.

But not powerful enough to hold France back, were she to decide to invade. That was the trouble.

There was going to be a fight about this, though. Sir Hugh would be appalled to learn that he was to be left here alone. He'd be more unhappy to hear that he was himself to be sent, because that would mean his death warrant, but when Edward left to go to France, it might well have the same impact.

Everyone knew how much the barons loathed Despenser, and that might result in his murder as soon as the King was out of the country. King Edward knew this only too well. There was little he could do to protect poor Hugh while he left the land, but what else could he do? He was the King, he had a duty to protect his realm from the ravages of the French. Dear Christ, but he wished there was some other way of doing it. Of protecting his son's inheritance.

It was possible that he could make his son the regent while he was abroad. Maybe then, if he gave Sir Hugh the task of protecting his son, the barons would be reluctant to try to hurt poor Sir Hugh. It was a possibility.

France. That was always the problem. His greatest enemy, and the land to which he was so closely bound, both geographically and by marriage. His wife was a clever woman, but she was also treacherous. Everyone told him that you could not trust a Frenchwoman. There was the risk that she might become a traitor in the English court, were she permitted. It wasn't to be borne.

Yes, he would have to go there, to France, into the heart of his enemy's camp, and run the risk of the death of his closest companion, friend, brother and confidant, Sir Hugh le Despenser.

He didn't know how he could bear to lose Sir Hugh. Poor, darling Piers Gaveston had been captured and slain while the King was away from his side, and he didn't know how he could cope without darling Hugh, if the barons were to take him away as well.

In Christ's name, he had had enough! All he wanted was some peace. He held up his hand to call a halt to proceedings. He needed some rest. His head hurt from the constant analysis of problems and threats.

\* \* \*

Baldwin felt the nudge. 'What?' he demanded less than amiably. He was trying to listen.

'Look. Them, over there. The Bishop of Orange and your man William Ayrminne.'

'What of them?'

'Ayrminne was just whispering in the Bishop's ear, and as soon as he finished, the pair of them turned and stared at us.'

'You're growing fearful of your own shadow,' Baldwin scoffed. 'What, do you think that they are joining with Sir Hugh le Despenser to attack you?'

'No, of course not, but what if they were both involved in the theft of the oil?'

'Simon, the Bishop couldn't be. He was with us, wasn't he? How could he have left us, killed the monk a week before we landed, and then returned to France, eh?'

'Ayrminne was there before us, wasn't he? And he is an ally of the Queen,' Simon whispered urgently.

'Simon, that is simply ridiculous. Ayrminne and the Bishop are both men of God. Perhaps one of them could have murderous tendencies, but both? No. That is quite—'

'Wait, Baldwin, just think. What if they hatched the plot before even leaving France, so Ayrminne was to bring a man over here with him who could leave his party on the way from Christ Church to Beaulieu, and then hold the oil in Canterbury, and then the Bishop's party, with us, would follow on a short while later and, as planned, we would find the oil stolen, and then follow on . . . the men whom the coroner insisted we should bring with us are perhaps carrying the oil?'

'Yes? And then what? Do you mean to say that the two will return to the castle in Canterbury? Or will they take ship with the Bishop to meet with the Queen? Or perhaps they'll attach themselves to William Ayrminne's group and make their way to France?'

'Any one of those options would be likely, and quite possible,' Simon asserted. 'The Queen could want to embarrass her husband, couldn't she? You have seen her over the last weeks, just as I have. Ayrminne is an ally of hers, so perhaps he wants the oil for the same reason. The Pope is hardly an ally of our king, is he? I mean, he lives in Avignon, not Rome. He's only there on the sufferance of the French, isn't he? Perhaps the Bishop of Orange is going to be the means of shipment of the oil. He is going straight to the Pope after his sojourn here, isn't he?'

Baldwin shook his head, but even as he did so, his eyes were drawn towards Ayrminne and the Bishop of Orange. In so doing, he caught sight of the King's son, who was now staring at him without concealment. The Earl looked over at Richard of Bury, and then spoke a few words into his ear. Bury nodded, and began to make his way across the hall towards Baldwin.

'Sir Baldwin? The Earl of Chester would appreciate a few moments to speak with you after this audience.'

Baldwin nodded and inclined his head to the Earl.

He looked just like any other young boy. It was cruel that life should thrust the cares of the realm on such small and insubstantial shoulders.

# Chapter Thirty-Three

Ayrminne was angry as he left the hall. The King's meeting had lasted much longer than usual, and now he was in that terrible position of having too much to achieve in a very short period of time.

The King was an obnoxious little man. Preening himself up there on the throne as though he was in some way deserving of respect and support from the barons. But few, if any, of the barons saw fit to give him more than a little word or two of support now. Nobody wanted to see his reign continue if it meant retaining Despenser at the very summit of power in the realm.

He'd already done his best to ruin so many, and now Ayrminne could feel his clammy hands on his own collar. Despenser was no ally of his. Ever since that first time that Ayrminne had stood up for the Queen, he had seen the way that Despenser's cold gaze turned to him, as though he was measuring Ayrminne for a coffin already. That was a good nickname for him, 'The Coffin Seller', because wherever he went, the sale of funerary items was sure to increase.

He left the hall and strode on to Westminster Abbey, around the church itself, and on to the little room at the southern side, near to the wall that bounded the Abbey precinct, where he had been given a room. Soon afterwards there came a knock at his door, and a quiet voice called.

'Canon?'

Ayrminne threw open the door. 'Get in here! Now, speak!'

Jack smiled easily. 'There were two guards with me when I came here with the Bishop. He's arranged for the oil to be stolen.'

Ayrminne curled his lip. 'You say that the emissary of the Pope has become a thief? Out of my way, you are wasting my time!'

'It would give him a bargaining counter against the King, if he had the oil,' Jack said. He gestured with his hands, palms down. 'Just hear me out.'

While Ayrminne tapped his foot, Jack told him what had happened at Canterbury: the dead monk, the stolen oil, the disappearance of Pons and André. 'The man who killed the monk was probably living there, in Canterbury. The Bishop of Orange's party arrived a week or so later.'

'Everyone said that it was the herald, Yatton, who stole the oil.'

'I knew Yatton. He wasn't a murderer. No, I think that he was the victim of an outlaw, nothing more. I was there at Canterbury. I know what happened. The Bishop's men were held up for attacking some locals, and next morning took flight – even though they were found innocent by the coroner. Why would they do that, if not because they had something on them and didn't want it found?'

'You said they didn't arrive until a week later!' Ayrminne said, trying to find holes in the tale.

'That's right. The thief kept it that long, and passed it on to them when we all arrived. In a city the size of Canterbury, it'd be easy to meet with the man who had the oil. He gave it to them, and they took it and ran.'

'It is an interesting theory.'

'More than that, it's likely,' Jack said smugly. 'Now, what we must do is get the oil back.'

'What will you do with it?'

'Bring it to you so you can take it to the King.'

'Good.'

'Unless . . .'

Ayrminne held his face carefully blank. 'What?'

'Unless you felt it better that you took it to the Queen.'

'Me? Why should I wish to do that?'

'I know you are in her favour. And then, when I get back to France, you can ask her to look on me favourably. I'll have saved it for her son, so he can use it at his coronation.'

'What makes you think she wouldn't punish you for keeping what was her husband's?'

Jack grinned. 'It's *you* who'll take it to her. I'll just keep in the background until you tell me to come to her. Is it a deal?'

In answer, Ayrminne opened his travelling chest, he took out the little soft leather purse and hefted it in his hand. Not quite a king's ransom.

'Be careful. The King is keen on the story of St Thomas. He would dearly like to bring punishment down on the head of the man who killed a monk down there in the priory where Henry II had seen to the slaughter of the saint.'

'Oh, I'll be careful,' Jack said. It would be the last sentence he spoke to Ayrminne.

Baldwin and Simon were wary as they approached the King's son.

All Simon could think of was how young the Earl looked. His own first-born son would have been how old now? About ten? This lad was two years older than that, if he was right, and yet he hardly looked it. He held himself well, though. His manner was haughty, and he had a cold eye for Baldwin and any others he glanced at. He wasn't impressed by rank, clearly. No reason why he ought to be. He had as many servants looking after him as any king, and he had knights and bannerets in his household, too.

'Your Highness, you asked to see us?' Baldwin said.

'I noticed that you had taken some interest in my behaviour at the King's hall just now.'

'No, I was merely looking about the hall to see who else was there,' he said.

'You were both watching me and my friends,' the Earl corrected him. 'And I wish to know why.'

Simon kept his head down, but his mind was whirling. The Earl must be perfectly used to being observed by others at all times, surely.

Baldwin was more conciliatory. 'My Lord, I was not aware I had caused you any offence.'

Bury was bristling with righteous indignation. 'You stare at the Earl and think you do him no insult?'

'Does my glance occasion such an insult?' Baldwin said, staring fixedly at Bury.

Bury was quiet for a moment, and then opened his mouth to speak, but before he could, the Earl held up a hand. Instantly Bury was stilled.

The Earl eyed Baldwin closely. 'If I were King, I could consider your attitude to be insolent.'

'When you are King, I shall be more cautious, I swear,' Baldwin said, but he was smiling, and he lowered his eyes to avoid the Earl. 'I promise you, upon my honour, that I meant you no harm and didn't mean to insult or offend you. I was only looking about the hall.'

'Why?' the Earl snapped.

'Because it occurred to me that among the men of the hall may be the man who had murdered the monk at Canterbury, and stolen your father's oil. And I caught your eye because I was reflecting to myself that the oil itself, were it to be recovered, may be extremely valuable to you.'

'You suggest that I stole it for myself?'

Baldwin shot a look upward, and stared a moment. 'My Lord, the oil would be valuable to you, I said. I meant that, were someone to try to blackmail you by demanding money in exchange for the oil, you might feel forced to agree to pay.'

'I might be more inclined to take the bastard's head off for stealing what would be mine anyway. As well as declaring him to the King for treason, in stealing what is the King's.'

'And perhaps also for bringing about another instance of embarrassment at Christ Church.'

'Yes. The man who killed the monk there was obviously not a friend to the King,' the Earl said. He was eyeing Baldwin with a speculative expression now. 'You are saying all this for a reason, are you not? What is your interest in this?'

'I am a humble knight,' Baldwin said. 'But I do have my own interest.'

'I thought as much. What is that?'

'Your father's friend has instructed me to investigate the matter for him. He has his own reasons for wanting to know where the oil is.'

'Despenser, you mean?' the Earl said with a raised eyebrow. 'You may tell him from me that you do not need to investigate further on his behalf. I will not have the oil in his hands.'

'I . . .' Baldwin was for the first time in a long while confused. It would have given Simon some pleasure, were it not for the fact that his own life and security depended upon his not upsetting Despenser.

'I would prefer you to seek the oil, find it, and bring it to me,' the Earl said.

'But, my Lord Earl, that is very difficult. I cannot simply—'

'You can decide whether to obey him, or me. He is the ally of my father the King – but that position could change at any time. The other alternative would be for you to support me. And those who do so will become my firm friends for the future. You understand me?'

'Earl, I am afraid that the Despenser has already demanded my help in locating the oil, and if we do not help him, he has sworn to make my friend here suffer the direst consequences.'

The Earl gazed at Simon with a pursing of his lips. 'Let me guess – that he'd take your house?'

'And rape my wife and see to my death,' Simon said quietly.

'You love your wife?'

Simon was about to respond with a wild demand to know what Chester meant to suggest, when he reflected that the Earl had seen his own parents' marriage dissolve under the pressures of politics and the King's infidelities. He swallowed back his angry response, and merely nodded. 'Yes. I love her dearly. I would not do anything that could endanger her.'

The Earl looked at him, then back at Bury. 'Then I shall have to consult to see how best to ensure that you are safe, Master Bailiff. I am sure that there must be a way.'

'What do you think?' the Earl said to Richard of Bury as Baldwin and Simon backed away from him.

'I would find it difficult to like that knight. He does not seem a sympathetic soul,' Bury said scathingly, adding, 'I doubt he owns a single book.'

'Do you think so? I should have said he was quite an educated fellow. Still, no matter. The main point is that I felt sure he was honest. I would trust him.'

'He has already confessed that he is working for Despenser,' Bury said warningly.

'And gave good reasons why he and his friend were forced into it.'

'It is hard to trust a man who is the ally of your enemy.'

'Sir Hugh is not my enemy – yet!' the Earl said with a faint grin. 'And aren't you always saying that I should have faith in my own judgement of a man? I judge this one to be honourable and decent. And as you know, my mother was herself complimentary about him. She had some experience of him, and then was happy with him as her guard on the way to Paris.'

'True. And yet—'

'And yet nothing! I trust him well enough. That is enough.'

André and Pons were both seated at a bench in the gatehouse tavern, when the messenger arrived. Jack looked about him at the people inside for some little while before he recognised the two. He smiled to himself, and then crossed the floor to them.

'Friends, I think you are fortunate today,' he began.

Pons looked at him, then across at André, before looking back up at Jack. 'What do you want?'

'I think you can guess that, can't you? I am like you two: a man-at-arms for the Bishop. I shared your journey all the way to Canterbury, where you two decided to flee. I have had a hard life, you know. A little money would go a long way for me. But I have the problem that I am not now a free man to take whatever I want. So I have to seek an accommodation if I want ready cash.'

André sniffed and reached out with an elegant hand to pick

up his drinking horn, a green pottery thing shaped roughly like a horn, but with two legs to convert it into a cup that could stand on its own. 'I don't think I understand you, my friend.'

'I got to thinking that if a man was to steal something from a priory, he'd have to run soon after. Especially if he killed someone to get it. You took the King's oil and fled. Only to bring it to your master, of course. The question is, have you still got it, or is it given to the Bishop already?'

Pons looked at his companion again, then shrugged. 'We have no oil.'

'That is a shame. Because I've been offered ten English shillings to get it back from you. With my three-shilling share, that would still leave you with three and a half each.' Jack smiled and sat opposite them.

André smiled with an easy calmness. 'And that would indeed be a wonderful present, if we had the oil. But, my friend, we do not. So, you rise, please, and leave us.'

'Are you trying to tell me you never had it?' Jack grinned. 'That's a shame. I reckon I can get the King to think you did have it. And the Despenser, too. You want him to come looking for the oil? Perfectly possible. I can see to it.'

André eyed him with a cold, calculating expression. 'You threaten us with this? I think you do not know what you are doing, friend. Pons, do you think the Bishop would miss one man-at-arms on the way homewards?'

The shorter man responded in swift colloquial French, and Jack suddenly felt wary. He had his knife ready under the table, in case these two decided to try to silence him, and now he wished he had kept to a seat nearer the door. He sat more upright, moving his legs underneath him, his left hand on the bench. 'Well?' he said.

Pons spat something that sounded like a deeply insulting

reference to his mother, and suddenly the two had lifted the table and it was moving towards his face. Jack leaped up and back, hurling the bench away, as the table rose and hit his cheek, but his knife hand was already on it, and he jerked it down and away, slamming the heavy wood down, the edge striking André on the foot and making him howl. Pons was right beside the table, his dagger out. He pushed the table, which now hit Jack's hip, the weight driving him backwards, while Pons jumped forward, the sharp tip of his dagger snagging in Jack's linen shirt. Jack felt the prick of the blade in his belly even as his heels both struck the bench he had shoved back, and he began to fall backwards, his eyes on that damned blade.

He hit his rump, then his back, and tried to roll away, but the knife was very close. And then he snapped his legs away, and was on his flank, drawing his legs underneath him, pushing with a hand to lift himself up again, and . . . felt the knife at the back of his neck, the point tickling just under his skull, where he knew a sharp thrust would cut his spinal cord and end his life in an instant.

'Now, friend, perhaps we should go and talk somewhere quieter?' André said. And this time there was no humour in his tone. Only fury – and hatred.

Baldwin and Simon were crossing the New Palace Yard when they saw the three bundling out from the tavern, and Simon was sure he saw a blade glinting wickedly in the grey light. 'Baldwin!'

The knight swore under his breath and nodded. They both began to run to the group. 'Halt! You three! Stop!'

There was a flurry of fists, and a sharp cry, and Baldwin saw one man drop to the ground, and then he had his own sword drawn, the blue steel shining clean and pure. 'Hold there, I say, in the name of the King!'

The two men standing threw a look at him over their shoulders, and he recognised the two from Canterbury. 'Christ Jesus, Simon, they've killed again!' he shouted as he pelted towards them.

They looked a little indecisive, then started to run. But to Baldwin's surprise, they didn't try to bolt for it, out through the main gate, which stood only a few yards from them; instead, they ran the other way, across Baldwin's and Simon's front, heading to their right, back towards the main palace.

Baldwin and Simon looked at each other, baffled by this new turn of events, and they were about to set off in pursuit, when a black body hurtled past them. It was Wolf, and he bolted along, looking like a lumbering brute, but covering the ground with speed. He was past Simon and Baldwin, and overhauling the two with ease, when one of them turned and saw the beast. It was Pons, and he gabbled something in a hurry, staring over his shoulder. Then Baldwin saw André stop and pull a dagger from his belt. He tossed it up, caught it by the point, and was about to hurl it at Wolf, when a stone hit his temple. It stunned him, and he dropped his dagger, falling to his knees.

'Who the hell?' Simon cried, but even as he said it, he saw the man over to his right, a king's man, as was apparent from his tabard, who had stooped to pick up another stone. Then he recognised Thomas.

There was no need. Wolf gave a leap, and both forepaws thudded into Pons's back. He crashed to the ground with a loud gasp that Simon and Baldwin could hear even as they ran, and then they heard the low rumble of Wolf's growl.

'Wolf, *Wolf*,' Baldwin shouted, anxious that his dog should not kill the man, but he need not have worried. Wolf remained still, standing over Pons, his muzzle touching the back of Pons's neck, but apart from growling in a blood-curdling manner, he didn't harm the man.

Simon had already reached the languid figure of André, who was trying to climb to his feet, and then toppling back, as regular as the sweep of Wolf's tail, up and down.

'Keep still,' Simon snarled and thrust hard with his boot. André fell back and stared up bemusedly. His dagger was forgotten a foot or two from his hand, and Simon pushed it further away with the point of his sword.

Baldwin allowed Pons to stand, while Wolf looked on disapprovingly, a growl rumbling deep in his throat every few moments. Pons eyed him with apparent terror, but made no move to escape again. He stood quietly, hands at his sides.

'So, tell me, master. What made you want to kill the man over there?'

'He came into the tavern and threatened us. What would you have us do?'

'Well, friend, firstly I'd have you tell the truth. You see, what I saw, as Keeper of the King's Peace,' Baldwin said conversationally, 'was you pulling a man from the tavern and stabbing him several times, without hesitation, and without provocation. It was witnessed by a king's bailiff, too, my friend over there.'

'I am the servant of the Bishop of Orange.'

'I know – if you recall, I was with you at Canterbury before you fled. So, that does not help you. Another dead man, and clearly a man whom you murdered intentionally. And while you were missing, another king's man was killed. This begins to look rather as though you are desperate to have yourself arrested. In God's name, man, why kill someone here, in the open, in the King's new palace? You must be a fool or mad.'

'You have no authority over me. I am here with the Bish—'

'So you said, yes. But I am here with the King, on urgent business from the Queen. I think my word will carry more weight than yours, my fine fellow.'

# Chapter Thirty-Four

It was obvious that Jack was not going to survive. Even as Simon and Baldwin reached him, Thomas behind André and Pons to prevent their escape, he was rolling on his back, his hands grasping, bloody talons in the air over his belly and chest. Baldwin could not see how many wounds there were on his body, but from the blood that lay spilled over the ground, it was clear that he had been mortally wounded. He could not speak above a whisper, and as Baldwin knelt beside him, he managed to mutter, 'Ayrminne. His money. Tell him who did this. He'll av . . . enge me.'

'Why would these men attack you?' Baldwin asked, and repeated his question three times, but even when he bent and put his ear to the dying man's mouth, there was not enough energy in him to do anything more than hiss.

It was no good. Baldwin bellowed for a priest, and was startled when one materialised from behind him. The fellow knelt immediately to give the King's man his last questions and offer him salvation.

'What now?' Simon asked. He had his sword to André's neck, while Thomas had his own at Pons's.

'Now,' Baldwin said, looking from one to the other of his captives, 'I think we tell the King that these two have slain one of his guest's guards in broad daylight, such as it is, and in front of our eyes. I don't think he will be enormously impressed. Do you?'

'We are here with the Bishop of Orange. We demand to see him,' Pons said. André was still looking a little bemused, shaking his head and blinking. His face had gone a pasty, yellow colour, and Baldwin was more than a little concerned that the blow to his head might have concussed him, but for now he was not being sick, and had not lost consciousness, so he reasoned that the man should be all right.

'Shut up!' Thomas grated, giving Pons a swift punch to the side of his head.

'You may be assured that I will tell him all,' Baldwin said, taking Thomas's fist in his hand and preventing any more blows. 'Meanwhile, unless you tell us what was happening in that tavern, I will be forced to go straight to the King to tell him you have killed a man in his own palace yard. He will not be sympathetic to you.'

'We have nothing to say to you. Only to the Bishop,' Pons said, giving Thomas a baleful look.

Baldwin was not loath to deliver the two to the King's guards down at the steps to the undercroft near the chapel. He watched the two being led down, still demanding vociferously that they should be allowed to speak with their bishop, but to no avail.

'What will happen to them?' Thomas asked harshly. He thrust his sword away regretfully.

'For now, little enough, I expect. Sadly, I think that even if the King tries to question them, the Pope's man will have them escape risk of life and limb. They can sit in there for a while, though. Do you know them?'

'No, but I know this other fellow. The one they killed. He was a friend of mine.'

'He was with the Bishop too, wasn't he?'

'Yes, but he befriended me in Beaulieu.'

'Yes?' Baldwin prompted.

Thomas looked at him from the corner of his eye. This keeper was known to him by face, but he had no idea of Baldwin's allegiance, and in this land it was dangerous to mention Despenser. If you were insulting about him to a stranger, you might later learn that the 'stranger' was a close friend of Despenser who'd told him everything. The first you'd usually know was when someone arrived at your house in the middle of the night with a flaming torch.

'Friend,' Baldwin said, 'all I am trying to do is discover why your friend was murdered. If you don't want me to learn that, tell me nothing. However, if you were his friend, please tell me all so that I can make sure his killers actually pay for their crime. If you don't help me, they will probably escape. If you help me, I swear I'll take the matter up, even if I have to go to the Devil himself.'

Thomas nodded slowly, and made up his mind. 'Very well. I am called Thomas of Bakewell. I was brother to Sir John, who was killed at the coronation when a wall fell on him.'

'I recall,' Baldwin said. 'A terrible accident.'

'It was. I was there. Not only John died, of course, but he was the noteworthy figure. The others were all unknowns. But it was dreadful. I can remember lying beside him, choked by the dust and muck, and all I could do was reach to him as he died, poor John, but my hand was kicked away.'

'Who would do a thing like that?' Simon asked.

'Despenser. He was furious. I think it was the way that the coronation had been allowed to be so disturbed. That was the first time I met him.'

'You wear the King's tabard,' Baldwin noted.

'Yes. The Queen saw me, and she was wonderful and kind to me. So from that day, I have lived with her household. I became one of her messengers a few years ago, and she has protected me even when her household was disbanded. She saw to it that I was given a job with her husband. Of course, that means I've had to see more of Sir Hugh le Despenser.'

'And I imagine that would be painful for you.'

'Yes. Especially since he seems to believe that I stole the oil from Canterbury,' he explained.

'Did you?' Baldwin asked.

'No! I was late back from my last journey, but that was simply because my horse went lame. I don't know anything about the oil. What could I do with it? But Despenser took me aside, threatened me, ripped up all my belongings ... if it wasn't for Jack, I'd have had nothing. He was good enough to look after me. He lent me a blanket and food for the journey here. I don't know what I'd have done without his help.'

'Can you tell us where to find his pack?'

'Of course. What about those two? Will they be safe in there? They won't be released while we're gone?'

'They can wait there. They'll need the order of the King to get released. They escaped one excess of violence back in Canterbury – they will not escape this one too.'

'The pair seem inured to violence. Do you think they could have stolen the King's oil?' Thomas asked.

'I fear not,' Baldwin said. 'They were with the Bishop's entourage, so they arrived with us the day after the theft. Still, they are trying to hide something. Let us find Jack's belongings and make sure they're secure, and then we can search for their packs too, and see what they were carrying.'

It took them little time to get to the house where Jack had been staying. The Bishop and all his men had been put up in a merchant's house just outside the palace walls, and when Baldwin and Simon hurried there, they found one of the other men from the Bishop's retinue sitting outside, yawning widely. He had been on guard the night before, and blinked blearily at them as Baldwin explained why they were there.

'Do you know them?' Baldwin said, after describing the dead man and the two he had arrested.

'Sounds like Jack and André and Pons,' the guard agreed. 'Those two bastards don't surprise me at all. They'd slit your throat for the price of an ale, they would. Fools! And Jack's dead? He was a good man, too. Hard, but competent.'

'Can you show me all their baggage?'

Jack's was very light, and it took little effort to go through it. There was nothing of any value, indeed little of any sort whatever.

Thomas sniffed and had to wipe at his eyes. 'Everything he had, he shared with me,' he said.

'What of these other two?' Baldwin muttered to himself.

Pons's bag was a thin linen scrap which held a small knife for eating, a worn stone for honing it, and a skimpy shirt, also of linen. There was a St Christopher in lead, a pilgrim badge like those owned by Richard de Yatton, but nothing else which caught Baldwin's eye. André's roll was different, though. It had a small pouch, and when Baldwin looked inside, he found a ring. 'Look at this!' he said, holding it up.

'A ring? What was he doing with that in his bag?' Simon wondered.

'There's more,' Baldwin said. Tipping up the bag, he found that there were two gemstones inside. One was a ruby, from the look of it. He sifted through the contents with a frown on his face, lifting up a soft woollen shift. 'This looks a little too good for a mere guard, too.'

When they went back to the rolls, there was more. Carefully concealed inside André's blanket Baldwin found two pewter plates, of the kind that would be very easy to sell or pawn for ready money. 'Our friend appears to have been well-provisioned with money,' he said.

Thomas was frowning as he looked down at the valuables, then up at the keeper's grim face. 'What does this all mean, though?'

'I think it means that our friends were prepared to be on the road alone for a while. They had pewter with them, so if they were forced away from the Bishop's entourage, they had something to sell. But then I think that temptation came in their way, and instead they robbed a church or two. That's what these jewels look like, anyway – jewels from a cross or a box of relics.'

'I haven't heard of any thefts,' Simon said.

'Perhaps these were taken from a church in Sussex, or Kent, though, Simon. Why should we have heard of them? It is no shock to think that these two may have been so dishonest as to steal in order to keep themselves funded, is it?'

'I don't understand,' Thomas said.

'It is very simple. They knew that when they came to England, they were likely to be left to their own devices for a while. The Bishop told them that they would have to be prepared in case they were told to leave his party. And strangely enough, that is what happened to them.'

'What does it mean, though?' Thomas demanded.

'It means that Simon and I need to talk to André again at least, before we go and speak with another man.'

André shivered a little. Up in the open air, the weather may have been grey, but it was at least mildly warm. Not so down here. The undercroft felt as though the very walls were made of ice. A damp squelching and sucking noise was his constant companion, and when he moved his feet, there was a slap of water underfoot. Already his boots had begun to leak, and now he was feeling the cold seeping into his arms as well. He held them wrapped closely about his torso as he walked back and forth.

Pons was huddled on a timber at the far side of the chamber, scowling down at the black water that lay all about. It was repellent, noisome, and foul to the touch, that water. André could believe it came straight from the privies. At least he hadn't heard or seen any rats.

The door opening was blinding at first, even though the day was so dull, and André had to shield his eyes.

'You! Get out here!' a harsh voice bellowed.

André stood undecided a moment or two, and it was apparently enough to infuriate his gaoler. The man sprang inside, gripped him by the shoulder, swiftly lashed him over the back three times with a short whip, and had him out through the door and the door slammed and relocked, before he knew what was happening. As he stumbled over a loose stone, falling headlong, he was aware only of the shrieking pain in his back from the whip.

'Get up, Frenchie!' the gaoler snapped, and André saw the whip rise again. He whimpered and threw an arm over his face, but even as he did, he saw a hand stop the gaoler.

'Leave him, man. He's mine now.'

André felt himself being lifted gently, and then he was led up the stairs once more and into the daylight. It was that knight again, the one who'd arrested him.

'We have had an interesting last hour or so,' he said.

André shook his head. 'I have not.'

'We found these,' Baldwin said, and beckoned. Simon stepped forward with a leather bag, which Baldwin took and opened. 'Recognise these?'

André did. 'They are mine. Where did you get them from? You have been rifling through my belongings? I shall have plenty to tell the Bishop when I—'

'This is very interesting. However,' Baldwin said, reaching into the bag and bringing out the small jewel-purse, 'I think he will not be happy to learn that these have been looted from a church. Do you?'

André was silent. There was no way that this knight could have heard about the church, surely. They had been so careful. 'Why do you say that?'

Baldwin carefully stowed the stones back in the bag, and then gripped André about the throat. 'Listen to me well, felon! I want clear and honest answers from you, right now! I have enough here in this bag to have you hanged by the Archbishop of Canterbury. Understand me? You came here knowing you were going to be sent away from the Bishop of Orange's party, didn't you? You knew because he supplied you with pewter plates to sell so you could subsist after you left his party. And then, later, you returned to him at Beaulieu so that you could remain under his protection. But you made the mistake of trying to silence poor Jack.'

'Poor Jack? You say so? He was a fool who wanted to blackmail us, nothing more. Yes, the Bishop gave me the pewter to look after, but not because he said I was to be forced from the party. He just said that if we were to become separated, this would give us some money to protect us.'

'And then you robbed a church as well.'

'We needed some aid. We couldn't go to a pawnbroker immediately, and we had nothing!'

'So you robbed a church, and still had nothing.'

André was silent. Better to allow the knight to think that they had robbed a church than the truth.

'What was Jack blackmailing you over?' Simon asked.

'He said we had the oil and he wanted it. But we don't have it!'

'Why kill him for that?'

'Why do you think? If he was to go about the place saying that we had the stuff, what would happen to us? We would be arrested and tortured, wouldn't we? We are French, and your King has no love for our people since our King has taken back his lands.'

'Fair enough,' Baldwin said. 'Although if you had the oil and had sold it, that would make a more sensible reason for you to try to keep his mouth shut.'

'No, we—'

'It was like that, wasn't it, Baldwin?' Simon said. 'They had Jack, but as soon as they saw us, they killed him. Right there in the open, even though they knew they'd be seen.'

'Yes. It was almost as though killing him was bound to be less dangerous than allowing him to talk.'

'Letting him talk and accuse us of possessing the oil was a great deal more dangerous to us than silencing him forever.'

'Because the Bishop of Orange could protect you.' Simon nodded, but with the disgust plain on his face.

'*Oui.*'

The simple answer was infuriating to Thomas. He had listened to almost all their conversation without flinching, but now, to hear his friend had died from mere expediency, made his blood boil over. He moved forward, and it was only Simon's speed that prevented him from spitting the Frenchman right there.

'Later, friend. You will have your chance later,' Baldwin said firmly, grasping his right hand before he could draw his sword.

Gradually the anger left him, and while André cowered, Thomas grew calmer. 'To think that a slug like this could harm a gentle, kindly man like Jack is almost more than I can bear. I swear, man, I pray to see you swinging by your neck.'

# Chapter Thirty-Five

'There is still Master Ayrminne to speak to,' Baldwin said. 'He was mentioned by Jack as he died. Do you think we should go straight to him?'

'I would go anywhere rather than back into the King's hall,' Simon said, with a glance over his shoulder at all the men filtering back towards the chamber where the discussions were to continue.

As he spoke, Ayrminne appeared through the little gate in the Old Palace Yard wall from the Abbey grounds. 'There he is, let us speak with him now,' Baldwin said.

Ayrminne was less than delighted to see them approach him. 'What is it, Sir Baldwin? I am to attend to the King's debate.'

'Yes, of course. And so are we, so perhaps we could walk there together?'

'Why?' Ayrminne said as they set off together.

There was a thick crush of men entering the doors, and Baldwin waited a moment, studying the canon as he considered the best means of getting the responses he needed.

Ayrminne was a political man from his boots to his shirt-collar. He had achieved a great deal in his life, rising to canon. He could hope to win a bishopric, if he won the right patron. It wouldn't require much. 'Master, you are a bright man, and I could try to deceive you with flattery or simple lies, but there is little point, I think. You know what the game is here as well as I do.'

'And it is?'

'Whoever finds the King's oil, this fabled oil of St Thomas, will have the King's regard for ever.'

'Oh?'

'And you seek it.'

'How do you . . . what makes you think that?'

'Master Ayrminne, a dying man just told me so. I doubt very much that a dying man would do so without good reason, don't you?'

'Who was this?' Ayrminne said with a frown.

'Your friend Jack, the man-at-arms to the Bishop of Orange.'

'Dear God!' Ayrminne said, and blanched. He took a deep breath. 'Are you sure of this? I mean—'

'We all three saw him fall, and caught his murderers. I am sure you know of them – they, too, were with the Bishop's entourage.'

'The two who had run?'

'The same, yes. Now, I don't know what you planned with Jack.' Baldwin paused, hoping for the canon's elucidation, but he said nothing. 'Whatever it was, the two have not got the oil.'

'How can you tell?'

'I have gone through all their belongings. Not the clothes which they wear now, however,' he added thoughtfully, 'but I doubt that would help. If they had the oil, they wouldn't risk dropping it or losing it. No. I don't think that they have it about their persons. Which means they don't have it at all, unless they've cleverly concealed it somewhere else.'

'Which means?'

'That most likely, in my view, they have already disposed of it. And you know how they are likely to have done so, don't you?'

'They will have given it to the Bishop, I expect. They are his men, after all.'

'Yes. So if you are keen to retrieve it, we shall have to try to recover it from him. And that will not be easy.'

'No,' Ayrminne said shortly.

'There is one thing, though,' Baldwin said, smiling. 'I have to ask you, to whom were you intending to give it, once you had retrieved it?'

'The King, obviously. Whom else would a man give it to?'

Baldwin was watching him closely, and saw the tell-tale twitch in his cheek. He immediately knew that Ayrminne was lying. It wasn't the mark of a coward; rather, it was the proof of a man who was a reluctant liar.

'I see, Master. If you ask me that, though, there are many answers. It is probable, I think, that the man who has the oil now is the Bishop of Orange, and I believe he intends to pass it on to the Pope. That to me seems most likely. Then again, there are others, no doubt, who would seek to have the oil to give to Sir Roger Mortimer. He would be grateful, would he not?'

'Yes, yes, very interesting, no doubt—'

'While others might wish to help their own patron. Some would probably give the oil to, say, the Queen.'

And there it was again, as the canon opened his mouth to deny that he would ever have any interest in such an action, the little tic went off by his right eye.

'Your patron is the Queen, isn't she, Master?' Baldwin asked firmly.

Ayrminne looked at him intently for several seconds.

Baldwin knew better than to make any further comment. This was one of those moments when a man could break a witness into honesty, or, by speaking, could lose the witness for ever.

'Yes. Yes, she is,' Ayrminne said at last.

'You were meaning to take it to her, then?' Baldwin said.

'Yes. That man Jack came to me with a cock-and-bull story about it, but it was clear he was convinced he knew exactly where it was, and he told me how much he wanted. I agreed the price, and he was going to bring it to me.'

They stood huddled together near the tavern at the palace gate: Simon, Baldwin, Ayrminne and Thomas. There were no benches or stools here, but no one to overhear their conversations, either.

'You knew Jack,' Baldwin said, turning to Thomas. 'He couldn't have already got the oil, could he? Ah, but then what would have been the point of his going to the two in this place. No, he must have thought that they still had it. Otherwise he wouldn't have been in here at all.'

'I don't think he had it,' Thomas agreed. 'It's not in his bags, either. You saw that.'

'Yes, we all saw his pack,' Baldwin agreed pensively.

'So where can it be?' Ayrminne said plaintively. 'So much harm done for this blasted oil – and no one thought it worth a second look a little while ago.'

Simon nodded, but he was keeping his own counsel. It was a trait Baldwin had seen and appreciated before in his friend. He didn't press Simon now, but instead looked at Ayrminne. 'What do you think we should do, then?'

'You ask me?' Ayrminne said with a grin. 'Since you already know that if I find it, I'll take it to the Queen, why ask me that?'

'Oh, I am sure that you are an honest man, canon. And if

you take it when I have discovered where it is, I will do nothing whatever about it.'

'Nothing?'

'Nothing. Bar telling Sir Hugh le Despenser what became of it. You see, that is my deal with Sir Hugh. He will stop persecuting me and my friend here, in return for which I will find this oil for him. It is not a pleasant task, but one I swore to try to achieve.'

'If you tell him—' Ayrminne began.

'He will do all in his power to find it,' Baldwin said flatly. 'Yes. And that is why I would greatly prefer to find it myself and bring this whole matter to an end.'

'Well, I cannot help you. Both from lack of personal knowledge, and also from inclination. It is my strong belief that the oil should be saved and protected. To throw it away on our king would be . . . he is already anointed. More oil on him would serve no purpose.'

'Then who can use it, if not the King?'

Baldwin stopped. Suddenly his eyes widened, and his mouth fell gaping. Recovering swiftly, he nodded curtly, and then made his apologies and walked out with Simon.

'What on earth is the matter with them?' Ayrminne wondered aloud.

'They are a strange couple, Master,' Thomas offered.

'Come, Baldwin, what were you thinking in there?' Simon demanded as soon as he felt out of earshot of any spies.

'What occurred to me was that there was one other fellow who would perhaps be keen to acquire the oil,' Baldwin said. 'The Earl of Chester.'

'That is what I thought too,' Simon said. 'I wasn't going to say anything because I didn't know if I was being stupid or not.'

'Why stupid?'

'Well, the idea that the Earl would steal from his own father, and take that which he was going to have anyway when he became King in his turn seemed a little far-fetched.'

'The more I think of that family, the more I appreciate being a rural knight,' Baldwin answered. 'The parents hate each other. Both were much in love, or at least trying to give that impression, when the boy was born twelve or thirteen years ago, but now there is no affection whatever between them. And look at their son! All he can do is try to walk a tightrope between them, balancing precariously, trying to satisfy both, trying always to keep his relationships balanced with them both, not showing too much love to either in case he is used later as barter in their little power-games. What sort of a life can the lad have?'

'A miserable one,' Simon offered. 'With only riches, security, diversions of all kinds, and the promise of a throne as soon as he comes of age and his father dies.'

Baldwin looked at him. '*Security*, you say? In this country? We have ever more barons determined to take any semblance of security from the King and his family. He will be rich, yes, but he will be seated on his throne, with another man like Despenser at his side, no doubt. No man he speaks with can he ever trust, because he knows all men will flatter and fawn before him, hoping to be granted some of his wealth, and when they are, they will flatter and fawn again, hoping against hope that he will honour them with more. It starts with a small purse of money, Simon, and then a post, and then the holding of a royal castle, or the privileges to a city, and before long the man is one of the privileged number who owns nothing but what he has been given.'

'It must be a miserable existence,' Simon said with a dry smile.

'Yes. It is. And the only escape is by death. There is no other way out for a king. This lad, the Earl of Chester, is embarked upon a journey in which there is nothing he can do but bend to the will of others.'

'Who rules the country, then?' Simon said, his smile broadening.

'Do you think the King does now?' Baldwin said sharply.

No, Simon didn't. Nobody who had spent any time at Westminster could think that. The man who held all the strings, and pulled them to his own tune, was Despenser. That was where the real power rested.

'So what do you want to do?' Simon said, serious again.

'There is only one thing we can do. Build our case and see where it takes us,' Baldwin said. 'And the first thing we must do now, is speak to the two men who replaced Pons and André and learn why they were there. There is more, much more to all this than I comprehend.'

They found the two in a lodging-house not too far from the palace, along the King's Street towards the Bishop of Exeter's house.

It was a good little place, run by a man called Jacob le Brewer, who stood only five feet at most, but whose girth spoke of his love for his produce. He was able to point out the two men whom Simon and Baldwin wished to see. The smiling Peter and another who might have been his son, John.

Simon was immediately struck with a sense of the power of the two men. There was something about the smiling face of Peter that set a warning bell tolling loudly in his head. If he were to enter into a battle with Despenser, this was the sort of man he would like on his side, but not on Despenser's. There was a controlled energy about him that was unsettling.

Not as unsettling, however, as the sense of uncontrolled, raw power he got from the other man at his side. Where Peter smiled at the world with eyes that were like flints, John glared balefully, without humour.

Baldwin had a single thought about him. He thought the man was just like one of the torturers of the Templars in those terrible, far off days when they had been arrested and incarcerated in their own castles. It set him on edge before he began to speak.

'Sir Baldwin. We haven't seen you since your departure for your home county,' Peter said. His mouth smiled easily, but Baldwin could see little actual pleasure in his eyes.

'I have been asked to learn what I can of the theft of the oil from Canterbury.'

'That is interesting. Who are you speaking with?'

'Just now, with you.'

'Us?' Peter said, and glanced at his companion. 'Hear that, John? He wants to learn about the oil, but he's come to us. Now why would he do that, do you reckon?'

'Maybe he's got lost?' the younger man said, scowling unblinkingly at Baldwin.

'You were added to the Bishop of Orange's party in Canterbury. I think it is because you had the oil with you. The other two were removed because you two needed to get to Beaulieu. I think you were taking the oil with you.'

'Now why would you think that, Sir Baldwin?' Peter said.

'At first I wondered what could have happened to the oil. It might have been taken away from the city that same night, of course,' Baldwin reasoned, 'but the fact that the coroner and your castellan went to so much trouble to have you inserted into the Bishop's party seemed to argue against that. There was a reason for Pons and André being taken out of the

Bishop's group. I think it was simply that you two had to join him. Why?'

'They thought we would make better guards than those two, I suppose,' Peter said mildly. 'We are very good, you know.'

'I am sure you are. But in the meantime, let's just continue. So, if it wasn't to make up numbers, since it was the coroner's fault that the numbers dropped in the first place, there was another reason. I think you were taking the oil to your master and protecting it en route.'

'Who is our master, then?'

'I would think that is obvious.'

Peter smiled more broadly. 'So what now?'

'Is it safe?'

'That depends on what you mean by safe.'

'In God's name, man, just answer a question without prevarication!'

'Yes. It is safe, sir. Safe enough.'

Simon was scowling. 'Safe how, exactly? It would be safe if it was back in the hands of the King, or the Prior of Christ Church, rather than dumped by you somewhere.'

Peter looked at him, and for the first time his smile faded. In its place a pitying look came over his face. 'You don't understand, master, do you? It'll be very safe where it is.'

Baldwin was nodding. 'Whose castle is Canterbury?'

'It is the King's own, Sir Baldwin. Definitely the King's.'

'And yet—' Baldwin stopped suddenly. His eyes narrowed. 'Simon, Despenser told us where Yatton was riding when he was killed. Do you remember where he said?'

'Leeds Castle, wasn't it?'

'Leeds, yes. The castle of Badlesmere, until he lost favour with the King. You remember that, Simon? He was one of King Edward's most respected men, but he grew despairing about Despenser's influence, so he threw in his lot with Earl Thomas of Lancaster, just before the Lords Marcher rose in rebellion. At about that time, the Queen was passing by on her way to Canterbury, and asked for lodging for a night. Since Badlesmere was away, his wife rightly refused entry, saying that she could not allow anyone inside without her lord's permission. When the Queen tried to force her way inside, Lady Badlesmere had her garrison open fire, and six or seven of the Queen's men were slain. The castle was taken, and the King exacted a vicious price for their rebellion.'

Peter was still smiling. 'He had Badlesmere's wife and children taken to the Tower. First women ever to be held there.'

'And gave the castle itself to his consort,' Baldwin agreed. 'The Queen held it since then, and only gave it up recently.'

'It's wrong to take away all her possessions for something her brother did,' John said.

Simon glanced at him. 'Oh, he can speak?'

'Hush, Simon.' Baldwin was watching Peter closely. 'You were in the castle for the Queen?'

'Aye. And then I went to Canterbury. No point staying in a castle when your patron's gone, eh?'

'Now I understand,' Baldwin said quietly. 'De Yatton was on his way *back* when he was killed. He had gone to Leeds – did he go on to Canterbury?'

'I think so. I think he was there.'

'And someone stole the oil there. Presumably, someone who also wanted to take it somewhere safe. For example to the Queen herself?'

'Yatton didn't want to kill that monk, you know,' Peter said. 'He really didn't. He was a gentle soul. But when he was there, the monk told him that he was going to tell Despenser unless he was paid. No one knew it before, but that bastard Brother Gilbert was the son of one of Despenser's closest friends. A small country, this!'

'Despenser has allies all over it,' Baldwin said heavily. 'So he took the oil, and brought it to you two?'

'What're you suggesting, *knight*?' John demanded.

Peter looked at John, 'There's no need for that, John. We're safe enough now. Yes, sir. That's right. And we took responsibility for it, taking it with us to Beaulieu.'

'On behalf of the Bishop of Orange so he could take it with him to France,' Baldwin finished with a sneering tone.

Peter blinked. 'What?'

'Isn't that what you intended?'

'Christ's beard, no!' Peter burst out, and then laughed quietly. 'Dear God, our master wouldn't be happy after going to all that trouble, if we were merely to pass it on to someone else!'

'But it was the Queen who—' Baldwin stopped and closed his eyes. 'The Earl,' he said.

'Aye.'

'I should have realised,' Baldwin breathed. 'So you intended bringing it here all along?'

'Not exactly, no. We thought he would be meeting us at Beaulieu. And then things in France grew worse, and the King decided to hold this set of meetings up here at Westminster. That made us change our plans.'

'So instead you brought it here? Where is it?'

'Delivered.'

'The Earl has it already, then?'

Peter smiled again. 'If you wish to think so, I am sure that is fine. So long as you keep it to yourself. The Earl wouldn't want it discussed too widely. A man who spoke to others about whether or not he had the oil would soon learn whether or not the young Earl has the spirit of his grandfather.'

Baldwin ignored the threat. 'What of Yatton? Was it him who was at Canterbury?'

'He was there, he collected the oil for us, and then he left.'

'Why him, though? Why use him to fetch it for you? Surely there were others who would have been less conspicuous?'

Peter shrugged and threw a look at John.

It was John who replied after a moment's silence. 'He wasn't selected at random. Richard de Yatton was keen to help the Earl. We all were.'

'What could he have had against the King? Why would he want to steal the King's oil?'

'Richard de Yatton was named for his birthplace, Sir Baldwin,' Peter said.

'Where is Yatton?'

'Just down the road from Wigmore. Where Mortimer comes from,' John told him with a curl of his lip.

'You mean to tell me that the Earl was happy to make use of a man loyal to his father's worst enemy?' Baldwin said, torn between being aghast that his son could treat the King in such a manner, and doubt that John was speaking the truth.

'Not entirely, no,' Peter said, glancing at his companion with an expression that bordered on frustration, Baldwin thought. He continued, 'The Earl didn't know Yatton was one of Mortimer's men, but that doesn't matter. Men change their allegiance all the time. Especially knights in the King's household, eh?'

'Some men change their allegiance, yes. Not all,' Baldwin said pointedly. 'So the Earl wasn't aware of Yatton's background?'

'Master Yatton made his oath to the Earl,' Peter said. He

toyed with a splinter of wood on the table in front of him. 'Yatton wasn't exactly happy when Mortimer stood against the King. What else would a man do, when something of that nature happens? Once Mortimer was arrested, he immediately had to seek a new patron. And he thought it would be best for him to serve the Earl.'

'Why not the King?' Simon asked. 'Or was he too religious to want to serve such a man?'

'What would religion have to do with it?' John snapped. 'You mean because the King is more interested in men than women?'

'I meant because he has deserted his wife,' Simon said coldly.

'His religion would hardly get in his way anyhow,' Peter said. 'I never saw him as a greatly religious man.'

'But,' Baldwin frowned, 'he had the necklace full of pilgrim badges. I saw it.'

'Oh, I know he had that, yes. He collected the badges quite seriously, but I don't think that had any bearing on his religion. Like any man, he would go to church on a Sunday, but he wasn't one of those who wrapped themselves up in Christianity every day of the week like a warm robe. He could happily sit in a church, but when I saw him, it was often because he wanted a doze, nothing more.'

Baldwin shook his head. 'Everyone else has said how religious he was.'

'They didn't know him, then. He was no more deeply committed than I.'

Simon looked at Baldwin. 'Then why did he take so long on his journeys?'

Peter shrugged. 'It's not my concern. All I know is that my earl wants the matter forgotten.'

'And that's why you've just told us all?' Baldwin said directly.

'No. I've told you this to stop you asking about the oil,' Peter said. 'I had a choice of telling you the truth and hoping to silence you, or removing you. The Earl seemed to feel it were better to feed your inquisitiveness, rather than kill you. He told us to tell you all, and ask you to hold this secret.'

'We should tell the King,' Baldwin said.

'It's up to you. The Earl asks that you don't. The matter is soon to be irrelevant, anyway. Why stir up such nonsense again?'

'Because the King wants to have it returned.'

'He's already anointed. He had his chance to use it before,' Peter said. The bells were tolling for the next session with the King, and all four stood. 'He didn't believe in it and so he didn't make use of it. The Earl, however, is determined that his own coronation will be more auspicious. He will make a good king.'

# Chapter Thirty-Six

The King walked through the assembled nobles and took his seat on his throne once more, letting his gaze range coldly over the men before him.

Once again, Despenser stood and read from a scroll, calling on all present to speak without fear or favour, his tone that of a steward in court, confident, strong, full of authority.

I wish I could speak with such a voice, the King thought. But he couldn't. His authority was eroded by the wars with the Scottish, the losses in France, and the rumours which persisted – that he was a supposititious king, a peasant's child inserted into the cot in order to weaken the Crown. He was nothing in the eyes of so many. His barons despised him: he could see it now in their eyes. The Church abhorred him for his frivolity, as they put it. Singing, dancing, swimming, all were frowned upon. His brother-in-law in France detested him for his friendship with Sir Hugh.

If there had been a little more respect for him, perhaps he would have enjoyed more success as a king. As it was, there was nothing he could do now. It felt as though his reign was set on a road that would end ultimately in shamefulness. Appalling to think that he could be responsible for the loss of so many territories. First he had the trouble with the Scottish, and now with his lands in France. There was no let up. Enemies were on all sides.

Men spoke. Their voices washed all around him, and there was no conclusion. He should go to France; he should remain in England. And all the while at the back of his mind was the proposal that his son should go in his place. Would that help him? How could he tell? All he did know was that his closest and best friend, Despenser, feared for his life were he, the King, to go.

The pressure was intolerable. He wished only to do what was best, but the competing demands were so insufferable that he hardly knew where to turn. If he could, he would throw it all up. There was no one in the land who could comprehend the immensity of the stress that a man must endure in his position. It was not something that he *could* give up, though. He was in a position granted to him by God. Not some secular body: *God*. What God had given, no man could take away.

Not that there weren't plenty of men there in that room who'd have been only too happy to take it away from him, he thought, looking about him at them all.

His gaze landed upon his son, the Earl of Chester. Twelve years old . . . or was he thirteen now? It was so hard to keep track. How could he send the boy over to France on his own? It would be madness. Apart from anything else, he didn't want to see his boy over there while Isabella was still there. She had to come back first. That was certain.

Baldwin found Richard of Bury clutching at his sleeve as he and Simon left the great hall. 'Yes?'

'My Lord. The Earl of Chester would appreciate a few moments of your time, Sir Baldwin.'

'Would he? Very well. Take us to him,' Baldwin said. However, he rested his hand on his belt like a man ready to draw steel in his own defence.

Bury took them along a long corridor, up to a second level, and thence to a chamber that lay near the Queen's cloister. Here they found themselves entering a pleasantly lit and warmed room that was filled with hallings of rich colours. There were hunting scenes on the wall near the door, but it was noticeable that the tapestries on the other three walls all contained scenes from the Gospels.

There was a roaring fire in the hearth, and the Earl stood before it, with his back to the flames.

'Today has been the wettest this year,' he grumbled. 'Miserable weather. I got drenched on the way to the audience first thing, and I'm still not dry.'

'Your Highness,' Baldwin said, bowing, Simon copying him at his side.

'You know all, I believe.'

'We have spoken with your men, your Highness.'

'You think there is more to learn, then?' Earl Edward said testily.

'No, no, my Lord. I am sure that your men will have been entirely honest with me,' Baldwin said.

The young Earl suddenly giggled, and for the first time Baldwin appreciated just how young he was.

'Well, if Peter was, it'll be the first time in his life.'

'That was rather the impression I formed as well.'

'But you do know much. I would ask that you don't share what you know with my Lord Despenser, nor with the King. It is a matter for me, not for him.'

'It is the King's oil, your Highness,' Baldwin pointed out.

'Actually, no, it's not. I believe the prophecy spoke of the King after him rather than he himself. In any case, he had it for his coronation and chose not to use it. Now it is up to me to be able to use it for my own coronation, I think.'

'What if the King learns of it? He is most angry already, is he not?'

'I think I can satisfy him on that,' the Earl said.

And he could. His father was always gullible. He would soon be presented with a phial containing a little oil, its scent altered by the addition of a little oil of sandalwood and myrrh. He would be content with that. And meanwhile Earl Edward would keep the real oil in his own little phial, ready to be used on the day that he went to the abbey and knelt to be crowned in his place.

'So what do we tell Despenser?' Simon demanded as they walked from the Earl's chamber.

Baldwin shook his head, desperate to think clearly. 'What can we tell him? That the King's son has it? That would be ludicrous. The Despenser would laugh at us, and then renew his assault on your house, Simon. We cannot do that.'

'Maybe he won't? He might bow to the fact that he was unable to do anything and subside quietly.'

'Simon, he asked us to look into the matter. Have you not wondered why?'

'No.'

'I think it's because he wants to have a little victory for the King. A small proof that he is still the King's greatest ally and confidant. If we go to him and tell him that the victory has actually been stolen from him, and that the King's son has the oil, I can envisage him considering even removing the son in order to get his own way.'

'That is a large supposition.'

'Yes. But he has an enormous awareness of his own self-value. Do not underestimate him as an enemy, Simon. He is very dangerous!'

'I do understand. So what do you propose, Baldwin?'

'First, I will tell him that we have investigated as far as we can. Second, that so far as we know, the herald who stole the oil is dead. Third, that he acted on behalf of another, but the oil was one of the items stolen from his body when he was killed. And fourth, that it was lost. Perhaps the outlaws had it, perhaps not. But either way, the man died and his secret died with him.'

'You believe that?'

Baldwin looked at him, and then a little smile crossed his lips. 'No.'

*Vigil of St Boniface*[1]

Despenser was already looking up when Baldwin entered the room. 'And?'

'You wanted us to report.'

'Yes. What has happened to the oil?'

Baldwin looked about him. There was a stool at the wall behind the door, so he took it and sat before Despenser. 'You have lost it.'

'*I* have lost it? And how did I manage that, precisely?'

'It was stolen by the herald we found dead at the side of the road in the great forest, Sir Hugh. I have no idea what became of it then. Perhaps he sought to save it, and threw it from the outlaws? I have heard of other men who have done the same, throwing their money away to ensure that it never benefits those who sought to steal it. Perhaps he did that, and threw the oil deeper into the forest. With the undergrowth there, you could well seek it for years and never find it. I am sorry. I think you have lost it.'

---

[1] Tuesday, 4 June 1325

'The King has lost it, not I.'

'Of course. If you do not find it, how can he?'

Despenser nodded slowly. 'I do not think I like this conclusion, Sir Baldwin. I told you that I would leave your friend Puttock and you alone, if you helped me on this matter – and yet I get the feeling that you are not being entirely truthful. Why should that be?'

'I am being as truthful as possible.'

'I wonder. I shall be forced to cope with the King's temper over the matter, but perhaps it is all for the best. The King would have liked to have had himself anointed again, but for him to do so would expose himself and the kingdom to risks he barely comprehends.

'If he were to seek the oil and then have another ceremony, it could lead the ill-disposed to believe that he had no faith in his initial coronation. And that itself could prove to be a disaster for him. If others got the impression that he was less than confident of his original crowning, they might wonder whether he was in truth anointed by God. All sorts of treasonous and dangerous ideas might begin to circulate. We cannot allow that, Sir Baldwin. *I* will not allow it!'

Baldwin nodded. 'I do not intend mentioning this matter to anybody whomsoever, Sir Hugh. It is closed, so far as I am concerned. I seek no more information about it.'

'I am glad to hear it,' Despenser said. The two said nothing more. There was no mutual trust, no companionship, no friendliness between them. And there never could be. One sought his own aggrandisement at the expense of any who stood in his path, while the other had witnessed and experienced the most appalling injustice. Baldwin had seen all his friends murdered to satisfy the greed of the French King. There was no point at which their minds and values could meet.

Baldwin rose and left Despenser there a few minutes later, aware of a great relief that he had at least averted one potential danger.

# Chapter Thirty-Seven

'And?' Simon demanded when Baldwin appeared in the doorway.

'I do not believe that he trusted my word. But I do not think that there is anything I could have said which he would have accepted wholeheartedly. It is the sadness of a man like him that he is forced to look always for the motivation of men like you and me. He cannot understand that we merely want our lives to move on, unimpeded by difficulties of royalty or barons.'

'He is mad.'

'No, I am afraid not. He is merely a man driven by lusts, lusts which I am glad to say, you and I cannot understand.'

'So what happens now?'

Baldwin looked at him very seriously. 'For the present, we sidle away from the stage and hide ourselves back in Devon. Personally, I hope that we shall be able to do so and remain safe from being asked to intervene in national affairs again.'

'And him?'

Baldwin sighed. 'If Despenser wishes to make our lives hard, he can do so, Simon. There is no point pretending otherwise. He is the most powerful man in England after the King. We have to hope that we have satisfied his curiosity and anger against us for now.'

'And if we haven't?'

'Keep your sword oiled and easy in the sheath, Simon. If he's not content, we will soon know all about it.'

## Morrow of the Feast of St Boniface[1]

The King studied the little phial with interest. 'Are you sure?'

'As sure as we can be, your Highness,' Earl Edward said, still facing the ground.

'Get up, boy, get up!' the King snapped. 'There's no need to keep staring at your feet like that. When have I ever been unkind to you? So you are sure that this is the real oil of St Thomas?'

'I believe so, Father.'

'How can you be so sure?' Despenser demanded. His voice was like a well-oiled blade: well-formed, polished, and lethal.

'I relied on some of my men to find it, Sir Hugh,' Earl Edward said, with just the level of contempt to annoy without upsetting. He was the King's son, after all.

The King stood up and motioned to Despenser. 'Sir Hugh, please come here a moment.'

He waited until his closest friend was at his side, and then murmured softly, 'Do not ever presume to insult my son in that manner again in my presence, Sir Hugh. I will not have the future King of England browbeaten. Is that *clear*?'

'Perfectly.'

'Good. Now,' he said, turning back to his son. 'You may leave us, Sir Hugh.'

'What did you say to him, Father?' Earl Edward said as the door closed.

'It was a private matter. A private talk.'

'Yes. What did you say to him?'

---

[1] Thursday, 6 June 1325

The King smiled thinly. 'I warned him against insulting you. I will not have the future King of our land made to look foolish by him.'

'Thank you.'

'Now. About this oil,' the King said. He hefted the phial in his hand. 'It is a pretty bottle, is it not? Anything in a bottle like this must be enormously valuable.'

'I think so, my Lord.'

'Yes. It is the way that a boy *would* think. The more valuable the covering, the more important the oil.' As he spoke he pulled the cork and sniffed at it. He nodded approvingly before tipping the phial upside-down, and watching his son as the oil dribbled out on to the slabs of the floor.

'But, Father!'

'Do not assume me to be a fool. The oil was stolen, it was taken by that ingrate Yatton and lost in the forest when he was attacked by the outlaws there. I know this as well as any. I shall never see it again. This, this is an insult to me.'

'Father, I am sorry. I only—'

His voice softened. 'I know, my son. You wanted to make me happy by providing me with another phial. But I can accept the failure and the loss. My reign is a mess, Edward. When you accede to the throne, promise me this: you will reign more cautiously than me.'

'I swear it, Father.'

The King stared down at the phial in his hand. 'I shall keep this, though. It is a good little container. I have not seen its like before.'

'Really, Father?' said his son. He wondered at that, for it was the same phial in which the oil had arrived with him. Still, no matter. He was only relieved that he had rescued the real oil before coming here.

'And now, please leave me. There is still much for me to consider about this new treaty with the French,' the King said heavily.

'Yes, Father. Father? I am sorry.'

'So am I, my son. I could almost bend my knees now and beseech the Almighty to send me another phial of the same oil, just to try to protect us. Because I am as sure as I can be that the King of France is not going to aid us. Not from the look of the treaty he proposes.'

## *Friday after Feast of St Boniface*[1]

Baldwin and Simon clattered thankfully out of the great gate of the royal palace, and set their heads down Thieving Lane, and on towards the west.

'Home again at last,' Baldwin said.

'I am looking forward to seeing Meg again,' Simon said, smiling.

'And I Jeanne,' Baldwin said. He was quiet a moment. 'You know that the forest where the herald's body was found has now been cleared of all the outlaws who infested the place?'

'I would hope so!'

'It is a safe area to visit now – until the next marauding group settles there.'

'Good. I am glad to hear it.'

'I suppose it would be a great deal out of our way,' Baldwin said musingly, gazing down at his new dog.

Simon gaped at him. 'Are you serious? The woods are straight south from here, while home is westwards. What would be the point of going down there?'

---

[1] Friday, 7 June 1325

'I had a mind to see that woman again. You remember her?'

'Yes. The scared one. What of her?'

Baldwin looked at him. 'I wanted to visit them and tell the man that he is safe now. Everyone believes him dead.'

Simon opened his mouth to speak, but Baldwin continued in his quiet, insistent manner.

'You see, Simon, we were right in the beginning. I think it might have been you who said it. I wondered about it when I was looking at the tabard and pondering what on earth someone would have been doing, pulling the tabard on over his head, but we had the confirmation that it was Yatton, because of the other messengers and heralds telling us it was him.

'But as Joseph said – even his own mother wouldn't have recognised him in that state. No one could. He was so badly decomposed that it was mere guesswork to see who it was.'

'Who was the man, then?'

'Again, you had the right idea. It was the husband of the woman we met in the woods, I think. I don't know, but I'd assume she was unhappily married, and gradually over time she grew to hate her man. And at the same time she came to know a man who kept riding past, a King's herald, a fine man on horseback, always smart and with coin in his purse. Is it any surprise that she and he began to talk? You set my mind on that path when you asked me about his being so religious. You recall, we were told originally that he was intensely religious, and then we heard that it was untrue. If that was the case, why was he spending so much time away from his duties? I think he was spending as much time as he could with his woman, the woman in the forest.'

'So he rode past, all the way to Canterbury, stole the oil from Gilbert . . .'

'Who then tried to blackmail him into paying more for the oil, threatening to tell his father's best friend, Despenser.'

'And then rode back to the forest, where he set upon the man and killed him, dumping his body in the woods, and, as an afterthought, placed his own tabard over him?

'But not before he had given the oil to someone else. Perhaps to the castellan at Canterbury, or the coroner. Then, when we passed through, the oil was given to Peter and John, who carried it with them in our party, and only when we reached Beaulieu did they realise that the Earl was not to arrive, so they proposed to the Bishop of Orange that they should continue with him and come to London too. And once here they could give the oil to Earl Edward.'

'And the true murderer lives on in a wood south of London?'

Baldwin pulled a grimace. 'Perhaps. And yet, who can tell? Perhaps Gilbert sought to attack him, and he killed the brother in self-defence? And the husband was murdered by his own wife. Or perhaps died naturally, and she dragged his body into the woods, anxious that anyone finding it at her home would automatically assume her to be guilty of his death? It may have been nothing to do with Yatton whatever.'

'And I may be a bishop.'

'Do you want to know the truth of it?'

Simon looked south towards the Thames. The river flowed sluggishly here, grey and slumberous, but it was an obstacle he preferred not to dare. 'No,' he said with certainty. 'The man is alive or dead. It matters not a whit to me. All I know is, I want to see my wife again and make sure that she is perfectly safe. If you want to follow this fellow, I think I shall have to ride on alone, Baldwin.'

Baldwin stared west, then south, and at last he nodded. 'You know, I think you may be right this once.'

* * *

Despenser walked back into his chamber and saw that Wattere was already there. 'Well? What do you want?'

'I have been investigating that bailiff you wanted me to remove. If you still wish it, my Lord, I think I have found a way to remove him legally.'

'Speak!'

'His house is not his own outright. He owns it on a seven-year lease. Usually, it would be perfectly safe for him, but he has spent so much time this year in France and here, that I am sure he will be in arrears with the rent.'

'Who owns it?'

'A man who could be persuaded to sell it to you.'

Despenser nodded to himself. He walked to his chair and sat. 'Buy the lease, and then begin efforts to recover the full amount. And if he cannot pay at once, I suppose I shall have to evict him.'

'That is what I thought, my Lord,' Wattere said, bowing his way out.

And what I hoped, he added to himself. Now, Bailiff, let's see who's still laughing when we're done with you!

# The Templar, the Queen and Her Lover

## Michael Jecks

1325: An atmosphere of dread and suspicion hangs over England.

The last years have been god-awful. A man was hard pushed just to survive with the realm stretched so taut with treachery and mistrust and the war with France.

When Isabella, Queen of England, is dispatched to Paris to negotiate peace with the French King, Sir Baldwin de Furnshill and his companion Simon Puttock travel with her to ensure her safety. But it seems no one can be trusted, not least those in the Queen's own retinue. Murder, betrayal, adultery and cold, calculating evil are just the beginning of Baldwin's tempestuous journey into the dark heart of the world's most powerful realm. Baldwin and Simon must fight to survive as the Queen struggles to stop a vicious war between her husband and her brother . . .

Acclaim for Michael Jecks' mysteries:

'The most wickedly plotted medieval mystery novels' *The Times*

'Atmospheric and cleverly plotted' *Observer*

978 0 7553 3284 7

## headline

# The Malice of
# Unnatural Death

## Michael Jecks

1324: The English kingdom is in uproar. Roger Mortimer, once the king's most able commander, but now his most hated enemy, is plotting to assassinate the King. But he's not the only one with murder on his mind . . .

When the remains of a local craftsman and a King's messenger are found in the city of Exeter's streets, Sir Baldwin de Furnshill, the Keeper of the King's Peace, and his friend Bailiff Simon Puttock are implored by the Bishop to find out who was responsible. The dead messenger was carrying a dangerous secret that may prove fatal, should it fall into the wrong hands. Baldwin and Simon must find the murderer before he can strike again. But when murderers can use magic, no one is safe . . .

Acclaim for Michael Jecks' mysteries:

'The most wickedly plotted medieval mystery novels' *The Times*

'Really difficult to put down' *Historical Novels Review*

'A gem of historical storytelling' *Northern Echo*

978 0 7553 3278 6

**headline**

# Dispensation of Death

## Michael Jecks

1325: England is a hotbed of paranoia under the reign of the increasingly deranged and unpredictable Edward II and his lover, Sir Hugh le Despenser.

When the Queen's lady-in-waiting is slaughtered and a man murdered in the Great Hall at Thorney Island, the King demands to be avenged. Sir Baldwin de Furnshill, a new member of his parliament and experienced investigator of murders, is appointed to track down the killer, aided by his friend, Simon Puttock.

As Baldwin and Simon's investigation deepens it becomes obvious that the murderer could be among the most influential men in the land. In an age of corruption, when the king's friends can use blackmail and murder to promote their ends, uncovering the truth could be fatal . . .

Praise for Michael Jecks:

'The most wickedly plotted medieval mystery novels' *The Times*

'A gem of historical storytelling' *Northern Echo*

978 0 7553 3281 6

**headline**

# A Friar's Bloodfeud

## Michael Jecks

March 1324 – the cruel winter is far from over . . .

In the rural idyll of Iddesleigh, a gang of men break into the home of Bailiff Simon Puttock's servant, Hugh, and attack his family.

When word reaches Simon, he and Sir Baldwin de Furnshill, Keeper of the King's Peace, find Hugh's cottage burnt to the ground, the bodies from within already buried. It seems that Hugh must have perished in a dreadful accident – but when they learn of the territorial battles between two neighbouring manors, Baldwin and Simon begin to suspect a deeper, darker truth.

Iddesleigh had seemed a harmonious village, but it becomes clear that evil lurks in this land, and pain and bloodshed are far from over . . .

Acclaim for Michael Jecks' mysteries:

'The most wickedly plotted medieval mystery novels' *The Times*

'Great characterisation, a detailed sense of place, and a finely honed plot make this a superb medieval historical' *Library Journal*

978 0 7553 2300 5

## headline

Now you can buy any of these other bestselling
books by **Michael Jecks** from your bookshop
or *direct from the publisher*.

FREE P&P AND UK DELIVERY
(Overseas and Ireland £3.50 per book)

| | |
|---|---|
| The Leper's Return | £6.99 |
| The Mad Monk of Gidleigh | £7.99 |
| The Templar's Penance | £6.99 |
| The Outlaws of Ennor | £6.99 |
| The Tolls of Death | £7.99 |
| The Chapel of Bones | £7.99 |
| The Butcher of St Peter's | £7.99 |
| A Friar's Bloodfeud | £7.99 |
| The Death Ship of Dartmouth | £6.99 |
| The Malice of Unnatural Death | £7.99 |
| Dispensation of Death | £7.99 |
| The Templar, the Queen and Her Lover | £7.99 |

TO ORDER SIMPLY CALL THIS NUMBER

**01235 400 414**

or visit our website: www.headline.co.uk

Prices and availability subject to change without notice.

*By Michael Jecks and available from Headline*

The Last Templar
The Merchant's Partner
A Moorland Hanging
The Crediton Killings
The Abbot's Gibbet
The Leper's Return
Squire Throwleigh's Heir
Belladonna at Belstone
The Traitor of St Giles
The Boy-Bishop's Glovemaker
The Tournament of Blood
The Sticklepath Strangler
The Devil's Acolyte
The Mad Monk of Gidleigh
The Templar's Penance
The Outlaws of Ennor
The Tolls of Death
The Chapel of Bones
The Butcher of St Peter's
A Friar's Bloodfeud
The Death Ship of Dartmouth
The Malice of Unnatural Death
Dispensation of Death
The Templar, the Queen and Her Lover
The King of Thieves
The Prophecy of Death

Michael Jecks gave up a career in the computer industry to concentrate on writing and the study of medieval history, especially that of Devon and Cornwall. He is a regular speaker at library and literary events, was the Chairman of the Crime Writers' Association in 2004, and judges the CWA Ian Fleming Steel Dagger. All his novels featuring Sir Baldwin de Furnshill and Bailiff Simon Puttock are available from Headline. Michael lives with his wife, children and dogs in northern Dartmoor.

Acclaim for Michael Jecks' mysteries:

'Captivating . . . If you care for a well-researched visit to medieval England, don't pass this series' *Historical Novels Review*

'Stirring intrigue and a compelling cast of characters will continue to draw accolades' *Publishers Weekly*

'Michael Jecks has a way of dipping into the past and giving it the immediacy of a present-day newspaper article . . . He writes . . . with such convincing charm that you expect to walk round a corner in Tavistock and meet some of the characters' *Oxford Times*

'A tortuous and exciting plot . . . The construction of the story and the sense of period are excellent' *Shots*

'This fascinating portrayal of medieval life and the corruption of the Church will not disappoint. With convincing characters whose treacherous acts perfectly combine with a devilishly masterful plot, Jecks transports readers back to this wicked world with ease' *Good Book Guide*

'Jecks' knowledge of medieval history is impressive and is used here to great effect' *Crime Time*